TETHERED SOULS

A NINE MINUTES SPIN-OFF NOVEL

BETH FLYNN

Tethered Souls
Copyright © 2018 by Beth Flynn
All Rights Reserved

Edited by Amy Donnelly and Cheryl Desmidt
Format by Amy Donnelly at Alchemy and Words
Cover Design by Jay Aheer at Simply Defined Art
Proofreading by Judy Zweifel at Judy's Proofreading

ISBN-13: 978-1718906297
ISBN-10: 1718906293

Tethered Souls is the second spin-off novel from The *Nine Minutes* Trilogy. It can be read as a standalone, but would most likely be more enjoyable if read after *Nine Minutes, Out of Time, A Gift of Time, and The Iron Tiara*. It contains major spoilers from the trilogy, and although not necessary, the reader might benefit by understanding the background stories of the main characters that are described in the series. There are many twists and turns in all my books that can best be connected if read consecutively.

Tethered Souls is a coming of age story for the grown children of parents with dark pasts. The childhood friends who are now adults were forbidden to see each other because of their parents' transgressions and buried secrets. Tethered Souls consists of two parts and probably could've been published as a duet, but I decided to keep the story as one so you don't have to wait! My heartfelt wish is that you enjoy both parts of Mimi and Christian's story.

If you'd like to familiarize yourself with the rest of my books, the recommended reading order is as follows:

The Nine Minutes Trilogy
Nine Minutes (Book 1)
Out of Time (Book 2)
A Gift of Time (Book 3)

The Nine Minutes Spin-Off Novels
The Iron Tiara (Book 1)
Tethered Souls (Book 2)
Better Than This (Book 3)

Thank you for your support and readership!

For Kelli and Katie

Map of Southeastern United States

North
Carolina

Pine Creek

Pumpkin
Rest

Mimi's
College

South
Carolina

Georgia

Atlantic Ocean

Jacksonville

Florida

Gulf of
Mexico

Alligator
Alley

Naples

Ft.
Lauderdale

Part One

"I Want You To Want Me"
Cheap Trick

PROLOGUE

SOUTH CAROLINA 2007

"Ten days is too long, Mimi," Lucas whispered in my ear after breaking our kiss.

Lucas, my boyfriend, and I were standing in my dorm parking lot. He'd stopped to see me before I left for my annual spring break retreat and before he headed for his family home in Charleston.

I looked into his dark eyes and smiled. "It'll fly by, I promise." I did my best to sound convincing.

"Maybe for you," he quickly countered. "I'll be spending spring break doing hard labor."

"I hardly think working in one of your father's stores is hard labor, Lucas." He pulled me closer and gave me an exaggerated sad puppy dog face.

"Any day I don't get to spend with you is hard labor, Mimi." He kissed the tip of my nose and sighed, resigned. He picked up the overnight bag I'd set on the ground, and taking my hand, steered me toward my car. Nodding at my Montana license plate he asked, "When will I get to meet your family?"

Like I'd done for the last several months, I expertly avoided his question. This time I did it by using the key remote to open the trunk. I watched as he arranged my overnight bag among two cases of bottled water, jumper cables, a laundry basket filled with clean clothes, a gym bag, and a pile of scattered books. I'd never intended to be so evasive with Lucas.

I was certain he would follow suit and do what every guy I'd ever dated had done. Once I let them know sex was off the table, they couldn't get away from me fast enough. My original decision to keep my virginity hadn't been so honorable. It had almost been taken without my consent, fueling my decision to hold onto the one thing that was mine and mine alone. There were a few who considered my intact hymen a challenge, but when they realized I was serious, it didn't take long for them to hightail it away from me and my "closed to the public" lady parts.

Introducing a boy to my family had never been an issue. Then again, no other guy had dated me long enough to want to meet them. Lucas didn't press me into a sexual relationship and that scared and excited me at the same time. It's not like he hadn't tried. We'd messed around a little bit, and he'd attempted to go further, but we never did. And still, when we got to a point I refused, he still stayed. I often struggled, wondering if he could be the one. I'd asked myself this more than once. My heart wanted to believe the answer was yes and I secretly wondered if I may have been falling in love with Lucas Paine.

Glancing at the laundry basket filled with clean clothes, he added, "I know your parents and brothers and sister are in Montana, but your grandfather is only a couple of hours away. You've never asked me once if I wanted to go with you to meet him."

He was right. I'd never invited him, and I'd deliberately chosen to tell a half-truth, letting him and everyone else believe that my grandfather was my nearest relative. It explained how I could leave some weekends with a basket of dirty clothes and return with a clean pile.

The sound of the trunk closing broke through my thoughts. "It's funny you brought up my grandfather. He mentioned having business near the college in a couple of weeks and wanted to take me to lunch. Do you want to come with us?"

He gave me a look that told me he knew I'd just made the lunch date up. "C'mon, Mimi. You've met my family. Are you embarrassed by me?" His tone was so sincere, I felt a sliver of guilt.

I shook my head and avoided his gaze as I headed for the driver side door. Opening it, I turned around to look at him. "Of course not. You're perfect, Lucas." And he was. With one exception.

"Then what is it, Mimi?" he pleaded.

"This isn't a conversation I can have right now." Looking at my watch I quickly added, "A conversation I don't have time for. Can you trust me that it's not you?"

He brushed his hand through his short, dark-blond hair, gave me a crooked smile, and pulled me in for a hug. I welcomed his embrace and his spicy scent. I smiled and explained, "It's not you. I swear it's not. It's my family. They're…" I paused, trying to come up with a description that wouldn't scare him off. "They're different."

Taking my face in his hands, he gave me a long, lingering kiss. He stepped back and let me climb into my car. I started it up and rolled down the window. He rested his forearms on the roof and leaned inside the window.

"If I didn't know better, I'd think you were harboring fugitives the way you're so secretive about them."

"Of course the criminal justice major in you would immediately jump to that conclusion," I teased as he backed away from the car. I rolled up my window, shifted into reverse and sighed a breath of thanks that he hadn't probed further.

If you only knew, Lucas, I thought. *If you only knew.*

IT WOULD TAKE me a little over two and a half hours to get to Camp Keowee, the Christian youth camp where I'd volunteered as a counselor for the past three years. I was looking forward to the long drive as it would give me time to collect my thoughts and try to figure out how to bring Lucas into the mystery that had been my life for the past five years.

Lucas assumed, as did everyone else, that I was from Montana. After all, that's what my vehicle plate said as well as my college ID, Montana driver's license, and all other forms of identification. As far as everyone was concerned, my name was Miriam D. Hunter. Years ago, I'd left Florida as Miriam Ruth Dillon and began a new life in North Carolina under my new name. It wasn't a stretch as far as aliases went, but it was still an effective deterrent since very few people from my past knew me as Miriam, and none of them knew my biological father's surname, Hunter. In addition to switching that up, I'd purposely stayed off of all social media, and even though I wasn't always successful, I did my best to avoid having my picture taken in the event it might be posted somewhere. I didn't want anyone finding me.

That hadn't always been true. There had been one person who I'd hoped might've cared enough to find me. I sighed out loud and rolled down my window, hoping the mountain breeze would distract me. I hadn't let myself think about him for a long time. So why was I allowing myself today?

Shaking my head as if doing so would toss all thoughts of my former teenage heartbreak to the wind, I focused on my current predicament. How was I going to introduce my boyfriend to my family? The family that didn't live in Montana, but in fact, lived only a couple hours away from my college, just over the North Carolina border.

Having been raised listening to '60s and '70s music, I stuck a homemade CD into the player and turned it up. It was an odd mixture of my mother's bubble gum ballads and both of my fathers' preferences for hard rock. Metallica's "I Disappear" blasted through the speakers as I continued to ponder my strange family situation.

My parents harbored a huge secret and I was adamant about protecting them. Lucas was a criminal justice major, making the entire situation more than ironic. It was the only flaw I could see in our relationship. And if I wanted Lucas to become a permanent part of my life, it would have to be dealt with. But not today. Today I would think about how much I'd looked forward to this retreat. I'd stayed in contact with a few friends that I'd met at camp over the past three years. Since our college spring breaks didn't always match up, I never knew who I'd run into.

It would also be the first time that my second semester midterms coincided with the birthday of my twin brother and sister. Ruthie and Dillon had just turned four and I'd missed their birthday party. Since I was leaving directly for camp, I let my family think I would bring their presents on my next trip home. I intended to leave the retreat a day early and stop at home for a surprise visit to make the special delivery.

Before I knew it, I arrived at my last stop before reaching Camp Keowee. Pumpkin Rest was barely a dot on the map and the last place I'd be able to get a halfway decent cell phone signal. The tiny township consisted of a small grocery store, gas station, pharmacy, and diner, all situated in the same building that sat on the northwest corner of the town's only named intersection. One so small the local folk referred to it as a crossroad.

I filled my gas tank and headed inside to buy one of my most anticipated guilty pleasures—a homemade biscuit with honey. After paying for my treat and gas, I pulled out my cell phone and dialed my mother as I walked toward my car. A sticky biscuit in one hand and my phone in the other, I hit the speed dial and smiled when I heard the worry in her voice when she answered.

Just like I'd done for the last three years, I would be spending the next ten days at a retreat and would have no communication with the outside world. Not only was it the camp's policy, it was almost an impossibility due to the mountain location and lack of cell towers. Calls rarely made it through, but oddly enough some text messages did. I promised to text my mother as soon as I arrived and reminded her that I would turn in my phone to be locked up for the duration of my camp stay. She could always call the camp's landline in the event of an emergency.

I was still on the phone trying to reassure her when I spotted an old friend.

"Oh my gosh!" I shouted into my mother's ear as I approached my car. I recognized the bright yellow Miata parked behind my green 2005 Ford SUV and the long blue dreadlocks of the girl whose back was facing me while she pumped gas. The three charms I knew she always wore in her hair, a cross, a dove, and a heart winked at me as the sunlight kissed them.

My outburst startled my mother and I did my best to put her at ease during our crackly connection. I was only hearing every other word when we were disconnected. Trying not to drop what was left of my biscuit, I texted with sticky fingers, "Sorry. Awful service. Will text you later. Love you."

I smiled when her immediate text reply came through. "Love you too."

"Bettina!" I shouted as I approached her. She stood up straight and did a swift turnabout, a wide smile lighting up her beautiful face. She quickly walked toward me and we collided, our friendly hug lasting longer than normal. I drank in her familiar scent. Bettina smelled like something clean, fresh and innocent. I had an instant déjà vu from almost four years ago of slathering baby lotion on the twins after their baths. *That's what Bettina smells like,* I thought.

It wasn't until she pulled away from our hug that I noticed she'd been crying. "Bettina?" I asked, my concern obvious. "What's wrong?"

"You haven't heard?" Bettina's words came out quivering. "You didn't get a text or phone call from Mrs. Mackie?"

"Heard what?" I asked, my attention solely focused on Bettina. I wondered what was so important that Mrs. Mackie, the camp administrator, would've needed to alert campers. I absentmindedly tossed what was left of my biscuit in the trash can we passed as we walked back toward her car.

"I got to the camp about the same time I got the text," Bettina explained through misty eyes. "Camp Keowee's been quarantined. Everyone is being turned away and they're trying to get the news out as quickly as possible."

She'd barely finished the last word when my phone buzzed and the text from the camp came through. Without reading it, I asked her, "Why?"

She sucked in her breath as she struggled for the words. "It's Josh."

Josh was one of the counselors at Camp Keowee. He volunteered every year that I'd attended and was one of the camp's valued and trusted leaders. Only a little older than me, Josh wanted to go into ministry. Without giving me time to reply, she continued.

"They thought he had the flu. But that's not what he has. It's so much worse." She paused and closed her eyes. I watched her swallow. The click of the gas pump turning off seemed to startle her and her eyes popped open. "It's meningitis and Josh is in critical condition," she explained as she robotically disengaged the nozzle from her tank and returned it to the pump. Turning back to face me she said, "He can die from this, Mimi. And it's highly contagious. The camp has to stay closed until it's thoroughly disinfected and given the green light by the Department of Health."

My eyes went wide as I felt the impact of what she told me. A horn interrupted us and we both turned to see an old man who'd pulled in behind Bettina's car. He gave us a kind look and indicated that he'd like for us to move so he could use the pumps. We both got in our cars and drove the short distance to the front of the grocery store entrance. Getting out of our vehicles, we stood behind mine and continued our conversation. After about ten minutes we'd calmed down enough to exchange hugs and say our goodbyes.

I was about to text my mother the change of plans and that I would be heading home, when Bettina whispered, "Hot guy alert." She nodded toward the grocery store entrance. "He got out of his truck and has been leaning against it, staring at us the entire time," she informed me. Not feeling any inclination to care about a random ogler, I returned my attention to my phone when her next words stopped me cold. "I guess we're closer to the Cherokee Indian Reservation in North Carolina than I thought."

I knew it was him. I don't know how I knew it or how it was even possible, but I could feel the heat from his eyes as they penetrated my back. As if in a dream I turned around slowly. I aimed my gaze toward the entrance of the store and saw Christian Bear.

The next few minutes were a blur as I once again hugged Bettina goodbye and tucked my phone in my pocket, completely forgetting I was going to call or text my mother. After waving to Bettina's retreating Miata, I turned back to the store entrance convincing myself that what I'd seen couldn't have been real—I was wrong. When I made eye contact with Christian, he walked toward me, his intense gaze mesmerizing me. He looked exactly as I remembered him from over five years ago, except he was much wider and taller. His vivid blue eyes stood out in stark contrast to his black hair which he still wore long, and I noticed a lot of tattoos as he got closer. I didn't remember him having so many when he was a teenager.

This couldn't be happening, I kept telling myself. Couldn't be real. It was almost as if thinking about him on the drive I'd somehow conjured him up out of nowhere. And speaking of nowhere, that's exactly where we were. In the middle of nowhere.

"Mimi?" He smiled hesitantly. "Is that you?"

Before I could answer, he asked, "It is you, isn't it? Mimi Dillon?"

"C-Christian?" I stuttered. "What in the world are you doing here?" Captivated by his intense stare, I had to concentrate on not allowing my knees to buckle.

"It is you!" His tentative smile turned brighter than the sun. He came at me for a hug and before I knew it my face was pressed into his chest. He smelled so good. I closed my eyes and inhaled deeply. Memories of his rejection rescued me from the moment, forcing me to tear myself away from him and look up. I didn't hold a grudge, but I also knew I wouldn't let myself get sucked back in. I knew the moment he recognized the change in my attitude as I nervously fiddled with my earring and looked around.

"So," I said as I rolled back on my heels and thrust my hands into my pockets. "Fancy meeting you here." I had to remind myself that we were both adults now, and he'd obviously forgotten what had transpired between us. I'd been able to move past it as well, but I'd be lying if I didn't admit that seeing him brought memories back from that place in my heart where they lay dormant for years. Unlike my earlier musings during my drive, seeing him in the flesh added a dimension to those memories I hadn't expected. It felt like a hundred raw nerves had been exposed and with them my humiliation. I felt a blush creeping up my neck. I hoped it wouldn't reach my face.

"I'm here on vacation with my family." He rolled his eyes as if he found the admission embarrassing. "We're staying at a house by the lake." He nodded toward his truck. I noticed the bed was filled with bicycles, a small kayak, and fishing poles. "I didn't want to come but now I'm glad I did. Mom sent me out for a bag of ice. Damn, I wish she'd come with me. I know she'd love to see you. What are you doing in South Carolina?" His voice was deeper than I remembered. "I thought you said your family was moving to Montana."

Warm memories of Christian's family replaced the angst I was feeling. I couldn't help but smile. "I go to college here. I spend my spring break at a camp up the mountain." I nodded toward the intersection and one of the roads that led away from Pumpkin Rest. "I always stop here for gas before I head there." I was so shocked by his sudden appearance that I forgot to mention the camp was under quarantine.

"Come back to the house with me before you head to your camp." His eyes were sincere. "Please, Mimi," he pleaded. "Ten minutes. It'll take ten minutes to see my family and say hello. You can follow me and be on your way after you see them."

I looked away nervously. Christian's parents knew my family's secret. Seeing them for a quick visit wouldn't be revealing anything they weren't already aware of. Except, of course, they believed we'd moved to Montana. There was no reason to say anything different to them. It was totally believable that I drove my car from Montana to attend college in South Carolina.

I made the quick decision that I would accept Christian's offer, convincing myself it was only because I wanted to see his family. I was so engrossed in watching the sway of his long hair against his wide shoulders as he strode confidently toward his truck, I missed the slight clenching of his jaw when he'd turned away from me. I'd also missed that he didn't stop for ice from the machine that sat just a few feet away.

CHAPTER 1

FORT LAUDERDALE, FLORIDA 2007

Two Weeks Earlier

C hristian Bear leaned back against the cushions of the worn couch and closed his eyes, letting the rhythm of her motions and the teasing of her tongue take him to a different realm. He could smell diesel fuel and grease as it drifted through the open door that separated the garage from the office.

He should've been grateful Axel had given him a job. After being released from prison, he'd had the option to work on his father's landscaping crew or suck up to Axel for another chance at car and motorcycle repairs. He had to stay off the law's radar, and it seemed like blending back into society as a mechanic was a good start. He was crashing at his older brother, Slade's, house in the guest room until he could figure out what he wanted to do with his life.

He chanced a glance down at the girl who was furiously trying to spin magic between his legs. It was working until she felt his stare and stopped what she was doing.

"You haven't even asked me my name," she said coyly, still holding his hardness with one hand. She batted her eyelashes and tried to look away shyly.

He rolled his eyes and roughly shoved her away. They were done.

Not another one. Another one who didn't understand a blow job was just a blow job. Not a fucking marriage proposal. He'd just turned twenty-three, but he knew the type. How he kept getting tangled up with these women, he didn't have a clue. She would want to talk and connect with him. She'd tell him she understood the depths of his pain and could heal him from the inside out.

So many had wanted to try. So many had been kicked out on their slutty asses as soon as he realized they thought they could be more than just a lay.

There was only one who could've been more. Only one he'd had feelings for.

How many times had he berated himself over the years thinking about how tongue-tied he'd been around Mimi? He'd barely been able to communicate back then, and missed more than one opportunity. By the time he was able to finally tell her how he felt, it was too late. Her mother was moving her away to start a new life in another state.

He remembered how back in 2002 when he was seventeen, his mother had invited Mimi's family over for a final goodbye. Except he hadn't known it was final. He'd thought it was just dinner. Apparently Mimi's mother, Ginny, had sold their house and had already shipped their personal belongings to their new home. They'd be spending the night in a hotel, starting the long drive to Montana the next day.

He almost dropped his fork mid-bite when he realized they were talking about leaving the very next morning. Everything had been set in motion.

How had this slipped by him? How had he not known? How could he not have heard his parents talking about a cross-country move by one of their closest friends?

There was no way his parents hadn't known about this, he concluded. They had purposely kept it a secret, and he wanted to know why. Being caught off guard like that had pissed him off to no end. As everyone stood in the foyer of his parents' house hugging and saying their final goodbyes, he'd slunk off to his room to fume, beyond angry.

He was throwing darts with his back to the bedroom door when he heard a soft knock. He gritted his teeth. If his mother thought she was going to try to smooth things over, she had another thing coming. His parents were guilty, and he planned on playing judge, jury, and executioner.

He heard the door open and was surprised when he heard Mimi's voice.

"Christian?"

His arm had stopped mid-throw, letting the dart drop to the floor as he slowly turned around to face her.

She was taking something out of her backpack.

"I never had a chance to give this back to you." She gave him a small smile.

He absently reached for the jacket he'd loaned her so many months ago. Mimi had looked at him with her big brown eyes as they both stood clutching the jacket, neither one willing to let go. He slowly tugged, and instead of releasing it, she held on and let him pull her closer. He saw something in her eyes then. He saw recognition. She was realizing at this very moment how he felt, how he'd always felt about her, even though he'd never been able to express himself.

"You have to go?" he heard himself ask her.

She nodded. "I want to go," she said in a soft voice. Her forehead crinkled. "At least, I think I do."

A pause. She looked at him with uncertainty and wonder.

Just then, her younger brother, Jason, poked his head into the room breaking the spell.

"Mimi, Mom said c'mon." They could hear his footsteps as he ran off.

"The guy that Jason mentioned at dinner, James. Is that why you're leaving? Your mom is seeing someone?"

"He's part of the reason. I'm glad my mother has fallen in love again. I want her to be happy, and I just don't think she can stay here."

"James who?" Not that he cared. He was just trying to think of conversation to prevent Mimi from leaving, if only for a few more minutes.

"Just James." She looked away.

Christian nodded. He was honestly happy for Mimi's mother and respected her privacy. She was a good woman, and Christian thought she deserved some happiness. But Ginny's happiness was taking his happiness across the country and out of his life.

"Mimi, I've waited too long, and now it's too late." His words were quiet.

She'd finally let go of his jacket, and he now held it in a crumpled ball.

Mimi laid a hand on his arm. "No. It's not too late, Christian. Look —we're going away to start over. Mom doesn't want us connected to anything from her old life. I don't blame her. We're going off the grid"—she emphasized the phrase with air quotes—"but it won't be forever. I know how to get in touch with you, and I will. You'll hear from me, okay?"

"When?"

"I honestly don't know, but I'll figure out a way as soon as I can. I have to go now. They're waiting. It won't be long. Trust me."

She'd stood on her tiptoes and softly kissed his cheek.

"Mimi," he'd called after her. She stopped and looked back at him, her hand clutching the doorknob. "Were you disappointed Slade wasn't here tonight? You know, to say goodbye?"

"No." She dipped her chin and peered up at him through her eyelashes. "I wasn't disappointed at all."

And then she was gone. That was five years ago.

And he'd waited.

And there was nothing.

Days slowly became weeks, which became months and finally stretched out into years, and there was no word from Mimi. She left, and he'd never gotten over her. Never forgotten that he'd seen something in her eyes that night. Something maybe she didn't even know was there. Something he'd wanted to pursue and would have—if she hadn't driven out of his life the next morning.

He was no longer the tongue-tied teenager who couldn't bring himself to ask Mimi out. Now he was a man. A man who knew what he wanted. A man who could finally admit that he'd always been in love with Mimi.

Shaking off the unhappy memory from five years ago, he barely noticed when what's-her-name pouted her way out of Axel's office and slipped out the back door of the garage. It was a Sunday, and the place was empty.

He absently looked around the small room and wondered if Axel had any liquor stashed. He rummaged through drawers and file cabinets until he came to the last one. It was an old metal number that had seen better days, and the drawers gave a loud screech when he opened and closed them.

The last and final drawer didn't contain files. A brown paper bag was sitting on top of something black. Maybe there was a bottle buried in here somewhere. He grabbed the bag, but could tell by its weight that it was full of paper. He wasn't interested and tossed it aside. Next, he came to a black leather jacket. Maybe there was a bottle of booze wrapped in its folds. Christian carefully lifted it out, but it wasn't concealing a bottle either.

He started to put the jacket back when he noticed part of a patch. Was this Axel's old club jacket? Standing up from his crouched position, he grabbed the jacket by both shoulders, stretching it out so he was looking at the back. He studied the patch. It was a sinister skull with devil horns. A naked woman was draped over the top of the skull. She had dark hair and dark eyes. He knew it was an image of Mimi's mother when she was a teenager, but he saw Mimi.

The suppressed feelings from his past started rising to the surface. She had told him to trust her. He'd waited. Trusted. And she'd never come back.

Christian was tired of waiting. He knew he could have someone find her. Yes, he would have someone track her down. Life wasn't fair, and there were too many rules.

He didn't play by the rules.

It was no secret that Mimi's biological father, Grizz, had her mother, Ginny, abducted back in 1975. It was no secret that Christian's father, Anthony, had taken his mother, Christy.

He'd grown tired of waiting. It was now time for Christian to take what he wanted.

And he'd always wanted Mimi.

CHAPTER 2

FORT LAUDERDALE, FLORIDA 2007

After leaving Axel's garage, Christian immediately sought out his computer geek friend, Seth. They launched a plan to find Mimi Dillon. He'd given Seth the only picture he had of her. The photo was of the entire family at the going-away dinner his mother had planned. Christy Bear had insisted on taking pictures that night and after she'd had them developed, Christian snuck one out of the processing envelope without her knowing. He'd trimmed it down to fit in his wallet where it had been tucked away for the past five years. He pulled it out and handed it to his friend.

"It's pretty worn, dude." Seth examined the photo, his forehead creasing as he frowned. "I'm going to try a facial recognition program that might help."

Eight hours later, Christian was back and standing behind his friend, staring at the computer screen.

"Is that her?" Seth was pointing at a cluster of friends who were all smiling for the camera.

Christian didn't answer at first. All he could do was stare. It was Mimi and she was no longer the young teenager he remembered. She was a woman, and he felt a stirring that was almost animalistic. The need to possess her, to own her, overwhelmed him with a soul-exposing intensity.

"Yeah, it's her." His voice sounded hoarse.

"I'm pretty sure they're all students at a college in South Carolina based on this dude's sweatshirt," Seth informed him as he pointed to one of the guys in the photo. "I also enhanced the picture and was able to confirm the name on one of the buildings in the background. I hacked the school's database and couldn't find a Mimi Dillon. She might not go to school there. Then again, she might be using a different name. Normally, when someone assumes an alias they still use a form of their real name. I found two possibilities, but they're a stretch." He swung around to face Christian. "Mary D. Dixon and Miriam D. Hunter."

Christian had an instant memory of being with Mimi when they were children. They'd been playing in the back yard and her mother had been trying to get her attention. After Mimi continued to ignore her mother's calls, Ginny had cried out in frustration, "Miriam Ruth I'm talking to you!"

Without taking his eyes off the screen, Christian replied in a low voice, "Her name is Miriam. The *D* could stand for her real last name, Dillon, and I can't say for sure about the name Hunter, but it's definitely her." Christian felt his back go rigid as the thought that Mimi might have gotten married crept into his mind.

"She's a senior and will be graduating this year—history major," Seth added.

Christian thanked him and headed out the door. It was time to put the next part of his plan into action.

A little over a week later and after paying a small fortune, Christian was handed an envelope that told him everything he needed to know about Miriam D. Hunter. He felt his jaw relax when he read the word single for her marital status. He wondered if she still went by Mimi. He dismissed the thought as he scoured through the information provided by the investigator he'd hired. The timing couldn't have been more perfect. Mimi would be finishing up her midterms in a week. In addition to details about her academic life, part-time job, and other information, the P.I. confirmed that Miriam Hunter drove a green Ford SUV with a Montana license plate. But more importantly, a lot of digging revealed that she was signed up to attend a retreat during her spring break. The same retreat she'd attended for the past three years. Christian carefully read each detail as a plan started to form in his mind.

He mapped out a route to the camp from Mimi's college. After careful consideration, he decided the best place to cross paths with her would be at a little town called Pumpkin Rest. She had no choice but to pass through there to get to Camp Keowee. He would wait at

Pumpkin Rest and look for her car. If she didn't stop, he would follow her and somehow get her to pull over. He didn't know if she would have anybody with her, and he would determine the best course of action for that possibility during the long, lonely drive to South Carolina.

The next day he was packed and minutes away from leaving when his older brother, Slade, came through the front door. Frowning at Christian, who'd been crashing in his guest room since being released from prison, he asked, "You're not going to smoke that in here, are you?"

Concentrating on the joint he was rolling and without looking at his brother, Christian replied, "It's for the road."

Slade shook his head knowing that Christian had skillfully managed to pass random drug testing by his parole officer. Proving once again that anyone could manipulate the system. Slade laid his briefcase on the coffee table and asked Christian, "Going somewhere?"

Christian stood and stuck the joint in the pocket of his tee. "Job prospect up in Jacksonville. I want to get out of Fort Lauderdale. I'll be gone at least a week. I already okayed it with Axel and my parole officer."

Slade raised an eyebrow and smirked. "Did you okay it with your women?" he asked sarcastically.

"I didn't tell Mom. I'll call her and Dad from the road."

"Did you tell...?" Slade prompted, but his words died off under Christian's glare. "Autumn?" Slade added.

"Autumn can screw herself," Christian replied as he picked up his duffel bag and headed out the front door.

Christian's first stop was Jacksonville, seeking a favor from a friend he'd made while in prison. After giving the man his cell phone, strict instructions, and a wad of cash, Christian continued his drive north. He arrived at Pumpkin Rest two days before Mimi was supposed to start her spring break. He'd already had Seth find him an isolated house to rent. After checking out the house, he returned to the crossroad and buddied up to one of the women who worked at the town's only gas station.

Through casual conversation he found out that the crossroad's one surveillance camera was only for show. It hadn't worked for over a year. He'd made up a story about looking for an old military friend who once mentioned coming this way during the same week every year to fish. When the clerk didn't recognize the man's name, Christian asked if it would be okay if he hung around. It was possible his friend might show up or pass by. She told him she didn't care and neither would anybody else.

After another exploratory mission of the small town and surrounding area, Christian was back at the rental house where he broke the locks off the owner's private shed and loaded up the bed of his truck with a couple of their bicycles, fishing poles, and a small kayak. He drove back to Pumpkin Rest and backed his truck in at the grocery store entrance so he could face the road. And he waited.

CHAPTER 3

W hile following Christian's truck I'd started to call my mother when a thought stopped me. Even though she wouldn't consider speaking with the Bear family a threat, what if she didn't agree with my decision? Wasn't it easier to beg forgiveness rather than ask permission and be told no? It didn't matter anyway. I wasn't getting a signal and I still had time. If I'd continued to the camp, my parents wouldn't be expecting a text for another hour. That was plenty of time to say hello to Christian's family before I headed for home.

We'd turned off the main street and were making our way along a neatly graveled road. It seemed like forever before the gravel gave way to just plain dirt and Christian stopped his truck and got out. I rolled down my window as he walked toward me. He pointed to a small pull-off covered by trees. "You should park your car over there and ride the rest of the way with me, Mimi. The road gets worse and I don't know if your car can handle it. You could break an axel. It'll be fine under those trees and I'll drive you back."

If I'd been anywhere other than a rural area I might've questioned his logic to leave my car. But because my family's home was in the Blue Ridge Mountains for the last five years, his request didn't seem out of the ordinary. My experience told me that city folk who vacationed in the mountains deliberately selected accommodations that were away from civilization. And more times than not, those paths were riddled with dust and fraught with divots and bumps. I returned my phone to my pocket, grabbed my purse and locked my car. I climbed into Christian's truck and looked over at his profile. I was instantly reminded of the last time I'd been in a truck with Christian. It had been an older model than the one I now rode in, but the memory washed over me.

He must've felt my gaze because he looked over at me and smiled. "How have you been? What have you been doing?" he asked before returning his eyes to the road.

I decided to share a little about myself, opting to keep what I told him at a minimum. I stuck to safe subjects like school, the camp I was supposed to be attending, and my part-time job. His next question caused me to pause.

"Did your mother ever marry that guy she was seeing? The guy who was one of the reasons behind your move to Montana?" A beat passed. "What was his name again"—before I could answer he asked —"James, wasn't it?"

I wondered why he was asking me this when he already knew the answer. I swallowed thickly and looked out the window, praying he didn't see the panic in my eyes. Maybe this wasn't such a good idea. Figuring Christian had forgotten what I'd shared with him five years ago I refused to look at him. Instead, I answered plainly, "Yes, she married him."

"What does he do for a living?" he nonchalantly asked me.

Racing through my memories, I tried to recall if I'd ever mentioned anything specific to Christian about James. It'd been more than five years since I last spoke to Christian and I didn't want to get caught in a lie. Seconds ticked by and I blurted out the first and stupidest thing that came to me. "He has an accounting degree. Like my mother." There. I didn't say he was an accountant, just that he had the same degree. Christian had no reaction, giving me the opportunity to quickly change the subject. I'd barely gotten the first sentence out when we rounded a curve and came upon a beautiful home set back from the road. We made our way up the long driveway. There were no other vehicles which gave me pause. "It doesn't look like anybody else is here."

Without missing a beat, Christian nodded toward a worn path that circled around behind the house. "They parked out back."

I relaxed and smiled knowing I was about to surprise his parents. I was also quite anxious to see his little sister, Daisy. I figured her to be about eleven or twelve years old by now. I almost asked if Slade was with them, but immediately tabled that question for later. After getting out of the truck, I followed Christian up the steps to the wide front porch. I stood behind him as he opened the front door, stepping aside so I could go in first. The loud click of the door closing behind us echoed off the walls.

I was immediately drawn to the view and strode through the huge family room toward the back of the house where enormous glass windows revealed a pristine lake. Beyond the lake was a mountain backdrop that left no doubt in my mind as to whether or not there was a master Creator. I'd seen a hint of a lake as we drove up, but what I gazed at now went beyond what I'd expected. It was massive and resembled a perfect sheet of glass. I smiled when I looked down at the boat dock. I turned around to ask Christian where his family was when he walked up next to me and peered down at the lake.

"I'm sorry, Mimi. The boat is gone. They must've taken it out for a spin."

He looked over at me, his eyes warm and I had an instant memory of our few moments together in his bedroom when we were teenagers. I quickly looked away.

"I know you need to head for your camp. Do you wanna take a fast tour of the house first? Maybe they'll come back while you're still here."

I nodded as I turned around and familiarized myself with the home the Bears had rented. Or maybe they owned it. Thinking that Christian might've spent family vacations just over the border from where my family lived sent a tingle of excitement mixed with mild trepidation up my spine. I needed to be cautious.

"This house is beautiful," I blurted out. "Are you renting or does your family own it?"

He smiled causing my heartbeat to speed up. I nervously nibbled at my bottom lip and avoided his gaze.

"It's a rental. C'mon. I'll show you around."

I followed Christian as he headed for a stairway that led to a finished basement. It was a huge space that not only included a seating area with a giant television screen, but pool and air hockey tables as well. One wall housed a wet bar, and the opposite wall was lined with video arcade games. There were two bedrooms on each side of the basement, four in all, and they shared Jack and Jill bathrooms. It was definitely a vacation house.

We made small talk as we walked through the basement and it wasn't until he waved me back toward the stairs that I made a closer inspection of some of his tattoos. I recognized the ink and wondered if Christian had been honest with me when I'd asked him what he'd been doing for the past five years. According to him, he'd graduated high school and instead of opting for college, he worked full-time in a garage specializing in motorcycle repairs. His ink told another story.

I'd wanted so badly to ask him about one tattoo in particular. It was a woman's name and based on the design, I knew that Christian loved her. I wondered if she was still in his life. Was she out on the boat with the rest of his family? How would I feel when I came face-to-face with the woman who had captured Christian Bear's heart?

Ignoring my churning stomach I pressed on as we arrived back on the main level and he ushered me toward the master bedroom. It was connected to an en suite bathroom that was bigger than any bedroom I'd ever had. I knew his parents had money yet lived modestly. Obviously they splurged when it came to vacations.

After making our way through the main-level guest bedrooms, bathrooms, and humongous kitchen we found ourselves in the great room again. Something was off and I couldn't place it, but I knew something wasn't jiving. This was wrong, but I couldn't figure out what would make me think so. Christian was different, but in a good way. He wasn't the serious teenager I remembered. The hair stood up on the back of my neck as something dawned on me.

"I'll be back in a minute." I brushed off any response from him with a wave. I practically ran to the master bedroom. I returned sixty seconds later, my breath coming out in huffs.

He was leaning against one of the huge beams that supported the tall vaulted ceiling. His arms were crossed in front of his chest and his head was tilted to one side. Expressionless, he stared at me.

"They're not here," I shouted. "Your family isn't here."

I didn't give him a chance to deny it as I babbled on, my voice rising with each syllable.

"A duffle bag on the bed, no toothbrushes or toiletries in the master bath. No personal items on the dresser, no clothes in the closet, no other suitcases. None of the bedrooms or bathrooms look like anybody has used them." Staring down at the hardwood floor, I was rambling more to myself as I mentally ticked off everything that wasn't fitting the scenario.

"And the road was smooth. We never hit any bumps. My car could've made it up here. You didn't want me to have access to my car." I finally looked up and my breath caught in my throat. Gone was the smiling, welcoming man I'd met at Pumpkin Rest. Gone was the childhood friend who seemed excited to surprise his parents by inviting me to their rented lake house. Gone was the amicable long-lost friend who'd just given me a tour of this huge lake house.

I raised my hand to my chest as he slowly walked toward me, his icy blue eyes revealing nothing.

"W-where's your f-family?" I clung to an iota of hope that I was wrong. Maybe they'd just arrived and didn't want to unpack before they took the boat out for a spin.

I made a quick scan of the room, my eyes resting on the open kitchen area. Not a pot or placemat out of place.

"In Florida," was his cold reply.

"Why did you lie to me?" I slowly backed up. I was momentarily startled when my back hit one of the huge support beams.

"Why did you lie to me?" he shot back.

His question caught me off guard and I blinked. He came at me slowly and I could feel my pulse quickening. "Lie to you? I never lied to you, Christian."

"When you left Florida five years ago, you said you'd be in touch," he growled. "And you're not leaving here until I find out why you didn't follow through on that promise. Was it all just a game for you, Mimi? Or was it even less than that? Was I less than that?"

He was now so close I could smell him. It was a mixture of the clean scent I'd detected at Pumpkin Rest and something raw and masculine. It assaulted my senses in a way I hadn't expected. My eyes were level with his chest, and when I raised them I could see the pulse beating in his neck. Before I had the chance to answer I felt his hands on my hips and realized he was digging my cell phone out of my pocket. My immediate reaction was to swipe it from him, but he was faster, holding it well above my reach. He backed away from me as he glanced at my phone.

"No passcode," then under his breath, "dumb."

"Give that back!" I cried as I walked toward him. "Why are you looking at my phone?"

He gave me a level look. "I'm making sure you didn't call or text anyone since Pumpkin Rest. And I see that you haven't. Good girl."

I bristled at the condescending endearment, and bit back a retort about the cell phone service being awful anyway. "Give me back my phone," I insisted. "And I'm not anyone's good girl."

"Not even Lucas Paine's?" His voice dripped with sarcasm.

His mention of Lucas halted my rush of thoughts. The realization of how articulately this must've been planned caused my heart to beat faster. Had he followed me all the way from school? And if so, how did he get ahead of me and park at the grocery store with a truck bed full of vacation paraphernalia? A million thoughts jostled for a front row seat to the movie playing in my head. I could see my choices for removing myself from this situation dwindling as I battled with not only the reason behind why this was happening, but to what end? What were Christian's intentions?

Some things I knew were certain. My mother would be waiting for a text from me to let her know I'd arrived at camp safely. When she didn't get that text, she would call the retreat administrators to verify I was there. And when she discovered the camp was closed, she probably wouldn't panic at first, assuming I'd turned around and was headed home and forgot to call. But if more than a few hours passed without me checking in, she would contact the authorities to report me missing. Authorities that would have to interview my parents extensively. Authorities that could discover my family's secret. I couldn't let that happen.

Without acknowledging his comment about Lucas, and refusing to show any fear, I raised my chin and demanded, "Take me back to my car."

"I'm going back to your car, but you're staying here."

Faster than lightning, he whipped out a pair of handcuffs that must've been tucked in the back pocket of his jeans. Before I knew what was happening, he'd slapped one on my right wrist and proceeded to pull me back toward the support beam I'd bumped into moments earlier. I fought him, kicking at his shins and punching on his solid chest with my free hand. I tripped over my feet and felt myself falling to the hardwood floor. Using one arm he had wrapped around my waist, he lowered me to the ground. If I hadn't known better, I would've thought he was trying to soften my landing. You'd think my dead weight would've slowed him down, but it didn't. He effortlessly pulled me back toward the post as I glided on my rear end across the glossy wood floor.

"Don't do this, Christian!" I screamed. But it was too late. I felt the cold metal as the handcuff was slapped on my left wrist, leaving me no choice but to hug the solid post to my chest. My hips moved from the force he used to dig in my other pocket. He stood and looked down at me.

"I'm going back to get your stuff out of your car," he informed me as he dangled my keys in front of me. "You'll need your things since you'll be staying with me for a while."

I scrambled to my feet clumsily, focusing on him with intense fury. Any concern I had to protect my family was now forgotten. "My father will kill you for this." My voice was low with a menacing quality that surprised even me.

"Which father? The one that died on death row?" Christian asked mockingly. I'm certain my eyes looked like they were popping out of my head. "Yeah, I know Grizz was your real father, Mimi." His eyes narrowed. "Or Tommy Dillon? The one killed in a botched robbery?" His lip curled. "We both know neither one of them will be coming to your rescue."

His comments forced my stunned silence. I didn't know how to answer him, so I stared, my jaw slack.

"Or maybe you're talking about James, the man your mother ran off with, who I'm sure is a putz," he sneered. "I know they're in Montana so I can't say that I'm too worried." He waited for my reply, and when I didn't give one, he continued. "Is that the best you've got, Mimi?"

He turned and stomped to the door. He didn't look back, ignoring my screams as I shrieked his name before he slammed the door behind him.

CHAPTER 4

FORT LAUDERDALE, FLORIDA 2002

Five Years Earlier

A teenaged Christian glared at his parents, Anthony and Christy Bear. Mimi and her family had walked out of their lives. Permanently. Just twenty minutes earlier, Mimi had reassured him that she would contact him. But he was angry to have been excluded from such a monumental secret. It caused his blood to boil.

"You knew they were moving!" he screamed at both parents. "You both knew, and you purposely didn't tell me. I want to know why?"

Anthony stared angrily at his son and without breaking his gaze said in a low whisper, "Christy, why don't you get Daisy ready for bed? Christian and I will finish this conversation in the garage."

Still staring at his father, Christian realized his seven-year-old sister, Daisy, may have been within earshot. He lowered his voice and said, "Something isn't right. You used to ask Mimi to babysit, and I don't believe for a second she got too busy. You didn't want us to hook up, and now I know why. You knew they were moving. And you didn't want me to know that. Why?"

"Don't be so hard on him, babe," Christy said to Anthony as she gave her son an understanding yet sad look. She knew that beneath the anger, Christian was feeling the pain of unrequited love. She had watched him silently pine over Mimi for years. And he was right. She and Anthony had discouraged any contact between the teens since last year. They even let Christian sit in jail for one of his minor stunts longer than necessary to keep him distracted and away from Mimi Dillon. And they'd had a very good reason. They knew the day would come when Ginny would move away from Florida. Their friend would be disconnecting herself from everyone and everything associated with her past. It was imperative that she leave the state, and the reason behind it was huge. They also knew it was something they could never share with another soul, and that included their sons, Slade and Christian.

Mimi's mother, Ginny, had a secret that would've been impossible for her to continue concealing. Especially in South Florida. Anthony and Christy felt they needed to respect the family's decision to move away and cut themselves off from their old life in Florida. The family had to sever all ties. And that would include ignoring the feelings they knew Christian had for Mimi since they were children.

They were standing in the kitchen, and as Christy walked away, she saw Anthony roughly shove Christian toward the door that led out to their garage.

"If you ever raise your voice to your mother like that again, I'll knock your teeth down your throat. You got—"

Anthony's voice floated away as he shut the door behind them.

Storming into the garage, Christian swung around to face his father, fists clenched at his sides. Anthony Bear was an imposing man. He was a full-blooded Native American with a muscular build who stood at six feet six inches tall. He was covered in tattoos and had jet-black straight hair that reached his belt. The slight streaks of gray at his temples were the only thing that contrasted his dark skin, hair, and eyes. Right now, those eyes were boring into his son's.

Nearing six feet tall, a soon-to-be eighteen-year-old Christian Bear wasn't intimidated. Just as dark and foreboding as his father, it was Christian's blue eyes that contrasted his dark features.

"I'll apologize to Mom later," he huffed. "But you two were wrong to keep this from me. I can't believe they're moving to Montana so that Aunt Ginny can be with some jerk named James. And why all the secrecy? What's the big deal, Dad?"

"You know the horrors that family has been through this past year. You know that Mimi's real father, Grizz, died on death row. You know the only father she's ever known, Tommy, was killed in a robbery gone wrong. You also know that before Tommy died, he was being dragged into some court case involving the murder of Blue's ex-wife. And I sure as hell know you know that Mimi was almost raped last year."

"Of course I know all that. And about Mimi's attempted rape—if it wasn't for me, it would've happened. And besides, I'm the one who told you about it!" Christian growled.

"Can you blame Ginny for wanting to move, son?" Anthony asked.

"I didn't think Aunt Ginny knew what had happened to Mimi," Christian replied, his tone calmer.

"She doesn't know, and she never will. Breaking ties with us, and from South Florida, will guarantee that. She wants to start over, and we're respecting her wishes, Christian. It's your own fault for slacking for so long in the romance department. Maybe if you'd been more aggressive with your feelings for Mimi, things might be a little different. Maybe you'd have been trusted with their specific destination. You're taking it too personally." Anthony crossed his arms and leaned back on Christy's car.

"Tell me how I can get in touch with Mimi. What's their new address in Montana?" Christian demanded.

Anthony didn't answer.

"Fine. Mom will give it to me," Christian said haughtily.

"Your mother and I don't know it," Anthony countered.

"Bullshit!" Christian replied, his voice going up an octave.

"Christian, we don't have a forwarding address. Ginny left no way for us to contact her. When and if she's ever ready, she'll be in touch with us." Anthony would never tell Christian that Ginny told them they could be contacted through her friends Carter and Bill. The Bears would only use this resource in the case of an emergency. Unfortunately, Christian's broken heart didn't qualify.

"Why do I have the feeling if I were Slade asking you this, I'd be getting a different answer?" Christian demanded, his voice cracking.

Anthony raised an eyebrow. "Slade would be getting the same answer you're getting. We don't know how to get in touch with her. And what is your problem with your brother? Are you still mad that he didn't put Mimi's attacker in the hospital?"

"Damn straight, I'm mad!" Christian hissed. He stood taller and took a more assertive stance, thrusting his fists on his hips.

Anthony pushed off the car and stood to face his son, looking down into his angry blue eyes.

"Your brother was smart. Smarter than you," he said in a low voice. He watched Christian wince in reaction to the words.

"So, because he's in college he's a big damn deal to be worshiped and adored?"

"First, he was taking college courses at night while still in high school. When he moved out to start at the university, he already had an associate degree under his belt. Does that make him smart? Yeah, it does. But it means more than that. It shows he has ambition. He is driven. He's willing to work for what he wants." Anthony stopped and pointed his finger at Christian. "Second, should you be worshiped and adored for screwing up with Axel and losing your mechanic job? Or for sitting in jail for stealing Escalade hood ornaments that you could sell to your idiotic friends to wear around their necks? I don't think so, Christian." He lowered his hand and moved closer to his son, giving him a look that dared him to challenge his last comments.

"The hood ornament crap was stupid. It was nothing, and I still don't know who tipped off the cops resulting in me getting pinched. I never get caught," he sneered. Then he recognized a look in his father's eyes. "Shit, Dad! It was you, wasn't it? You tipped off the cops. You're the reason I went to jail, and you let me sit there too!"

Anthony didn't deny it, and before he knew it, he was deflecting a punch aimed for his face. In a flash, he managed to twist his son around and slam him hard against the hood of the car, pinning his right arm tightly against his back.

"Your temper is your biggest weakness, Christian. You keep this up, and you'll be stealing car parts the rest of your life to get by. If you don't spend it in prison." Anthony had bent to whisper in Christian's ear, his voice deep and serious.

"You were the leader of a motorcycle club in Naples. I know what you're capable of," Christian growled over his shoulder. "And you prefer a son with a college degree who's going to sit behind a desk and take orders from some snot-nosed corporate shit?"

Anthony released his son and took a step back as Christian turned around. He was impressed. He knew that he was close to breaking Christian's arm, but Christian never flinched, whined or gave any indication that he was in pain.

"I prefer a son who uses his brains to be successful, and more importantly, knows when to use his brawn and when not to. I'm not telling you not to be physical. I'm telling you to be smart about it. Anything done in haste and anger will come back to bite you."

Christian gave a derisive laugh. "In other words, you want a son who's a wuss?"

Anthony didn't reply. He shook his head as Christian pressed the garage door button and headed toward his motorcycle parked in the driveway. "I don't need anything from you or Mom. Mimi said she'd be in touch with me and I believe her," he called out over his shoulder. "And there's nothing you can do about that."

Anthony watched Christian jump on his bike and speed off.

"You don't know how wrong you are, son," he said to no one as he took a deep and calming breath before heading inside to kiss his little girl goodnight.

CHAPTER 5

PUMPKIN REST, SOUTH CAROLINA 2007

"Christiannn!" Mimi screamed as he slammed the massive door to the lake house and headed down the steps toward his truck. Her voice echoed in his brain and it wasn't until he closed his truck door that he was able to clear it from his head.

As he drove down the dusty and lonely road that would take him to Mimi's car, Christian mentally berated himself for handling her the way he had. Swiping his hand through his long hair, he tried to ignore the scent that filled the small space. Mimi still smelled the same. Unlike his mother, who could detect the aroma of a rainstorm miles away, Christian wasn't a man who could identify a particular scent. Yet he never forgot one either, and Mimi's essence had lingered in his soul all these years, taunting him.

He'd had plenty of time to think during his long drive to South Carolina and was certain he'd put his original anger about the past behind him. He'd been genuinely happy to see her at Pumpkin Rest and considered coming clean with her and hoping she'd have a civil conversation with him. It wasn't until she got in his truck that the anger started to simmer again. Memories of their last night together and the empty promise that he'd clung to for five long years threatened to boil to the surface when she stared out the truck window and started concocting lies about her new stepfather, James. Once they reached the house he decided to give her another chance and was enjoying their lighthearted banter during the tour of the house. It wasn't until he started asking her questions that he'd already known the answers to, based on facts from the private investigator's report,

33

that he began to change his mind. Those facts weren't particularly important, yet Mimi still felt compelled to lie about them. When she figured out the ruse about his family's visit, he used his anger as an excuse to restrain her and whipped out the handcuffs before he could stop himself.

He shook his head as he pulled up to Mimi's car. *How did I go from being angry enough to make the drive to South Carolina to find her, to being glad to see her, to handcuffing her to a post?* The answer was simple. His feelings for her were stronger than he cared to admit, yet he knew they'd always been there. Only Mimi could have this effect on him. He didn't give one shit about any other woman he'd been with. Not one. The irony wasn't lost on him that the only female who did get to him, was the only one he'd never been physical with. He'd never even kissed Mimi. What was this hold she had on him since childhood? Whatever it was, he would confront it over the next couple of days and then bury it. Along with anything he might've thought he felt for Mimi Dillon.

After Christian lifted the hood of her car and disconnected crucial wiring, he rifled through her trunk and grabbed her bag. Noticing the laundry basket filled with clothes, he tucked it under the same arm. He slammed the trunk closed with his free hand, got in his truck and headed back to the house.

He thought about moving her car to the rental house but decided against it. It wasn't because he thought she might give him the slip, it was because it wasn't necessary. This road wouldn't be traveled by anyone other than him. And on the off chance someone could see it from the air, the green car blended in perfectly with the canopy of trees that covered it.

He made the drive up the solitary road, pondering the challenge he faced at the end of it. Tossing aside the memories of the deep feelings he'd harbored for years and the mixed emotions he'd been juggling since his trek to Pumpkin Rest, he decided the best way to deal with Mimi would be to treat her like he'd treated all females. He would get the answer to his question and have her apologizing before dinner. And like every woman he'd ever encountered, she'd be throwing herself at him before the night was over, no doubt waking up in his bed tomorrow morning.

He told himself that Mimi would just be another meaningless lay. All he had to do now was convince himself he believed it.

CHAPTER 6

PUMPKIN REST, SOUTH CAROLINA 2007

The silence in the beautiful lake house was resounding. Or maybe it wasn't the silence, but the pounding of my heart reverberating in my head.

My wrists were almost raw from tugging at the handcuffs. Rawness that matched my sore throat from screaming Christian's name for a full five minutes after I heard his truck drive away. I knew he couldn't hear me, but yelling made me feel like I was doing something since I wasn't getting anywhere with freeing myself from my restraints.

Wishing I hadn't wasted so much energy, I slowly slunk back to the floor. I wrapped my legs around the beam and pressed my forehead against it. It was then that I noticed the stinging in my forearms. Casting a wary glance at each arm, I realized that the tender insides of both of them were bright red and filled with splinters. I'd been so engaged in my useless tug of war, I hadn't noticed that my arms were teeming with scratches that were deep enough to draw blood.

I sighed as I glanced around the tastefully furnished room, unconsciously admiring the soft leathery couches, the vibrant wall tapestries portraying mountain scenes, and the black baby grand piano nestled in a far corner. It reminded me of my own home in the foothills of the Blue Ridge Mountains, just over the border in North Carolina. The home where my family was going about their daily routine, having no clue of what I had gotten myself into.

"I suppose it could be worse," I said to no one. At least it wasn't a cabin with no plumbing or electricity. I shuddered when I thought about the kinds of creatures that took up residence in some of those old hunting shacks.

"You're handcuffed to a post in the middle of nowhere and you're thinking about plumbing and spiders?" I scolded myself out loud.

I forced myself to take a calming breath and considered what Christian had said moments before leaving me chained to the beam. He'd accused me of lying to him when my family moved away from Florida five years ago. I hadn't lied to him. I'd honored what I'd told him. He had some nerve flinging accusations at me after what he'd done. It was bad enough that I'd been rejected by his older brother, Slade. But the pain Christian inflicted had been much worse. He'd shattered my heart into a million pieces.

Five Years Earlier

It had been only a couple of months since my family had made the move to North Carolina. I sat on the front porch swing and wrote in my journal as I reflected over the summer. I was elated that my family chose to only go as far as North Carolina instead of moving all the way to Montana. The lazy creaking of the swing was comforting, soothing, as were my happy memories of my first summer in the mountains.

The previous two months had been filled with cementing new and lifelong friendships. Most of them with my cousins. Cousins with whom I'd be starting my senior year in high school. Cousins I hadn't known existed this time last year. I'd also caught myself thinking about someone who would never be part of this new chapter in my life. Thinking of and missing this person so badly my heart physically ached. My father, Tommy Dillon. He wasn't my biological father, but he was the man who'd raised me. The man I'd called Daddy. The man who'd died last year leaving me, my mom, and my younger brother, Jason, alone. That was until my mother discovered that my biological father, Grizz, was still alive and wanted very much to be part of our lives. The only way that was possible was for us to leave South Florida. We'd left soon after my mother tracked down Grizz's family, insisting that he meet them. The family Grizz hadn't known about until last year.

So here we were, cut off from all of our ties to South Florida. Cut off by choice and thriving in our new home near long-lost relatives.

Yes, I thought to myself, *North Carolina definitely feels like home. With one exception.*

Him.

Christian Bear.

How had I not seen it when I was still living in Fort Lauderdale? I remembered feeling attracted to him the morning he drove me home after babysitting the night before for his little sister, Daisy. The same night I'd suffered a humiliating rejection from his older brother, Slade.

The months following that encounter seemed like a blur. I remembered calling Christian's mother, Christy, several times asking if she needed me to babysit again. But the answer was always the same. She would keep me in mind and let me know. I remembered thinking that maybe she was trying to help me get over Slade's gentle rebuff, guessing that my mother had probably mentioned it to her. But that wasn't why I wanted to babysit. I realized that I was hoping to run into Christian again—to gauge my feelings for him.

Months passed and there hadn't been any occasions to see the Bear family. After not getting any replies to the texts I sent him, I convinced myself the ride home Christian had given me was just that, a ride home. And I believed it. Until our last night in Florida. My mom, my brother, Jason, and I spent that last evening in Fort Lauderdale having dinner at the Bear home. I tried to act casually while we were eating, but noticed Christian's demeanor change after his mother mentioned it was a going-away dinner for my family. He left the table without giving any of us a backward glance.

I finished the meal in silence and was secretly disappointed that he hadn't returned to the table. I'd excused myself from the after-dinner goodbyes and went to his bedroom, knocking lightly on the door. When he didn't answer, I opened it and went inside. He'd been throwing darts, and I remembered a lump formed in my throat when he turned to look at me, dropping the dart to the floor with a thud. I'd been so startled by what I saw in his expression I forgot to ask him why he'd never responded to any of my texts. I'd stopped sending them after the fifth or sixth one went unanswered.

I'd relived those last two minutes with Christian a million times. I'd fantasized what it would have been like if he'd kissed me that night. What it would've felt like to run my hands through his black silky hair, breaking from that kiss anticipating what I would see in his eyes.

I shifted my position on the porch swing and it gave a louder than usual groan. Swatting away an annoying insect, I continued to ponder everything that had led up to this moment. As far as everyone knew, my family had started a new life in Montana, breaking contact with everyone from our past. That night in his room, I'd promised Christian that I'd keep in touch with him, and I'd been wracking my brain for the last few months trying to figure out a safe way to do it. I'd confided in my cousin and now best friend, Rachelle, telling her I needed to get a message to a friend and provide a way for him to communicate with me.

Rachelle had come up with an excellent plan a few weeks ago.

"You can't text because you dumped your old phone and don't have any contacts," Rachelle said matter-of-factly. "Besides, you said he never answered the ones you sent before you moved." We were sitting cross-legged on my bed. The windows were open, and the fresh mountain air, along with the smell of whatever my grandfather, Micah, was roasting in the fire pit, had wafted in.

I nodded.

We heard the sound of bedsheets flapping on the clothesline. My mother insisted on hanging our linens outside to dry. She swore the mountain air made them smell fresher than any dryer sheet could. I smiled when I remembered watching Grizz carry the heavy load of wash to the clothesline. He didn't want Mom doing laundry at all, let alone hauling it around. He doted over her like nothing I'd ever witnessed. Even more so after they found out my mother was pregnant with twins. Their love was so obvious that seeing it sometimes caused an ache in my chest. Is this what I could've had with Christian if only I'd seen it sooner?

"Earth to Mimi!" Rachelle snapping her fingers in front of my face broke through my thoughts.

I shook my head and smiled. "Sorry. Yeah, I don't have any contacts from my old phone, and before you ask, I don't have a clue if Christian has an email account. I highly doubt it." I looked hopefully at my cousin. "What else ya got?"

"Do you know his address?"

"Umm, yeah, I know his address. Even if I didn't, we could find it online. But I can't mail a letter from here, Rachelle. Even if I didn't put a return address on it, it would still be stamped with a North Carolina postmark. I can't let him know where I am. I have to honor my parents' wishes. I promised them I would." I knew the tone in my voice conveyed my disappointment. "Besides, he thinks we're in Montana."

I jumped when Rachelle sat straight up on my bed. "It won't have a North Carolina postmark! It'll have a California postmark!"

Her excitement was brimming, though she wasn't making sense. She ignored my confused expression.

"I'm going to California before school starts. Remember? You write him a letter. Don't put a return address on it. I'll mail it from California." She beamed at me, and slapped her right thigh.

"That's an awesome idea!" I said, my excitement joining Rachelle's. But another thought followed, and I felt my shoulders slump in defeat. "But how can he get back in touch with me? I can't give him my new phone number this soon. I'm still trying to be careful. And you know there's no way I can give him an address to write back to me."

Not one to be deterred, my cousin's enthusiasm returned as she burst forth with another plan.

"Okay, here's what we're gonna do," she said quietly. "We are going to drive down to South Carolina. I mean, we're what, eleven miles from the border? We'll open a new email account at any public library. But you cannot sign into that account from any computers at our school, your house, anywhere in our state. You can only check that email when you're not in North Carolina. Think about it, Mimi," she challenged as she stared at me with wide eyes, "we are in the perfect location for this. You can drive from here in any direction and be in Georgia, South Carolina or Tennessee within thirty minutes to an hour. You write him a letter and tell him to send you an email." She sat back against the headboard and crossed her arms in front of her, satisfied with her suggestion. "And the next time we go to the mall in South Carolina or Dollywood in Tennessee or river rafting in Georgia, we'll swing by a public library, and you can check your email account. It's that simple."

I slowly nodded as I started to see how this could essentially work. I would explain in my letter to Christian how he should do the same thing; create an email address only to be used from a public computer. That way there would be no chance of someone in his house happening upon an open email. I didn't understand how people could be traced through their computer addresses, and I highly doubted we needed to go to the extreme that Rachelle suggested, but it was a good idea. It also made me feel like I wouldn't be in too much violation of the "breaking all contact" rule that my family had established. Besides, Christian Bear was my oldest friend, and there would certainly be an exception for him.

"I think this might actually work, Rachelle!" I whisper-yelled, as I remembered the open windows and my parents' presence at the clothesline right outside.

I swatted at a yellow jacket as I was brought back from the memory of almost a month ago. I closed my journal and laid it next to me on the porch swing as I reflected on how Rachelle had visited California and was now back. Christian definitely would've received my letter by now. Rachelle would be picking me up in less than an hour, and we were driving over the state line into South Carolina. We would be stopping at the same public library I'd used to set up an email address before giving Rachelle the letter to mail to Christian from California. The anticipation of logging onto the computer and finding an email from Christian gave me a heady buzz. I was so excited I could barely contain myself.

CHAPTER 7

PUMPKIN REST, SOUTH CAROLINA 2007

I heard Christian's truck outside and stood up. There was no way I would allow him to see me slumped on the floor in defeat. I glared at him as he came through the door, carrying my things. It was a wasted effort since he completely ignored me as he strode toward the master bedroom.

He walked out of the bedroom, and gave me a level look. "You think you can behave yourself if I unlock the handcuffs?"

He wanted me to behave myself? I was surprised he could walk because he apparently had balls the size of a lion. I swallowed back a nasty retort knowing that if I lashed out, I'd stay attached to the beam. I opted for a slight nod. He nodded back and approached me. I couldn't see his face, but could feel his movements as he started to unlock the cuffs from the other side of the post, but something stopped him.

"What have you done to your arms?" He almost sounded like he cared.

"It's nothing," I shot back. I felt the release of the handcuffs and pulled back, rubbing the sting out of my wrists.

"It's not nothing, Mimi," came his retort.

I looked up when he grabbed my left wrist and studied the inside of my arm. Making a fist, I aimed for his lower jaw and connected hard, the knuckles on my right hand throbbing. He barely flinched.

"You idiot!" I screamed as I stepped back from him, yanking my wrist from his grasp. My fury was unflinching. "Did you even think for one second that if anything had happened to you while you were gone, I would've died of dehydration or starvation before anybody found me here?"

"Nothing was going to happen to me," he spat as he started dragging me toward the master bedroom.

I started to fight him again, struggling to pull away, but he managed to get behind me. Forcefully, he wrapped his arms around me, pinning my back against his chest and my arms to my sides. As he steered me toward the bedroom door, I tried to bring my heel down on his foot, but my thin sandal didn't stand a chance against his heavy boot. I finally used the back of my head, thrusting it backward against his chin. I think it hurt my head more than his chin because he didn't react. Instead, he held me tighter and kept pushing me toward the master bedroom door. When we reached our destination, I lifted both feet off the ground and straddled the doorjambs, blocking our entrance.

"Put your feet down, Mimi." His warm breath caressed the side of my face.

"No!" I screamed as I tried for another reverse headbutt. This time I connected with his nose and heard him grunt.

"Damn it, Mimi! I'm just trying to get you to the bathroom where we can clean up your arms and get something on them before they get infected."

Without relaxing my legs I threw his words back at him. "Damn it, Christian! Why couldn't you just ask me to walk back here with you?" I lowered my legs at the same time he relaxed his grip on my arms. Free from his grasp I turned around to face him and saw a small trickle of blood coming from his nose. Good.

He glowered at me, grabbed me by my shoulders and whipped me around. Giving me a gentler nudge through the bedroom door, he growled, "I don't ask."

I SAT on top of the granite bathroom counter and watched the top of his head as he meticulously removed all the splinters from my forearms with a pair of tweezers we'd found in one of the drawers. He'd also managed to locate cotton swabs and peroxide left by the previous renters or the homeowners. Neither one of us spoke as he worked. I was grateful as it gave me time to think. I needed to get a message to my mother and I needed to do it sooner rather than later. And more importantly, I was completely on edge knowing the anonymous and quiet life my family had carved out in the last five years was at risk.

"I need to text my mother," I blurted out after he yanked out the last of the splinters.

Christian didn't say anything as he laid down the tweezers and picked up the peroxide and cotton balls. Before dabbing the wounds on my arms, he replied, "No."

"No? Just who do you think you are?" I yanked my arm away from him, causing him to look up.

"I know exactly who I am. And I'm telling you no." He gave me a serious look. "Besides, I saw the notification text from your camp telling you it's been cancelled. They won't be contacting your family when you don't show up."

"If I don't text my mother to let her know I arrived safely at the camp, she'll call there. And when they tell her it was cancelled and she hasn't heard from me, my parents will come..." My words died off as I realized I almost gave away that my parents could jump in the car and be at the camp in a little over two hours.

"You have to check in with your mother?" His tone was beyond sarcastic.

"As a matter of fact, I do, Christian. My parents care about me. The drive to camp is desolate."

He nodded his head as if in agreement, then his eyes narrowed.

"You can tell me what you want to say and I'll do the texting," he said.

I didn't answer him as I followed him out through the bedroom. We were once again in the great room when he pulled my phone from his pocket. He held it up high and told me, "The signal is almost nonexistent in here. It's a little better on the back deck."

I swung around and marched toward the French doors that led to the large wooden deck. I was once again almost mesmerized by the view, but shook it off as I turned around to face him. "You need to text 'I'm at camp.' And you need to spell it out. I never abbreviate my messages. She'll immediately know it's not me if you just type camp or use the at sign."

He rolled his eyes before returning his attention to my phone. "You'll find her under Mom," I quickly added.

"Thanks for the info. I never would've figured that one out on my own," he said without looking up.

I crossed my arms across my chest and waited for him to finish.

"Done," he told me.

"There's one more thing." I looked away. Before he could ask, I said, "I have a code word too." I could practically feel his eye roll this time.

"What is it?"

I didn't answer immediately.

"What is it, Mimi?" His voice was raised. "And this better not be a trick."

"It's not a trick, Christian!" I shot back. "I'm not a scheming, deceitful person!"

"Just give me the code word."

I could tell by his tone he was aggravated. Good. For some reason, it made me feel smug. My self-righteousness wouldn't last long. "It's Dreamy Mimi, all one word, all lower case and no snide remarks, thank you," I huffed in one long breath. I was embarrassed and he knew it.

"Done," came his reply. I was surprised. I'd not only expected some recognition in his expression, but also sarcasm about my silly code word which had also been a childhood nickname that I'd never shared with him, except in my letters. But there wasn't any hint of recall or nasty comment from him. Maybe he's not as much of a jerk as I thought. *He's definitely a jerk. He handcuffed you to a beam,* I reminded myself. But still, this is good. This tells me he can be reasoned with. I needed to have an adult conversation with him and figure out what this was all about. I stood up taller and tucked my hair behind my ear. I was going to demand an explanation as to why he deceived me when he asked, "Are you hungry?"

I was ready to tell him that food was the furthest thing from my mind when he started to walk back into the house. "Kitchen is this way," he said without looking back. I started to follow when I heard him say with a smirk in his tone, "Dreamy Mimi."

CHAPTER 8

PUMPKIN REST, SOUTH CAROLINA 2007

C hristian stood at the kitchen stove with his back to Mimi. She was sitting on a chair and he could feel her eyes following him as he moved around the room and heated up some food he'd prepared the day before. He tried to dredge up some of his earlier anger, but it wouldn't surface.

Seeing her bloodied arms had almost undone him. Yes, he'd metaphorically shattered some hearts, but he'd never physically injured a woman. Never. And the irony wasn't lost on him that the first woman he'd hurt was Mimi. And she was right. It was a stupid move on his part to leave her handcuffed to that beam. If something had happened to him, she would've been in serious danger. He didn't want to harm Mimi. So if he didn't want to hurt her, what exactly did he want? Did he truly believe that he only came here for an explanation for why she'd never contacted him? He shook his head when he thought about how juvenile that sounded. He wanted to kick himself in the ass for mentioning it to her. But that was how he rolled. Spur of the moment, hotheaded, and off the rails.

He smiled when he thought about the punch to his face and the head-butt that had bloodied his nose. Mimi was a spunky thing and he wasn't used to that. Women usually made sappy fools of themselves to get his attention. He never remembered one challenging him. Some had done their best to aggravate him, but challenge him? Never. And he could definitely say that a woman had never struck him. But she came at him a few times and as much as he wanted to use the punch and headbutt as an excuse to resurrect his ire, he couldn't. As a matter of fact, it had the opposite effect. It not only showed her as a strong woman worthy of respect, but it also made him see himself as she'd seen him. As a monster.

I am a monster, and to try and be something else to save face with Mimi isn't who I am, he told himself. With his back still to her, he gruffly announced, "Like I said earlier, you'll be staying with me a few days." He spun around and gave her a serious look. "Don't fight me on this. I don't want to use the handcuffs again, but I will."

She stood up from the chair, her hands clenched at her sides. "This is ridiculous, Christian. It's obvious you think I somehow betrayed you and you planned this. You had someone investigating me. I don't understand why you would go to such lengths. I thought we were friends, but you've taken this to a whole new level. You remind me of—"

"My parents? Your parents?" he cut in.

He could tell that his answer caught her by surprise. She was going to say something else, but he nailed it. And she knew it.

"Look, Mimi," he said as he leaned back against the counter and hooked both thumbs in his belt loops. "I was at a friend's house and he was messing around on the computer. I guess it was a one-in-a-million shot, but your picture popped up on Facebook with a bunch of kids from your college. Apparently, my friend and one of your friends had some connection. I knew the school where the picture was taken and tracked you down."

She cocked her head and frowned.

"I don't believe you," Mimi said through slitted eyes. "And even if I did, I don't see what any of this has to do with you methodically planning my abduction!" With her hands on her hips she moved toward him.

"I guess it doesn't have anything to do with it," Christian countered. "I wanted to see you and like I said earlier, I don't ask."

"Well, you've seen me, Christian." She held her hand out. "My phone and car keys, please. I can make it ho—back to college before it gets too late."

"No," he replied immediately. "And don't try to leave on your own. I hid the keys to my truck and your car outside before I came in. And if you think you can make it to your car and use a key you might have hidden, it'll be fruitless. I messed with your engine."

He watched her take a deep breath as she carefully measured her words. "You know what? I'll play along with whatever this is." She swept her hand through the air. "However, contrary to what you might think, other than averting a nuclear disaster of some sort or a life-and-death situation, I can't come up with one plausible explanation for what you've done."

Before he could reply they both heard her stomach grumble. In an attempt to avoid answering her question, he barked, "We'll eat first. Talk later."

Instead of being embarrassed, she tried to peek around him to see what was on the stove. Mimi realized then that the only thing she'd consumed in the past twelve hours was a few bites of a honey biscuit at the gas station. "Whatever it is, it smells good. I guess your mother taught you to cook." She eyeballed the food when he stepped to the side.

"My mother can't boil water," came his dry reply.

"If memory serves me correctly, your mother made the most delicious going-away dinner for my family the night we left Florida."

He scoffed. "My father made that dinner."

Mimi couldn't contain her surprise, and he gave her a crooked grin. "It's a family secret," he admitted. "Now sit down and I'll bring a plate over."

He watched her as she shook her head and went to sit at the table.

"Stupid jerk thinks he can order me around. Reminds me of someone else with testosterone overload," she mumbled as she took a seat and scooted the chair up to the table.

Christian set a dish full of food in front of Mimi and took the seat opposite her. After a few bites, Mimi prodded, "Any other family secrets I should know about?"

When he didn't answer, she continued, "How are your parents? What's new with your little sister? She's almost a teenager now, right?"

"Yeah, she'll be thirteen next year," he replied.

"What about your brother?" Mimi asked. "Did he end up becoming an attorney? I remember he mentioned that once."

She knew she must've hit a raw nerve when Christian set the glass down he'd lifted to his mouth seconds before without taking a drink.

"Slade's a prosecutor with the district attorney's office," he grunted, unable to hide his scowl of disapproval.

"By the look on your face I guess you're not very close with him?" she probed.

"I live with him," Christian snapped.

"You live with him?" She leaned forward. Setting her fork aside, she continued, "I guess he knows about all of this and gave his blessing?"

Christian leaned back in his chair and crossed his arms. "Slade doesn't know anything, nor would I tell him. He's too much of a goody two-shoes. He has enough criminals to chase without being involved with my shit. Why do you want to know so much about Slade?"

"I don't," she shot back. "I was asking about your family in general. He is part of the family, right?"

Christian didn't answer her, concentrating on his food instead.

They didn't speak during the rest of the meal, giving them both time to contemplate their current situation.

Mimi tried to draw on memories of Christian as a child. The few happy times she could remember helped her tamp down the anger she felt when she let herself think about the extremes he'd gone to in order to get her alone.

Christian was trying to reconcile his earlier thoughts about treating Mimi like every other woman he'd ever met and having her in his bed before morning. Recognizing that she wasn't like every other woman made the need to possess her even stronger. He wanted Mimi and he wouldn't let her leave this place until she wanted him too.

CHAPTER 9

FORT LAUDERDALE, FLORIDA 2007

Slade Bear sat at the trial counsel table and watched as the district attorney questioned a witness in the murder trial of a wealthy South Florida entrepreneur.

After having only been hired a little over two years ago by the State of Florida district attorney's office, this was the first capital felony case Slade had been assigned. And here he sat in Judge Celeste Marconi's courtroom and watched as the DA pelted the witness with questions.

This was the second week of the trial, and during that time, he'd observed not only the DA who'd earned Slade's admiration, but the judge who was currently presiding over the case. The judge was known as Maximum Marconi because she always meted out the maximum sentence in criminal cases. She had a vibe that had gotten under Slade's skin. He couldn't pinpoint it exactly, but she'd made him cautious. He told himself it could be one of two things. She wasn't pleased with how the prosecution was handling the trial, or she recognized his last name and knew that Slade's family hadn't exactly been model citizens. Or maybe he just didn't like her. She was fair, but there was an abrasiveness to her that grated on him.

He wouldn't let himself think about the sentencing his brother, Christian, would've received if he'd been tried in Judge Marconi's courtroom. Christian had been found guilty of his crime and was sentenced to five years in prison, but managed to get paroled after serving only three years. Slade would've liked to think that Christian had been released due to his rehabilitation and good behavior, but the sad truth was, the Florida prisons were overcrowded and they needed to make room for more dangerous and sinister criminals.

"No more questions, Your Honor," the district attorney said as he turned his back on the witness and headed for the counsel table.

Judge Marconi announced a ninety-minute recess for lunch. Slade knew that while the DA would be dining with his attorney friends, he would be ingesting whatever he could grab on his way to the law library. As second chair, it was his job to do the research and trial prep. Even though he'd prepared for this trial, he spent his lunch hours continuing to expand his research.

After spending a few minutes with the DA, Slade grabbed one of his files and his laptop and headed toward the courthouse library. He stopped by a vending machine and bought an apple, a bag of chips, and a bottle of water. He sat on a bench and made quick work of downing his less-than-satisfying lunch.

I wonder if she'll be there? he asked himself as he tossed the empty bottle in the recycle bin and made his way through the halls.

He took a seat at his usual table and glanced around the room. Ignoring his disappointment at not seeing her, he opened his laptop. An hour later while his head was buried in his research, he felt a rush of air whoosh by him and watched it take some of his papers with it. As he turned to grab the flying documents, he noticed an entrancing fragrance before finding himself staring directly into light-brown eyes.

"I am so sorry," she said, looking away shyly as she knelt on the floor and tried to retrieve the scattered contents of Slade's folder.

"It's okay, no problem." He scooted his chair back and started to help her. But she was too fast and was already standing up. He stood up too and watched as she tapped the papers on his table and returned them to the folder that was still resting at the edge of it.

Slade had used the courtroom library at least a hundred times and only noticed her for the first time a couple days earlier. She'd caught his attention because he was certain he was seeing the actress, Drew Barrymore, pushing a library cart and returning books to their shelves. She was the spitting image of the character that Miss Barrymore had portrayed in the movie *The Wedding Singer*. From her short, dirty-blond hair to her unassuming but stylish dresses and subtle makeup, she was a dead ringer. After convincing himself that Drew Barrymore didn't moonlight as a librarian he'd tried more than once to approach her, but the timing was always wrong. Not today.

He stuck out his hand. "I'm Slade."

She smiled and took his hand, shaking it delicately. "I'm Bevin. It's nice to meet you, Slade."

"Nice to meet you too, Bevin," he countered. Slade didn't have his father's dark, Native American good looks. Instead, he favored his fairer mother, Christy. But like Anthony Bear, Slade had a deep dimple in his left cheek.

He watched Bevin blush as she stared at it and quickly looked away. He took the opportunity to rake his eyes down her body and admired what he saw. Slade hadn't received his father's imposing height or width. He stood at five feet eleven inches. In her flat shoes, Bevin was eye level with him. Some would probably consider her tall for a woman. However, she wasn't overweight, which wouldn't have mattered to him anyway, her build fit her height. He noticed that she didn't wear earrings, had one tiny book charm hanging from her neck-lace, and wore a watch with a thin black band on her left wrist. Her unpainted nails were cut short and she wasn't wearing any rings. He wasn't certain but he thought he detected the scent of apples lingering in the air between them.

"You're new here?" he asked quietly.

"I'm moonlighting during spring break," she answered. Before he could question which school she attended, she added, "I'm the librarian at Citrus Acres Middle School. And you're an attorney."

"Yeah. What gave me away?" he laughed.

"I saw you coming out of Judge Marconi's courtroom yesterday. You looked upset. I know she's a tough one."

"They don't call her Maximum Marconi and other unflattering names for nothing," he scoffed as he ran his hand through his hair. "She is a real piece of work." Before he could elaborate further on his dislike of the woman who was presiding over the murder trial, Bevin interrupted him.

"Other unflattering names?" she questioned.

"They also refer to her as Maxi Pad Marconi," he said in a low voice. He immediately noticed Bevin's discomfort, quickly adding, "I don't like the woman, but I would never call her that."

Bevin tilted her head to one side. He took her inquisitive look as an invitation to explain further. "I have a mother and a sister and I respect women too much to pin a sexist nickname on a successful female who I may not like, but I appreciate." After an uncomfortable pause, he added, "And Judge Marconi seems to penalize rapists harder than any other judge in this jurisdiction. I admire her for that. I despise rapists. They're spineless cowards."

His phone pinged indicating he was due back at the courtroom. He was grateful because he was afraid he'd just given Bevin more information than she'd asked for. What would she care about his hatred for rapists? She wouldn't, but he wanted her to see that he wasn't a total jerk when it came to his feelings about the woman who was presiding over his trial. "I have to run, Bevin. Do you think you might like to grab a drink after work one evening? Maybe even tonight?"

He couldn't explain why, but the innocent-looking, apple-scented Bevin had intrigued him from afar, and even more so now.

She gave him a wide smile. "I can't tonight. But I can tomorrow night." She fought to hide her slight blush by tipping her chin down. "If you're available."

"Maybe we could have dinner instead of just drinks. If you want to," he said as he stood up straight, his laptop and folder already packed away in his leather satchel.

"That would be nice, Slade. I guess I'll see you tomorrow then?" Her smile was appreciative.

"I'll come by here to pick you up after court lets out. Sound like a plan?"

"Sounds like a plan." Her smile grew even bigger. Slade noticed she had two deep dimples of her own.

He was walking away when he quickly spun around. "Hey," he whisper-yelled. "I didn't catch your last name."

"Marconi." She didn't meet his eyes. "It's Bevin Marconi."

AFTER A GRUELING AFTERNOON in that courtroom, Slade welcomed the quiet of his home. His condominium on the Intracoastal had been a present from his parents when he graduated law school. He heated up some leftover takeout from the previous night and sat on his couch, hunched over his laptop that rested on the coffee table. He logged into his Facebook account, which he hadn't used in almost eighteen months, and immediately started searching for Bevin Marconi. Or was it Bevan? He'd never heard such an unusual name and wasn't sure how she spelled it.

Deciding after almost twenty minutes of searching that Bevin didn't have an account, he checked out what some of his friends had been up to. He smiled when he saw some of the pictures his high school and college buddies had posted. There was everything from wedding pics to new baby announcements. He continued to scroll and check out some more posts when he came upon a picture with a caption that read: *Can't believe my little bro will be graduating this year. Remember these days, dudes?* Slade was lifting a beer to his lips, but set it back down so fast it almost bubbled over. Not taking his eyes off the screen he leaned closer to his laptop. His friend had posted a picture of other college students. Apparently, one of them was his friend's younger brother. But it wasn't the brother that caught Slade's eye. He clicked on the picture to make it bigger and had no doubt that he was staring at Mimi Dillon. He immediately typed in her name and did the same type of search that he'd done for Bevin. And like that search, he came up empty-handed. He went back to the picture and saw that it had originally been posted weeks earlier.

He grabbed his beer and leaned back on the couch. He hadn't thought about Mimi Dillon in years. He remembered how attracted to Mimi he'd been the night he'd rescued her from a dangerous situation —one that had contributed to his disdain for sexual assault criminals. He also remembered how he'd tamped down those feelings because she'd only been fifteen years old at the time. He cringed when he thought about the last time he'd seen her. She'd been babysitting for his little sister, Daisy, and he'd stopped by his parents' house unannounced. Mimi had let him know that night that she had feelings for him. And he did what he knew he needed to do. Not wanting to hurt her feelings, he let her down as gently as he could. He found her attractive, but he didn't act on it because of the torch he'd suspected Christian had been carrying for years.

He sat up again and looked at the picture. She'd been a beautiful fifteen-year-old, but now she was stunning. The complete opposite of Bevin, he mused. Mimi had a dark and sultry look to her. He immediately determined that her appeal was solely because she wasn't trying to be sexy. She was naturally appealing. He shook his head to keep the thoughts from heading down a road that couldn't be traveled. Then his eyes landed on one of Christian's hoodies that he'd left slung over the adjacent dining room chair and a ridiculous thought jumped to the forefront of his thoughts.

Slade shot straight up from his seat and headed for the spare bedroom that Christian had been using. After rummaging around and finding nothing to confirm his suspicions, he returned to his computer and searched social media for Christian's name. As expected, he didn't find it and breathed a sigh of relief but couldn't let go of the foreboding thought. A picture of Mimi Dillon had been posted on Facebook weeks ago. Christian left a couple of days ago for a trip to Jacksonville. *No. He wouldn't. He couldn't,* Slade thought.

He picked up his cell phone and dialed a number. After barking an order to the man that answered, he hung up. And having no other recourse, he waited.

Slade paced the floor of his condo, dialing Christian's number every few minutes and getting voicemail. Finally, after what seemed like an eternity, his cell phone rang.

"What'd you find?" he asked, anxiously awaiting the answer.

"He's pinging off a couple of towers in Jacksonville. Has been for the last two days. He's definitely there," the man informed him.

"Keep checking it and if it shows up anywhere other than Jacksonville, call me." Slade commanded. And after a pause, "And thanks, dude."

After the man reassured him that he would continue to check the number in question, Slade hung up, relieved.

"It wasn't Mimi," he said to himself, and laughed. "My eyes were playing tricks on me." Now that he wasn't fretting over Christian, he could concentrate on his trial research.

He'd decided that Maximum Marconi couldn't possibly be Bevin's mother. He'd spent an afternoon in the shrew's courtroom and had never felt so physically drained. The DA had snapped at him after Judge Marconi had denied several motions he'd cited based on previous cases. Slade would spend the next several hours scouring the LexisNexis looking for something he must've missed. He took a quick shower and sat down at the kitchen table with his laptop, his books, and the folder he'd had in the library. He opened the file and had the second shock of the night. Right on top where she must've put it, was a printed note. Bevin hadn't accidentally knocked his folder off the table at the library. She'd done it on purpose. And if what he was seeing was put there by her, it was cause for a mistrial and the accused could go free. And she would know this. Why would Bevin want to sabotage his case?

Since he couldn't address it until the morning, Slade decided to open his laptop and sign back on to Facebook. He'd confirmed that Christian was in Jacksonville, so he didn't have a reason to look at the girl's picture again. He told himself it was to challenge his earlier assessment. The girl was not Mimi Dillon, and he wanted to confirm it. He went through his notifications and couldn't find the picture again, so he stalked the page of his friend's younger brother. But the photo with Mimi was gone. He shook his head and told himself he wasn't familiar enough with social media to know what he was doing. He closed his laptop at the same time his cell phone rang.

Erin was what most people would refer to as a MILF. An extremely attractive single mother, Erin was at least fifteen years older than Slade. She was a tiny wisp of a woman who wore her highlighted brown hair in a stylish bob. She had beautiful green eyes, and a smattering of freckles on her nose that made her look like she was approaching thirty instead of forty.

They'd met in the lobby of his building six months prior and had struck up a casual friendship. Erin lived two floors below him and when she knocked on his door one night wearing nothing beneath her coat, he had no problem giving her what she wanted and what he needed. They were two lonely beings who saw their infrequent time together as a type of therapy. College and law school left little time for him to have a social life, let alone a girlfriend. Which is why he even surprised himself when he asked Bevin to have dinner with him. His relationship with Erin was purely physical. He wasn't a kiss-and-tell kind of guy, and even though he knew they would never have real feelings for each other, he always treated Erin respectfully.

As he waited for her to arrive he couldn't help but wonder whose face he would see when he was buried deep inside of Erin. Would he imagine the sweet and kind eyes of the Drew Barrymore doppelgänger or the smoky and sultry ones of a woman whose Facebook picture reminded him of Mimi Dillon?

Erin's soft knock at the door interrupted his musings. Time to find out.

CHAPTER 10

PUMPKIN REST, SOUTH CAROLINA 2007

I was pleasantly surprised at how good the meal was that Christian had prepared. I told myself I didn't want to enjoy it, but my stomach and taste buds told me differently. He obviously knew his way around a kitchen. I was torn between using my head to determine the best way to give him the slip, or sticking around to see where this unusual reunion might lead. He seemed calmer, nicer than the man who'd handcuffed me to a beam and disabled my car.

Returning to an earlier comment he'd made, I stared down at my plate and muttered, "You didn't find a hide-a-key on my car because I'm not stupid." I immediately felt his eyes on me and looked up. He was smiling. My heart did a flip-flop in my chest.

"Good. It's the first thing a car thief would look for," he told me, his eyes steady. "Do you know that's how my mother got away from my father?" he asked.

Even though I hadn't known any details of his mother's kidnapping, I did know the circumstances had been different than those of my parents. I shook my head.

I listened, fascinated, as Christian went on to share the details of his parents' story.

"When did they know it was love?" I later asked as I stood at the sink and rinsed out my glass. My voice conveyed a dreamy quality that I couldn't disguise.

"I don't know," came his bland reply from behind me. "I guess you'll have to ask them one day."

The reality of his deception came crashing down. I spun around to face him. "I could've asked them if this ruse you planned had been the real deal!" I snapped. "Tell me again why you are under the misconception that I lied to you?" I demanded.

With his back to me, I watched him stiffen and shrug his shoulders while bending low to bag up the garbage. "Forget it. It was stupid. A misunderstanding."

"Stupid? Tell me how a stupid misunderstanding led to this?" I asked.

He stood up straight and turned around to face me. Dropping the garbage bag on the floor, he said, "It's simple. You lied. You told me that night in my room that you'd be in touch. You never called or bothered in any way. I thought there was something between us that night. I was obviously wrong. You left and never looked back. I've obviously made a big deal out of nothing."

"I didn't lie to you that night. And before we talk about that night, let's go back even further," I threw at him.

His only response was a raised eyebrow.

"Do you remember driving me home after I babysat for your sister?" I asked.

"Yeah, when you got your period in my truck," came his impassive reply.

"Thanks for bringing that up," I scoffed. "Do you know how many times I texted you after that? How many times I called your mother to see if she needed me to babysit for Daisy again?"

"I don't know if you're telling the truth about the texts, but it doesn't matter anyway. I lost my phone after I drove you home. My mom got me a new one with a new number."

I watched his expression start to change as if something jogged his memory.

"But that was almost a whole year before that going-away dinner, and has nothing to do with the promise you made that night in my room," he shot back.

"And you're accusing me of breaking that promise?" I asked, incredulously. Without giving him a chance to answer, I walked toward him and jabbed him in the chest. "I sent you letters, Christian. I went to extremes to make sure there was no possible way your parents would figure out they were from me."

He grabbed the hand that was getting ready to poke him again and leaned down until we were nose to nose. "Bullshit," was his only response.

"No, it's not bullshit," I spat and pulled my hand away. "I sent you letters, Christian!" I yelled in his face.

"I never got any letters, Mimi!" he yelled back.

"Yes, you did!" I screamed. I was thrumming with a fury so intense, I had to make sure I didn't hold my breath and pass out.

Obviously not one to back down, he got right back in my face, saying in a low, menacing voice, "There's no way you sent me any letters and even if you did, which I highly doubt, you have no way to prove it," he countered.

"Oh, I have no doubt I sent them and no doubt that you got them," I huffed. I could feel my blood pressure rising.

"And how is that?" he asked, his blue eyes blazing.

I stepped back and narrowed my eyes. With a hand on my hip, I shook my head. "I cannot believe you have the balls to deny this."

"Deny what?" he growled. "That you mailed some imaginary letters?"

"No, Christian. Deny that you got my very real letters!" I exclaimed. I was utterly amazed at his hardheadedness.

"I am denying it," he said through gritted teeth.

"I don't see how you can deny it since you wrote me back. Or did that little detail slip your mind?"

CHAPTER 11

FORT LAUDERDALE, FLORIDA 2002

Five Years Earlier

C hristian's mother sat at her kitchen table and stared at the letter she held in her hands. It was addressed to Christian and had a California postmark. It was written by an obviously feminine hand. There was no return address. She held it up to her face and caught the unmistakable scent of something fruity and fresh. Christian had never received a letter. Not once. This could only be from one person. Mimi Dillon. So, they'd settled in California. Christy thought the plan was Montana, but she wasn't surprised they changed it. What did surprise her was that if this letter was from Mimi, she was going against her mother's wishes by contacting Christian.

"How was your day, Owani?" Anthony asked as he came in through the garage door that led into the kitchen. He called Christy Owani, affectionately. It was his pet name for her that his sister had made up as a child; meaning someone who was cherished and prized above all else.

Christy hadn't heard his truck and looked up at him, her expression unreadable. She normally warmed to the term of endearment he'd been calling her for over twenty years. But she had something else on her mind.

He chanced a quick glance at her before opening the refrigerator and pulling out a bottle of water.

"Christy? Is something wrong, baby?" he asked as he walked toward the table.

She waved the envelope in the air and looked concerned. "This came today. For Christian," she said.

Anthony was raising the bottle to his lips when he stopped and looked at her. "Who's it from?" he asked.

"Don't know. No return address and it has a California postmark," she answered.

The timer on the stove dinged softly, but they both ignored it.

"Who does he know in California?" Anthony asked, his jaw clenching as the possibility that this letter might be from Mimi sunk in. Anthony cared enough about Grizz, Ginny, and their children to break off their friendship. Even at the expense of his son's feelings.

"I don't know if he knows anyone from California. I do know that he has never, not once, received a handwritten letter. From anyone. What should we do?" Her big blue eyes were concerned.

"We open the damn thing and see who it's from for starters," he stated.

Dear Christian,

I know it's been months since we moved and I'm sorry it's taken so long to get in touch with you. It's kind of complicated. My mom did marry the man you heard us talking about. James. He's a good man and I'm glad for my mom. I still miss my dad, but I like seeing my mother so happy.

The reason we didn't want anyone to know where we were going is because my mother is ready to start a new chapter in her life and doesn't want any sad reminders of our past. I know you understand what I'm talking about so there's no need for me to go into details. She didn't feel like we could have a fresh start if we stayed connected to South Florida. Jason and I were ready for a change anyway. I'm sure my mom told your mom how hard things were getting for him at school.

I'll be starting my senior year in a few weeks. I've already made new friends over the summer, so starting in a new school doesn't seem so scary. I guess you graduated this past spring.

I have some other news. My mother is pregnant! She's due next year, but the doctor says she might be early because she's having twins. We can hardly believe it. It'll be an adjustment having not one, but two babies in the house. I don't know if you remember the last time we played wedding. I don't know if you even remember that we used to play that. Anyway, seeing my mom with her big belly reminded me of it. I don't remember a whole lot, but I do remember one thing. Do you remember the ring you won for me out of the claw machine? I wish I still had it but I don't remember what I did with it.

I feel a little stupid writing about that memory and I wish I could remember more. But I did promise you I would contact you. I felt like we made a connection that last night before I left. I think I saw in your face that you felt it too. You said that you were afraid that you waited too long, that it was too late. I think you were talking about us. If I'm wrong, this will go down as the most embarrassing letter in history. But I don't think I'm wrong. At least I hope not.

I also promised my mother and James when we left Florida, I wouldn't look back, and I meant it. But then we had those few minutes alone in your room. I'm breaking a promise by writing this letter. I want to stay in touch with you and the best way, for now, is for me to give you my email address. I set up a new account on a public computer. I think that would be a good thing for you to do the same thing. If we can stay in touch over email for a little bit, maybe as time goes by things will change. You can email me at dreamymimi1985@aol.com.

I won't be able to check that email regularly, but I will as often as I can. Please email me back so I know you got this letter. I can't wait to catch up with you, Christian, and I'm sorry I didn't make more of an effort when I lived there. I hope you don't think that it's too late. Like I told you that night, and again in this letter, it's not too late for me.

Love,

Mimi

After quietly reading the letter out loud, Christy gently folded it and put it back in the envelope. She didn't have to ask Anthony what they should do. She knew that Christian would never see it.

"I thought we were successful in squelching anything that might've been brewing between them. I knew he acted differently last year after he drove her home. I got rid of his phone and after convincing him he lost it, I got him a new one in the event she tried to contact him. I even turned Mimi down every time she asked if I needed her to babysit." Christy brushed her hand through her hair and looked up at Anthony. "And you set him up to get busted and sit in juvie for a while." She blew out a long breath and said, "That last night at dinner, I didn't detect anything between them. If anything, I think I remember him stomping off to his room. I guess maybe we didn't do as good a job as we thought we did."

"We did just fine," Anthony told her. "And I know what you're thinking, Owani. Don't feel bad. Christian isn't mature enough to be trusted with their location or their secret."

Shaking his head, Anthony headed for the master bathroom to take a shower. Christy shoved the letter from Mimi into her purse. She would get rid of it later. She had to pick Daisy up from dance class. After turning off the oven timer, switching the temperature to low, and praying she wouldn't be ruining another meal, Christy grabbed her keys off the hook and headed for the garage.

"I'm so sorry, son. So very sorry," she whispered to herself.

CHAPTER 12

I don't know how long Christian and I bickered back and forth about the letters I sent him that he supposedly didn't get, and the letter I received from him that he insisted he hadn't written. When he pressed me for details of what the letter had said, my pride wouldn't allow me to elaborate. It had been too humiliating at the time and I couldn't bring myself to share it with him. Besides, I'd spent the last five years trying to forget about it. Why dredge up a painful reminder?

We'd made our way to the great room. I sat cross-legged on the couch while he paced back and forth. He'd stuffed his hands in his pockets and was staring at the floor as he walked. I couldn't help but admire the man he'd become—at least physically. I guessed him to be about six feet two inches tall with silky black hair that fell to the middle of his back. His smooth dark skin was flawless and he had very little facial hair. He had classic Native American good looks, like his father. A strong nose and a chiseled chin. And his eyes. His blue eyes, inherited from his mother, could hold a cobra captive. After catching myself staring at his tattooed muscular biceps, I gulped and tried to steer my thoughts away from his appearance.

"We both agree that my mother dissuaded you from babysitting," he said as he scratched his jaw. "And there's no doubt that my father let me take a fall for a stupid stunt I pulled that sent me to juvie for a while. We don't have any way to know if I lost my phone or my mother took it and made me think I lost it."

"But we both can agree there seems to be evidence that they didn't want our friendship, or whatever you might want to call it, to continue," I piped in. I swallowed and looked away, embarrassed that I'd hinted at the idea we had more than just a friendship. I looked back at him and was relieved that he was still pacing with his head down. "They were taking my mother's wishes to disappear very seriously. That much is obvious," I added without admitting that I knew the reason why.

He stopped walking and leveled a gaze at me. "I can believe that one of my parents might've intercepted the letters you mailed me, but I can't even imagine them writing back to you while pretending to be me. They wouldn't do that, Mimi. Especially if it was as hurtful as you're alluding."

"I got a letter that was signed by you, Christian. Who would do that? Who, other than your parents would have access to your mail?"

He didn't say anything, but stood there staring at me. Then it dawned on me.

"You still think I'm lying," I said, without breaking from his gaze.

He didn't answer at first, but I thought I saw a flash of anger in his eyes before he said, "You lied about other stuff. Stupid stuff."

I nodded in agreement. "You're right. I guess I was being tested on that little tour you gave me earlier. Now that I think about it, it was a test, wasn't it? Little nonsense questions that your private investigator could've easily dug up."

The anger I'd thought I'd seen seconds earlier was replaced with something else. It could've been a tad of admiration for guessing what he'd been up to. He gave me a slight nod.

"You know when we left Florida it was to start a new life." It wasn't a question but a fact. When he didn't reply I continued. "I didn't deliberately lie to you, Christian. I'm embarrassed to say that it's pretty much a habit I've adopted. I'm always on the defensive, waiting to be tripped up so the answers just come out of my mouth automatically."

"I would've thought I deserved the truth, Mimi. I can't say for sure, but I think I'm your oldest friend."

My heart did a somersault in my chest. He was right. My earliest childhood memories included Christian and I was immediately catapulted back to a happier time. As if in a trance, I hovered above the long-forgotten memory, and felt a warmth invade my veins.

"I'll push you on the swings, Mimi. C'mon!" Christian ran toward the swing set, his black braid swaying behind him.

I glanced at my mother, and after receiving a smiling nod of approval, I bounded happily after him.

"You have to promise not to push me too high, Christian!" I called out as I excitedly trotted behind him toward the swing set.

"I promise, Mimi," he yelled back at me.

Where had that come from? I was certain I'd buried those memories away years ago.

Shaking my head as if to clear it, I looked at Christian, my attitude softening. "You're right. I'm sorry. Do you want to start over? Ask me anything," I offered. And I made up my mind at that very moment that I would tell him as much as I could without revealing James's true identity. Even though Christian would never meet them, I would even share that my extended family lived just a couple of hours from my college. I braced myself for the barrage of questions that he would be throwing at me and said a silent prayer that I wouldn't give anything away about the real reason for my family's secretive move from Florida.

"Anything?" he asked.

I nodded. "Yes, Christian. Anything."

He walked to where I sat on the couch and looked down at me. Our eyes locked for what seemed like an eternity. *This is it, Mimi,* I told myself. *You have to answer his questions as honestly as possible without betraying your family secret.* I swallowed, and waited for the first, and what would turn out to be his only question.

"Are you in love with Lucas Paine?"

CHAPTER 13

FORT LAUDERDALE, FLORIDA 2007

"You're a million miles away," Erin whispered in Slade's ear. "Something you want to talk about?"

She'd just come out of his bathroom and was sitting on the edge of his bed, leaning over him. He turned to face her and gave her a sweet smile.

"Nah," he told her. "It's boring work stuff."

"You sure? Because I get the impression this is about a woman." She tilted her head to one side.

Slade sat up and leaned back against the headboard. "Erin, why would you say that or even think that?" He looked uncomfortable. "I didn't...I didn't..."

"No," she laughed. "You didn't call me by another name. It's just a feeling I got. Call it women's intuition. And it's perfectly okay. We established rules when this started, remember?"

He spent the next ten minutes filling her in on the enigma that was Bevin Marconi.

"Why wait until tomorrow morning to confront her, Slade? You should get dressed, look up her address, and drive straight to her house. This sounds important, and your whole case could be in jeopardy." Erin took the T-shirt off she'd been wearing and tossed it at him. "Here's your shirt back. Get dressed."

After pulling his shirt over his head, Slade sat up on the edge of the bed and reached for his jeans. He was putting them on when he stopped and gave her a look.

"Don't look at me like that," Erin insisted. With a big sigh, she said,

"Slade Bear, you are a first-class gentleman. You already know I don't require obligatory cuddling and pillow talk. I never have, and I've let you know it more than once. I don't consider you leaving to see another woman as disrespectful." She gave him a sweet smile and reached for her clothes. "Besides, it's late and I need to get home. I have to get some laundry started or I'll be sending my kids to spring break camp naked."

He was standing in front of her. She stood on her tiptoes and planted a kiss on his lips. "Go!"

FINDING BEVIN'S address took less than sixty seconds and, before he knew it, Slade was standing at her front door. He glanced around her porch, admiring the colorful potted plants, bird house and swing that made the entrance to her home more than inviting. Bevin lived in what could best be described as a retro beach bungalow that had probably been built in the late forties. It had been tastefully restored and showcased what looked like original windows and even a white picket fence. He looked at his watch. It was almost midnight, and even though he could see lights on inside, he didn't know if he would be waking her. It didn't matter. He pressed the doorbell.

He thought he saw a shadow making its way to the front door and before he had time to contemplate it further, he heard two deadbolts unlatching and it swung open.

Bevin stood in front of him wearing light-blue pajamas, a fluffy zebra print bathrobe and matching slippers. He thought she was utterly adorable.

"I had a feeling I'd be seeing or hearing from you before tomorrow," Bevin said as she stepped to the side and waved him in. "You found it." She nodded at the folder Slade clutched in his hand.

"You shouldn't be so easy to find," he said gruffly. "Your mother puts a lot of people away. Seems you should take better precautions in case one of her haters decides to get back at her."

"Thank you for your concern, but I'm a grown woman and can handle myself," came her response from behind him. He heard her lock the door, and he turned around to face her. He raked his eyes over her and was surprised by his instant reaction to Bevin. He felt a stirring in his groin before snapping himself out of it when she pulled her robe closed. Swallowing thickly, he remembered his reason for being there.

Slade peppered her with questions, not giving her time to respond. "Why did you put that paper in my folder, Bevin? Is this some kind of trick? Are you trying to tank this case? Did your mother put you up to this? Am I being tested?"

Bevin held up her hands as if to ward him off. "Slow down. It's not what you think."

"It's an important piece of information," he said louder than he'd intended. "It is my ethical duty to report it to your mother, the judge, and the defense could move for a mistrial." They were still standing in her small foyer and Slade had broken out in a sweat. It felt like the walls were closing in on him.

"Except that you don't have to share it with the defense," she quietly informed him. "They already have it, Slade. They're withholding it from the prosecution." She paused before muttering under her breath, "Well, at least one guy is."

Slade tugged at the collar of his shirt. "How do you know this?"

"Let's just say it was something I stumbled on by accident. I work in the library, and most people don't know I'm Judge Marconi's daughter. You didn't know who I was." She tilted her head to one side and a stray lock of hair fell across her pink cheek. "People tend to be careless in their conversations. And interns tend to be even more careless about what they leave around and don't shred. It happens more than you'd think."

"Why would the defense hold back this information? It could set their client free!" His exasperation was obvious.

She shrugged nonchalantly and looked at the ceiling before offering, "Maybe somebody on the defense doesn't want to prove his innocence."

He nodded slowly as understanding sank in.

"No, this is not some kind of trick. No, I'm not trying to tank your case. No, my mother did not put me up to this. Are you serious about that one?" She rolled her eyes. "And finally, no, you are not being tested. I'll leave it up to you to decide how you want to handle it, and I'll never say another word about it. And should you decide to share it with the judge and the defense, I'll deny it came from me."

She crossed her arms and leaned back against the front door.

"Your mother doesn't like me," Slade confessed.

"She knows about your family. And she has serious contempt for bikers in particular."

Slade's eyes went wide, but Bevin continued. "Your father was supposedly a pretty bad guy. Maybe still is. Your brother has been in prison and I'm almost certain he was attached to a motorcycle club before he was arrested. Still might be now that he's out."

Slade exhaled slowly, deflating like a balloon. It was obvious Bevin had done her homework.

"Which makes my mother admire you even more."

He looked up and saw that Bevin was giving him a half grin.

"What about your father?" Slade questioned. "I can't imagine what kind of man is married to the judge." He had to stop himself from rolling his eyes.

"I don't have a father," Bevin answered a little too quickly. "Okay, that's not true. Obviously. I know a man impregnated my mother, but she won't talk about him. I know absolutely nothing. Apparently, it was only one encounter and the few times I've asked, I get the impression she had feelings for him. He could be dead or alive. He could be living around the corner." She gave a nonchalant shrug as she stepped to the side and unlocked the front door. She opened it. Their little impromptu rendezvous was apparently over.

"Thanks, Bevin," Slade told her, his tone sincere. "I think." He raked his hand through his hair as he walked outside. Turning to face her he said, "I'm going to be up all night now." Bevin nodded her understanding.

"So, tomorrow night?" He gave her a quirky smile.

"I don't think so," came her soft reply.

"Because of this?" He waved the folder at her.

"No." She leveled a gaze at him. "Because you reek of Chanel No. 5. And since I'm assuming it's not your cologne of choice, you've recently been with a woman. And you've been close enough that you're carrying her scent on you, so I can only assume you're cheating on her by asking me out for drinks and dinner tomorrow night."

Slade's jaw dropped.

"I don't date cheaters, and I certainly don't like playing second fiddle to another woman." Bevin wouldn't break eye contact. "I guess she wasn't available tomorrow night so I'm a fill-in."

Slade couldn't think of a comeback. How could he explain Erin? How could he explain the gorgeous woman he'd been sleeping with?

But, Bevin was right. His shirt smelled like Erin because Erin had been wearing it. And less than an hour ago he'd been enjoying their tryst, but his heart hadn't been in it, and his mind had been elsewhere. He hadn't been able to get Drew Barrymore's twin sister out of his head, even while he'd been buried deep inside another woman. A woman who wasn't just his lover, but a trusted friend as well.

"And your lack of response tells me I'm right. Good night, Slade," came her firm dismissal.

Without giving him time to reply to her last comment, Bevin shut the door, locked it and turned off the porch light, leaving Slade in the dark.

CHAPTER 14

PUMPKIN REST, SOUTH CAROLINA 2007

O   f all the questions he could've asked her, he had to open with one about her boyfriend? He sounded like a jealous teenager.

Christian watched Mimi's eyes go wide and her mouth formed an O. She hadn't been expecting his question. He was finished caring about the reason he'd tracked her down. It was obvious she was still lying about getting a letter from him. When he asked her details about the letter he'd supposedly sent, she hemmed and hawed. But she also apologized and offered up a truce. Did he want to spend what time he had left with her squabbling over the past or did he want to start over like she'd suggested? He chose the latter and blurted out the only true question that had been haunting him since receiving that private investigator's report.

Mimi shifted on the couch. "I guess you probably already know I've been seeing Lucas for a few months."

"That wasn't the question." He huffed.

"Why would you ask me that, Christian?" she replied, pulling her long hair into an imaginary ponytail. She was doing her best to get over the shock she felt at his question and hoped he couldn't read it on her face.

"Because he's the only guy that you've been with for more than a few weeks. That tells me it's more serious than the others." Christian watched her swallow. The P.I. hadn't been able to do a complete background check, but thanks to the exorbitant fee he charged, he'd infiltrated Mimi's campus and had been able to find out that before Lucas

Paine, Mimi dated different guys and not for very long. The thought of her sleeping her way through college made the muscle in Christian's jaw tic.

Mimi's forehead creased when she told him, "Gee, your investigator sure did his homework. He would've had to ask around campus to get that kind of information."

"He's good," Christian snapped. Holding her captive with his penetrating eyes, he asked again. "Are you in love with Lucas Paine?"

Mimi tilted her chin up slightly. "This wasn't the question I expected, but I promised honesty and you'll get it."

"And?" He motioned for her to continue.

"I don't know if I'm in love with him. Maybe. I'm not exactly sure." She blew out a breath and waited for him to respond.

"Good," was all he said.

Mimi wondered if he looked almost relieved. Christian must've read the confusion on her face.

"If you're not sure, then you're not in love," he told her matter-of-factly.

"And you think it's good that I'm not in love with him?" She couldn't quite believe what she thought he was saying. Even the implication made it hard for her to swallow.

He reached for her hand and pulled her to her feet. He tentatively touched her face and softly caressed the side of her mouth with his thumb. "This way you won't be so conflicted when you fall in love with me."

She stepped back and looked up at him. "I don't remember you being so cocky, Christian." She took another small, hesitant step back, ignoring the heat that was coiling in her belly. It matched the heat in his eyes.

"And I don't remember you being so fucking beautiful, Mimi."

CHAPTER 15

PUMPKIN REST, SOUTH CAROLINA 2007

I didn't know what to say after Christian's admission that he thought I was beautiful. Was this the same man who'd handcuffed me to a post, then cooked me dinner, next accused me of lying to him, and then told me I was going to fall in love with him? I shook my head in the hopes it would clear away some of the confusion. Christian was an enigma and I'd have been lying if I didn't admit the whole situation was stirring up long suppressed feelings. But those were the feelings of a teenage girl. And I was no longer a girl.

"You look tired," he said, interrupting my thoughts.

"I am," I admitted, stifling a yawn. "It's been an exhausting day. And my arms are starting to sting again."

I thought I saw a flicker of regret in his eyes.

"Why don't we both call it a night?" he offered.

Nodding my head in agreement, I asked, "I'm going to get a shower. Which bedroom is mine?"

He motioned toward the master bedroom.

"Where are you sleeping?" My shoulders were beginning to feel as heavy as my eyelids and my arms were sorer than I'd originally thought.

Again he motioned toward the master bedroom.

My eyes widened, and I told him under no circumstances would we be sharing a bed. He told me that we would be and if I didn't like it, he would have no other choice but to handcuff me to one of the bedposts in another room.

I marched toward the master bedroom. He didn't follow me.

I picked up his duffel bag from the bed and slammed it on top of the dresser. After rifling through a few drawers I found a small stash of some of his clothes. I stuffed them in his bag and walked to the door. He was still standing where I'd left him and I could tell he was suppressing a grin. I threw the bag and it landed with a soft thud on the hardwood floor. I slammed the bedroom door shut and locked it. I grabbed my overnight bag and sifted through it for my pajamas and toiletries.

I languished in the hot shower for at least twenty minutes and was surprised at how rejuvenated and calm I'd become. A good night's sleep was what I needed. I was secretly grateful that I'd handled the text to my mother and was equally thankful that Lucas wasn't expecting to hear from me. *Where did that come from?* I asked myself as I towel-dried my hair and brushed it out. I hadn't put on my pajamas because the bathroom was steamy and I felt sticky. I flung open the bathroom door to let some air in and almost fell backward.

Doing my best to use both hands to cover my nakedness, I awkwardly kicked the door shut in Christian's face, but not before I caught the wide smile.

"How did you get in the bedroom?" I yelled through the door.

"Really, Mimi?" he scoffed. "I picked the lock."

"Get out!" I screamed.

"No," came his blunt reply.

I rolled my eyes. "I'm not coming out until you leave."

"I'm not leaving. I hope you find the bathtub comfortable. Want me to toss in a pillow and blanket?"

I looked over at the huge Jacuzzi tub and cringed. It would be lovely to have a hot soak in it, but not spend the night sleeping against its hard surface. My original exhaustion returned with a ferocity that I hadn't expected. I pulled on my panties and Beauty and the Beast nightshirt.

I calmly walked into the bedroom and found him stretched across the top of the bedspread. He was wearing a pair of navy-blue pajama pants. Lying on his side with his head propped against one hand, he laughed when he saw my nightshirt.

"Daisy would love that," he told me, as he sat up and crossed his legs.

"Your little sister likes Beauty and the Beast?" I asked him, surprised that he would know about the Disney classic.

He gave me a smile that sent a wave of heat down my spine. "I used to play with her when she was much younger," he confessed, not an ounce of embarrassment showing. He was proud of it.

"I'm going to assume you weren't Belle. Let me think..." I paused. "You played the overbearing and egotistical Gaston?"

My insult didn't affect him at all as he sat up straight and shook his head, sending his long hair flying around his face. In his most ferocious voice, he said, "You will join me for dinner. That's not a request!"

It was a line from the movie and he nailed it. I started laughing and sat down on the edge of the bed. We were both smiling and staring at each other. It was then that I noticed the tattoo over his heart. It was two chess pieces. A black king and white queen were connected by a pair of handcuffs. I gently placed my hand on it, and asked, "What's the significance of this tattoo?"

"You don't remember?" he softly whispered.

There was a memory trying to battle its way to the surface of my brain, but the day's drama kept it just out of reach. I slowly shook my head as I stared at my pale fingers against his dark skin.

He took my hand and lifted it to his cheek. "That's okay, Mimi. Sometimes the things we don't remember can be just as important as the things we do remember." A moment passed before he added, "It'll come back to you when the time is right."

Our eyes locked, and after a moment, I started to fidget. Pulling my hand away I stood quickly. "I guess I'll take one of the other rooms," I announced and headed for the door.

"I'll grab the handcuffs and be there in a minute," I heard him say from behind me as he jumped off the bed.

I stopped dead in my tracks and balled my hands into fists at my sides. I swung around and faced him. "You're serious about this," I barked. "You think I'm going to try and leave?"

"I didn't say that. I just want to make sure you don't," he said. He had his hands resting on his hips. After raking my eyes over his abs, I looked back at his face.

"I'm not going to sleep with you, Christian."

"I'm not going to make a move on you, Mimi. I just want you close by." He waved his arm toward the bed.

I was tired and the fight was slowly draining out of me. He followed me as I walked back into the bathroom. We wordlessly brushed our teeth and he dabbed more peroxide on my arms.

He climbed into bed first and patted the spot next to him. I crawled in and turned my back to him. He switched off the bedside light and I didn't resist when he pulled me into his arms. I was too tired to care. He told me he wouldn't make a move on me and in my exhausted state I needed to believe that. I could feel the heat of his chest through the back of my nightshirt and felt his warm breath at my ear. "Good night, Dreamy Mimi," he softly whispered. There was no hint of his earlier mockery and I smiled in the dark.

"Christian?" I whispered back.

"Yeah?"

"Will you tell me tomorrow about your prison tattoos?" My question wasn't accusatory. I wanted to know what he'd done that sent him to prison and hopefully get him to open up about the name on his right bicep.

"What makes you think they're prison tattoos?"

"I don't think they're prison tattoos." I looked back over my shoulder so I could see his eyes. A beam of moonlight cast a sliver of brightness over his face, making his cobalt eyes glow. "I know they're prison tattoos."

"What would you know about prison tattoos?" he asked, our eyes locking in the eerie stillness of the room.

Of course Christian had no way of knowing that I'd spent the last five years getting to know my biological father. The same father who'd lived fifteen years on death row in a maximum-security prison.

I returned my head to the pillow. "You'd be surprised by what I know," I quietly answered before letting sleep carry me away.

CHAPTER 16

PUMPKIN REST, SOUTH CAROLINA 2007

C hristian let the hot water soak into his hair, his neck, his shoulders. *I really should be taking a cold shower,* he thought as he rinsed the shampoo away. He reached for the soap and cast a glance at the unlocked bathroom door. *Maybe by staring at it long enough, I can will Mimi to walk through it,* he told himself. Just thinking about the frustrating night he'd spent holding her caused his hand to wander down to the body part responsible for his dilemma.

He almost scoffed out loud at yesterday's musings about having her in his bed this morning. He'd had her in his bed all night and never once touched her inappropriately. He'd even pulled back when he was betrayed by the body part he was now clutching. He closed his eyes and let out a groan, but stopped himself. He wouldn't want her to catch him pleasuring himself. Unless she was into that. He got even harder at the thought, then reached for the hot water valve and shut it off.

After a good dousing of cold water, he turned the hot back on and continued washing. He resumed thinking about the woman he'd held in his arms for the last several hours. She still smelled like heaven. More than once he'd panicked that she'd gone to meet her maker— Mimi slept like the dead. Even more startling, she didn't make a sound in her sleep. No snoring, no moans or sighs. Not only was she quiet, but she didn't move either. He'd gently placed his hand on her stomach several times to be sure she was breathing. He'd tried to rouse her to let her know he was taking a shower and to give her an option. She could shower with him or he would handcuff her to the bed post while he showered solo. When he couldn't get her to respond, he figured she'd be out for a while so he nixed the shackling strategy and decided to take a quick shower. Except it wasn't quick and he was now starting to wonder if he'd been slack.

She doesn't have keys to either vehicle, both phones are charging on the bathroom counter and even if she walked to town, it would take her hours on foot. Enjoy your shower and take care of business so you're not thinking about it all day. His release was quick and he found himself peering outside the bathroom door before toweling off. He didn't have a clear view of the bed, but he could see her body beneath the huge comforter, exactly as he'd left her.

He leisurely dried off. After throwing on his underwear and jeans, he made his way out to the bedroom. He was heading for the kitchen to put on a pot of coffee when he cast a sideways glance at the bed. Something was off. He strode quickly but knew before he even yanked back the comforter what he would find. And he was right. She was gone.

He would've liked to believe that the pillows were coincidentally stacked beneath the covers to resemble a body, and that she was in the kitchen or one of the other bathrooms. But he knew the bed had been staged.

He made a quick search of the house and without even putting on a shirt, flew out the front door and made a mad dash for the spot where he'd hidden both sets of keys. He held them in his hand and scratched his jaw as he looked around. Had she actually thought she could walk the distance to town before he would catch up to her? He was climbing in his truck and about to back out when he saw her car come into view. She pulled up behind him, parked and got out of her SUV.

She strode up to his open truck window and calmly stated, "I wasn't lying when I told you I didn't keep a spare key hidden somewhere on my car. I keep one in my wallet." She held up the solitary key. "And I knew that you wouldn't have disabled my car to the point that it would require a major repair later. I know a little bit about car engines. Not much, but enough to know how to reconnect a stupid wire."

She stood back and placed both hands on her hips as she waited for him to exit his truck. He slammed the door behind him and tried not to smile at her. She had brains beneath all that beauty. He'd never been so drawn to a woman in his life. The animalistic intensity he'd experienced when first seeing her picture pop up on Seth's computer returned with a vengeance. But Mimi was obviously no ordinary woman. She'd just made it clear that she wouldn't let him intimidate her. So he would have to seduce her another way. He would have to play nice. He didn't like playing nice. But if it meant winning the game, winning her, he would certainly give it a shot. He reminded himself, *I may not like playing nice, but I like losing even less. And I don't intend to lose Mimi.*

CHAPTER 17

PUMPKIN REST, SOUTH CAROLINA 2007

I couldn't tell if Christian was mad or amused. His face didn't betray his emotions as he turned his back to me and headed for the front door.

"I could've kept driving," I said as I tried to catch up with him.

"I would've come after you," he called over his shoulder.

"Stop! Stop right now and look at me," I demanded.

He turned to face me and didn't say a word, just stared at me like I was annoying him.

"I'm just trying to level the playing field, Christian. I don't like being bullied," I explained.

"I'm not trying to bully you, Mimi," he conceded as he scrubbed his hand down his face.

"Then what is this, Christian?" I shook my head slightly. "I've already agreed to move past your trickery and the handcuffs. Why do you still feel the need to be in control?"

His face softened. "I don't know how to be any other way, Mimi. I'm trying. But it's who I am." A moment passed. When he spoke again, he said, "I'm gonna put a shirt on and make a pot of coffee. You want some breakfast?"

I gave him a small smile and nodded. "I'm going to sit out here for a few minutes." I saw the hesitation on his face. "I'm not going anywhere, Christian. My word is good regardless of what you think I've done to you."

Without saying anything else, he went inside, shutting the door behind him. I walked up the front porch steps and took a seat on one of the rockers.

Before leaving for college and almost every other weekend for the past four years, I lived with the man Christian believed to be my step-father, James. In reality, James was my biological father, also known as Grizz. He was a man who never asked permission and never apologized. I'd only seen him behave, if that's what you could even call it, in my mother's presence. I might've even envied the hold my mother had on him. He loved her beyond anything I'd ever witnessed and in the deep recesses of my heart I wanted that kind of love. But I knew the cost.

My mother once told me that you could take a man off the street, but you couldn't take the street out of the man when that was all he'd ever known. I knew Grizz tried—he tried for her, but he wasn't always successful. Even though he knew my mother was well past wanting him to change, it still bothered him that he couldn't. It didn't have to bother him though. My mother found her place of acceptance with him and the lifestyle he'd not been able to give up entirely. No. He was no longer the leader of a motorcycle club. But he was still a leader who took charge of situations nobody else wanted to address.

Lucas was the complete opposite of my father and Christian. A criminal justice major, Lucas did everything by the book. He had a strict certainty in what he believed to be right and wrong. My world wasn't so black and white. I wouldn't even call my world gray. It could best be described as murky. Was I drawn to Lucas because he was the total opposite of my world? Or was I drawn to Lucas because he was the only man who'd respected my wishes to abstain from premarital sex?

Even during the most heated of my almost moments with Lucas, I wasn't as excited as I'd been with Christian in the last twenty-four hours. How many times had Christian said something or given me a look that caused my heart to dance in my chest? The reality of this felt like a shockwave. Especially since I'd never even kissed Christian. It was obvious that Christian had been through some dark times and done some not-so-savory things. I was used to living with a bad guy. Could this be my future? Did I want it to be?

Four Years Earlier

It was the summer before I started college. I'd been unloading the dishwasher and watching Grizz effortlessly change Dillon's dirty diaper. I couldn't peel my eyes away from his hands. They were huge, and I knew they were capable of unspeakable acts. Acts I'd heard about and understood to be true. I shivered when I realized that his knuckles were red and raw. I inwardly cringed when I realized I knew the reason why and that when I had a moment alone with him, I was going to confront him.

"I hate changing his diaper," Grizz offered, bringing me out of my thoughts.

I hadn't been aware that he'd been watching me as I watched him. "I don't think anybody likes changing a crappy diaper," I said nonchalantly.

"I don't give a shit about the, uh, shit," he answered. "I hate having to wipe it off his balls. I'm afraid I'm going to hurt him."

"You haven't hurt him yet, so I highly doubt you will," I replied without looking at him as I went back to emptying the dishwasher. I stifled a groan. I'd been recovering from an accident, and something as simple as bending over proved challenging.

I stole a sideways glance and watched Grizz lift Dillon up off the couch and press his mouth to the baby's fuzzy head.

Just then my mother came in from the laundry room carrying a basket of folded clothes with my thirteen-year-old brother, Jason, following her.

"Mom, it's not yours. I didn't go through your things," Jason whined as he padded along behind her. "I've had it since before we moved here. I found it bunched up in my sock and underwear drawer. You're the one who told me to start going through my clothes to see what I could give away." He turned red and added, "Not that I think anybody would want used socks and underwear, just that it's time to throw a lot of it out."

Grizz and I looked at them at the same time, and watched as my mother started down the stairs toward the basement bedrooms.

"What's going on?" Grizz asked as he stood up, holding the baby away from him. Dillon seemed to be fascinated by Grizz's earring and kept reaching for it.

Jason stopped and looked at Grizz. Pointing at the bandana on his head, he replied, "Mom thinks I took her blue bandana without asking. I told her I didn't. I've had it since we lived in Florida."

My mother stopped on the stairs and turned around to face Jason. She walked back up the stairs to the basement, standing in front of Jason. "I've bought all of your clothes since you were a baby, Jason. I don't ever remember buying you the bandana you're wearing when we lived in Florida. I'm putting these clothes away," she said, nodding to the basket resting against her hip. "And when I come back upstairs I will look in my dresser and see if my bandana is missing."

"Mom, you're going to find your bandana. This isn't yours." Jason was defensive and a little angry.

"Then where did you get it, Jason?" As was her habit she started walking around the room and absentmindedly tossed items that were usually stored downstairs in the basket with her laundry. "How come I never saw you wearing it in Florida?"

"I never wore it because after I found it, I stuffed it in one of my drawers and forgot it was there. It even made the move up here with us and still got buried. Shit, Mom. I don't know what the big freaking deal is about a stupid bandana anyway!" he screamed.

"Jason!" my mother yelled.

"What?" Jason nodded toward Grizz. "He says worse than shit all the time."

Mom couldn't argue that, so she didn't say anything. Walking toward Jason with her laundry basket, she set it down and calmly asked him, "Then where did you find it, Jason?"

"I found it in the garbage, Mom. Right on top of the trash in the compactor. I still remember the day. You took Mimi to the shooting range, and Dad told me to take out the trash before he dropped me off for my game. It didn't have any garbage or anything stuck to it, and I thought it was kind of neat, so I grabbed it. Again, what's the big deal?"

My mother and Grizz exchanged a glance. I understood what the look meant. My mother had shared with me the significance of the bandana Jason was wearing around his head. I knew she thought it was lost forever. It was the bandana that Grizz had been wearing the day he took her for her first ride on the back of his motorcycle in 1975. The same bandana Mom had found years later hanging on his motorcycle as a way for her to signal him if she ever needed him. The bandana she told me she'd thrown away in anger.

"I'm sorry, son. I'm sorry for not believing you." She reached for Jason and gave him a hug.

"It was my bandana, and I'd thrown it away. I guess since it was in the trash meant first dibs, so it's rightfully yours." She looked over at Grizz and without tearing her eyes away from his, asked my brother, "Will you give it back to me, Jason?"

Jason's head swiveled from Mom to Grizz and back to Mom.

Almost too quiet to hear, my mom pushed, "I'll buy you ten more if you let me have yours."

He pulled it off his head, holding it out for her to take. "Do you wanna just swap? You can give me the one you wear."

She cleared her throat and said, " I want to keep that one, too. Your father bought it for me. They both have a special meaning."

Jason and I shared the same mother, but we had different fathers. Our mother had been married to Grizz and was pregnant with me when he'd been arrested. Before he went on trial and was eventually sentenced to death row, Grizz insisted that she marry Tommy Dillon. Tommy was the man who'd raised me. And he and my mother had Jason when I was five years old.

"Sure, Mom, you can keep it. And I'm sorry for cussing in front of you."

"It's okay, Jason. And thank you. For the apology and the bandana," Mom told him as she wrapped it around her hand and then bent down to retrieve her laundry basket.

An hour later, Mom had taken Jason to soccer practice, the twins were napping, and I was alone in the great room exercising. Thanks to the car accident I'd been in months earlier, physical therapy had become a way of life.

Grizz had come inside from chopping wood and was reaching in the refrigerator for a beer when I stopped what I was doing and asked him, "Who did you kill?"

I watched him hesitate before closing the refrigerator. He turned to me and didn't break from my inquisitive stare as he twisted the top off his beer and leaned back against the counter. He took a long, slow swallow and asked, "What do you think you know?"

I walked to the kitchen and leaned up against the counter opposite him. He wasn't going to lie to me. I wasn't sure if knowing this came as a relief or scared me to death.

"I heard you and Micah," was all I said. Micah was Grizz's father, my biological grandfather. We'd been living in Micah's mountain home since we moved to North Carolina. He was also a beloved

89

preacher in the tiny community of Pine Creek where we'd permanently settled.

Grizz didn't ask how or when I overheard them. He just slowly nodded, and answered matter-of-factly, "I killed a distant cousin's abusive husband. I made it look like an accident. He won't be missed. I've done the family and his community a favor."

I'd heard about Tom Deems even before I'd eavesdropped on Grizz and Micah's conversation. It was thought that he fell in his woodshop and split his face and head wide open. Bled out before anyone found him.

"Micah wasn't happy that you killed him," I countered, breaking our standoff.

I was surprised when Grizz decided to give me a full explanation of Micah's original request and how the whole situation escalated. Apparently, Tom Deems was the grandson-in-law of one of Micah's cousins, Myrtle Blye, who lived two towns west of us. She'd been concerned about her granddaughter's abusive husband for years, but Tom was so mean-spirited and out of control, people avoided him instead of confronting him. Even the local law kept him at arm's length. He was a live wire that nobody wanted to deal with, including his family. Micah asked Grizz to scare Tom Deems into leaving town and never coming back. It almost worked. My father showed up on a day he was told Tom would be alone in his woodshed. Tom never saw him coming as Grizz approached him from behind and put him in a choke hold that was intended to disable him.

"I told him one of three things would happen," Grizz explained after taking another sip of his beer and giving me a level look. "I told him he'd never wake up and would remain in a coma for the rest of his life. Or he would wake up but have brain damage. Lastly, he would wake up and remember everything. And if that happened and he didn't pack up and leave, I would be back for him. He wouldn't know when or how or who. Just that he would always need to look over his shoulder." Seconds ticked by before Grizz added, "I promised Micah I wouldn't kill the man and I intended to make good on that promise."

I nodded, but gave him a hesitant look and added, "But they found him with his head bashed in."

Grizz took another long swallow of his beer before answering me.

"I let up on the choke hold just long enough for him to tell me he understood what I expected. But that's not what he told me."

I listened, transfixed as I waited for him to continue.

The muscle in Grizz's jaw strained, his teeth gritting together. "Instead, he offered me an hour with his eight-year-old daughter."

I gasped out loud and pressed my hand to my chest.

"Or his ten-year-old son," Grizz continued. "So I made an executive decision."

"Does Mom know?" Saliva was pooling in my mouth and I thought I'd be sick. I almost didn't want to hear that he'd kept it from her.

"She knows," he told me as he pushed off the counter. "Any more questions?"

"Why would you risk being found out? Going back to prison?" I asked incredulously.

"I'm a careful guy," was all he said.

And there it was. No remorse. No apology. He did what he believed needed to be done.

I was brought back to the present when Christian came outside carrying two mugs of coffee.

"Wasn't sure how you liked it," he confessed as he handed me a steaming cup and took the rocker next to me.

"What? It wasn't in the report from your P.I.?" I teased. "I used to douse it with sugar and creamer, but learned to take it black when cramming for exams. I can't go back now," I admitted.

"Ah," he said after taking a sip. "A girl after my own heart."

I felt a spiral of heat coursing through my insides at the innocent endearment. Taking a sip of my coffee, I balanced the mug on the arm of the rocker and blurted out before I could stop myself, "Have you ever killed anyone?"

I peered over at him as he lifted the mug to his mouth, but instead of taking another sip he looked over at me.

"Not yet," he told me with a mischievous smile. "But never say never."

CHAPTER 18

A fter a quick breakfast that was followed by an uncomfortable silence, Christian suggested they get out of the house and take in some fresh air. He didn't know how long he'd be able to keep his hands to himself and hoped the cool mountain breezes would stave off some of the physical tension he knew was brewing between them. He sensed that Mimi felt it too. For as strong and confident as Mimi appeared to be, he noticed she couldn't hold his gaze when there was a lull in their conversations.

He walked behind her as the sun broke through the trees casting rays that resembled sparkling shards of glass. As they made their way along the hiking trail that led away from the house, Christian couldn't take his eyes off her perfectly round bottom. She was wearing canvas hiking shorts that weren't tight, but couldn't hide she had an ass you could bounce a quarter off of. She wore tan hiking boots and her legs were flawless. Not a freckle, scar or birthmark kissed her smooth skin. He couldn't help but imagine them draped over his shoulders while he had his face buried—

"Look!" Mimi shouted. "It's still a little early, but I think these are wild strawberries!"

Grateful that her outburst interrupted the porno playing in his head, Christian looked up to see that they'd happened upon a clearing.

"C'mon," she yelled over her shoulder as she made her way toward a patch of the ripe red fruit.

Minutes later they were sitting on the ground enjoying the taste of the sweet berries and sipping on the water they'd brought with them. Mimi was wiping the juice from her chin when Christian told her, "I almost waited for you."

Mimi looked over at him. He was sitting with his back against a tree and his forearms resting on his bent knees, one hand dangling the bottle of water he'd just recapped. Her forehead creased with curiosity. "Waited for me?" she questioned.

"All those years ago." He squeezed the water bottle, the plastic crinkling in protest. "The morning after you babysat for Daisy. Instead of driving you home, you asked me to take you to the grocery store to meet up with your mom. Even though you told me not to wait for you, I almost did."

Mimi's posture immediately changed. He watched her take a deep breath. "Why didn't you?"

Christian slowly shook his head. "I honestly don't know. I wanted to, but there was a nagging sixth sense that told me not to. That maybe it would've made you mad."

Mimi chewed on her bottom lip and averted her gaze. How could she tell him that his sixth sense to leave had been partially correct? She wouldn't have been angry at him, but it wouldn't have helped that he might've come face-to-face with the secret she'd been harboring since that day. Christian would've seen Grizz, and even though Christian had never met Grizz, Mimi was certain it wouldn't have taken him long to make the connection.

"I wouldn't have been mad at you, but I was already embarrassed about what happened in your truck." She looked at the ground. "What I did to your leather seat."

He didn't want her to relive the humiliation of staining his truck seat with her menstrual blood, so he changed the subject.

"I saw you once. You were in the mall, sitting on a bench talking to some woman," he admitted. "I think it was about six months before Grizz's execution."

Mimi rolled her eyes. "That could only have been Leslie."

"Leslie?" He frowned before uncapping his water again and taking a long swallow.

Mimi shook her head and huffed, her exasperation obvious. "She was a reporter who was trying to get an inside scoop on my family. She persuaded me to convince my mother to give her an interview before Grizz's death." She closed her eyes and said, "I can't believe I fell for it. Then again, I was just a stupid teenager."

She shared with Christian the rift she'd caused in her parents' relationship when Leslie threatened to reveal a secret that even her mother hadn't known. Of course, the secret turned out to be false, but they hadn't known that at the time.

"One of the biggest mistakes of my life," she confessed as she looked past Christian's shoulder and stared at a deep gash in the tree he was perched against.

"One of the biggest?"

"Oh, there have been a lot more," she replied with a sheepish grin.

He stood and walked over to her, extending his hand. She grabbed it and was surprised at how quickly and effortlessly he yanked her to her feet, right into his chest. She slammed into him and started to bounce backward when he grabbed both of her upper arms to steady her. She chanced a glance up at him and her eyes widened when she met his stare. Christian's eyes made the bluebonnets she'd seen dotting the meadows appear dull and lifeless.

"You have strawberry juice on the side of your mouth," he lied as he let himself imagine the taste of her lips. He was looking for any excuse to touch her face—even an imaginary drop of juice if it meant he could pretend to wipe it off.

Mimi licked her lips and started to raise her hand to her mouth when he grabbed it. He saw her wince and his eyes darkened when he noticed the black and blue bruises encircling her wrist. The handcuffs.

"I'm sorry for this, Mimi," he said, nodding at her wrist. He quickly pulled it to his mouth and laid a gentle kiss on the inside of it. He thought he heard her suck in her breath.

"It's nothing," she answered a little too quickly. "I shouldn't have pulled so hard."

"I shouldn't have shackled you to a post." He chuckled, but she could tell he was pained he was the reason for the marks. Before she could answer he added, "But I'd do it again, Mimi. I'd do it all over again for the chance to be standing here with you at this moment."

Christian watched as Mimi's eyes slowly wandered down to his mouth. He let go of her wrist and raised his hand to her cheek, caressing it softly with his thumb. He began to lower his mouth to hers when their eyes met. He could see the battle raging behind her dilated pupils. She wasn't sure about kissing him. Was it because she didn't want to cheat on her boyfriend? It didn't matter.

The loud shrill of a bird caused her to jump, breaking the spell. She took two steps back and swiped her hand through her hair. Without meeting his eyes, she bent low and scooped up her bottle. Turning her back on him, she headed toward the trail calling over her shoulder, "I feel like this is one big loop and we'll be coming back up on the house."

The path was narrow so Christian had no choice but to follow her. He didn't mind. He would soak up as much of her as he could over the next few days. He would never tire of being with her. Just like when they were children, being with Mimi soothed his soul. He couldn't explain how he knew, even as a kid, that they were connected. There was an undercurrent that tugged at their souls. Even though she seemed to be in denial, he was certain she'd felt it too, but somewhere along the line it changed for her.

"What happened?"

"What happened to what?" She continued along the path.

"What happened to us? When we were kids? I know we lived on opposite sides of the state, but our mothers did a good job of making sure we got together regularly. And it couldn't have been easy for them. It was at least an hour and a half one way. But they made sure our friendship stayed intact."

Mimi finally stopped and turned around to face him. She reached out and subconsciously fiddled with a stray branch, stroking the leaves between her fingers.

"Maybe they were trying to make sure their friendship stayed intact."

He nodded. "Possibly. But even if that was the case, we were still best friends. Do you remember your mom driving to our house with a car full of Girl Scout cookies a couple of times?"

Mimi's face broke out into a wide grin. "Yes! And your mother took us to a few different neighborhoods. They walked along behind us as we pulled the boxes of cookies in a wagon and knocked on doors." She burst out laughing.

"What?" Christian asked.

"I remember you yelling at every person that didn't want to buy them until our mothers finally threatened to pack us up and drive us home if you didn't stop doing it."

"That sounds like me," he said with a sideways grin. "Do you remember when I tried to teach you to ride my bike? My dad had just had our driveway paved and you fell. You got pretty banged up. I remember you had tar and gravel embedded in your knees and elbows."

"I remember you trying to carry me back up the driveway and I was too heavy for you so you dropped me and then fell on top of me," she laughed.

"I didn't drop you!" he shouted. "I tripped."

"You dropped me. Admit it. You were what? Eight? You weren't strong enough to carry me then."

Mimi noticed the mischievous glint in Christian's eyes as he lunged for her and scooped her off her feet.

"Not strong enough, huh?" he teased as he broke into a full run.

"Stop!" she screamed, but the playfulness in her voice told him she didn't want him to.

Just like Mimi had guessed, the trail was a circle and Christian slowed down when the house came into view. He was now standing at the edge of the yard.

With her arms wrapped around his neck Mimi looked up to see why he wasn't returning her to her feet.

"So, what happened?" he asked, piercing her with his stare.

She swallowed and shrugged her shoulders. "I don't really know, Christian. Life happened? My mom had another baby and it was getting harder to pack Jason up and make the drive. And I think your mom was having a hard time controlling you. Do you remember the last time we came for a visit?"

He nodded. "I remember every detail of every visit with you, Mimi."

Mimi's eyes widened in surprise. "I think you were ten. The police showed up while we were there. You had stolen someone's motorcycle and hid it somewhere on your property."

With their eyes still locked he slowly lowered her to the ground. "I stole it for you. I was trying to show off," he admitted.

She tried not to smile. "It was a pretty big feat for a ten-year-old. How did you steal a nine-hundred-pound Harley?"

"I was almost eleven and it was a much smaller bike," he corrected. "But it still wasn't easy."

"I'm sure it wasn't." Her smile faded and her face grew serious.

97

"After that was a weird time for me, Christian." She kicked at the grass, distracted. "It all changed for me when I was about eleven or twelve."

"Yeah, so it was hormones for you too?" he asked.

She looked up. "What?"

"Hormones. We may have only been on the cusp of puberty, but didn't you feel like it was getting awkward toward the end? Like we noticed each other a little differently?"

"No." She shook her head. "I wasn't thinking that." She looked away and asked, "Have you ever screwed up so badly you convinced yourself that it actually changed the course of your life?" She stole a glance and saw him nod. "When I was eleven, maybe twelve, I made the first big mistake of my life. I thought I was a super sleuth. I even convinced myself that I wanted to go into investigative journalism." She tucked a stray hair behind her ear. "Anyway, I was trying to do something good, but it turned out all wrong. I managed to break into my parents' safe, and discovered my original birth certificate."

She felt his arms go around her as he pulled her into a hug.

"That's when you found out about Grizz." Christian pressed his chin against the top of her head. It was a statement, not a question and he felt her nod.

She pulled back and looked up at him. "Everything in my world changed at that moment, Christian. I was so mad at my parents for keeping it from me. It consumed me for the next few years. I shoved everything and everyone I loved away from me. I existed only in an angry vacuum I'd created. I didn't allow myself the luxury of remembering a happy childhood—our happy childhood."

Since it was already a source of contention between them she decided not to mention that she purposely suppressed more of those memories after she received his letter. With both hands Mimi reached for one of his and held it tightly. "I remembered seeing you in the hospital waiting room when my father was shot and how angry you seemed. After he died, my mother reminded me of our friendship. I made light of it because I had convinced myself that those memories were exaggerated."

"I was mad," he countered, an angry edge to his voice. He remembered the day clearly as they all waited at the hospital for word of Tommy Dillon's condition. "You were gushing all over Slade if I remember correctly."

She dropped his hand. "And that was a result of yet another one of my huge mistakes," she told him, her lips forming a thin line.

They both stared, each waiting for the other to say something.

Mimi crossed her arms in front of her. "Are you going to tell me that Slade never told you what happened to me? What he saved me from?"

"He didn't have to tell me because I already knew," Christian replied, giving her a sympathetic look. "I was the one—"

"Ugh!" Mimi interrupted. "I should've known it would've gotten out. Especially in the biker community. I mean, everyone but me knew that Grizz was my real father so why wouldn't they know about this too?" She threw her hands up in the air and turned her back on him before adding, "I guess I should consider it a miracle that my parents never found out what happened that night."

Mimi stomped off toward the house in an embarrassed huff, missing Christian's response.

"Slade didn't have to tell me, Mimi, because I was the one who told him to save you."

CHAPTER 19

PUMPKIN REST, SOUTH CAROLINA 2007

"So much for happy memories," I muttered to myself as I marched up the front porch steps and let myself into the house. I heard Christian say something to me as I walked away, but I couldn't make out the words and didn't want to hear them anyway. I was certain he would've only added to my humiliation. The memory of the horrible event that had inspired my decision to retain my virginity enveloped me as I headed for the kitchen. Like a madwoman, I started opening up cabinets and pulling out food.

I barely noticed when he came up behind me until I heard him say, "I guess it's a good thing I stocked up on groceries."

I swung around. I had an unopened package of Mallomar cookies in one hand, and clutched a bag of Cheetos to my chest with the other.

"I'm starving from our walk." I carried both goodies to the back deck and plopped down in an Adirondack chair. I started with the Cheetos and refused to look at him when he took the seat next to me.

"Are you gonna eat the whole bag yourself or are you gonna share?"

The deep timber of his voice stopped me mid-bite. Without looking over I passed him the Mallomars.

"You can start with these, but save me some. They're my favorite cookies," I confessed, still refusing to look at him.

"That's why I bought them," he replied.

My head snapped to face him and I stiffened. The enormity of everything that had transpired in the last two days felt like an anvil pressing down on my chest. I could feel my heart straining against muscle and bone as it threatened to burst out of my body. I recognized the look he was giving me. It wasn't anger or revenge or pain. It wasn't even lust or desire. Those emotions may have been there, but that wasn't what fueled Christian.

"How could you possibly remember that Mallomars are my favorite cookie?" I challenged, my voice shaky.

"I told you before, Mimi. I remember everything." His tone was smooth and casual but his eyes told a different story. They held a wildness that caused the hair to stand up on the back of my neck. I sat up on the edge of the chair, reeling at what I'd recognized in his expression. It was the same look I'd seen Grizz give my mother for the past several years.

Rolling up the almost empty bag of Cheetos, I folded my hands in my lap and looked at the boards of the deck. I immediately focused my attention on an ant that was staggering beneath the weight of a huge orange crumb.

And like that crumb, we staggered beneath the weight of the silence between us. I slowly looked up, and once again, met his penetrating gaze. Christian's eyes weren't those of a lovesick boy. Like my father's, they were the eyes of a man who didn't ask permission, apologize or make excuses for himself. Men who claimed ownership of what they considered rightfully theirs. Christian was a man who knew what he wanted, and took what he wanted without considering or caring about the consequences. Something resembling a cross between apprehension and longing lodged in my throat as I realized the magnitude of what Christian had done.

Christian had taken me.

I abruptly stood up, letting the bag of Cheetos fall to the ground. Swiping the pack of cookies from Christian's hand I briskly announced, "I'm sweaty from our hike. I'm going to take a shower."

He didn't say a word as I flounced off toward the bathroom chased by his sharp blue glare.

CHAPTER 20

PUMPKIN REST, SOUTH CAROLINA 2007

Once inside the bathroom I noticed our phones still charging on the counter. Not that it mattered. The lack of service was frustrating and Christian hadn't felt the need to enforce his cell phone ban since our truce. I'd used my phone twice since last night, texting Bettina to ask about Josh's condition, but it didn't look like they'd gone through. And if by chance they had, I hadn't received a response from her.

I sighed as I returned my phone to the counter. Glancing at the locked door, I picked up Christian's cell and was both disappointed and relieved that it required a passcode to open it. I wanted to search his contacts for the name tattooed on his arm. Maybe it was better that I didn't know.

After my shower, I headed for the kitchen where I found him sitting at the table, thumbing through a magazine that highlighted businesses in the surrounding area. He was wearing glasses and I marveled at how sexy he looked in them. I avoided his gaze as he watched me discard the empty container of Mallomars which I'd hastily shoved down my throat before my shower.

"You must've been starving," he observed.

"I was," I answered a little too brusquely. Turning to face him I leaned back against the kitchen island. Trying to avoid direct eye contact, I watched as he removed what obviously were reading glasses and laid them on the table. I stared at the dark frames, wracking my brain for a memory of Christian wearing glasses. Nothing surfaced.

I heard the scrape of his chair and my eyes cut to his. Slapping the magazine on the table he stated, "Looks like there's a bar and grill about an hour outside of Pumpkin Rest."

I nodded.

"I know you're probably not hungry now, but I was thinking if you'd like to go there maybe we could hit up a store on the way. I saw something on the news about a freak snowstorm that might blow in. I didn't bring a heavy jacket and wasn't sure if you had anything warm to wear just in case."

"I have some warm things in the laundry basket. And freak snowstorms aren't uncommon here. I've heard people talk about a blizzard that hit close to spring in the early nineties."

We decided to take my car since the back of his truck was still loaded down with the homeowner's recreational toys. I watched as he went to the spot where he'd hidden the keys he'd swiped from me that first day and got in the driver's side of my SUV.

We hadn't gone far when he gruffly announced, "Doesn't look like there's much of a choice for radio stations."

"I have some CDs I compiled." I pressed play on the car stereo. I saw a half smile when "The Weight" by The Band came on.

"We have the same taste in music," he said matter-of-factly.

"Yeah, I guess we grew up listening to the same songs as our parents," I told his profile, taking notice of his smooth dark skin and strong jaw. My eyes wandered lower to his right arm and the name I could see so prominently displayed across his muscular bicep thanks to the sleeveless tee he wore.

"You said it's about an hour to the restaurant?" I questioned.

"Yeah, looks like it."

"Maybe we could pass the time by trying to get reacquainted." The purpose behind my suggestion wasn't as noble as it sounded. I was being nosy. I wanted to know the reason behind those prison tattoos and the one in particular.

"Okay, how do you wanna do this?"

"I'll tell you something about me. And you tell me something about you that might relate to it. We could pretend it's a sort of game."

His eyes shifted to mine and he answered roughly, "You're trying to see what, if anything, we have in common."

"Maybe, yeah. It can't hurt to establish some commonalities. There's no denying we don't know each other anymore." I thought I saw his jaw tighten, but ignored it and pressed on. "We already know we like the same kind of music. What could it hurt?" His face softened as he watched the road.

"I'll go first." Without waiting I stated, "I'm a history major, but might go back to study archaeology after I get my degree. I recently discovered I have a fascination with artifacts and I'm particularly interested in digging up and studying old bones." I looked at him expectantly. He didn't say anything so I added, "Do you have any interest in history or archaeology?"

"Yeah. I guess so."

I sat up straight and turned my body to face his, the seat belt straining against my chest. "Really?" I prompted, my voice sounding hopeful. "What part?"

"The bones part," he said.

"You've dug up other people's bones? You have some experience with this?"

"Not digging up bones," he replied. "Breaking people's bones."

"You are not funny!" I barked through gritted teeth as I returned to my original position, crossing my arms over my chest.

"I'm not trying to be funny," he informed me without any hint of remorse. "It's your game. I'm doing what you said. Trying to find something related to what you told me about yourself."

I looked out the window so he wouldn't see me smile. He was right. Snapping my head around I said to him, "Maybe it's a stupid game."

He gave me a quick glance and offered, "There are other ways to get to know each other again."

I blinked, trying to ignore the warmth that was spreading through my chest and wondering what he meant. I didn't have to wait long.

"Maybe we could just talk. This time, I'll start. You told me you recognized my ink. And when I asked you how you would know about prison ink you told me I would be surprised. So tell me. How did you recognize that my tattoos were done in prison?"

A shiver of panic made its way down my back. How much could I say without telling him about Grizz? As far as Christian knew, I'd never met my biological father.

"My stepfather, James, did some time in prison. It's one of the reasons he and my mother wanted to make a clean break from Florida."

"He must've been one badass accountant," he said, his brows narrowed skeptically as he gazed out over the steering wheel.

"I guess he was," I replied, rubbing the side of my nose absent-mindedly. Without letting him speak I blurted, "Your turn. What did you do to end up in prison?"

"Aggravated battery," he said, his voice even. "They tried to get me on attempted murder, but as much as I wanted to kill the guy, having him live with a constant reminder of his transgression was my primary goal."

"Aggravated battery of who?" I asked, my eyes wide as saucers. "And what had he done?"

I noticed his knuckles were turning white as he grasped the steering wheel. I had a fleeting thought about whether or not I'd ever heard of anyone breaking a steering wheel with their bare hands.

"Who, Christian?" I probed.

Christian shot me a dark look, his eyes blazing with something primitive and wild.

"Nick Rosman. The piece of shit who tried to rape you seven years ago."

The only sound in the car was my loud gasp.

CHAPTER 21

FORT LAUDERDALE, FLORIDA 2003

Four Years Earlier

"Maybe you should think about selling the business and retiring," Christy told Anthony as she put towels away that she'd folded.

Anthony stepped out of the shower and reached for the towel his wife held out to him. Drying himself off he answered, "We've talked about this, Christy. What would I do with myself? Until Daisy graduates from high school, which won't be for several more years, we're tied down here. And I'm happy. I like working. I always have."

"I know," she replied. "Lately you just seem to come home more aggravated than not."

"That's because I've lost a lot of men recently and can only seem to find morons to replace them."

She gave him a hopeful glance, her bright blue eyes almost pleading.

"Don't even think about Christian taking over the business, Owani. Landscaping isn't his thing. I think we both know that."

"Is riding with Grizz's old gang his thing, Anthony?" It was difficult to keep the frustration out of her voice.

"That's his choice." He threw his wet towel in the hamper and reached for his clothes.

"You sent him there, Anthony!" she cried.

"They'll teach him what I apparently couldn't," he countered.

"To be a criminal?"

"To be responsible for his actions. Christian is a hothead. He'll either buck the hierarchy and someone will put him in the hospital, or..."

"Prison," Christy finished.

"We both know Christian is heading for prison, Owani. Maybe he'll learn enough discipline with Grizz's old gang to avoid it."

Christy walked into Anthony's massive arms. Hugging him tightly, she let out a sigh against his chest. "Well, at least I'm doing everything I can to make sure he doesn't end up in prison. And I'm pretty sure we've managed to divert the Mimi thing. I think she's finally given up trying to reach him."

"You're a good mother." He kissed the top of her head. "And you were right to throw her letters away, Christy," Anthony said while stroking her soft hair.

She looked up and gave a slight nod. "I know. But I can't help but wonder if Mimi would've been good for Christian."

"Not at the risk of Christian finding out Grizz didn't die on death row. He's eighteen but still not mature enough to be trusted, honey."

Christy pulled away and took his hand. "C'mon, dinner will be ready in ten minutes and Autumn will be bringing Daisy home soon."

"Is Autumn still trying to get her hooks into Christian?" Anthony asked as he followed Christy through their bedroom.

Stopping at the foot of their bed, Christy turned to face Anthony. "I know Autumn thinks she's in love with him and does whatever she can to get his attention. It doesn't help that he still lives here, at least part-time. God only knows where he crashes when he's not home."

Anthony was going to reply, but looked at their bed instead. "How long do we have until Daisy gets home?" he asked, giving Christy a mischievous grin.

Dropping to her knees and unbuckling his belt, Christy told him, "Long enough."

"DINNER WAS GOOD, OWANI," Anthony remarked as he walked behind her toward their family room. "Daisy scarfed it down."

"I think she scarfed it down so she could watch her favorite show. Besides, it's not too hard to mess up a four-ingredient Crock-Pot recipe, although I have ruined some of those in the past." Christy laughed.

As was their nightly habit, Anthony and Christy cleaned up the dinner dishes before retiring to the family room to enjoy a cup of coffee and watch the evening news.

"Daisy, you can finish watching that in your room. Daddy and I are gonna have our coffee and watch some TV," Christy directed Daisy as she set both cups on the table.

Daisy jumped up from her spot on the floor, and after giving each parent a quick hug, happily bounded off to her bedroom.

"I don't think I've ever encountered a sweeter or more agreeable child," Christy said as she took a seat in one of the leather recliners and reached for the remote and her mug.

"I agree," Anthony replied. "I sometimes wonder how she could be ours. Slade was a good kid, but even he had his moments."

After craning her neck to make sure Daisy had gone to her room, Christy said, "I don't know if I told you that I heard from Carter."

"Is everything okay?" He gave her a sideways glance.

"I'm sure it is. It amazes me that we never got to know Carter and Bill that well, especially with how close they were to Ginny." She paused and drank her coffee. "You remember we had lunch about eight months ago, right?"

"How could I forget?" Anthony asked. "I was shocked that Ginny called her, and that Carter told you about it."

"Ginny had a good reason to call Carter. Grizz killed that man, Anthony. Ginny had been holding it all in and was getting paranoid. I think she needed to talk to someone who knew about Grizz's history. And since Carter's husband is responsible for scouring the internet and burying anything remotely connected to Grizz and their family, I think she was nervous about possible rumors surfacing." Christy picked at an imaginary piece of lint on her pants. "I don't blame her."

Anthony gave her a sympathetic nod and added, "If Carter has anything interesting to share, I'd like to know."

"Of course, babe."

They settled on their favorite news station and commented to each other on the weather, the latest business report and a feature on tourists who were being targeted by local thugs.

We're coming to you live from Davie where three boys happened upon a gruesome discovery while fishing at this remote canal.

The reporter gestured to the area behind her.

The children alerted police to what they believed was a dead body, but turned out was only an arm that had been cleanly severed at the elbow. We can't show you a picture of the detached limb, but we can describe it in the hopes that someone will recognize the tattoo descriptions. Police tell us the forearm has what appears to be a religious cross with flowers intertwined around it. On the other side, and what may be the best clue to the victim's identity, is a heart with the name Edith inside it. If you think you may know someone who has tattoos like these, you are urged to contact law enforcement at the number at the bottom of the screen. Right now, police aren't sure if they're looking for a murder victim or the victim of a horrible accident—

"What a horrible thing to find," Christy remarked. "I can't imagine what kinds of nightmares those poor boys will have after finding an arm."

"The police will probably find the rest of the body soon," Anthony interjected. "If it was an accident it would most likely be ripped and torn, not a clean cut. The clean cut tells me it was deliberate."

"You would know," Christy huffed, giving him a knowing look.

They both heard the sound of Christian's truck pulling up the long driveway. Christy got up and nodded toward Anthony's mug. "Want a little more to warm your cup?"

She was standing at the counter giving them both a refill when the door that connected the kitchen to the garage swung open. She turned around to greet her son when both mugs she'd been holding crashed to the ground, splattering hot coffee across the floor and on the cabinets.

Anthony raced to the kitchen in time to see Christy patting Christian down. "Where is it? Where are you hurt?" she screamed in obvious terror.

"What happened?" Anthony barked.

"It's obvious he's hurt!" Christy cried. Christian was covered in blood.

"It's not my blood," Christian replied.

Christy stood back, her eyes wide.

"Whose blood is this, Christian?"

"Nick Rosman's," he said curtly.

It took Christy a moment to place the name, but when recognition dawned, she barely whispered, "Did you kill him?"

"No. I maimed him for life," Christian said, without a hint of remorse.

"The arm," was all Christy managed to say.

Christian nodded, but didn't ask how she'd known about the arm. He addressed his father. "I guess you'll tell me I'm an idiot for going after him."

"Not for going after him," came Anthony's stern reply. "You're an idiot for leaving evidence. I wouldn't have left an arm for somebody to find."

"Yeah, what would you have done?" Christian challenged.

"I would've put him in the ground. All of him."

CHAPTER 22

PUMPKIN REST, SOUTH CAROLINA 2007

I sat with my back against the car door, my jaw slack, staring at Christian. Not even the hopeful pinging of our cell phones as we drove closer into range could take my attention away from the shock I felt at what he'd revealed.

"You cut off Nick Rosman's arm?" My voice came out raspy, a frog lodged in my throat.

He leveled a look at me. "Yeah."

"Why?" I could feel my heart thudding as it threatened to beat out of my chest.

"I did it to get back at him for what he planned to do to you. He's lucky he didn't see you naked, because I would've gouged out his eyes. Or that he didn't actually rape you, because I would've cut off his—"

"I get it!" I cried, holding up both hands. "Slade told you what happened to me?"

I listened, stunned, as Christian revealed the story behind the night of my attempted rape by a guy I'd been dating. He explained in detail about overhearing a conversation weeks earlier between my father, Tommy, and Axel at Axel's garage. He told me how he infiltrated Nick Rosman's small gang of punks. And how, after learning the time and place for the sinister plan, he'd rushed to rescue me himself, but ended up getting pulled over by the police and hauled off to jail for smarting off to the officer. He went on to explain how he'd used his one jail-house call to contact Slade and insisted he race to the location to stop my attempted rape.

By the end of his story, my lungs burned from taking short, unsatisfying breaths. I had to calm myself and focus on deep breathing.

"Why his arm?" I asked. "And why years after what he tried to do to me?" My voice didn't sound like my own.

"I heard that he used the tattoo to trick you into thinking he was a nice guy. It probably gave you a false sense of security about him. It was a religious tattoo, right?"

I could only nod. He looked over at me and words wouldn't come so I nodded again.

"And as far as why it took a couple years, I can't say for sure." He shrugged his shoulders. "I just know that the few punches to the face that Slade gave him never seemed like enough retaliation. It gnawed at my gut for a long time."

"You went to prison for it." It was a statement, not a question.

"Yeah. I got five years for aggravated battery and got out in three."

"How long have you been out?" I asked.

"A couple months."

I shook my head. "But you said this happened in 2003 and this is 2007. That's four years."

"It took over a year to go to trial."

"How come they didn't charge you with attempted murder?" My mind wasn't only reeling that he'd mutilated Nick on my account and went to prison for it, but concern that my name might've come up in trial. As if reading my mind, Christian provided more details.

"It wasn't attempted murder because I wasn't trying to murder him. I used a tourniquet and drove him to the hospital after I hacked off his arm."

I cringed but didn't interrupt him, clearing my throat.

"When I got him there, I told the people at the E.R. that we were messing around with machetes and it was an accident. They rushed him into surgery and I waited until I was told he would make it. Then I headed home. By then, kids found the arm and it was all over the news. By the time the E.R. doctors got in touch with the police, they'd already been looking for who the arm belonged to. I didn't try to hide the crime."

"What did Nick tell the police?" I asked hoarsely. The frog had returned to establish residence.

"What I told him to tell them. They didn't believe it, but they didn't have anything to go on. Me driving him to the hospital

proved I wasn't trying to kill him, but I still did time for aggravated battery."

He looked over and finally answered what I was questioning in my head. "Your name never came up. I threatened to cut off more than his arm if your name was mentioned. And if I couldn't do it from jail, he knew enough about my father's history to believe my threat could be enforced. And I'm certain the money my family paid him to help in his *recovery* went a long way in keeping him quiet."

I shook my head in disbelief. Christian was the one who'd actually saved me that night, not Slade like I'd always believed. I winced inwardly when I remembered fawning over Slade for coming to my rescue.

"You went to prison." A moment passed as I breathlessly added, "For me."

"I'd do anything for you, Mimi. Anything."

He looked over at me and then back at the road. The words were out before I could stop them.

"Then who is Abby?"

He threw me another fleeting look and then raised his right arm and looked at the tattoo on his bicep. He didn't answer me at first and I wondered if he was going to. I can't say why, but everything seemed to hinge on his response. He may have hacked off a guy's arm for me, but he had another woman's name notably memorialized with a tattoo. It didn't make sense.

"My older half sister. You remember how we used to play at Abigail Ramirez Memorial Park when you came over to visit?"

"I don't remember the name of the park, and I certainly don't remember that you had an older half sister," I admitted, shaking my head.

"Abby was born years before my mother met my father, and she died when she was a baby."

Abby was a sister I'd never known about. The heat I felt spreading through my veins found its way to my chest and my heart gave a flutter.

"I thought maybe Abby was your girlfriend or something," I said, trying to keep the deep sense of relief out of my tone.

"I've never had a steady or serious girlfriend," he admitted. I couldn't tell if he was being boastful or if his tone was one of regret.

"Why's that?" I prompted. I absentmindedly picked up my phone and scrolled through texts so I had somewhere to look other than at Christian.

Instead of answering me, he reached over and turned up the volume on the CD player.

"Bad Time" by Grand Funk Railroad floated through my car speakers. The lyrics describing a bad time to be in love were almost as taunting as the texts I had scrolled through and chose to ignore from Lucas.

CHAPTER 23

W e found a small bargain store on the way and stopped to get Christian warmer clothes. I wasn't certain, but I could've sworn I detected odd glances from some of the male customers. I brushed it off, reminding myself that we were strangers in a very remote area and the local folk were probably wary of outsiders. I also noticed that unlike the men, the two women we encountered looked like they wanted to devour Christian. Giving them a dirty look, I sidled up closer to him and linked my arm through his.

He asked me if I was sure I didn't need anything warmer and I reminded him that I had long johns, sweatshirts, and a warm jacket in the laundry basket he'd retrieved from my trunk.

Back in the car, I looked at my phone again and let out a sigh.

"What's wrong?" Christian prodded.

"You know the friend from my camp that I told you was sick?" I blinked to ward off the tears and looked out the window. "He's not getting better. It doesn't look good for him."

Christian asked me for details about Josh's illness, the camp, and Bettina with the long blue dreadlocks from the gas station. Our conversation bordered on normal as he told me that he'd inherited his father's skill for auto repair, but preferred working on motorcycles. I told him about my college courses, my friends, and my part-time job at a used book store. Details he had to have already known from the P.I. but listened to again.

I was stunned when he told me the name of the person who'd

filled in his P.I. about my dating habits. It was a girl I had roomed with during my junior year. We were in a couple of the same classes this semester and even had several study sessions together. She was a straight A student, a sweet and unassuming wallflower with a secret. Apparently she had a serious addiction to prescription drugs. Proving once again that everyone has their price.

After discovering the restaurant from Christian's magazine was closed due to a kitchen fire, we found ourselves pulling into the next place we saw. Sitting by itself in a gravel turnoff, Chicky's was housed in what looked like an old gas station that had been converted to a bar and restaurant. It was obvious by the addition that the business outgrew its original building. It was a pleasant-looking place with a sign that boasted the best wings and burgers in the Carolinas. There were two motorcycles and one truck parked out front. I was relieved that we'd beaten the dinner crowd.

Christian opened the door and waved me in. Once inside he gently grabbed my elbow and bent low to ask me, "Do you want to sit at the bar, a table, or a booth?"

I didn't answer right away as I slowly perused the inside of Chicky's. The far wall had a long bar where a lone bartender was obviously getting ready for the after-five rush. One man sat at the end by himself nursing a beer. A table off to our right housed two bikers who were having a heated, but what sounded like a friendly argument. The one facing me caught my eye and stopped talking. His friend turned around and gave us both the once-over.

"The bar," I told Christian as I walked toward it.

After taking our seats at the opposite end of where the lone drinker was perched, the bartender loudly asked us if we would be ordering food. He was an older man with long gray hair, a stocky build and a ruddy complexion. Christian nodded, and he approached us with two menus and a smile on his face, but his expression immediately changed when he handed them over. The look was one of curiosity or maybe recognition. But that was impossible, I told myself. This man wouldn't know us. I looked over at Christian who already had his face buried in the menu. Since he wasn't wearing his glasses he must've been having a hard time reading it.

"You folks from around here?" the man asked. His voice sounded gruff, but I got the impression that was how he always sounded.

Without looking up, Christian answered, "Just passing through."

The man nodded and asked, "Do you know what you're drinking?"

I ordered a water with lemon and Christian ordered a beer. Before he could leave to get our drinks, Christian laid down the menu and said, "I know what I want."

"Me too," I added since I'd already decided on wings after seeing the sign.

After ordering, I asked Christian if he thought the guy gave us a funny look when he first handed us the menus.

"Maybe. It looked like he thought he knew us and then realized we weren't who he thought we were," he replied as he reached for a bowl on the bar filled with assorted nuts.

I slid my hand into my purse and pulled out some red licorice.

"Dessert before dinner?" he nonchalantly asked, popping some nuts into his mouth.

I nodded and chewed on my licorice, admitting through a mouthful of red, "I'm a snack-a-holic."

I climbed off my chair and tugged at his arm. "C'mon, there's a jukebox in the corner. Help me pick out some songs."

He stood, reached into his front pocket and said, "Let me get some change first."

"You don't need to. I'm the change queen," I laughed, handing him the wallet I'd retrieved from my bag. It weighed a ton and I could hear him chuckling as he carried it behind me. After relieving my little purse of its load and filling up the jukebox, I told him to go first.

He picked "Feelin' Alright" by Joe Cocker. I punched in "Seminole Wind" by John Anderson. He pressed the buttons for "Run Through the Jungle" by Creedence Clearwater Revival. We had one more selection and I chose "Time Has Come Today" by The Chamber Brothers.

His hand found the small of my back and he steered me toward our seats. The same hand that had used a machete to hack off Nick Rosman's arm.

"Do you know what became of Nick?" I asked out of curiosity

He took a sip of his beer before answering. Swinging around to face me, he said, "He visited me in prison."

My eyes went wide. "What?"

"He said that he'd completely turned his life around after he met a man who'd found God while in the slammer." Christian rolled his eyes before continuing. "The guy was out and wanted to do something positive with his life. Something that would prevent boys from getting into trouble and winding up spending their lives incarcerated. Nick had the money, thanks to my parents, and the ex-con had the vision."

He reached for his beer and took another swig. "Nick was there to tell me that he forgave me." Christian's lip curled. "Like I cared."

"So he's okay? He fully recovered and is doing well?" I questioned reaching for another piece of licorice.

"Yeah, they opened up a camp or retreat for troubled teenage boys. I think he said it was called Diamonds in the Rough." He took another long swallow of beer and added, "Or something like that."

The bartender was back, but not with our food.

"I wouldn't have recognized either of you if you weren't together. You're Grizz and Bear's kids, aren't you?"

Completely caught off guard, neither of us responded, but I detected a change in Christian's posture. The man's expression softened, and focusing on me, he said, "I'm sorry. It never occurred to me that you might not know that. You know...that Grizz was your father."

I shook my head slightly. "No...no, it's okay. I've known since I was twelve. But I'm more curious as to how you know them?"

He broke into a wide grin and looked from me to Christian and back to me.

"The name's Mike. I used to tend bar for Grizz at The Red Crab and Razors back in Fort Lauderdale."

I nodded, recognizing the names of Grizz's places.

"How did you know who we were?" Christian asked. I immediately detected the annoyance in his tone and laid my hand on his knee.

"You're the spitting image of Bear, minus the eye color. And you," he said, turning to look at me, "could pass for Kit's twin." A moment passed before he added, "But I still don't know if I'd have recognized you if I hadn't seen you together. Something just clicked."

He left to check on our food and I turned my stool toward Christian. "This bothers you?"

"It doesn't bother you?" he asked stiffly.

Since Christian didn't know Grizz was alive, I couldn't share my concern with him about having someone from my father's past living only hours away instead of several states. But I also knew my father didn't venture far from home and when I saw him again, I would warn him.

"Not really," I told him. "It might be fun to hear some of Mike's stories."

"Whatever," he replied shrugging nonchalantly.

Mike returned with our food and even Christian couldn't resist laughing at some of the tales Mike shared.

"Your fathers were some clever SOBs," he said. "They had everybody thinking for years that they were enemies. I even thought it for a while!"

Mike laughed and then his face turned melancholy when I asked him how he ended up working at Chicky's. He looked away and concentrated on wiping down the bar while he told us about the woman who owned the bar and named it after herself. I was no expert, but I would've bet a million bucks that Mike had been in love with Chicky. She was a waitress at the same bars where Mike worked in Fort Lauderdale, and she left Florida after my father's trial. She opened up her own place and married an older man named Ed. She'd traveled back to Florida and visited my father while he was in prison and on one trip, she made it a point to stop at The Red Crab to see Mike. She offered him a job and it only took him a week to quit the job he had, pack all his belongings, and make the move to South Carolina. Apparently, he didn't care that she was married. He even spoke fondly of Ed, and stayed on to work for the heartbroken man after Chicky succumbed to cancer. Eventually, Ed fell ill too, and left the bar to Mike since Chicky's grown daughter from a previous relationship didn't want it.

I changed the subject and started asking him questions that made him smile, the corners of his eyes crinkling. I could tell that Mike was a good guy and that his crow's feet weren't so much from age as they were from grinning.

Christian and I had both finished our meals and tried to pay our tab, but Mike waved us off, insisting it was on the house. I stood and was getting ready to excuse myself to use the restroom when I sensed a presence standing on the other side of Christian.

"If I'd known we'd be blessed with a big handsome hunk of a man like you, I'd have shown up earlier."

I immediately felt myself stiffen as I peeked around Christian to see who'd made the comment.

"You're late, Tina. As usual!" Mike barked, causing me to flinch.

I watched as Tina slowly moved her hand up and down Christian's left arm, and didn't seem the least offended when he shirked her off.

Who does she think she is laying a hand on my man while I'm right next to him? I thought.

Did I just think of Christian as my man?

I glared at the woman. She was tall, shapely and had rainbow-colored hair. Her big brown eyes were focused on Christian, and they weren't the only big things. To sum it up, she was drop-dead gorgeous. I gritted my teeth.

Before any of us could remark, we heard a deep but whiny voice behind us.

"'Bout time you got here, Tina. I've been trying to get Mike's attention for another beer, but he's been too busy with Crazy Horse." His words were slurred, but that didn't stop him from continuing. "I didn't know they let them off the reservation. They need to stay on their own side of the border."

I was instantly transported to that day at the playground, watching a memory from my past unfold.

"So, are you and your squaw gonna live in a teepee?" the intruder sneered while swiping at his sweaty face with his arm. "Wait, she can't be your squaw. She's a pale face, and you're too dark."

I looked at Christian with a puzzled expression. He was staring hard at the older boy when I asked, "What's a squaw?"

"It's a dirty injun's wife," the boy laughed. "You are an injun, right?" he sneered at Christian. "You have a long braid and dark skin. Where do you keep your bows and arrows?"

"Hey, Sal!" Mike shouted, at the same time Christian stood up. "You're talking to biker royalty. Go back to your table and park it, and Tina can bring you another beer."

Mike's yell brought me back to the present as I skirted around Christian's barstool and poked Sal in the chest. "You," I snapped, "are an ignorant, racist jerk!"

Sal didn't have time to reply as Christian's right fist connected with his face. The sickening crack of Sal's jawbone was horrifying, and Sal was out before he hit the ground.

Tina giggled while Mike apologized for Sal's rude behavior and told us not to worry because Sal had it coming. He also told us we should probably leave before more regulars showed up. He didn't need to tell me twice. I looped my arm through Christian's and headed for the door, aggravated that he didn't feel the same sense of urgency as I did. The man who'd been sitting at the table with Sal when we first walked in stood up, but raised both hands in the air and said, "Ain't lookin' for trouble. Just goin' to check on my friend."

We'd only driven about two miles when Christian looked over at me, his eyes blazing.

"What did you think you were doing, picking a fight with that drunken slob?" he demanded.

"I needed to do something, to deal with it, so you wouldn't. I did it to protect you," I snapped, my chin jutting out.

"Protect me?" he shouted. "And poking him in the chest was your way of dealing with it?"

"Yes," I said defiantly. "I was giving him a warning. If he went for me, I would've broken your beer bottle over his head."

"If he went for you, I would've killed him," came his reply, his voice low and menacing. "Which is why I coldcocked him before he could retaliate against your poke." His tone was mocking and I felt my face flushing with anger and embarrassment.

"Look," I huffed in exasperation. "Maybe I didn't handle it right. What I'm trying to say is that I know you just got out of prison so you must be on parole. If you had picked a fight with him and the police were called you would be going back to jail."

He gave me a hard look and returned his eyes to the road. "You think I don't know that? And so you know, I was doing my best to control my temper. Not because I didn't want to get hauled back to jail, but for you." He banged his fist hard on the steering wheel. "I wasn't gonna confront the guy until you picked a fight with him, Mimi. I don't care about jail. I care about you and I don't want to give up the time we have left together."

I nervously twined a finger in my hair, and tried to ignore his last comment. It unsettled me in a way I hadn't expected. Christian would've walked away if I hadn't confronted Sal. And he only knocked Sal out because he knew he would've gone too far if Sal had reacted against me. Christian might've killed a man because of me.

Brushing the thought away in an attempt to not read too much into it, I muttered, "I guess it's a good thing you knocked the guy out and the law didn't have to get involved. Because if the police were called they'd be getting in touch with your parole officer and he'd probably lose his job for giving you permission to leave the state so soon after your release."

Christian narrowed his eyes at me and looked back at the road.

He didn't need to say anything. I saw it in the set of his jaw.

"Your parole officer doesn't know you're here." It wasn't a question. I was giving him a stern look.

"He thinks I'm in Jacksonville applying for a job."

"Uh!" I exclaimed. "You didn't ask him if you could take a trip to South Carolina?"

He kept his eyes on the road, his right hand tightly clutching the steering wheel while his left elbow rested on the open window.

"I've already told you, Mimi. I don't ask."

CHAPTER 24

PUMPKIN REST, SOUTH CAROLINA 2007

W e were less than ten minutes into our ride when I insisted Christian find a place for me to use the restroom since I'd missed my opportunity at Chicky's.

Afterward, I climbed back into my SUV and decided we were in dire need of a change of subject and mood. I tried to lighten the tension by suggesting another game. Only this time, my motives were slightly different. Up until now, I was under the impression that everything Christian had done had been purely selfish on his part. When he admitted that he intended to let Sal's comments slide for me, I sensed a shift in my feelings about our situation. For some reason that I couldn't fathom, I wanted to share a nugget of truth with Christian about my family. I'd been willing to do it when I'd made the offer to answer any question, and he'd caught me off guard by asking about Lucas.

"Tell me something nobody else in the world knows," I coaxed.

He looked over at me, and I gave him a sincere smile. He pulled the edges of his mouth into a wide grin that caused my skin to tingle. I expected him to insist that I go first so I was totally surprised when he asked, "Do you have any memories of us playing wedding when we were kids?"

Yeah, I thought. *I even mentioned it in one of my letters.* Instead of going down that road again, I nodded and let my mind drift back to that innocent time.

"Let's get married by the water fountain this time," I told Christian.

"Why?" he asked as he returned the ring to his pocket and scooted into the tube that would eventually deliver us to the ground.

"Because I'm thirsty," I replied. I gave him a shove and jumped in behind him.

After taking turns at the fountain, we made our way to a small shaded area, waving to our mothers as we went. Still within their protective view, Christian yanked his white T-shirt over his head and handed it to me. The first time we played wedding, we got some help from Aunt Christy who showed us how we could turn a shirt into a makeshift bridal veil.

While I tucked my hair up under Christian's shirt, he picked some flowers that may or may not have been weeds.

The wedding preparations were complete, and it was time to take our vows.

"Some," I admitted. "I remember you showed me a ring with a huge blue stone. I think you said you got it out of one of those claw machines."

I watched him nod and then say with a laugh, "It was a big gaudy thing, wasn't it?"

"Yeah, I think it was," I agreed. "I'm sorry I don't remember what became of it," I sadly confessed. Recalling my earlier question, I prodded, "You were supposed to tell me something that nobody else in the world knows but you."

"I was getting to that. It took me a couple of years to figure out we weren't really married."

I busted out laughing and he quickly added, "Give me a break, I was only six."

I twisted around in my seat and leaned back against the door, thoroughly enjoying the playful side of Christian. He'd left Florida without permission and that nagged at me, but I couldn't deny the thrill I felt that Abby was his half sister, and not a girlfriend. Or that he'd not given Tina from Chicky's a second glance. Or that he was going to let Sal's racist statements slide because he didn't want to get in a brawl that could've separated us. And that's when it occurred to me that the looks I'd seen being thrown Christian's way at the store held the same disdain as Sal's remarks. I'd wondered if the comments were aimed at Christian because he was Native American or because his skin was so much darker than mine. Or maybe a little bit of both. Ignorant idiots.

"Your turn." His deep voice rumbled, gaining my full attention. His voice alone made me borderline giddy.

"My mom found Grizz's real family and they live just a few hours away in North Carolina." There. I said it. I shared a truth about myself. It was as if a yoke had been lifted from around my neck and I suddenly felt lighter.

"Your mother lives in North Carolina?" he asked. Even though I was staring at his profile, I could see his brow crease in question.

"No!" I answered louder than I'd intended. "But she thought it was important that I establish a relationship with them since Grizz was my biological father and they are really the only extended family I have. It's one of the reasons I go to school in South Carolina. I can spend weekends with my cousins and grandfather. His name is Micah."

I sucked in my breath, worried that I may have gone too far. But I was pleasantly surprised when Christian showed only mild curiosity, asking me how much they knew about Grizz's past, what they thought of it, and were they sorry he'd died on death row before they could meet him.

After giving him the best explanation I could, I closed with, "My grandfather was humbled when my mother and James gave my little sister the middle name Frances. It was Grizz's mother's name."

"Your little sister?" Christian interrupted.

"Yeah, Ruth Frances." A beat passed and I added, "I told you in my letters about Ruthie and Dillon."

"Dillon?" He sounded confused and I saw his forehead crinkle.

"Christian. You said you remember everything. How could you not remember that I mentioned in at least one of my letters that my mother and James had twins? A boy and a girl."

He looked over at me and there was no hint of recognition in what I'd just revealed about the twins. I knew instantly that he'd never received my letters.

"Tell me what it said," he demanded.

"What what said?"

"The letter I sent you. What did it say, Mimi?"

CHAPTER 25

I was somewhat reluctant to share what I remembered about the letter I'd gotten from him so many years ago. It was too humiliating so I was mildly relieved that I couldn't recollect all of the details. I still had the letter, but hadn't looked at it since the first and only time I'd read it. I could've made the trip home in a few hours to retrieve it, but it didn't seem necessary now.

Christian reassured me he'd never received or sent a letter and I knew he was telling me the truth.

Christian finally believed me.

And I believed him.

He shocked me when he unexpectedly pulled over to the side of the road. Turning to me, he reached across my chest to unhook my seat belt. He pulled me toward him and tenderly pressed my face between both of his huge hands. His eyes were filled with concern when he quietly said, "I could never even think those things about you, Mimi. Let alone write them."

I tried to blink back the tears, but they couldn't be stopped. They trickled down my cheeks as I confessed, "I really believed you hated me all these years. That I disgusted you." I choked back a sob, and tried to swipe my arm across my cheeks, but he was still holding on to my face.

And then he did something that I'd thought only happened in romance novels. He kissed away my tears. I closed my eyes as I felt his feathery kisses on each eyelid, cheek, and I stifled a moan when I felt his tongue lick the saltiness that had made its way down to the corner of my mouth. He pulled back as I blinked, and stared right at him.

Our eyes locked in a battle of longing and desperation, and true to form, Christian didn't ask when his mouth collided with mine. Bold at first, the intensity of our kiss was hurried and heated as if we both feared it wasn't real. Eventually, he slowed the pace as he continued to explore the inside of my mouth, our tongues warring for dominance. I finally relented and let him take the lead.

Kissing Christian Bear had felt as natural as breathing and I quickly ignored the stab of regret I felt at all the wasted years. Even after he broke the kiss, he held my face in his hands and I realized I was tightly clutching his wrists, reluctant to let go. I stayed in my dreamlike state with my eyes closed and my breathing heavy. When I finally opened them he was smiling at me.

"When did you brush your teeth?" He slowly let go of my face, kissing my bruised wrist before separating us.

"At the last stop," I laughed, amused by his question. I was still trying to catch my breath while Christian was curious about its minty freshness. "I always carry a travel-size toothbrush and mini toothpaste in my purse."

"You are full of surprises, Dreamy Mimi," he teased as he shifted into gear and pulled back on to the road. I refastened my seat belt while reveling in how our kiss seemed to melt away years of pain, misunderstanding, and pent-up anger on both our parts. And it was obvious that the kiss was going to be responsible for allowing us to easily slip back into the comfort zone we'd had as children. I prayed that it wasn't an illusion. A tug on my heart wanted and needed to believe this was real.

After more discussion as to who could've intercepted my letters and responded to them, we both came to the sad conclusion that it could only have been Christian's mother. I had a difficult time reconciling the sweet and caring woman I'd always called Aunt Christy as the author of the words that had shredded my teenaged heart into pieces.

I could see by the clenching of his jaw, that Christian was not happy with our concluded suspicions so I assured him that even though it was terribly mean-spirited, his mother was only following my mother's wishes. He seemed to calm down and I popped a new CD in the player and turned up the music.

I burrowed deep into my seat, secretly reveling in how natural his hand casually resting on my left knee felt. I listened to the words of Paul Davis's "Sweet Life" and changed the song, its lyrics bringing up a sadness and truth I hadn't wanted to face. "I Saw the Light" by Todd Rundgren started and I hoped the melody would distract me enough to stamp out the memory of the day I received the counterfeit letter from Aunt Christy. But it was of no use. My mind couldn't stop itself from dredging up the hateful words I'd read so many years ago, and even though I now knew they hadn't been Christian's words, thinking about them brought me back to the day I'd decided to forget I'd ever known Christian Bear.

Four Years Earlier

"You need to shoo!" Aunt Tillie commanded the four of us from the kitchen. "All of you! We have this under control."

"I pumped enough milk for—" my mother started to say.

"I know this, darlin'. You've already told me and then told me again, and I'm pretty sure you told me again. These babies will be fine, and all of you need a break," Aunt Tillie replied, her voice a little gentler. "It's only three days. Now go!"

Aunt Tillie was Grizz's aunt, my grandfather, Micah's, older sister. And in typical Aunt Tillie fashion, she decided on her own that the family could benefit from a small respite away from the twins. Like a drill sergeant gathering the troops for roll call, she'd organized an around-the-clock babysitting regime of aunts and cousins who would stay at the house and care for the infants.

The four of us said our goodbyes and shuffled out of the house carrying our overnight bags. My mom headed for the car when Grizz grabbed her arm.

"We're not taking the car," he stated.

"How are we supposed to get there?"

"We're taking my bike. The kids are taking the car to Becky and Dave's," he answered matter-of-factly as my brother and I loaded our things into the family's SUV. Becky was Grizz's first cousin. She was the mother of DJ and Rachelle, best friends to Jason and me.

"We had a plan. We're supposed to be going to Gatlinburg," Mom reminded him as Jason and I made our way over to her.

Grizz took the bag from her and said, "We're still going to Gatlinburg. But these two," he nodded at us, "aren't coming with us."

"We don't want to hurt your feelings, but we'd rather stay at Aunt Becky's," I volunteered. "Besides, we already planned it without you. We don't need to go off the mountain to get a break, but I think you and Grizz do."

My mother swung around to stare at Grizz who was squatting and rifling through one of her bags. He looked up and gave her a quick wink. I could see the love in her eyes as she watched him. At six feet five with a full head of golden locks that had slight streaks of gray that fell below his shoulders, even I had to admit my father was an impressive sight. Mom confided in me that she'd thought it the first time she climbed onto the back of his motorcycle in 1975, and I could tell she still thought it now.

Mom swiped her hand through her hair and smiled. "We haven't ridden in years. It'll be nice to be on the bike again. This is a lovely surprise. Thank you," she told me and Jason as she grabbed us for a collective hug.

I was heading back toward the car, keys in hand when something occurred to me. I spun around and said, "Umm, Mom, I was just wondering..."

My mother stopped walking toward the motorcycle and turned around to face me.

"What is it, Mimi?"

"I'm curious. What kind of Native American is Uncle Anthony? Did we ever know that?"

Grizz had been crouching by his bike and stood up. He exchanged a quick look with Mom.

"Why would you want to know about Uncle Anthony?" she asked, the curiosity on her face attempting to mask her concern.

"No reason," I reassured her. "Just that with us being so close to the Cherokee Indian Reservation, I was thinking about the Bears and couldn't remember if I ever knew what Uncle Anthony's background was. That's all."

"Cherokee and Seminole," Grizz answered, his deep voice floating over the sweet- smelling mountain air.

"Really?" I wasn't able to keep the excitement out of my one-word reply. They both noticed and exchanged another fleeting look.

"Not a North Carolina Cherokee, though," Grizz quickly added.

"Maybe originally. Bear was descended from a band of Cherokee that had migrated west in the 1800s. Oklahoma, I think."

"Oh," was all I said as I tried to hide my disappointment.

Jason, who had already stuffed his thirteen-year-old growing-like-a-weed body into the car, opened the passenger door and got out.

"I forgot something," he yelled as he ran back into the house.

Again I approached the driver side while putting in my earbuds. I hadn't turned up the music yet when I overheard my mother ask Grizz, "What do you think that was all about?"

Instead of getting into the car, I leaned up against the side of it and pretended I was listening to my music, bobbing my head to the silent tune.

"Not sure. Probably nothing. I don't see her curiosity as unusual. We're so close to the reservation. I thought about the Bears more than once myself since we've moved here."

I looked at the ground but could see with my peripheral vision that he'd walked toward Mom and pulled her close, wrapping his muscular and heavily tattooed arms around her. "Hope you don't mind my scheming to get you alone," he said as he buried his face in her hair.

"I don't mind at all. I'm excited. I've missed being on the back of your bike. It's been a long time."

I knew they'd planned to ride last summer, but after discovering Mom was pregnant, Grizz didn't want her on his motorcycle. Not to mention, she'd been too overcome with morning sickness to be able to enjoy herself. Then as she got larger, it wasn't practical. I knew this would be the first time in almost twenty years that they would be cruising together. I didn't have to see my mother's expression to know she was getting excited.

"Why is my breast pump unpacked?" she asked, looking over at the small pile Grizz had apparently made on the ground next to his bike.

"Can't fit it on the bike, baby," he told her without letting go of her.

"I need it, Grizz. I don't think I can go three whole days without pumping. My boobs will explode. I need a way to get the milk out."

I looked up and watched as she pulled away from him and started to walk toward the pile. But he grabbed her arm and swung her around. Staring at her chest, he gave her a wicked smile.

"I can think of more than one way to get the milk out, Kitten."

That'll teach you to eavesdrop, Mimi, I scolded myself as I made a mad dash for the car door and suppressed a groan of disgust. Everyone knew their parents did stuff. But hearing my father's comment only exacerbated the reality, and I was secretly grateful I'd never accidentally walked in on something.

Once inside the car, I laid on the horn. "C'mon, Jason!" I yelled through the open passenger window, unable to look back over at my parents. I'd never been so grossed out in my entire life.

AFTER DELIVERING Jason to Aunt Becky's, I drove Rachelle to check her mailbox at the local post office just like I'd done almost every day since mailing my final letter to Christian.

Rachelle had gone to extremes to provide a way for him to reply to me and keep my location a secret. She gave the last letter I'd written to her friend who'd mailed it from Ohio during her family reunion. Rachelle even worked it out so that her friend Ariel, who lived in California, let us use her address for Christian to send a reply. He'd never contacted me via email so assuming he wasn't a tech kind of guy, Rachelle hatched another plan. If she received a letter from Christian, Ariel agreed to mail it to Rachelle to give to me. It had already been a few weeks since I sent my last letter to him. Maybe it was just too much subterfuge to manage. Or maybe he wouldn't be replying to this one either.

I was sitting in my car waiting for Rachelle to come out of the post office. I gazed out the open window and swiped away a piece of hair that had blown in my face. The breeze was warm, and the air smelled like wet asphalt. A shower had doused our tiny town earlier, causing steam to rise from the ground as the sun burned the fresh rain off the road. Movement to the right caught my attention. It was Rachelle, running while wildly waving a piece of mail with a grin so huge her eyes practically disappeared. I knew it was for me. I was almost bouncing in my seat by the time she jumped into the car.

"It's from him!" she cried as she shoved the letter at me.

I took a deep breath and stared at the letter with the return address and postmark from California. Not wanting to get my hopes up, I said, "Maybe it's a letter from Ariel to you."

"Mimi, shut up and open it. If you don't, I will!" she screamed.

I carefully opened the letter and let out a shriek of excitement when I saw that it contained another note inside. I took it out and glanced over at Rachelle as I pried open the envelope. I could feel her anxious eyes on me as I slowly read Christian's words. The back of my eyes started to burn and I willed myself not to cry. A physical punch to my gut would've felt better than the metaphorical one I was experiencing. It was sharp and debilitating.

"Mimi? Mimi, are you okay?" Rachelle asked me as she watched tears slowly spill down my cheeks. "Tell me those are happy tears," she said as she softly stroked my upper arm.

In less than thirty seconds my pure joy and exuberance had been replaced with confusion and sadness, followed by heaping doses of grief and humiliation.

"I'm almost too embarrassed to let you read this," I sniffed, wiping my cheeks with my left hand as I awkwardly tried to fold up the letter with my right.

Rachelle swiped it from me.

"Don't read it out loud. I don't think I can bear to listen to it," I pleaded, my skull pounding from an instant headache.

"Your supposed friend Christian is nothing but a *bass hole*," Rachelle spat. I usually laughed at her unique ways to avoid cussing. But at that moment, I couldn't imagine ever laughing again.

I wished my parents weren't going to be gone for three days. As much as I needed my cousin and best friend to console me, the thought of hearing her bash Christian all that time was too much. I knew she would be doing it to make me feel better, but it wouldn't work. The only thing I wanted to do was erase Christian Bear from my memory along with my embarrassment and heartbreak.

And that's what I'd intended to do when my parents returned, and Jason and I went home. Instead of throwing the letter away, I'd folded it up and hidden it in my Bible. I remembered asking God to erase my feelings for Christian, and more importantly to put the pieces of my heart back together. I thought He had because as the years passed I found myself thinking about Christian less and less.

"Mimi. Mimi!"

I was startled out of my memory as Christian waved his hand in front of my face.

"The last place to stop before we get home is coming up. Do you need to use the bathroom again or need anything for the house?"

I shook my head and let it rest against the seat as I silently watched him drive. I never opened that Bible again. It stayed on the bookshelf in my bedroom, eventually getting buried behind other books. As the years passed, I tried to convince myself that God had healed my heart.

I could see now that my heart had never healed from the sting of what I perceived to be Christian's rebuttal. If anything, it had been held together for years by my own makeshift bandage. Until now.

It had taken over four years, but I was beginning to believe that my original prayer was finally being answered. But not in the way I'd expected. God didn't erase the feelings that I'd had for Christian. If anything, God now allowed them to reveal themselves. I knew without a doubt that Christian Bear had established permanent residency in the center of my soul long ago. I could feel the bandages I'd wrapped around my heart disintegrating as the real healing began.

CHAPTER 26

PUMPKIN REST, SOUTH CAROLINA 2007

I t was dark and chilly by the time we pulled up to the rental house. Once inside, Christian headed for the thermostat to turn up the heat, and I set out for the bedroom to dig through the clothes basket that held my warmer things. I put on some long johns under my nightshirt and proceeded to the great room where I found Christian standing in front of the fireplace with his back to me. He'd built a fire and the crackling wood and roaring blaze couldn't compete with my nervous anticipation of what that kiss meant and where it might lead.

As if sensing my presence he slowly turned around and looked me up and down. A lazy smile spread across his face and it occurred to me that it probably wouldn't lead anywhere since I was dressed for bed like a ten-year-old.

"I haven't showered since our hike this morning," he informed me. "Give me ten minutes and we can spend the rest of the night however you want." He grabbed me by my upper arms and pulled me toward him and planted a kiss on my forehead. A nice, loud, brotherly kiss.

I watched his backside as he strolled toward the bedroom and I blew out a long breath. *Maybe it's for the best,* I thought. We've been together a few days. Was I willing to give up what I'd protected from every other man when we would be going back to living our separate lives in different states? I spotted the baby grand piano in the corner. *An expensive instrument to have in a rental house,* I thought, but then again, it fit beautifully in this home.

True to his word he was back in ten minutes.

"I was gonna ask you to play for me," I heard him say from behind me. "I made sure to rent a house with a piano." He paused before adding, "For you."

I felt his hands on each of my shoulders, before he kissed the top of my head.

Of course he would remember I took piano lessons when I was a child.

"Any requests?" I asked without turning around.

He named a few songs and I was glad I knew them. I added a few of my own and he busted out laughing when I started banging away to "Linus and Lucy" from the Charlie Brown Christmas Special. I laughed too when I remembered watching the cartoon as a kid and trying to imitate the dances I'd seen the Peanuts characters performing on their school stage.

Christian, who had been poking at the fire while I played, closed the gap between us and once again rested both hands on my shoulders. I immediately transitioned into Jefferson Starship's "Count On Me." I closed my eyes and shivered in anticipation when he moved my hair off my neck and bent low to kiss it.

My fingers stopped working and I turned slightly on the bench. He took my hand as I stood up and walked me around the bench and right into his arms. The opposite of our kiss in the car, this was gentle at first but grew more heated as our hands explored each other's bodies. Our groping quickly became more fevered than our kisses, and before I knew what was happening, we were undressing each other. I had pulled his T-shirt off and was going for his pajama pants when he stopped me. He removed my nightshirt and undershirt in one long tug over my head. He stared at my breasts and I started to cover them, but he pulled my hands away.

"No, Mimi. Especially not with me," he reassured. He bent low to kiss each one and I ached for more but he didn't give it to me. I was a virgin, but I was still a woman, and I mourned the loss of his hot mouth as he got on his knees and slowly rolled down my long john bottoms and panties. He stopped, and I knew what he was seeing. I froze.

I peered down and saw him staring up at me.

"I thought you saw it when you walked in on me in the bathroom that first day," I quietly said, my voice raspy with unquenched passion.

He shook his head. "What happened?"

Christian listened as I quickly explained the vertical scar that went from my belly button to my pubic bone.

"I was in a car accident right before my high school graduation. A guy crossed the yellow line and almost hit us head on. My cousin, who was driving, swerved and then overcorrected. Long story short, I fractured my pelvis. I have so many pins and screws inside me I'm afraid to go near a metal detector," I teased, trying to make light of my situation so as not to ruin the mood. But he persisted.

"Looks like a serious scar." His eyes were concerned. "Does it still bother you?"

"Nope," I lied. "Six months of rehab is all it took." I looked away and started to wonder where, if anywhere, this was going. I didn't have to wait long to find out. Just like he'd kissed away my tears in the car, I could feel his mouth right below my belly button, gently making its way lower as he planted soft kisses on my scar. When he kissed my most private place, I lost all modesty and any trepidation I felt, moaning loudly as I grabbed hold of his hair and ground myself into his mouth.

I surprised even myself when my release came quickly and I heard him whisper, "I knew you would taste good."

He pulled me down to my knees so we were almost eye level. I was waiting for him to stand and I prepared myself to reciprocate. I'd only performed oral sex on Lucas, and not very often. I knew without a doubt that Christian was experienced, and I couldn't bear to think that I wouldn't measure up to what he was used to.

"I've waited my whole life for this moment. And it might seem rushed, but I'll make it up to you, baby. I promise," he whispered. "I can't wait to be inside of you, Mimi," he said as he laid me back on the fluffy rug.

His hand found its way between my legs and after feeling my wetness, he added, "And you're more than ready for me."

In two swift movements he expertly removed his pajama pants and situated himself between my open legs. He gave me a long, lingering kiss, only stopping to tease each breast with his tongue. He made his way back up to my mouth and after another kiss, he stopped. I opened my eyes and saw him staring at me.

"I can get a rubber." He sounded like he was in pain.

"You brought condoms?" I asked him.

"I didn't bring condoms," he corrected. "I pretty much always have them with me. But I haven't used them since I've been out of prison."

I guess this was his way of telling me he hadn't had sex with anyone since he'd been released. I wasn't sure how to respond so I went with the truth: "I don't have an STD, and I won't get pregnant."

I couldn't be certain but he almost looked disappointed when he said, "Good. You're on the pill."

I didn't answer him. I just stared into his eyes trying to gauge what I'd seen in his expression. The moment passed and he once again lowered his mouth to mine. I had my arms wrapped around his neck and was running my fingers through his silky hair. He ended our kiss and gave me a smile that had probably broken a hundred hearts. Slowly, he started to enter me.

And I panicked.

I suddenly remembered how he'd told me on the drive to the restaurant that he'd never had a serious girlfriend. *He's probably broken a hundred hearts,* played like a mantra in my head as I found myself leaning up on my elbows and trying to scooch away from him. *What are you doing, Mimi? A few kisses, one orgasm and you're ready to give your virginity to a man who is going to get in his truck in a few days and drive away from your life?*

"Mimi?"

I couldn't tell if I was seeing anger or hurt in his eyes as I scrambled out from beneath him and reached for my nightshirt.

"What's wrong?" he asked. He'd leaned up on his side and was watching me.

Yanking my shirt down over my head I reached for my panties and tried to untangle them from my thermal underwear.

"Nothing's wrong," I lied. I couldn't meet his eyes when I blurted, "This is just too quick for me. I'm sorry. I'm not a tease. I'm just not sure about sleeping with you this soon."

"This soon?" he asked. He sounded hoarse. "In my mind, this should've happened years ago."

I wouldn't look at him, but sensed when he got to his feet and pulled on his pajama pants. I didn't answer as I tried to think of where I could escape to.

"It's Lucas, isn't it?" he growled.

Lucas who?

"I'm sorry, Christian. I didn't mean for this to happen." *Of course you did,* my subconscious screamed.

Our gazes locked and I sensed a dangerous shift in his attitude. Something raw and feral appeared behind his eyes, and for a moment, I wondered if he was going to force himself on me. Never. *Christian would never hurt you,* I told myself. But I knew what I was seeing. I was witnessing a man who was trying to restrain himself. The animal instinct was there and he was doing his best not to pounce.

"I'll sleep in one of the spare rooms tonight." His voice was unrecognizable. "I can't sleep in the same bed with you again, Mimi."

I nodded, and without looking back, made a beeline for the master bedroom. Once inside I sat on the edge of the bed and stared at a painting over the dresser. What was I doing?

I leaned forward, stuck my elbows on my knees and plopped my head in my hands. I'd only been sitting that way less than sixty seconds when something caused me to look over at my pillow. And there it was. Its vivid color in stark contrast to the white case it rested on. Bright and blue and as gaudy as I'd remembered.

My eyes got wide as I gazed at the ring, the big, blue artificial stone overshadowing the tiny plastic gold band it was attached to.

"It's so beautiful, Christian," I cooed. "Did you get it because it matches the color of your eyes?" I asked adoringly.

"No," he answered matter-of-factly. "I got it 'cause it was the only one in the claw machine."

We'd played wedding almost twenty years ago and he still had the last ring he'd tried to give me. And he must've laid it on my pillow after he came out of the shower and before he found me sitting at the piano. I picked it up and tried to put it on, but my fingers were too big. I finally managed to squeeze it halfway up my left pinky finger.

I immediately sensed his presence in the bedroom doorway. "I need to brush my teeth," he informed me. "I won't bother you."

"You kept it," was all I said.

"Yeah, I kept it."

"Christian, are you a lost soul?" I knew my voice held an edge of sadness.

"You think I'm a lost soul?" he asked as he walked toward me. He didn't look angry or hurt. He looked...he looked...I had trouble coming up with a word. And then it dawned on me. He looked amused.

I was once again at a loss for words so I just watched him approach me. He was now standing directly in front of me and I had to raise my head to face him.

"The term lost soul is overrated," he told me. I tried to raise an eyebrow. I always envied people that could ask a question by raising one eyebrow. Unfortunately for me, it didn't work, and I'm certain I just came off looking surprised. Or stupid.

"I'm not a lost soul, Mimi. I never have been. A bad one? Maybe. But not lost. I knew when we were children that our souls were tethered. I know you felt it too, but you lost it or forgot it somewhere along the way."

I think I must've swallowed my voice because it was suddenly gone.

"I know despite our rocky start a few days ago, you feel it too. I've seen it in your eyes several times over the past couple of days. You really are Dreamy Mimi, aren't you?" he teased.

Before I could stop it, a childhood memory slammed into me with such ferocity I felt it pressing on my chest. I instantly remembered the significance of the tattoo over his heart. And just like that, my fears and doubts about him—about us—fell like dominos and formed a perfect circle around my instantaneously healed heart.

I jumped up so quickly I almost knocked my head into his chin. I grabbed him by the hair and tugged until his mouth met mine. He welcomed my advance and pulled me hard against his chest.

He broke our kiss and said, "I'll still sleep in the other room if you want me to." He didn't look sincere, but I knew he was making an effort so I decided to give him a full explanation.

"What happened earlier has nothing to do with this," I told him as I stepped back and waved my hand back and forth between us. "It's me."

There was the eyebrow raise I envied.

"I've not...I've never..." I stammered. "I'm still a virgin," I finally blurted out.

He couldn't have looked more shocked if I'd told him I was really a man.

"But, Lucas...all the guys you've dated." It was his turn to stammer.

"I never slept with the guys from college, or any guy for that matter. And that was why my relationships were so short-lived. They weren't getting it so they went somewhere else. Lucas is the only one who has stuck around." I looked away, embarrassed, surprised that his detective hadn't uncovered that tidbit.

He didn't say anything so I looked back at him. He had an odd look on his face.

"What?" I asked.

"Do you really want to know?" he prodded.

"Whatever it is, yeah, I want to know."

"Lucas stuck around because he's getting laid elsewhere." He crossed his arms in front of him and continued, "He's been cheating on you."

I stepped back again, and this time the back of my knees hit the bed, almost causing me to topple backwards. He grabbed my elbow and steadied me. It was my turn to be stunned. "Why didn't you tell me this before?" I asked him.

"Because I want you to want me. On your own. Not because your boyfriend is cheating on you."

It was back. The sense of relief that came with knowing where I belonged.

"Why are you still a virgin?"

His question caught me by surprise, but I had a ready answer.

"It was a decision I made after Nick almost raped me. After that, I was very cautious about dating and getting physical with a guy. I guess I was always waiting for the next Nick to rear his ugly head." I gripped the back of my neck and rubbed it. "After a while, I realized that I was starting to grow spiritually, and my faith was making it easier to abstain." I looked at the ground and confessed, "I kind of tried to make a bargain with God. I believed that if I waited, He would let me know when I met Mr. Right. Who would, you know…"

"Love you enough to marry you?"

"Yeah, I guess so." I looked up, wrapped my arms around his neck and tilted my head to one side. "But I don't want to wait anymore. What was it you said about our souls being tethered?"

He abruptly reached behind his neck and disengaged my hands. I was stunned as he walked around the bedroom, muttering, "What did you do with it? Where is it?"

"Where's what?" I asked, still in shock over his behavior.

He stopped and looked at me. "When I first brought you here I went through your stuff. There was a Bible in your bag."

I rolled my eyes. Of course he went through my things. "It's in the nightstand on my side of the bed. Why?"

He opened the drawer and pulled out my Bible. It was the new one I'd gotten four years ago after hiding away the one that contained his letter. Clutching it in his right hand he grabbed me with his left, and started pulling me out of the room.

"W-wha..where are we going? What are you doing?" I exclaimed as he trudged toward the French doors that opened onto the deck, dragging me behind him.

He let go of my hand long enough to open one, and a cold blast of air almost knocked me over, but I was too immersed in Christian's odd behavior to notice the cold.

Grabbing my hand again he pulled me onto the deck and asked me, "You believe God made all of this?" He waved the Bible in the air and I looked up into a beautiful starlit sky. The moon was full and it cast a glow off the lake that looked surreal.

"Yes," I answered. "Of course I believe it."

"What does it say about marriage? About husbands and wives?" he demanded. I was once again caught off guard when he snapped, "What does it say, Mimi?"

"It says a lot of things, Christian," I managed to reply.

"Tell me some of them."

I was never good at memorizing Scripture, and I cringed at the thought of bumbling it. I paused and a lightbulb went on.

"In Genesis it says a man shall leave his father and his mother and hold fast to his wife, and they shall become one flesh." I blinked at him, not knowing where this was going when another one occurred to me. "Also, there's one about what God has joined together, let no one separate."

"Marry me," he said, his eyes flashing.

"What?" *Did I hear him right?*

"I never ask, but I'm asking you. To marry me. Tonight."

"How? Where?" I stammered, trying to recover from the shock. "And more importantly, why?"

"Here. Under the stars that God created. And why? Because I love you, Mimi. I've always loved you, and I'm not going to let you break an oath you made because of me."

"It won't be a real marriage," I whispered.

"Who says it won't be real?" He looked up at the sky and yelled,

"God, if You're real and You're listening, then You know I've been in love with this woman my entire life. I'm asking You..." he hesitated and held my Bible up high while he sought the right words, "by the power of what it says in here to let Mimi know that our marriage will be real and that You give Your approval."

I smiled at him and shook my head. I might have lost my mind. But if I'd had doubts before, they were now gone. I knew I was looking at my soul mate. A man who, like both our fathers, had done awful things, and was capable of even worse, yet wasn't afraid to profess the love for me he'd clung to for years. My man. Love swelled up from my chest and threatened to bubble over. I feigned a cough so he wouldn't notice what a sap I was.

"It doesn't always work like that, you know." I walked toward him and reached for his empty hand. Holding it against my chest, I told him, "Yes, I'll marry you tonight, but don't be disappointed if you don't get His approval." I nodded toward the sky with a lopsided grin. "He doesn't always give us the signs we're hoping for."

And before Christian could answer me, I felt something cold land on my cheek.

It was snowing.

CHAPTER 27

A fter we said our spur-of-the-moment vows to each other, Christian picked me up and carried me inside to the bedroom. I should've been freezing, but I was warmed from the inside out in anticipation of what would come next. We once again undressed each other, slower this time. When he laid me back on the bed and straddled me he mistook my shivering for something left over from the freezing cold we'd endured on the deck.

"I'll always keep you warm, Mimi," he whispered in my ear before showering my face with kisses. He stopped to look down at me and asked, "When I went down on you...when you came on my face..." His eyes were searching and I knew what he wanted to know.

"No, it wasn't my first orgasm," I offered. I thought I saw a flash of disappointment mingled with anger, "But," I quickly interjected. "It was the first time I came like that."

I didn't want to go into an explanation of how I'd let Lucas down there only once and it ended up being more awkward than passionate.

I sucked in a breath and looked over his shoulder, avoiding his eyes. "And you might as well know that I don't have a whole lot of experience reciprocating." I was afraid to look back and see frustration at my lack of experience, but he looked relieved. "I can't stand the thought of another man touching you, or vice versa," he admitted. "But I'm also glad you'll have some firsts with me. And they'll be the lasts too, because you belong to me, Mimi. No other man will ever touch you."

I didn't challenge his comment about belonging to him because I was too impatient for what was happening between us to continue talking. I wrapped my arms around his neck and pulled his mouth hungrily to mine. He eventually made his way to my throat and I missed our broken kiss but couldn't stifle a groan when he made his way even further down my body, this time giving the attention to my breasts that I'd craved earlier. And I thought Lucas's sloppy attempts at teasing my nipples felt good? In retrospect it was like comparing Cogsworth to the Beast, I mused. My Beast.

He used his tongue to slowly make his way down my stomach and once again focused on the place that provoked so much pleasure less than an hour earlier. I screamed his name this time and was still trying to catch my breath when he made his way back up to face me. I opened my eyes and smiled, reaching for his hardness but he shooed my hand away. I guess I looked surprised because he explained, "Like I told you before, I don't want to wait any longer to be inside of you, Mimi."

I smiled and spread my legs wider, finally wrapping them around his waist. I felt his body meeting mine, and braced myself for what I knew would be a mixture of pleasure and pain, but he suddenly stopped.

Before I could ask why, he said, "Tell me."

I blinked, confused. "Tell you what?"

"Tell me what I told you before we said our vows." His eyes were serious, almost hard, and I knew what he wanted to hear—what he needed to hear—and I said it without hesitation or reservation because I meant it.

"I love you too, Christian."

He entered me slowly, not taking his eyes from mine so he could evaluate my reaction. He stopped when I gave a slight wince, but I breathlessly told him, "It's okay. Keep going."

So he did and our bodies met in unison, eventually finding a pace that left us both breathless and sated.

We spent the rest of the night talking, and exploring, familiarizing ourselves even more with each other. Making up for years that had been lost. We made love twice and he refused me a third time, insisting that he didn't want to make me sore. But that doesn't mean we didn't find pleasure in other ways.

"Don't look so disappointed, Mimi. I'll be making love to you for the rest of our lives," he assured me.

He fell asleep in the same position that he held me our first night together. With my back against his chest and his arms wrapped around me from behind. I could feel his breath on my neck as sleep evaded me. I remembered our last-minute made-up vows on the snowy deck and I smiled when I thought about the ones we'd made so long ago on a playground that had been dedicated to the sister he'd never met, and I'd never known about.

Apparently, being with him was unlocking memories that I'd deliberately chosen to forget. But they were slowly making their way to the surface. In this particular recollection, I'd been the one to recite my vows first after Christian handed me a clump of flowers. At least I think they were flowers.

I'd looked at Christian adoringly before saying, "I will always wear my ring and be your bestest friend ever. And I will be your wife and live with you when we get older, and we get jobs, and you make us a house." I paused to consider my next words. My mother had been very pregnant at the time with Jason, so I knew having babies was a part of marriage. "And if we go to the doctor and he puts a baby in my belly, I will be the mommy, and you will be the daddy when the baby comes out."

I smiled big at him and waited expectantly for his response.

He took a deep breath and said, "I will always win more rings for you. I will win ten hundred rings with different colored diamonds, and you can have one for every day. I will be your husband, and I will make you a house, and I will eat soup every day if that's all you can cook. And if the doctor doesn't put a baby in your belly, then I will put one there. I don't know how, but that's how I think babies get in the mommies' stomachs. The daddies put them there. That's what Slade told me, but he didn't know how either." He paused before shyly adding, "And you'll belong to me, and I will love you forever, just like my daddy tells my mommy."

"Why aren't you asleep?" he whispered in my ear, startling me out of my memories, part of which caused an ache to surface.

"How did you know I wasn't asleep?"

"Because you sleep like the dead, and I'm a light sleeper. You've been fidgeting and it woke me up."

"I was thinking about what you said earlier, about me belonging to you," I told him.

"What about it?" he asked.

"A person can't belong to someone, Christian," I quietly replied. "That's claiming ownership and you can't own someone."

"Yes, you can, Mimi. You've owned me all these years." He kissed the back of my head.

"How have I owned you all these years?" I whispered.

"By holding me hostage," he answered.

"I think you need to reverse your thinking on that comment." I couldn't keep the attitude out of my voice. "I'm not the one who slapped handcuffs on you."

"Yes, you did," he countered.

I quickly shifted around to face him and like that first night, the moonlight helped me find his eyes. When I did, they weren't challenging me. They were filled with longing and what I thought was vulnerability. Vulnerability from Christian Bear? Surely not. I must've been misreading him.

"What makes you think I held you hostage?"

"Because that night you drove out of my life with your mother and James, you took my heart with you."

CHAPTER 28

PUMPKIN REST, SOUTH CAROLINA 2007

Christian lay awake long after Mimi finally fell asleep, and thought about the woman he held in his arms. She was full of surprises. Never in a million years would he have guessed she'd never slept with a man. It only confirmed in his mind what he'd always believed. *Our souls have been tethered, and she's always belonged to me.*

He got hard again when he thought about Mimi's body coming alive beneath him. She'd obviously been storing up a shitload of passion over the years. He could tell that each touch, each kiss, each caress sparked a fire in her that almost caused him to spill his load too soon.

He smiled when he thought about her awkward attempts at a blow job. She wasn't lying when she said she had very little experience. But he didn't care. For the first time ever he wasn't interested in skill, because this definitely wasn't just about the act. It was about the woman performing the act. Just knowing that it was Mimi's warm and perfect mouth holding him prisoner was enough to keep him satiated for the rest of his life.

She's perfect. So damn perfect.

He shifted uncomfortably in the bed when the impact of that thought slammed into his chest. She had no flaws that he could see. The exact opposite of him. And to add insult to injury, he still had secrets that he hadn't shared yet. Like before he was arrested he'd joined Grizz's old gang. He wasn't kidding when he told her he'd broken bones. That had been his job—his specialty. Going after the people that didn't pay their loans. He'd been a debt collector with a message. Pay up or suffer.

Did he believe that Mimi would come back to Florida with him, make their marriage legal, and play devoted wife to an ex-con, bone-breaking, hotheaded, motorcycle gang member? It was obvious he hadn't thought this out when he hatched the plan to find and confront her. He'd not allowed himself the luxury of thinking beyond the anger that had originally driven him. He knew deep down he'd been in love with Mimi for as long as he could remember, but when had he crossed over from exerting his will on her to the lovesick fool who'd confessed she'd stolen his heart years ago? True? Yes, but that didn't matter.

And neither did the fact that their situation looked hopeless. He knew without a doubt that her mother and accountant ex-con stepfather wouldn't approve of him, but he didn't care. With his mind made up that he always got what he wanted, he decided not to worry or think about their future. As far as he was concerned, it was sealed.

CHAPTER 29

PUMPKIN REST, SOUTH CAROLINA 2007

We woke up the next morning to a thin blanket of pristine snow covering the ground. If we had any intentions of leaving the house it would have to be after the snow melted, but neither of us cared. We both preferred to continue pursuing the intimacy we'd missed out on over the years.

I lay in Christian's arms and lightly traced the tattoo on his bicep. I turned to face him and leaned up. With my head propped on one elbow I prompted, "I guess you work out a lot. I'm a sucker for big muscles."

"Didn't have much else to keep me occupied in prison," he said gruffly, the memory obviously not one he liked to indulge.

"It worked out for me because I love how big your arms have gotten since I saw you last."

He gave me a sly smile and said, "And I love how big your boobs have gotten since I saw you last."

I rolled my eyes and playfully slapped at him. He caught my hand and studied my wrist. The bruises were bolder, and I watched his mood go from spirited to dark. In an effort to not let him go down that road, I got up and peered down at him. Tilting my head to one side, I asked, "Shower with me?"

Without waiting for him to answer I headed for the bathroom and was inwardly delighted when he immediately joined me.

After an exploratory dousing that took way longer than a regular shower, we eventually succumbed to the cold water and turned it off.

Besides, the drain was starting to back up and I was concerned that it might overflow into the bathroom.

Later, I was making us breakfast when he came in and rummaged around in one of the kitchen drawers. He looked over at me and asked, "Do you remember me waking you up last night?"

I quickly glanced his way, and returned my attention to the pancake I was getting ready to flip. "You didn't wake me up last night."

I heard him chuckle and say, "Yes I did. I thought I heard someone on the porch, and I woke you up—which wasn't easy—and told you I was going to check it out. You really don't remember?"

I peeked over at him and shook my head.

"You told me it was probably a bear or some kind of animal and I shouldn't be worried. You also said your grandfather doesn't even lock his doors at night because there's no place safer than the mountains."

"That's all true, but I don't remember having this conversation, Christian," I confessed.

"Do you remember yelling at me when I took my gun out of the nightstand?" he prompted.

I turned to him and placed one hand on my hip and waved the spatula I was holding at him. "Are you kidding me? You brought a gun with you? You shouldn't even have a gun, Christian. You're a convicted felon. If you get caught it's an automatic trip back to prison!"

"That's what you told me last night," he laughed, giving me a wicked smile. "Found it!" he quickly added and held up a screwdriver.

"You are exasperating," I huffed. "And what do you need that for?" I asked, turning back to the griddle.

"Something needs fixing," he called back to me as he walked away.

I flipped the last pancake onto a plate, and contemplated the irony of our relationship. A Bible in one nightstand and a gun in the other. *Sounds like my parents*, I mused, as I set the table for breakfast. But instead of being intimidated at the prospect of being with someone so completely opposite, I warmed to it. My parents weren't perfect, but they were in love, and their marriage—as odd as it might seem to an outsider—worked. I was starting to feel hopeful, but wouldn't let myself get too excited. I still had many secrets that needed to be shared with Christian. And I could only hope that those secrets wouldn't cause him to reevaluate our newly established relationship. At least with Christian, what you saw was what you got. He didn't hide things. If anything, he was a little too bold.

After calling out to him twice that the pancakes were getting cold, I went in search of him.

"You must really be engrossed in whatever you're fix..." My words died off as I entered the bathroom, and found him hunched over the shower drain. He had a disgusting heap of hair piled next to the opening, but it wasn't the hair that sent a wave of shame over me. It was what clung to it that stopped me cold.

Our eyes clashed, and I could see the questions in his.

"I didn't do this, and I know it's not left over from whoever stayed at this house last." His eyes weren't accusing, but warm and concerned.

"I was sick that first night..." I stammered.

"Don't," he interrupted. He stood up and said, "I knew something was up with you, but couldn't place it. You do this a lot, don't you?"

"I don't want to talk about this now," I stated as I headed back to the kitchen. He was right on my heels, and grabbed my elbow, whirling me around to face him.

"Tell me about it, Mimi. I know there's a name for it, but I'm not sure what it is. All that food I've watched you shovel down over the last few days. It's not staying down, is it?"

I shook my head, but couldn't meet his eyes. "No. Not all of it."

"Why not?" His eyes were challenging, but not accusatory. He really cared.

My shoulders slumped as I tried to appear smaller, and a wave of tears followed. He pulled me to him and guided me toward the leather couch, taking the seat next to me. He sat on the edge and rested his elbow on his knee and with his other hand, grabbed mine tightly. The concrete walls that'd been holding in my family secret finally started to crumble, and I told him how my shame began, and why I continued to nurture it.

I explained how it all started with an innocent comment from a girlfriend when I was a senior in high school. We'd been looking at pictures from an outing at the lake. There were about six of us, and a stranger offered to take a group photo. There I stood in my bathing suit next to the tallest, thinnest guy in the class. His name was Rodney, and he was the school's star basketball player. Rodney was over six feet tall, and was extremely slender, to the point of looking gangly. My girlfriend said something to the effect that even though I wasn't, I looked huge when standing next to him. She didn't mean anything by it. She wasn't a mean girl at all, but the comment stuck. I'd never been overly concerned about my weight. I'd always thought I looked okay, but that remark burrowed its way into my subconscious, and revealed itself again after I'd suffered a nasty stomach bug and lost six pounds in one week. My jeans felt a little loose, and I wondered how I would look in a smaller size. I knew what I had to do to achieve that. I knew it worked, so I gave it a shot.

I told Christian how I felt that I was in control, and I could stop binging and purging anytime I wanted. What I hadn't realized was how my eating disorder manifested itself in a different way.

"Binging and purging?" he asked, obviously not familiar with the terminology.

"Eating whatever I want, as much as I want, and making myself throw it all up," I explained, as I focused on the dark, callused hand that was holding mine tightly.

When he didn't say anything, I cut my eyes back to his and I could tell by his crinkled forehead that he was trying to understand. Instead of attempting to explain the psychology behind why I would do this, which I wasn't sure I even understood myself, I blurted out the excuse I used for continuing to do it.

I told Christian that my biological father, Grizz, was very much alive and living just over the border in North Carolina. Christian stared at me, the shock evident in his expression as the air between us crackled with unspoken tension.

"Grizz?" he asked, his chiseled jaw tightening. "The man you've been calling James and referring to as your stepfather? The one your mother left Florida to be with?"

I nodded.

Dropping my hand he stood up and looked down at me. "He didn't die on death row?"

Tilting my head up to meet his eyes, I shook it.

"How?" He scratched at his chin, and let his eyes wander around the room. Was he concerned that Grizz might show up? I didn't see fear in his eyes so I dismissed the thought.

Taking a deep breath, I told him, "When I asked Grizz the same thing, he said that anybody could be bought for the right price. I don't need to tell you the kind of wealth he accumulated during his tenure as the leader of a powerful motorcycle club. When you consider that he lived in a run-down motel until he built a house for my mother, he had nowhere to spend his money. I can only assume he's responsible for giving several people in the prison system an early, extremely comfortable retirement."

I watched as he took it all in, his head slightly bobbing as the mental cartwheels found a place to land. Then his brow creased and he countered, "What does that have to do with you throwing up? Purging, right?"

Nodding, I blew out a long breath and looked at the floor. "I guess keeping Grizz's secret has had more of a negative effect than I let myself believe. When I had my accident, my father couldn't visit me in the big city hospital that was an hour and a half away from our home. He wanted to, but my mom begged him not to. He won't be coming to my college graduation. I would never be able to bring anyone home to meet my parents for fear he be recognized." I looked up, and my voice rose an octave. "Look at the guy we met in Chicky's who knew him!" I slapped my hand on my knee.

I craned my head to look at the ceiling. "And what could I possibly have been thinking by dating a criminal justice major? That was just a disaster in the making." I paused. "But Grizz isn't responsible for my binging and purging. I found that when those things bothered me or I would dwell on my situation, I would stress eat. A lot of food. And weight gain wasn't a concern because I knew how to expertly conceal what I was doing. I throw up in the shower when I don't want to be heard. If something solid comes up, I ground it down into the drain." Taking a deep breath, I quietly added, "It obviously didn't make it down this drain thanks to the hair clog."

"When we stopped on our way home from Chicky's..."

"I went in the bathroom to throw up my dinner. Seeing someone who knew my father unnerved me."

"So you don't do it all the time?" he asked, sounding somewhat relieved. He leaned his back against the beam where he'd left me shackled just days before and crossed his arms.

"No." I shook my head. "But I'm always prepared just in case."

"How?" He cocked his head to the right, and his long hair covered Abby's name tattooed on his bicep.

"The orange Cheetos. The red licorice. I usually eat them, and other brightly colored foods, as a marker."

He shook his head, not understanding. "A marker?"

"I ate the red licorice on the way to the restaurant, before I ate the wings. That way, if I chose to vomit later—and by later I mean within thirty minutes of the meal—I have a way to know when I've completely emptied my stomach. I kept puking until I saw red."

I waited for his reaction, not sure if I could bear to see disdain in his eyes. *He hacked a guy's arm off. Cut yourself some slack, Mimi.* I sat up a little straighter.

Christian noticed the change in my posture, and a hint of a smile formed at the corner of his mouth. "Is that it, Mimi?" Pushing off the beam he walked toward me, extending his hand. "A father who's not really dead and an eating disorder?" He softly yanked me up from the couch.

Releasing a long breath, I shook my head. "There's one more thing you should know."

Christian handled my last and final confession with words of comfort and reassurance, and then asked me again, "Is that all of it?"

"Isn't that enough?" I cried, trying to avoid his eyes. I thought he was going to pull me into his arms, but he didn't. Instead, he tucked a strand of hair behind my ear, and lightly held my face between his hands.

Kissing the tip of my nose, he said, "I'm not going to pretend to understand the eating disorder thing, but it doesn't change how I feel about you. And I'm assuming you can get some help with it?"

I blinked and gave him a slight nod. "Yes, there are therapists who specialize in it, but I've never seen one."

"We'll make sure you do." He gave me a wide smile. "Your undead father and the last thing you mentioned don't change my feelings either. As a matter of fact, I can't think of anything you could tell me that would cause me to not love you or think less of you."

The relief must've shown on my face because he added, "If anything, I'm sorta glad."

I stepped back, my eyes wide. "Glad?"

"Not glad like you think. I'm just glad you aren't flawless, Mimi. I need you to not be perfect. Thinking that you didn't have any faults kind of nagged at me."

"I think I get that," I admitted. "Do me a favor?"

"Anything," he replied.

"Don't keep an eye on me or what I eat. I won't be able to handle you thinking you can do something to fix it. I already feel stronger after telling you about Grizz. That was a heavy load to carry. Thank you for not freaking out."

"I got you, Mimi," he said, pulling me into the warmth of his rock-hard chest. "I'll always have you."

CHAPTER 30

PUMPKIN REST, SOUTH CAROLINA 2007

W e ate our pancakes and wandered downstairs to the basement. I'd never played pool and Christian decided he would teach me. We ended up making love on the pool table instead. I didn't complain, but had to finally admit that I was starting to get tender.

We were putting our clothes back on when he asked me, "So you said something before about not coming when Lucas went down on you."

I stiffened, embarrassed. "Yeah, what about it?"

"But you had come before, right? Just not like that?"

I whirled around to face him. He was buckling his belt. "Yes, I've come before, Christian. I know what an orgasm is. You don't go as long as I have without sex, and not figure out a way to compensate for it." I rolled my eyes and yanked up my jeans.

"So do you use your fingers or something with batteries?" he teased.

I busted out laughing. I'd already put on my jeans and was reaching for my bra when I inquired, "This is turning you on, isn't it?"

"Everything about you turns me on, Mimi. I want to watch you make yourself come."

"Now?" I asked, incredulously.

He shook his head. "Nope. I'm gonna save it for our honeymoon." His smile was like a flash of blinding sunshine.

I may have been sore, but just the thought of what he wanted to watch me do caused a rush of heat that hit me right between my thighs. "Aren't we kind of already on our honeymoon?" I asked, as I slowly removed my jeans and panties and kicked them to the side.

After another round of exploratory lovemaking we went upstairs and found that the light veil of snow had already melted away and the noon sun was shining bright and warm.

"The snow is gone." Christian looked down at me, bewilderment in his expression.

"It's not that unusual," I explained. "Besides, we didn't get as much as they predicted. I'm sure other places got slammed but we got barely a dusting."

"But snow in spring is normal?"

"It's technically not spring. Yeah, I'm on spring break, but this is still a winter month."

"You were wearing shorts yesterday, it snowed last night, and it's already warming up."

I nodded. "Yeah, it took a while for me to get used to it, but we're in a southern state yet still at a high elevation. The forecast isn't always accurate. We've had predictions of a dusting and we get twelve inches. Last night they were saying to expect almost six inches, and we got barely a flake." I shrugged my shoulders. "And the temperature is supposed to dip again tonight."

He nodded before asking me, "Wanna ride?" He scratched his chin. "It feels warm enough."

"Ride what?"

"I brought a motorcycle."

"You brought your bike with you? Here?" I knew I sounded skeptical.

"Yeah. Um, no. It's not my bike." He gave me a wicked grin.

"Whose bike is it?"

He shrugged his shoulders. "Some idiot in Georgia who didn't have the smarts to lock the damn thing."

I tried not to smile as he continued with his explanation.

"It was sitting in the middle of nowhere with a for sale sign on it. I'm driving my buddy's truck and it's the kind with the extended bed. And he happened to have a piece of wood in the back."

"Happened to have a piece of wood in the back?" I interrupted. "Why do I get the impression your buddy has it there for a reason?"

"Because he probably does," he answered in a flash. "Anyway, I stopped and rolled the motorcycle right up into the bed." He waved toward the rear of the house. "It's around back."

I put my hands on my hips and tried to look stern. "So, you want to take me for a ride on a motorcycle that you stole in another state?"

"Yeah, that pretty much sums it up."

"Give me time to pack us a lunch," I laughed as I headed for the kitchen.

I WAS grateful that South Carolina didn't have a helmet requirement. It would've given law enforcement a reason to stop us should they have seen us. I cautioned Christian on the roads.

"I know the snow has melted off, but we should be careful anyway," I warned. My parents would be having a fit if they knew I was on the back of a bike without a helmet, but since South Carolina didn't have a helmet law, I wasn't too concerned.

I clung to Christian, not because I was concerned with how he was handling the road, but because I wanted to. Just like being in his arms and in his bed felt right, so did being on the back of his stolen ride. There was no denying it. Being with Christian was where I belonged.

With my arms wrapped tightly around him, I pressed my cheek against his back and inhaled the scent of his hair, his jacket, him. Like the proverbial son who finally found his way home, I knew I'd found my way. Back to my soul mate. Back to Christian Bear.

We rode for almost an hour when he finally pulled over and asked if I wanted to find a picnic table somewhere outside.

"You sure you're warm?" he asked.

"The sun feels glorious!" I shouted. "Besides, I feel like I'm hugging a space heater. I'm almost too warm," I laughed over his shoulder.

"That sign a few miles back said we're coming up on a state park. I was gonna say we could turn around and head back to that diner if you want to."

"The park," was my response, and he pulled back onto the road.

We found a secluded spot and sat down at a table that was in the sun. I took out the lunch I packed, and silently thanked the bike's owner for having saddlebags.

"Are you keeping the motorcycle?" I asked, giving Christian a sideways glance as I unwrapped our sandwiches.

He was fiddling with his phone and answered, "Nah. I don't need a bike. When I saw it I imagined you on the back of it and took advantage of the opportunity." His eyes cut to mine and he added, "But I'm not returning it. I'll leave it somewhere so it can be found."

"I was just curious," I admitted. "I wasn't trying to give my opinion on what you should do with it." I sat down in front of him. "I just don't want you to get caught with it."

He flashed his pearly whites at me, and I thought I felt butterflies in my stomach, but it ended up being more of a lion instead. When my stomach growled, he chuckled, and took a bite of his sandwich. After a few more bites he asked, "What is this?"

"It's a veggie sandwich. What? You don't like it?"

"It doesn't have any meat on it?"

"That would be the definition of a veggie sandwich." I wasn't being sarcastic, just goofy. "We were out of almost everything. Do you have to have meat?" I took a swig of my bottled water.

"The last time you saw me naked I had testicles, right?" he scoffed.

I spit out my water, laughing. "So where you come from, meat and testicles are synonymous. Got it."

After we cleaned up our mess, I reached for my phone. "Did any messages or calls come through on yours?"

He shook his head. "Not anything new." He proceeded to answer my unspoken questions by offering up details as to how he'd managed to avoid having his phone traced in the event someone knew what he was up to. "And I called my mom yesterday when we stopped on the way home from Chicky's."

"And she didn't suspect anything?"

"Nope." He downed the last of his water. "Any more messages from Lucas?"

"Yes, but nothing from Bettina about Josh." I'd already shared with Christian that even though Lucas wasn't expecting me to reply, he'd been sending me daily texts about how much he missed me. If I'd had even the slightest guilt concerning Lucas, Christian's revelation had squelched it. But Lucas wasn't my concern. I'd explained to Christian over breakfast that in addition to Josh's illness, my bigger worry was my parents' friend, Bill Petty. When we left Florida, he was the man who'd assumed responsibility for scanning the internet and detecting any searches or inquiries on me and my family.

I nervously fiddled with the cross on my necklace and looked at

Christian. "I'm still a little shocked that your friend searched the internet to find me and it didn't alert Bill."

"Maybe it did." His answer was casual, like he didn't have a care in the world.

I shook my head. "No. My mother would've immediately called or texted. She doesn't know."

Our conversation somehow circled back to my parents, and then zeroed in on my father's former motorcycle club. I was surprised when Christian admitted that he'd been riding with my father's old gang, until his arrest and subsequent prison time. I should've been shocked when he told me what he did for them, but I wasn't. It was almost as if I'd already known it somewhere deep inside.

"Are you still a member or did they kick you out for getting arrested?"

He threw his head back and laughed. "Are you kidding me? I was their inside guy in prison while I did my time. So I guess I'm still a member, but I haven't seen them. Besides, it was a condition of my probation." He waited for me to say something and when I didn't he continued, "And before you say anything, this is different."

I cocked my head to the side and asked, "Leaving the state and kidnapping isn't a condition of your probation?" He didn't reply so I added, "Not to mention the stolen motorcycle. I guess it's a good thing we're in another state. I highly doubt they're looking for it here."

His answer was a mischievous wink.

He filled me in on some details about the gang, which I'd thought had disbanded when Grizz supposedly died.

"They floundered for a while. Especially after Grizz gave Blue a pass to leave, which is unheard of in the biker community. But too many people respected your father to hold Blue accountable. Besides, he's back. He's been their prez for a few years now."

Shocked, my ears perked up and I sat up straight.

"I didn't know he was back with the gang. I wonder if my father knows?" Before Christian could reply, I added, "My mom ran into Blue right before Christmas."

It was Christian's turn to be shocked. Without any prompting I continued, "To make a long story short, my mother and her sister, who she only met for the first time a few years ago, took a trip to Florida. My father wasn't thrilled with the idea, but he understood that my aunt Jodi, who'd never known her real mother, wanted some type of connection to the past." I tapped my fingers on the picnic table. "It was only a two-day trip where my mother promised to avoid familiar neighborhoods and old hangouts. She was planning on showing Aunt Jodi the house she lived in, her school, where their mother worked. Stuff like that. Mom happened to drive by Razors, and mentioned to Jodi that Grizz used to own it."

"It's not a biker bar anymore," Christian interrupted. "It's like a bistro or cafe or something, and Blue owns it now."

"Yeah, that's what my mom told me. Unfortunately, Aunt Jodi convinced her to stop for lunch. It wasn't her fault. The chances of them running into any bikers from the old days were slim. Of course they never counted on Blue owning it or being there that day. He saw my aunt Jodi coming out of the ladies room and thought it was Mom. It could've been a disaster, especially after my mother stepped in to formally introduce them and he let on that he used to be Grizz's number one guy." I looked heavenward and rolled my eyes. "My aunt despises bikers, and was really awful to Blue. But Mom said he didn't seem offended, and apparently he respected Mom's privacy with her new husband enough not to probe further."

I saw the question in Christian's eyes. "No, he absolutely, positively does not have a clue that Grizz is actually Mom's new husband. He thinks we moved to Montana like she told him when we left South Florida. She felt she owed him that much. Even though we didn't see a lot of him, I was raised thinking Blue was my uncle."

Christian nodded his head. He apparently already knew that story.

"So tell me," I said.

"Tell you what?"

"Tell me more about Blue."

CHAPTER 31

FORT LAUDERDALE, FLORIDA 2002

Five Years Earlier

Keith "Blue" Dillon stood in front of his bathroom mirror and scowled at his smooth-shaven face and short hair. Blue had cleaned up for his so-called girlfriend with the ridiculous name—Detective Dicky Fynder—only to come to the surprising realization she hadn't wanted him on the straight and narrow. He shook his head and scoffed at himself when he reflected on the sacrifice he'd been willing to make for her, and grateful that Grizz's blessing allowed him to remove himself from the gang without repercussions. After Grizz's death by lethal injection, Blue could've automatically assumed his right as club president. A position he thought he didn't want. He'd been wrong.

Even though Blue had distanced himself as much as possible, he was still welcomed by some of the older members who respected him. Those that didn't were too afraid to cross him. Maybe he still had some pull after all. The younger, newer members of the group had heard the stories about their glory days. The ones that knew what Blue was capable of kept their distance. The ones that didn't, risked mouthing off and catching him on a bad day.

He leaned away from the sink and ran his hand through his short hair as he thought with self-disgust how soft he'd become. The old Blue would've put that seedy little shit in the ground that attempted to rape Mimi. Instead, Blue tried to give Mimi's father, Tommy Dillon, a courtesy call to let him know what he'd heard on the street, but he'd been too afraid of messing things up with Dicky to do what he should've done himself. Blue was certain that Mimi had no way of knowing that Grizz was her real father. But that shouldn't have mattered anyway. Dead or not, Blue owed Grizz his loyalty. Nick Rosman shouldn't be alive.

In the end, Blue's decision to fade away from gang life, not retaliating for Mimi's attempted rape, even his altered appearance were all for naught. After realizing that Blue left the club, Dicky flat-out dumped him. He was only as good as the information he could unwittingly feed her, and if he was no longer involved, he was no longer privy to the info she craved. And since he would never be a deliberate informant, not even to keep her in his life, he was useless to her, and she let him know it. *Never again*, he told himself. *Never again will I let myself care for another woman.*

An hour later he pulled up to the back of a run-down warehouse that was a front for the gang's headquarters. An old member who'd done his time and was released ran Grizz's old crew now.

Apparently, Mickey Moran had learned a lot while serving out his sentence in a maximum security prison. He used to go by Monster back in the day. A nickname he'd lived up to. A calmer, more composed Mickey emerged from behind bars and after slowly immersing himself back into the group, convinced them they needed a fresh start. He'd given them a new name, and a new patch which at first they were reluctant to accept. But after earning the respect of the new members, and surprising some of the older ones with his newfound leadership skills, they finally relented. Blue should've objected when Mickey showed back up after Grizz's execution, but he'd been so relieved to have an out without feeling guilty, he'd passed the baton to the man without so much as a backward glance. He was now regretting that decision. Not because Monster wasn't doing a good job, but because it was Blue that should've been doing it. He was certain that Grizz would be turning over in his grave to learn who was now running the old crew.

He revved his bike and watched as the tall set of metal doors lifted. He slowly drove in and noticed a young guy he instantly recognized. The man nodded at Blue, and then pressed the button so the door would slide back into place. Blue was certain he was looking at one of Anthony Bear's boys. Which one, he wasn't sure. He didn't remember ever knowing their names. He did know that it was because of one of them that Nick Rosman hadn't been able to carry out his misguided attempt at filming his sexual assault on Mimi.

After pulling into the warehouse, he parked his bike with the others and headed for the meeting room. So different from the days when they'd conducted business around a fire pit at a run-down motel.

He walked into the ramshackle office and headed for the refrigerator in the small kitchen area. He grabbed a beer and plopped himself down in a chair. Several men nodded, including Mickey, who no longer went by the name Monster.

"Glad you're here, Blue," Mickey said. "We could use some input on the Phillips' deal. It's a little more delicate than what we're used to. Maybe some of our old gang tactics might be useful here. You were around back then. What do you think?"

Blue took a swig of beer and set the bottle down on the table. He wasn't sure if he would ever get used to the new Monster, and sure as shit couldn't say if he would ever trust him.

"You were with our crew back then, Mickey. How do you think it should be handled?" Blue asked, the confrontation obvious in his reply.

There was no indication in Mickey's expression that he heard the challenge in Blue's voice. As a matter of fact, his smile seemed sincere when he replied, "I was too busy fucking and fighting back then to pay attention."

After business concluded, the senior members wandered out to where the bikes were parked. Several more had shown up during the meeting and were now sitting around in chairs or standing off to the side.

One yelled out, "When are the whores getting here?" Almost all of them were engaged in conversation with each other, except for one.

Blue approached the guy who was leaning up against a pallet of stolen computers.

"Are you Bear's oldest or youngest?" he asked Christian.

"Youngest. I'm Chris," he told Blue. "I already know who you are."

"Isn't this a school night?" Blue asked a little sarcastically.

Christian tensed and told him, "I graduated, and before you ask, I'm not the college type."

"Does your dad know you're here?" Blue asked, this time in a voice that was more curious. "I know that he moved here from the other coast to distance himself from his old crew. Heard he's completely clean now. Runs a successful business. I'm surprised he'd allow this."

"He didn't allow anything," Christian sneered as he pushed himself away from the pallet. Walking away from Blue he called out over his shoulder, "He's the one who sent me."

CHAPTER 32

FORT LAUDERDALE, FLORIDA 2007

S lade Bear drove up the long driveway and was relieved to see both his parents' vehicles in their open garage. His mother had been insisting for days that he stop by, and when he'd called this morning to see if he could bring lunch, she hadn't been sure if his father would be around, but insisted Slade come anyway. He normally wouldn't visit them in the middle of a work day, but something had been nagging at him. It was as good a time as any to casually approach them, and get a feel for their thoughts on Christian's trip to Jacksonville. He knew there was the distinct possibility that Christian was up to no good, and could bring unwanted attention to him, his family, and the motorcycle club he'd joined as a teenager.

Letting himself in the front door, he called out, "Who's hungry for lunch?"

Christy came out of the hallway wiping her hands, and Slade immediately detected a hint of the lotion she applied to them a couple times a day.

"Your call this morning was a nice surprise!" Christy exclaimed as she approached her son and pulled his face down to kiss him on the cheek.

Slade gave his mother a knowing grin. "Not like I had much choice. You can be very persuasive."

"Are you on your lunch hour?" Ignoring his comment, she looked at her watch and mentally gauged how much time they would have for their visit since the courthouse was a good distance from their home in the suburbs.

"Yes, but I have more time than usual. I don't have to be in court because my case has a forty-eight hour continuance." He held up the bag he was carrying. "Brought your favorite Italian subs. Where's Dad?"

"He came home from work when I told him you called. He's in his shop now. I'll call him. My phone is charging in the kitchen."

Slade followed his mother and could see his father walking toward the house through the glass doors that opened onto their deck.

Christy saw him too and commented as she pulled out plates and napkins, "I guess he saw you drive up."

After Anthony met them inside, and Slade explained once again that he had some free time away from the trial, they sat at the table and dug into their sandwiches.

"Tell me about the girl you mentioned you saw in the law library," Christy said before taking a sip of her drink.

Slade had been getting ready to take a bite of his sub and stopped. "There's nothing to tell. I talked to her a little bit. She's a librarian at a local school and works in the law library during her school's spring break."

"You talked to her enough to find all of that out?" Christy looked at her son, her eyes wide and hopeful.

"Don't, Mom," Slade said and took a bite of his sandwich. He slowly chewed his food, and watched Anthony signal his wife to let it go. As much as Slade appreciated his mother's concern for his non-existent social life, the last thing he wanted was to have her hovering around it. He could've kicked himself for mentioning Bevin. A little over a week ago, his mother had asked if he'd met anyone at the courthouse who he found interesting, and like an idiot, he gave up that he'd spotted someone in the law library that he might like to meet. He should've known Christy would follow up. Time to steer the conversation toward his real reason for caving into her insistence he make time to see his family this week.

"Have you talked to Christian since he left for Jacksonville?" Slade casually asked.

"Yes." Christy reached for a bag of chips and tore them open. "Twice." Pouring chips onto her plate, she remarked, "Once when he first left and again, yesterday."

"He called you from his phone?" Slade paused. "Or answered his?"

Both Anthony and Christy stopped what they were doing and gave Slade a suspicious look.

"What is this really about, Slade?" Anthony asked, his eyes narrowed.

Slade shrugged his shoulders. "I'm just worried about him," Slade confessed. Without giving his parents time to comment, he quickly added, "He answers my texts, but doesn't take my calls. I can't figure out what's in Jacksonville that he would even consider moving there. Especially with—"

"No," Christy interrupted. "He didn't call me from his phone. Both times he told me that his was charging, and he had to use his friend's phone. He sounded upbeat. Actually, a little too happy now that I think about it." She cast her husband a worried glance.

"It doesn't mean anything," Anthony reassured her at the same time the doorbell rang.

After trying to disguise their shock at seeing Carter's husband, Bill Petty, standing at their front door with his laptop under his arm, Anthony and Christy invited him in and asked him to make himself comfortable in their great room.

Bill and Carter Petty had been close friends with Grizz and Ginny. Bill willingly took on the responsibility for maintaining the façade that Grizz had died by lethal injection in 2000. He was a computer genius who could hack any system, create false information, and cause the real stuff to permanently disappear. Not to mention the myriad of other computer skills that would frighten the general public into tossing their electronics in the garbage. Bill had once written a program that allowed him to manage an airborne helicopter's controls from the ground. He hadn't created it because he intended to use it. He only did it to see if it could be done. And the results scared even him.

Prior to Grizz and Ginny's move out of Florida, Bill had written several programs that routinely scanned the internet for any inquiries about Jason "Grizz" Talbot or his family members. The program he designed did one of two things. Depending on the query, it either rerouted the user to bogus sites, sending them down bottomless rabbit holes that led nowhere, never revealing any information about Grizz or his glory days as one of South Florida's most feared motorcycle club leaders. Or, it zapped the user's computer with a virus that shut it down. The two years after Grizz's supposed execution, followed by the tragic death of Ginny's second husband Tommy "Grunt" Dillon, had been the busiest. But as time passed and the macabre fascination died down, Bill's program had mostly been used to block queries from curious ex-classmates and friends of Ginny's children, Mimi and Jason Dillon. However, with social media evolving at an alarming rate, Bill had to continuously update his program to detect these searches. And it was becoming more difficult.

After setting his laptop on the Bears' coffee table, he sat down and clasped his hands together. Looking from Slade to Anthony, to Christy he said, "What I need to discuss with you is sensitive." He shot a glance back at Slade.

"Time for you to leave, Slade," came Anthony's brisk response. There would only be one reason for Bill Petty showing up at his home. Anthony knew this had to do with Grizz.

"No," Christy interjected, giving Anthony a challenging look. "He's mature enough to be trusted with what we've kept secret for six years. Who knows how it might one day affect this family. And if by some chance it does, he should be prepared. One of our boys should know the truth, Anthony."

Bill deferred to Anthony who nodded.

Christy could see on her husband's face that Anthony knew she was right. She also knew Anthony had always considered Slade the less temperamental of their two sons. Slade was the responsible son. The ambitious son. The smart son who made his decisions based on facts, not feelings. Besides, Bill showing up in their living room with his computer would only pique Slade's curiosity, and might even send him down a rabbit hole of his own.

Nodding his head, Bill opened his laptop. "Okay then. You both know I keep tabs on Grizz and his family." It was a statement, not a question and all three of them cut their eyes to Slade's to see if the comment registered. Slade's expression didn't reflect surprise or curiosity.

I wonder if he's known or suspected all this time? Christy thought before returning her gaze to Bill.

"Normally, my programs monitor and deal with all internet searches on the family and shuts them down before they go anywhere. I get a printed report every time this happens. It's unsettling how fast technology is growing, and it's getting increasingly difficult to stay ahead of it even with my programs continuously being updated.

Using recent pictures that Ginny provides, I keep a facial recognition program running at all times." He swung his laptop around and showed them the picture of Mimi with her friends. "My program didn't catch this picture of Mimi for a couple weeks, but when it did, it took it down."

"Okay." Christy tucked a stray lock of hair behind her ear. "That's a good thing, right?"

"Yes." Bill hesitated. "But there's more and you're not going to like it."

Anthony, Christy, and Slade listened as Bill explained how it took some time, but his facial recognition program detected another similar program that linked to the picture he'd just shown them.

"So someone else was looking for Mimi," Anthony interrupted.

Christy noticed Slade stiffen in his seat.

"I traced the software to a kid named Seth. I did a search on Seth and found a connection to your youngest, Christian."

"And?" Christy prompted.

"After hacking every camera near Seth's home, I found this." His fingers clacking on the keyboard resounded in the quietness of the room. He once again swung the laptop around to face them and watched their expressions as they saw a grainy picture of Christian getting out of his truck.

"Christian isn't in Jacksonville, is he?" Christy sighed. Purposely avoiding her husband's hard stare, she looked from Bill to Slade and back to Bill again.

"His phone is," Slade chimed in. "I ran a trace on it and it's been showing up in Jacksonville. Mom, you said he called you but not from his phone."

"I traced his phone too and got the same result," Bill added. "It's in Jacksonville. What number did he call you from?" His gaze was focused on Christy.

Christy got up and ran to get her phone in the kitchen. Returning quickly, she handed it to Bill, and stood over him watching him type.

"How long will this take?" she asked.

"He's in South Carolina," Bill announced after getting an immediate response for his search.

"Why would he be in South Carolina?" Christy asked, a worried frown on her pretty face.

"It's where Mimi goes to college," Slade and Bill said at the same time.

All three of them glanced at Slade, and he shrugged. "It's a palpable assumption."

"You always were the smart one," Anthony said under his breath, not intending for anyone to hear, but it was clear they had by the nasty look Christy shot at him.

Bill explained that after discovering someone had used a cutting-edge program to find Mimi, he'd tried to conduct a wellness check on her. He told the Bears that she attended a retreat in South Carolina every spring break and when he checked with the camp to verify her whereabouts, he was told the camp had been closed due to a medical quarantine.

"And she hasn't returned home or to college," Bill offered. "She's still somewhere close to the camp. At least her car is. She doesn't know Grizz put a tracker on it that I monitor. And I suspect she's staying at a house that Seth rented." Before anyone could comment, he continued, "Yeah, I hacked the hacker and found out he rented a house with a bogus credit card near her camp."

"Christian would never hurt Mimi," Christy practically shouted. "But we need to go get him, Anthony."

Anthony closed his eyes and pinched the bridge of his nose between his fingers. "You think he took her against her will?" He opened his eyes, but wasn't addressing anyone in particular.

"Does it matter?" Slade barked. "He's obviously violated his parole and somehow covered his tracks so that his phone is in a different state."

"That's exactly what he did," Bill agreed. "He had to have given his phone to someone who lives in Jacksonville, and is driving it all over the place. Have you tried contacting him, and if so, does he respond to texts or phone calls right away?" he asked Christy.

"No," she said, her voice wilting. "It always takes a while to get a text from him. And even longer to get a call."

"Because he's instructed whoever has his phone to notify him at the number he called you from. And he's telling this person how to reply to your texts. The couple of times he's called you, he's probably given you an excuse as to why he's not calling from his phone. He's had you convinced that he's calling you from Jacksonville while using his friend's phone, when he's really three states away using a phone he probably bought along the way." Looking at Christy, Bill continued, "Am I right?"

She nodded.

"Christian was in prison for three years," Anthony said, changing the subject. "Can you pull up the inmates who were there with him and cross reference who's been released against any of them who might have a current Jacksonville address?"

The search took a few minutes, but Bill was able to tell them Christian had served time with a man named Reed Boyle who'd been released, and resided in Jacksonville.

"What's Christian's license plate number?" Bill asked. "I hadn't thought to look for Christian's truck, but if we can find it, it just might provide more concrete evidence of the lengths he's gone to pull this off."

When the three of them looked at him, he quickly added, "Never mind. I can find it faster."

Christy was now pacing, shooting nervous looks at Anthony who sat in his recliner, remaining calmer than she'd expected. It seemed like an eternity before Bill finally spoke.

"Here," Bill said, once again turning his computer around to face them. "This program scanned cameras near Boyle's address and detected Christian's vehicle by the type and license plate. And it's obvious it's not your son who's driving it."

"No, it's not," Anthony confirmed.

"Christian swapped trucks with Boyle," Bill commented.

"How do you know Reed Boyle owns a truck?" Slade asked.

Without looking at Slade, Bill answered, "It's all here." He closed his laptop and stood up.

"I have a responsibility to notify Grizz and Ginny," he informed them, giving them a compassionate look. "But to keep Grizz from coming out of hiding, I'll give you a head start. Right now, I'm certain Grizz doesn't know about the camp being quarantined, and that Mimi is missing. Otherwise, he would've contacted me to activate the tracker he has on her car."

Anthony gave a curt nod. "We can get there faster from here than he can from Montana anyway. I don't like to fly so it'll take us two days by car. Less if we drive straight through." He shot a look at

Christy, and told her to line up a babysitter to come stay at their place. "We can leave as soon as Daisy gets home."

"Yeah, except that I should probably tell you that Grizz isn't in Montana." Bill looked from Anthony to Christy. "If that camp's quarantine gets news coverage, or he somehow gets word of it and he can't reach Mimi, he will be calling me and I'll have to tell him the truth. I'll have to tell him what I know and give him the address where she is."

"Where is Grizz?" Slade asked.

"He lives in North Carolina. Right over the South Carolina border, just hours away from where I suspect your brother and Mimi are."

They all heard Christy suck in her breath. "If he gets to Christian and Mimi first…"

"He won't ask questions," Bill finished for her. "Grizz will act. And there's no telling what that might entail."

"And Christian won't be expecting it…" Christy added in a shaky voice.

"Because he thinks Grizz died years ago," Anthony growled. He gave his wife a glance that caused her to cringe.

"Wait!" Slade yelled as he jumped up from his seat. Motioning his hands as if to tamp down erroneous conclusions. "Why can't you get ahead of this and call Grizz to tell him what's happened? Maybe he already knows. How do you know that Mimi hasn't been in contact with her parents and is spending time with Christian willingly?"

"Because I've looked at the texts she's exchanged with her mother," Bill piped in. "She doesn't mention seeing your brother, the camp being closed, or that she's staying somewhere near it in a rented house. As a matter of fact, she's not sent any texts to her mother since the last one, and that was to confirm that she arrived at the camp, which we all know is a lie."

"And Christian probably sent that text or convinced Mimi to send it." Christy's voice was fading as quickly as the color in her cheeks.

Slade returned to his seat as Anthony scrubbed his hand down his face and addressed his son. "And you think I should call to tell Grizz that Christian, who was just released from prison for a malicious act of violence, went to unbelievable extremes to find his daughter and is keeping her at a remote location in the middle of nowhere?"

"If there is any chance of Christian bringing harm to her, I have to contact Grizz," Bill interjected.

"No!" Christy insisted. "As unreal as this may sound, Christian has loved Mimi since they shared a playpen. There is no way on this earth he would hurt her. I know he wouldn't. Right, Anthony?" Christy wrung her hands as her eyes appealed to Anthony to confirm her statement. "And we still don't know if it's against her will." Her voice was hopeful.

Nodding his head, and trying to keep the irritation out of his tone, Anthony replied, "I agree. But I think we need to fly up there. Driving will cost us hours we don't have."

Bill sat back down and opened his laptop. They watched as his brow creased in frustration. "I can't get you a flight anywhere near where they are. They had an unexpected winter blast and even though it doesn't look like the house where they're staying got hit very hard at all, the two closest airports did. They're closed and it doesn't say when they'll be reopening."

"How about a private jet?" Christy inquired.

"It doesn't matter what kind of air transportation you want to use. It can't land at a closed airport. There are a few other airports, but the drive will be longer."

"Not longer than if we drove from here," Anthony interjected. "Get us on the best flight you can, and have a rental car waiting for us."

"Please," Christy added before giving Anthony a cross look for barking out orders to Bill.

A few minutes passed before Bill announced, "Done." He closed his laptop and stood. "I'm sorry to bring this down on you. I'll do what I can to hold off Grizz on my end should I hear from him."

After thanking Bill for coming to them first and reassuring him that he and Christy were certain Mimi wouldn't be in danger, Anthony walked him to the front door while Christy headed for the bedroom to throw essentials in a suitcase and call the sitter.

Before opening the front door to leave, Bill turned around and addressed Anthony. "Christian not only found Mimi Dillon, but managed to evade or trick his parole officer, and cover up his true whereabouts by leaving his phone and truck in Jacksonville. When you think about it, his plan is flawless with the exception of not knowing Grizz is close enough to hurt or even kill him. And that's not his fault because he would have no way of knowing about Grizz."

Anthony nodded. "You're right."

"And you think he's the smart one?" Bill added while nodding toward Slade. "Seems like your youngest son has outsmarted us all."

"That he has," Anthony replied, unable to conceal the grin that was tugging at the corners of his mouth. "That he has."

CHAPTER 33

B efore heading back to the rental house, Christian shared a few more details with me as to how Blue became the club's leader after Mickey Moran had been diagnosed with pancreatic cancer and died shortly thereafter. Immediately following Mickey's death, Blue had been reinstated as leader. But not long after it was discovered that Blue was only second in command. He was reporting to someone else.

The old crew had been involved with prostitution, theft, loan sharking, and street drugs. This new leader—only referred to as The Ghost—ran a more sophisticated gang behind a desk in an office that nobody had ever visited. Yes, there was still prostitution, but not the typical hooker you'd find on a street corner or hanging at a bar. These were high-priced call girls that were on retainer for clients with very deep pockets who needed to remain faceless. Clients who could be blackmailed for money, information, or favors. The loans to itinerant gamblers were no longer being arranged from the back rooms of pawn shops, but were being managed by a well-placed insider at the local casinos and racetracks. Yes, the gang had stepped up their business, and still kept the right amount of law enforcement in their debt.

The Ghost was smart. The new club headquarters was a highly respected South Florida HVAC business. Shielding the club's illegal activities with an air conditioning company was brilliant. This gave gang members, some who were now HVAC employees, access to almost any building they wanted. If they weren't repairing the units, they were installing new ones. The point being that almost every building in South Florida had an air conditioner that needed to be repaired or replaced, or in the case of new construction, installed. And people lived and worked in these buildings. All kinds of people. Rich, poor, black, white, men, women. People that were flawed. People that took drugs, cheated on their spouses, hid gambling addictions and so much more.

"So, does anybody know who this Ghost is?" I tilted my head to one side and frowned. "And where did they come up with the name The Ghost?"

Without answering, Christian stood up from the picnic table, walked toward a large tree and stepped behind it. I didn't realize what he was doing until I heard the unmistakable sound of liquid spattering against bark. I rolled my eyes and stood up, disengaging myself from the picnic table.

"No. Nobody has a clue who The Ghost really is," he called out from behind the huge oak. He came around the side of the tree and was zipping his pants when he said, "And the name Ghost is obvious. Nobody has ever seen him. But he wasn't always The Ghost. He used to go by some weird name that was hard to pronounce." He paused a moment and looked thoughtful before adding, "Verkozen."

"Ver...what?" I asked, scrunching up my nose.

"Verkozen. I think it's Dutch and means elected one. I guess it was mispronounced enough that it was shortened to just Kozen, which became Koze, which eventually became Ghost. Probably because it's easier to say, kind of rhymes and makes more sense." He shrugged his shoulders and added, "Don't know and definitely don't care."

"Has Blue met this elected one?" I asked using air quotes.

"Blue communicates by cell phone or computer."

"Has he ever said if he recognizes the voice?" My curiosity was more than piqued.

Christian shook his head as he reached for my hand and we walked toward the motorcycle. "I've been told it's one of those robotic voices. It could be anybody. Blue could even by lying. Maybe there is no Ghost." A few seconds passed when he added, "Or maybe there is, and it's somebody who's supposed to be dead."

The implication was obvious. We'd reached the bike, and I grabbed my jacket that I'd left draped over the seat. He held it up for me to slip on. I had my back to him and said, "No way. It's not Grizz."

"How can you be sure?" he asked, as he reached for his jacket. I'd turned around and was fastening mine when I shook my head. "He's too busy. He'd never have the time, and he's not exactly a poster boy for technology. If anything he hates it."

"What does he do all day?" Christian climbed on the bike and waited for me to get on behind him.

"When he's not helping my mother raise two four-year-olds, he trains and rehabilitates dogs. And when he's not doing those things, he spends time making our home self-sustaining. He's had solar panels installed for power, wells dug for fresh water. Stuff like that."

Christian didn't reply. He started the bike and moments later we'd pulled out onto the main road and were heading back to the house.

The long ride gave me time to think. Could my father be The Ghost that gave orders from behind a computer keyboard? I couldn't picture him doing it. Everything I'd told Christian was true. Grizz kept himself very busy, and when he had free time, he used it to ride his motorcycle. But that didn't mean he couldn't find time to slip away by himself. He could have a laptop hidden somewhere or maybe use Mom's when no one was around. After her nagging and then insisting he'd finally relented and gotten her one. She only used it to look up recipes or browse parenting forums. I knew he was very interested in the stock market and traded, but I never asked how. Maybe he used her laptop. And if that was the case, I'm sure there was some kind of technology that Bill used to make it untraceable. Heck, he could even be doing what I did all those years ago when I'd tried to establish contact with Christian—using public computers. My father using a public computer? I immediately dismissed the thought. Unless…what if Grizz's disdain for technology was nothing but a cleverly designed ruse that allowed him to still run his old club?

The thought poked at me the entire ride home. Apparently, something had been poking at Christian as well, but it didn't have to do with The Ghost. We'd pulled up to the house and I'd just gotten off the bike and was heading for the front porch when I heard him say, "I think I should go back to school with you to help you pack."

I slowly turned around to face him. He had dismounted, too, and was removing his jacket as he approached me.

"Help me pack? For what?" I wanted to know.

"To come back to Florida with me," he answered matter-of-factly. "I don't see why we need to wait until you graduate. You can transfer schools and finish up there."

"Who says we're going to live in Florida?" I couldn't keep the attitude out of my voice.

He stopped in his tracks and frowned at me. "Who says we're not?"

"Don't you think it's something we should at least talk about?" I huffed.

"What's to talk about? We're married. We belong together. And I can't leave Florida until I'm finished with my parole."

I nodded. "Okay, I understand the parole issue," I conceded. "But there is no way I'm transferring schools right now to finish up the last few months in Florida." I shook my head and glared at him. "Not that I'd even consider it this late in the semester, but I don't even know if it's possible this close to graduation."

He gave me a smirk and said, "I'm sure we can figure it out. A couple of bucks in the right bank account can make it happen."

I was suddenly filled with annoyance. If I didn't think stomping my foot on the ground was tantamount to a full-blown juvenile hissy fit, I would've done it. I wasn't an errant child, but I was a seriously ticked-off adult at his controlling assumption.

"You can't buy everything, Christian," I spat. "And you can't always have things your way. Did you ever once consider what an inconvenience it would be for me?"

"You're my wife now, Mimi. I want you with me."

"You can't have everything your way, Christian! You certainly can't disrupt me attending school. I'm graduating!" I yelled. "And besides, we're not really married!"

I saw a flash of anger in his eyes, and I braced myself for an argument. An argument that didn't come as he turned his back on me and headed toward the stolen motorcycle. I stood with my hands on my hips and watched him drive off.

I let myself in the house, and paced for a good twenty minutes before I grabbed an empty basket off one of the shelves and headed outside. I found my way back to the field of strawberries we'd stumbled on earlier in the week in the hopes of salvaging some that may have survived the dip in temperature. While I plucked the decent ones and tossed them in my basket, I found that my earlier anger had subsided. When I allowed myself to recall our conversation I realized that Christian hadn't approached the topic in a demanding or bossy way. He may have been confident about his assumptions, but that was all. And considering Christian hadn't gone to college, what would he know about the hoops I'd have to jump through to transfer? He wouldn't, which is why he'd offered the only solution he was familiar with. Bribery. I'd been quick to unfairly assume he was issuing an order when he was only telling me what he figured was the best way to handle our situation. I was the one who escalated the conversation into a quarrel. I stopped picking strawberries and stood up when I realized we hadn't had a quarrel. I had angrily jumped down his throat in a nasty and ugly manner. And he never once raised his voice or challenged me. Instead, he'd driven away.

I looked at my watch and gulped. He'd left almost an hour ago. And if he'd returned, I would've surely heard his bike. I looked up at the sky. The sun would be setting soon. An emptiness laced with a tingling of fear descended on me. My eyes started to burn when I remembered my parting shot at him. *And besides, we're not really married.*

What had I done?

I trudged back toward the house and was staring at the ground when I was startled by Christian. He'd appeared out of nowhere and came barreling at me with what looked like an expression of relief on his face. I dropped my basket when he pulled me into a tight hug. After releasing me he took my face in his hands and kissed my nose, my cheeks, my eyes, my forehead.

"I couldn't find you anywhere, Mimi. I thought you left," he admitted before letting out a long breath.

I was a bit breathless myself when I said, "But you must've seen my car still parked in front of the house."

"Yeah, I saw it. But, I was gone long enough for you to call a cab or maybe run to the main road and hitchhike, or..." He stopped and pulled his hand through his long hair. "I thought you were gone."

I took a step back and retrieved the basket I'd dropped. Holding it up I explained, "I was picking strawberries." He gave me a smile that turned my insides to mush. "Wait...why didn't I hear the motorcycle?"

"I left it where it would be found." He took my hand and started tugging me toward the house.

"How did you get back?" I asked as I struggled to keep up with his long strides.

The house came into view and I saw a pickup truck idling in the driveway. Apparently, the driver had waited for Christian to return and gave him a wave before driving off. Before I could ask he told me he helped a guy get it started in return for a ride.

"About earlier. What I said when you drove off. I—"

"Forget it," he interrupted as we made our way up to the front porch.

I looked up at him, but he must've seen something in my expression that caused him to continue.

"I've wasted my entire life holding grudges. Being with you this week has shown me how much I've missed out on real happiness." His deep voice was laced with regret.

"I'm not perfect, Christian. And neither are you. We've still got a long way to go, and let's face it, we both know that our families will probably be placing bets on how long we'll last."

"Then let's make sure we prove them wrong, Mimi."

"We still have a couple of days left before you have to go back to school," Christian said as we watched the truck head down the long drive round a curve and disappear from view.

I looked up at his profile and he must've felt my stare because he turned and looked down at me. I was certain he was going to tell me that he wanted to spend the few days we had left in bed. His answer surprised me.

"We're going to pack up and go to Pine Creek, North Carolina. I want to meet your family before you go back to school and I head back to Florida. And you told me your grandpa is a minister. We should ask him to marry us."

I fumbled for words that didn't come.

"Am I wrong to assume you want to make our marriage official?" he asked.

This was supposed to be the part where the guy tells the girl that it wasn't real and he enjoyed their time together, then makes fun of her for thinking they were really married. But that's not what Christian did.

"You're not wrong," I whispered. I wanted my grandfather to marry us, but I was concerned about the resistance I knew we would get from my family. "I'm not sure if asking him to do it this soon would be a good idea. I think both of our families would probably take us more seriously if we waited until I graduate in a few months."

"I didn't mean he had to marry us immediately, Mimi. I would make it official tomorrow, but I understand if you want to wait until summer."

"I think it's for the best," I assured him.

"Are you having doubts about us?"

"No!" I blurted. And I was telling the truth. Our romance may have been fast, but I had no doubt it was real.

"Good." A few seconds passed before he added, "And I was wrong to make an assumption about school without talking to you, Mimi."

I blinked. Stunned at his admission.

"Shocked?" he asked with a lopsided grin. "Don't be. You're the only person in the world I'd do anything for. I wasn't being cocky when I told you before that I don't ask. I don't. I never have. But for you, and you alone, I'll try."

"Thank you for that, Christian. I'll do my best to be patient when I think you're giving orders or being bossy. I'll remind you nicely when I think it's something we should decide together."

"You look worried." He hesitated before adding, "Are you doubting if we can make it work?"

"No. Not at all," I answered, while shaking my head. "I'm not worried about us. I'm worried about bringing you home to meet Grizz." I chewed on my bottom lip as the horrible-things-that-could-go-wrong scenarios played in my head. There were too many to count.

"YOU HAVE to keep ice on it, Mimi!" Christian practically yelled as he bent over me. The frustration in his tone was apparent.

"But the ice hurts more than the injury when it's been on too long," I whined.

Immediately following our earlier conversation about visiting my family and announcing our wedding plans, we made the decision to leave first thing in the morning. We used what little daylight we had left to unload the bed of Christian's borrowed truck with the home-owner's personal recreational toys. He was tugging at the kayak when it caught on something. Without realizing that I was standing right behind him, Christian gave a hard yank that dislodged the kayak with unexpected momentum. It hit me in the face with enough force to cause me to stumble backwards and land with a thud on the ground.

I was stunned, and even winced when I tried to smile as another childhood memory descended on me.

"Mimi, do you wanna get married again?" Christian asked me as I followed him through the maze of jungle gym tunnels. He stopped crawling and turned around, accidentally kicking me in the face. I was startled, but not hurt.

"I'm sorry, Mimi! I'm sorry. Did I hurt you?" he cried as he tried to wiggle closer to me in the tight space.

I gave him a wide grin and said, "Yeah, it kinda hurt, but not bad."

Christian looked relieved and started to turn back around when I answered his earlier question, "I forgot to bring my ring with me. I didn't know if you wanted to play wedding again."

Christian had given me a plastic ring that he'd won at a carnival and I'd worn it every time we saw each other.

"That's okay," he told me as we ventured out of the maze and were now standing in a small cube-shaped part of the structure that had open windows. He proudly pulled something out of his right front pocket. "I got this one for you out of the claw machine at the grocery store. It has a bigger diamond and it's blue!"

It was the same ring that he'd held onto for years and put on my pillow last night.

After holding the ice to my swollen face for what seemed like forever, we ate a simple dinner, and turned on the TV to discover that even though snow wasn't in the forecast, the temperature was supposed to dip that night. It was about that time we realized the heat in the house wasn't working, and he didn't want to call the realtor to send a repairman.

Christian's solution was simple. He dragged the master bedroom mattress out to the living room, piled it high with blankets, and built a roaring fire.

"As much as I don't want to, I think we need to sleep in our clothes tonight. The fire will go out when we fall asleep, and I don't want you to freeze."

I gave him what I could only assume was a crooked smile. My face was numb from all the ice packs. We decided to turn in at ten o'clock so we could get an early start in the morning. Our plan was to be on the road at sunrise; he would follow me to Highway 11. There was a gas station where we could leave his truck. We'd drive my car up into the foothills of Pine Creek. We concocted a story that had nothing to do with abduction, but of two old friends running into each other, deciding to spend time together. We were going to keep the story short and simple. Christian was there to fish with a buddy who never showed up, and after running into him at Pumpkin Rest and discovering Camp Keowee was closed, I made the decision on my own to stay with him. We realized we've always been in love, and picked up where we left off. We had an impromptu wedding, but wanted my grandfather, Micah, to make it official after I got my degree.

"You look awful, Mimi," he said shaking his head, disgusted with himself. We were on our improvised bed and he was sitting up, looking down at me. "What will your parents think when we walk in with you looking like you've been in a car wreck?"

I reached for him to pull him down to me and said, "I'll go in first and explain there was a mishap, an accident. Then I'll tell them I brought someone home for them to meet. Believe me, that'll shock them enough that they won't even be thinking about my face."

He nodded and settled next to me on the mattress. He was on his side, softly stroking my neck when he asked, "Does Grizz still go by James?"

I took his hand and kissed it before answering. I looked up at the ceiling and tried to explain.

"When my dad bought his way off death row, he was given a new identity." I looked at Christian and his eyes were serious. I looked back at the ceiling. "It was James something. I don't remember the last name he was given," I told him shaking my head. "The story of how my mother found his real family is long, but I'll give you the edited version. Before dying, Grizz's birth mother gave him the first name Jamison, which was her mother's maiden name and what would be his only link back to her family and a father he never knew. My mother's search ended in Pine Creek, North Carolina, where she found Grizz's real father, Micah Hunter. So, Grizz's real name is Jamison Hunter."

"That's where you got the Hunter from in your alias," Christian interrupted.

"Yeah, though technically," I informed him, "it's my real name."

He nodded his understanding. "So is he Grizz or James or Jamison?"

I looked over at him and smiled. "He's all of them. For the most part, James was the man my mother left Florida to marry, and people call him that. And it's understandable because it can be short for Jamison. My grandfather calls him son, except when he's mad at him. Then he's Jamison." I laughed before continuing. "My mother calls him Grizz, but not in public. And it took me a while, but I call him Dad."

"I'll be back in a sec," Christian told me as he jumped up and made his way to the master bedroom.

I took the few minutes he was gone to stare into the fire, and was immediately mesmerized by the flames. I sat up and watched as sparks flew off the burning timbers and disappeared. I'd never given much thought to the color of a fire. I thought they were mostly a combination of orange and red, but this one was different, and I suddenly realized why. I didn't recall where I'd learned it, but I remembered knowing that the hottest fires burn blue. The same blue I saw in Christian's eyes. The intensity I felt from his stare was hotter than any flame I'd set my eyes on. And everyone knew that if you played with fire you got burned. There was no fear in my revelation. Because I knew with every fiber of my being that Christian would never burn me. I felt the weight of the mattress as he sat down behind me, and I turned to him. He was holding his gun that he'd obviously retrieved from the nightstand.

"What do you need that for?" I asked. Our makeshift bed was pushed up against one of the couches. He shoved the gun beneath a seat cushion before curling next to me and pulling me into his arms.

"I like to know it's close by."

"Please don't bring it inside my parents' house tomorrow," I pleaded.

"I wasn't going to," he replied, then asked, "but why not?"

"Because I'm seriously concerned about how my father will react to all this. And I don't want to have to worry about anybody getting hurt."

"I'm not going to hurt your father, Mimi." His breath tickled my neck as he nuzzled it.

"It's not my father I'm worried about, Christian. It's you."

He laughed. "I can handle Grizz, and I won't need a gun to do it."

The last thought I had before falling into a deep sleep was, *I pray you're right, my love*, followed by, *but you don't know Grizz*.

CHAPTER 34

"Again, Grizz?" Ginny ran her hand up and down her husband's arm.

They'd made love twenty minutes earlier, and were enjoying the rare solitude that came with having the house to themselves. They were completely nude, on top of the covers, and had the bedroom door wide open. Thunderclap Newman's "Something in the Air" was softly playing from an iPod that was connected to a speaker on their nightstand.

"Are you asking or telling me, Kit?"

His voice was low and deep and the tone never failed to send a spiral of heat flowing through her blood. Mimi was at camp, Jason was on a hunting trip, and the twins were spending the night with cousins. Even Grizz's father, Micah, who'd moved in with them, recognized they needed some time alone and made an excuse to stay a couple nights with one of his many relatives. It wasn't very often they were minus children, but they were tonight, and were taking full advantage of it.

Ginny sat up, and gave him a wicked grin. "You're the one who likes to hear me scream. And because there's always someone in the house when we make love, I normally have to bite my knuckles off trying to shove my hand in my mouth so I don't make so much noise. But not tonight." She lightly caressed his muscled and heavily tattooed bicep.

Ginny recognized when his eyes turned from teasing and playful to intense and heated. Her gaze roamed down her husband's hard chest and she shook her head with a smile as her eyes wandered lower. "It never ceases to amaze me how fast you get hard." Ginny looked back at him and saw him swallow, his eyes never leaving hers as he guided her on top of him.

"I'll still be getting hard for you when I'm in my nineties." His voice held its low rumble. "Besides, I'm still in my fifties and I have a lot of lost time to make up for."

"You won't be in your fifties for long," she laughed. "Your birthday isn't that far off."

Disregarding her attempt to tease him, Grizz's voice was thick with need when he asked, "Kit, do you wanna scream for me again, or not?"

"Make me," she challenged, her voice husky.

And he did.

Later, they were tangled together in bed talking when Ginny stifled a yawn.

"Go to sleep, baby," Grizz said as he kissed the top of her head. She'd been twining his long hair around her finger, and when she didn't object, he helped her untangle it.

She felt him pull away and she opened her eyes. "Aren't you tired?"

"Nah," came his reply as he stood up and stretched. "I'm gonna check my stocks, and maybe watch the news. Where's your laptop?"

"I left it on the end table in the great room. It should be fully charged."

He leaned down and kissed her on the forehead. Pulling on his thermal long johns, he headed out to the great room, and found her computer where she said it would be. He sat in his recliner, opened up the laptop and then picked up the remote to turn on the television. He missed the eleven o'clock news, but knew they would rebroadcast it shortly.

When he first allowed himself to test the waters with the computer, his huge fingers were clumsy and awkward on the keyboard, but as he became more familiar with the act of typing, it got easier. He didn't know how long he'd been staring at the computer screen, when he thought he heard the words "Camp Keowee" coming from the TV. Slowly closing the laptop and setting it aside, he reached for the remote and turned up the volume on the television. He wasn't sure if what he was hearing was true, but he couldn't take his eyes away from the screen. When the clip ended he raced into the bedroom and flipped on the light.

"What? What is it? What's going on?" Ginny asked, alarmed. She sat straight up and watched Grizz jog to the safe hidden in their bedroom.

"I need to talk to Bill," he huffed.

Grizz had a phone that he used only to communicate with Bill, and he rarely touched it. This was important, and Ginny could feel her heart racing as she climbed out of bed and ran to her husband.

"Tell me!" she cried when she got to him. "Tell me what's wrong. Why do you need to talk to Bill right now? What's so important?"

Ginny listened, stunned, as Grizz explained how he'd just seen a news broadcast about a man dying from a serious illness.

"The anchorman said he was a counselor at Camp Keowee, and the camp is under quarantine. That's Mimi's camp, right?" he asked.

Ginny nodded and quickly added, "I'll check my phone to see if she texted. I'm sure she'll be heading here. They can't keep her there, can they?" She turned her back on him as she headed for her phone on her nightstand.

Grizz grabbed her arm and spun her around. "You don't understand, Kit. They closed it down and wouldn't let anybody in."

Ginny breathed a sigh of relief, but something about the comment confused her. "Wait. What are you saying? They're not letting anyone else in? Or they're not letting the campers and counselors out?"

Grizz gently grabbed both of Ginny's forearms. "Baby, they closed the camp and turned everyone away over a week ago. Mimi never got there. Do you understand what I'm telling you?"

Ginny gasped as the significance of what Grizz was saying sunk in. "I need to call her. She must have her phone, right?"

"Don't call her yet," Grizz demanded. "Let me call Bill and have him activate the tracker on her car. If she's back at school, then you can call her. Maybe she didn't want to come home, and didn't want to hurt our feelings."

Ginny shook her head. "No. No. Mimi wouldn't do that, Grizz."

She could tell by his expression that he knew she was right. "Give me five minutes. Okay?" What he couldn't say was that if Mimi not arriving at the camp had anything to do with his past, he wouldn't want to alert whoever his daughter might be with. The person whose neck Grizz planned on snapping.

"Yeah, okay," Ginny said as she wrapped her arms tightly around herself. It was then that she realized she was still nude. She made her way to her dresser and pulled out some clothes to occupy herself while Grizz opened the safe and made the call.

Less than twenty minutes later, they were in their truck and heading toward an address provided by Bill.

"Slow down, Grizz!" Ginny screamed. "You're going too fast on these roads. It's below freezing."

"We didn't get that much snow and what we did get melted off. The roads are fine," he answered, looking over at her. "Bill knows more than he's telling me," he growled.

"What makes you say that?" she asked, her eyes wide as she watched her husband's determined profile.

"It's just a feeling, Kit. And I don't have to tell you that it's not sitting well with me."

"Grizz, if Bill isn't telling you something, I think we can assume it's for your own good. Or Mimi's own good. He's been your most trusted ally since you were in prison." She swept her hand through the air. "He plays the most important role in keeping up the façade of your death. He's the only reason we can use a laptop." She sighed before adding, "I doubt we'd be able to go online if I didn't have the laptop Bill made especially for us. It's untraceable, no microphones or cameras. You know, all that computer stuff I don't understand."

Ginny noticed when her words started to sink in and she saw Grizz's jaw relax. "If Bill thought Mimi was in danger, he would've sent a helicopter to pick us up!" she added. Ginny knew her suggestion sounded outlandish, but not where Bill was concerned. Her words to Grizz were reassuring, and a calmness settled over her before she added, "Please don't speed, Grizz. The last thing we need is for you to get stopped for speeding in South Carolina."

He reached over and squeezed her thigh. "You've always been my voice of reason, baby."

She smiled and reached for his right hand which had found its way to her left knee. She started to grab it when he pulled it away.

"But not tonight, Kitten," he told her as he clutched the steering wheel with both hands and pressed the gas pedal to the floorboard.

CHAPTER 35

PUMPKIN REST, SOUTH CAROLINA 2007

I was dreaming and I couldn't see anyone, but I could hear them. "Oh, Christian, tell me you did not do that to her face." I hadn't heard her voice for years, but in my dream, I immediately recognized it as belonging to Christian's mother, Aunt Christy. "And her wrists. Is that bruising?"

"Of course I didn't do that to her face," came Christian's reply. In the fogginess of my dream I could tell he'd been offended by her comment. "Not deliberately," he quickly added.

It sounded like there was a scuffle of some sort when I heard Uncle Anthony's voice. It was low and menacing. "What does not deliberately mean?"

"Let him go, Anthony!" Aunt Christy shouted. "Stop it!"

My eyes popped open and I sat straight up. I had to be dreaming. But I would quickly realize what I'd heard was all too real. My gaze immediately landed on Uncle Anthony who was towering over Christian, who had him by the scruff of the neck. The material of Christian's long-sleeved T-shirt collar was scrunched up tightly in his father's big, brown fists.

"Don't!" I yelled while simultaneously rising from the makeshift bed. The mattress was soft beneath my feet and I started to lose my balance when I felt a hand grab my arm. It was Aunt Christy. She looked exactly as I remembered. An attractive blonde with chin-length straight hair and engaging blue eyes. Just like Christian's.

I watched as Uncle Anthony relaxed his hold on Christian. In turn, Christian brought his hands up between his father's and roughly knocked them loose. Uncle Anthony's expression darkened, and I thought he was going to retaliate at Christian's dismissal, when Aunt Christy shouted, "Enough!"

The next few minutes were a blur as conversations were scrambled and we all talked over each other.

"Quiet!" I shouted above the commotion. All eyes turned to me and I launched into the fictional explanation I'd prepared to tell my parents. I should've known better. I wasn't dealing with two people who would've been oblivious to Christian's history.

"I'm pretty sure Christian hasn't picked up a fishing pole in his life," Uncle Anthony countered, giving me a stern look. "And if he did, he wouldn't have violated his parole for the catch of the day."

I exhaled loudly and slowly shook my head. "I'm sorry. You're right. But it's not my place to explain it to you. And before you give Christian a hard time, please understand that I'm not a victim here." Pointing to my face, I added, "And so you know, this really was an accident. The bruises on my wrist weren't, but Christian can tell you everything." I looked from Uncle Anthony to Aunt Christy, whose face softened. Looking back at Christian's father, I noticed that his hadn't.

I glanced around the room and realized that a very subtle glow was coming from the skylights. The sun was starting to come up and if the light hadn't been a reminder that it was time to rise, my full bladder was. It also dawned on me that I wasn't wearing a bra and I quickly crossed my arms over my chest. I chanced a peek at Christian who was smiling at me. I secretly thanked God that we hadn't fallen asleep without our clothes on. This could've been so much worse. I knew he'd read my mind when he winked at me. I stifled a smile.

"I'll leave the three of you to talk." I excused myself and scurried toward the master bedroom. Once inside I grabbed a bra and headed for the freezing bathroom. "Thank goodness for overhead heat lamps," I whispered to nobody as I hastily put on my bra and pulled my thermal top and nightshirt back on. I was curious as to how Christian's parents were handling his explanation as I washed my face, brushed my teeth, and combed my hair. *I wonder how they knew we were together and where we were? Would Bill have figured it out and contacted them without going to my parents first?* I stopped mid-stroke and laid down my hairbrush. Something felt off. I opened the bathroom door and suppressed a gasp.

Their voices were unmistakable as they drifted in from the great room. My parents were here. There was a cacophony of voices and words jumbled together, but one stood out above the rest. It was my father, and he was mad.

"Where is she?" he shouted.

"She's in the bathroom. She's fine, Grizz," came Aunt Christy's soothing voice. "And we're just as upset as you. We didn't know and just found out ourselves. We flew in as soon..."

"You don't look very surprised to see your old friend is still alive." It was Christian's voice, and it was laced with sarcasm. I knew he was talking to his parents. But I didn't want to divert attention away from our situation. I wanted to address it head on. It was time to make myself known.

I made my way to the open bedroom door and assessed the room. My mother and Aunt Christy were standing off to the side of the men, talking in whispers. Uncle Anthony was standing next to Christian who had his arms crossed and his chin raised. My father was right in his face, and his shouting had died down to a low rumble.

"I don't know what the fuck is going on here, but as soon as I talk to my daughter—"

My father's words were cut off when my mother gasped. She'd noticed me standing in the doorway and I could tell by the look on her face that she'd made the same wrong assumption about my bruised face that Christian's parents had.

It all happened so fast, I couldn't have stopped it if I'd tried. My father's eyes cut to my mother. He turned around and followed her gaze, his mesmerizing green eyes landing on me. I'd never seen such rage in my life.

I started to walk quickly toward him, my words coming out fast. "It's not what it looks like, Dad." My explanation fell on deaf ears as he turned his back on me, his fist connecting with Christian's jaw.

The next sixty seconds happened in slow motion as I watched my father beating on Christian. Uncle Anthony tried to pull him off, but he was no match for my dad's heated fury. My mother and Aunt Christy were both screaming, but knew better than to go near the three men. An end table and lamp were knocked over. Not even the ceramic bear that shattered against the wood floor could break up the riot that was playing out before me.

In the chaos, I realized that Christian was not defending himself against my father. He hadn't thrown one punch to stave off the angry fists that were raining down on him. I knew what I had to do. I ran for the couch and reached for the gun hidden between the cushions. I fired two shots in the air.

The commotion immediately ceased as all eyes turned to me. But I only had eyes for one person. I watched as Christian swiped his arm across his face, the blood from his nose and cut lip leaving a streak across the fabric of his long-sleeved T-shirt.

Taking a deep breath, I lowered the gun and said, "We will either have a civil conversation or I'm going to have to ask you all to leave." I looked at each person. My father raised an eyebrow. Uncle Anthony and Aunt Christy seemed relieved. My mother was looking at me like she didn't know me. And my husband was trying not to grin. I knew he was comparing my suggestion for all of them to leave with the poke I'd given Sal at Chicky's.

"I didn't know you could handle a gun, Mimi," Christian said, while the others just stared.

I set the gun down on a side table. "I am my father's daughter."

My father kept quiet, but couldn't keep his angry glare at bay, as Christian and I launched into our explanation. We left a lot of the details out. As far as we were concerned the only important thing was that we wanted to be together.

When there was nothing left for us to say, my mother spoke up.

"Listen, there is obviously more to this story, and I think we could all benefit from digging in a little deeper. I'm sure we all have questions that need to be answered, but I'd rather not do it here." She turned and looked at Aunt Christy. "I think it would be a good idea for all of us to go back to our house. It's only a couple of hours away. We are all friends," she added with a smile. "It would be nice to spend some time together."

My father and Uncle Anthony started to object when Aunt Christy piped in, "I agree with Ginny. We're old friends, we're adults, and maybe we can hash all of this out. And it would be better to do it in a more familiar environment." She nodded at my father, and I knew she was alluding that he probably shouldn't have ventured so far from home.

I watched my father's face relax, but only a little.

"I'll put on some coffee while you two pack your stuff," Aunt Christy added, addressing me and Christian. "I need caffeine."

"I could use some too," my mother chimed in. She gave me a look that I knew meant she intended to have words with me. "Mimi, I'll drive back to our house with you in your car. Your father can drive his truck, and—"

"No!" Christian and I both shouted at the same time.

"I'll drive Mimi in her car," Christian said, his eyes landing on everyone in the room. "Dad can drive my truck."

"It's not your truck," Uncle Anthony spat. "I'd just as soon leave it here."

Ignoring his father's comments, he gave him a hard stare and said, "Mom can drive whatever car you drove." He then nodded at my parents. "And you two can drive whatever you came in."

"You're in no position to be spouting orders," my father practically growled.

"It's not an order," Christian conceded. "I'm not giving up even a second of the time I have left with Mimi. Besides, I know what all of you are thinking." He looked around the room. "Divide and conquer. It ain't gonna happen. Mimi stays with me."

I watched my father's fists as they clenched at his sides. My mother noticed it too.

"That's fine," my mother quickly added. "But when we get home, we will have alone time with our daughter, just like your parents had the benefit of talking to you without anyone around."

"Yes, ma'am," Christian replied with a curt nod.

"C'mon," I said to Christian. "Let's pack."

He started to walk toward me when I heard my father say under his breath, but loud enough for everyone to hear, "Didn't know you raised such a wuss, Anthony. The boy didn't even know how to defend himself."

Christian stopped and turned to look at my father. "I was only being respectful. I didn't want to get off on the wrong foot by beating the shit out of my father-in-law."

CHAPTER 36

PINE CREEK, NORTH CAROLINA 2007

"Are you okay, Mimi?"

I didn't immediately answer, but sniffled and reached for another tissue. Just like Christian had insisted, we were driving my SUV to my parents' house. I glanced in the sideview mirror, and could tell even from a distance that my father, who was driving behind us, was clenching the steering wheel with a death grip.

"Am I okay?" I replied with a scornful tone. "That depends on which part of the last hour you're asking about."

I saw Christian nod as he watched the road. I reached toward his right cheek and tried to dab at the blood with my tissue. It was slowly seeping below the bandage that was straining against the swelling from the beating my father had given him.

"It really needs stitches," I told him.

"I've had worse," he countered. He took his eyes off the road long enough to give me a regretful glance. "I'm sorry about your friend."

"I am too." I took a deep breath and watched the beautiful scenery that seemed to mock the darkness gripping my heart.

It wasn't too long after Christian's not-so-subtle announcement of our nuptials that I got around to asking my parents how they knew I wasn't at the camp. The heated intensity that our makeshift marriage had incited in all four parents had immediately been squelched when they told me about Josh's death. Out of the corner of my eye I noticed my mother and father as they approached me, but Christian was the closest and he gently tugged me into a hug and steered me toward the bedroom. He closed the door behind us and sat on the bed, pulling me down onto his lap. He stroked my back and hair as I sobbed into his chest.

It had all been too much. Watching my father beat on the man I loved. Seeing the disapproval in our parents' eyes after Christian explained his father-in-law comment. The relief in their expressions that followed when we described our wedding under the stars that wasn't legally binding. And finally, hearing about Josh's death. When the tears subsided and the hiccups commenced, I told him I was ready to pack.

After loading the cars and hitting the road, Christian and I rode in silence for a few miles.

Finally, he broke the silence. "Will you be able to go to the funeral?"

At that moment our phones hit signal range, and Bettina's texts started pinging, painfully confirming what my parents had told me. I slowly shook my head and glanced down at my phone. "No. His mother, who flew in from California as soon as he got sick, is leaving immediately for home and taking Josh with her."

I knew what he was going to ask next, and I already had an answer. "Lucas must not have heard. There's nothing here," I waved my phone in the air, "other than his mushy missing me crap. Listen. I want you to tell me more details about his cheating. I have no problem breaking up with him as soon as I get back to school. But if he gives me a hard time and I have to use it against him, I want proof to substantiate my claims."

"I'll show you the report from the P.I.," he answered evenly.

I thanked him, and returned my gaze to the passing scenery. His next comment startled me.

"I can go back to school with you before I head for Florida," Christian replied gruffly.

"Absolutely not!" I shouted a little louder than I intended. Before he could react, I immediately launched into an explanation that he couldn't fault.

"I have no doubt that if I bring you back to college with me, there will be a scene. We both know it's true. And with your record, and you weren't supposed to leave Florida, and Lucas being a criminal justice major, it's a recipe for disaster."

He couldn't argue with my logic.

"I should be with you," he huffed.

"We have the rest of our lives to be together. And we will be. I can handle Lucas Paine."

He gave me a lopsided grin. "I know you can, baby. But if he does anything, I mean anything..."

"I know, Christian." I smiled reassuringly and patted his arm. "I know what you're capable of. My goal is to never let that happen."

Two hours later, the six of us stood on the main level of my home in Pine Creek, North Carolina.

The air was fraught with tension until Aunt Christy broke the ice by saying, "That was a very long, solitary drive up the mountain. I can see how this kind of isolation works for your situation."

My mother brushed her hand through the top of her hair and admitted, "It gets harder, though. I'm always concerned about tourists who retreat to the mountains to escape the big cities." She blew out a breath and added, "The more people who find our little town, the greater the chance of him being recognized." She nodded toward my father.

"Not gonna happen, Kit," my father confidently reassured her as he draped his massive arm around her shoulders.

She shrugged. "Is anybody hungry? It's almost time for lunch."

My father stepped away from the embrace and answered her with a serious glare. "Our daughter was abducted and you want to feed everybody?"

Before she could answer him, I burst out, "I could've gotten away from Christian, but I didn't because I wanted to stay." I slowly and deliberately made eye contact with all of them, eventually locking eyes with my father.

I didn't give him a chance to reply when it occurred to me that the house was eerily silent. "Where is everybody?" I looked at my mother and waited for her response.

"The twins were already spending the night with cousins. I called on the way back here and asked if they could stay an extra night. Micah is staying with one of his nephews, Jason is hunting with Dave and DJ, and my sister never made it here."

I could tell by my mother's expression that something other than the current situation was bothering her.

"Is Aunt Jodi okay?" I asked, not able to keep the concern out of my tone.

"Let's just say she has an unexpected houseguest and she can't seem to get rid of him," came her exasperated reply.

"Forget Jodi and Blue," my father barked. "Do you know that your husband..." His eyes narrowed at me before he continued, "has been in prison?" He looked around the room and added, "I had a conversation with Bill on the drive back up the mountain."

Ignoring the revelation about my aunt and Blue, I crossed my arms, and addressed my father. "Yes, I know Christian's been in prison, and you should talk! Do you know why he was in prison?"

"No. Bill didn't get to tell me because the call dropped, but it doesn't matter why," my father spat. "He's a criminal, out on parole, and took you against your will."

I'd heard enough. I dropped my hands to my sides, my fists clenching.

"Yeah, Dad, he's a criminal. And so are you and so is Uncle Anthony!"

I didn't give anyone a chance to object when I spat, "Christian put someone in the hospital. You on the other hand have put people in the ground." I looked at Uncle Anthony and back at my father. "Don't try and deny that you two haven't left a wake of missing persons posters and broken lives in your rearview mirrors."

I could see my mother and Aunt Christy in my peripheral vision. They were both trying to contain their shock at my accusations. Denial of the claims wasn't in their expressions because they knew the men they'd married. It was because I was delivering them that led to their surprised faces.

"So what did you do?" Grizz asked Christian, his tone filled with derision.

"Hacked a guy's arm off," came Christian's even reply.

I heard my mother's sharp intake of breath, but I didn't care. I was not going to stand there and let Grizz accuse Christian of bad behavior when our fathers had written the book on it. My father's lip curled. His disapproval was obvious.

"And you cut out a woman's tongue!" I screamed, pointing at Grizz.

I started to walk toward him when I felt Christian grab my wrist. He managed to uncurl my fist with his fingers and enveloped my icy cold hand in his warm one. I felt the tension leaving my body. With a calming breath and a milder tone, I launched into an explanation as to not just the assault Christian had perpetrated against Nick Rosman, but the reason behind it.

When I got to the part describing Nick's original intentions all those years ago, my mother cried out, "Oh, Mimi!"

I wouldn't look at her as I waited for my father's reaction. Aunt Christy and Uncle Anthony hadn't said anything up to this point. I knew they'd kept it from my parents and I wondered if they were concerned about their reaction to finding out.

"You cut off his arm?" My father glared at Christian. "You should've buried him neck-deep in the ground and run over his fucking head with a lawn mower!"

"Grizz!" my mother shouted at the same time I screamed, "Dad!"

Christian let go of my hand and walked toward my father. I cringed when I thought about how painful his already-beaten face would feel if my father launched into another attack. Apparently, he wasn't as concerned as I was.

"I've let you have your say," he calmly said to my father. Tilting his head to the side, he stated, "And I respectfully let you pound on my face." He paused and looked back at me. "For Mimi's sake."

"Let?" Uncle Anthony and my father both asked simultaneously.

Christian peered over at his father. "Yeah, I let him do it. I know you two are still in good shape and you've got experience, but I've got youth and speed." Christian looked back at Grizz and narrowed his eyes. "Know this. I won't just defend myself next time, I'll do damage. After all, I learned from the best." He nodded his head toward Uncle Anthony before adding, "It'll be like fighting yourself thirty years ago. You wanna go up against your younger self?"

I watched my father's expression change from anger and rage to what could only have been described as an iota of admiration, and maybe even some respect. Christian didn't give him a chance to comment when he explained his reason for not killing Nick Rosman.

"Dad also didn't like that I didn't put Nick in the ground," he said, raising his chin. "But it's a different world than when you two were wreaking havoc all over South Florida. There's a camera on every corner. I made the decision not to hide behind my crime. And that bastard will have to live every day of his life with a tangible reminder of what he tried to do to Mimi."

The room got quiet. Our dog, Rocky, got up from his bed and sauntered over to us. He made a show of lazily stretching his legs followed by a wide yawn, and an explosive expulsion of gas.

Aunt Christy burst out laughing. My mother followed suit, but hers was more of an embarrassed giggle as she shooed Rocky toward the doggie door. All three men hadn't cracked a smile, but they also didn't look like they wanted to kill each other so I made my way to the kitchen and started pulling things out of the refrigerator in a lame attempt to break up some of the tension.

In less than ten minutes, the six of us sat around the huge kitchen table that was piled high with a variety of lunch meats, cheeses, breads, condiments, chips, and my mother's homemade potato salad. It was decided that the Bears would stay overnight and drive their rental car back to Florida, stopping in Jacksonville so Christian could exchange trucks with the man with whom he'd traded his. I was relieved when Dad and Uncle Anthony started reminiscing about the past, while Mom and Aunt Christy chatted about the twins. It didn't escape my or Christian's notice that his mother specifically asked after Ruthie and Dillon. Of course, my mother could've told her about them while Christian and I were packing back at the rental house, but something told me that hadn't happened. I knew Christian thought the same thing. I laid my hand on his thigh and gently squeezed. This wasn't the time or place to confront his mother. Besides, we had something else to address and the sooner it was out in the open, the better.

"As soon as we're finished with lunch, I'm going to call Grandpa and ask him about planning a real wedding."

I watched as my dad slowly set his fork full of potato salad down and looked at my mother. The scraping of her chair was loud as she stood up from the table and discarded her napkin. "I'd like to have the benefit of a private talk with Mimi," she announced.

I could feel Christian's eyes on me as I stood and followed my mother into the master bedroom, shutting the door behind us.

She turned around to face me and I could see her carefully measuring her words. "Mimi, you really don't plan on going through with this marriage, do you?"

"Actually, Mom. Yes, I do."

"But you can see how this looks, right? There is no way you and Christian could've fallen in love in less than ten days." She waved her hand through the air. "He has to go back to Florida and you have to go back to school. It's not going to work."

"Are you even interested in why I love him?" When she didn't answer me, I decided to tell her anyway. "In addition to him being my best friend from childhood, he's also the man who insisted on marrying me before he touched me."

She gave me a condescending look. "That wasn't a real marriage, Mimi."

"It was to us," I insisted. "You know what else I love? I love that he's not afraid of Dad and that he let Dad beat the crap out of him when we both know he could've fought back and probably won. I love that we don't have to hide who Dad is because Christian and his family know him already. I love that he's not afraid to admit his weaknesses. And despite how horrific the crime was, and not that I condone it in any way, shape or form, I love that he went to prison for me. For me, Mom!" I beat my hand against my chest. "Just like Dad went to prison for you. Or have you forgotten that?"

"But still, this isn't real, honey. It's what people refer to as the honeymoon phase of a relationship. It's all romantic and enthralling, but it's an illusion. You don't even know each other anymore."

I knew that her words weren't meant to hurt me. They were said kindly and lovingly because she cared. But I also knew my heart. And it belonged to Christian Bear. I nodded as if to agree with her and asked, "Do you know that I've been dealing with an eating disorder since high school?" Her eyes went wide and without letting her answer, I continued, "Christian figured it out after only a couple of days." I saw the hurt behind her eyes and I gently added, "You couldn't have known. I hid it well."

I could see her brain scrambling for a reply when I asked her, "You know I was saving myself for marriage, right?"

She smiled. "Of course I know that. We've talked about you waiting. I guess this means that Lucas hadn't made any advances? He'd been respecting your wishes?"

"He's been screwing my friends behind my back," I replied. There was no hurt or dejection in my voice. I was glad he was giving me a solid reason to dump him. "Do you know that every single guy I dated still tried to get me to sleep with them after they knew I wanted to wait? Every guy except for Christian. When I told him I was a virgin he immediately found my Bible, dragged me out into the freezing night and married me, his way, under the stars. I know by the world's standards, our marriage would seem rushed, out of the ordinary.

What do they call it?" I asked, snapping my fingers to try and think of the right word. "Insta-love. But I say, why wait when you know your heart? I've known I've loved him since we were children."

She tried to skirt around my question by changing the subject. "I guess your upbringing in the church served as a positive influence to help you stick to your—"

I cut her off. "I'd like to think that too, Mom. At least that's what I told myself. I used what Nick almost did to me as an excuse to keep boys at bay. And then I used my faith as a safety net to justify it. But there was always something missing with the guys I dated, so it wasn't difficult for me to not sleep with them. I must've known deep down that I was waiting for someone. And that someone is Christian."

"Okay, so you believe Christian is the one. I understand why you think this, Mimi, but why do you want to rush talking to Micah to make plans for a wedding? I think a year is considered a proper engagement."

"Why would I hesitate when I know something is right?"

"Because," she huffed. "You. Don't. Know. Him. Anymore." She'd said each word slowly and deliberately to make her point, and followed it up with, "You just think you do."

Instead of arguing with her, I smiled. "I've always known Christian, Mom. I just forgot that I did."

"You're not even making sense, Mimi. How did you just forget that you've always known Christian?" She was becoming frustrated, and instead of launching into accusations about how finding my birth certificate had turned my world upside down causing me to cut myself off from the important people in my life, I offered the simplest explanation that made sense.

"It's similar to driving somewhere and before you know it, you arrive at your destination. But you can't remember any of the lights or stop signs in between. That's what it feels like, Mom. I've been driving my entire life toward this moment, and Christian has always been my destination. I know with every fiber of my being I'm supposed to be with him."

Her eyes couldn't betray that she thought I was making the biggest mistake of my life, and I watched her fight against tears that were threatening to spill down her cheeks. "I'm asking for you to take your time with this. Hold off on talking to your grandfather. Go back to school. Gauge your feelings."

I silently relented. I walked toward her and hugged her tightly. I felt the tension seep out of her body when I whispered in her ear, "It's okay, Mom, I'll talk to Christian. We were thinking of asking Grandpa to marry us after I graduate, but maybe we'll use the summer to plan it and get married in the fall."

Her relief was obvious when she exhaled loudly, and a wisp of warm air brushed my neck.

Breaking the hug, I told her that I would let everyone know what we talked about, but not until I talked to Christian privately about it. She smiled and swiped at her eyes.

"I'm so relieved, Mimi," she said, reaching for a tissue on her nightstand. She blew her nose. "Your graduation is right around the corner, and we both know your father would never allow you to marry him that soon."

Never allow? That was the wrong thing to say to me.

When we returned to the group I was happy to see Christian was helping Aunt Christy put the food away while both our fathers seemed to be having a serious conversation by the fireplace.

I felt Christian's eyes on me as my mother and I walked toward the kitchen to help. Minutes later, we all joined my father and Uncle Anthony in the great room and I noticed that both sets of parents were trying not to yawn.

"I know that the four of you probably haven't slept. Why don't you take some cat naps while I take Christian to meet Rachelle and Travis?"

I saw the skepticism in my mother's expression. "What?" I challenged. "You think we're going to take off down the mountain and find a courthouse? I already promised that I wouldn't call Grandpa."

"No. Of course not. I just don't understand..." she began.

"Don't understand that I want my best friend to meet the man I'm going to marry? Look, Mom. It may not happen today, but it's going to happen. I suggest all of you start working on accepting it."

I didn't give anybody time to respond as I grabbed Christian's hand and pulled him out the front door.

CHAPTER 37

PINE CREEK, NORTH CAROLINA 2007

We arrived at Rachelle's house in less than ten minutes. My cousin and best friend looked like she was about to give birth to triplets as she clumsily hugged me and waved us both inside. She waddled toward the couch as she rubbed her back. She wasn't due for three weeks, but I wouldn't have been surprised if she popped out her second baby during the next ten minutes. Her husband and childhood sweetheart must've been in the barn out back because I saw his truck when we pulled up. Their eighteen-month-old, Travis Jr., was napping in his playpen. Without introducing Christian, I jumped right into a quick explanation of what had transpired over the past several days, closing with why both of our faces were purplish, Christian's more so than mine.

"This is the *bass hole*?" she asked, her eyes going wide.

I couldn't contain my grin as I gave Christian a sideways glance and explained, "She's the only other human being who read the letter that was supposedly from you."

He nodded his understanding as I went into even more detail with my cousin. Less than fifteen minutes later her phone rang. "You're spot on," she told me as she made her way to the landline that was perched on the kitchen counter and looked at the caller ID.

"Hi, Aunt Ginny," she answered in her normally bubbly tone. "Uh huh, yep. Sure. Do you want to talk to her?"

I took the phone out of her hand and asked, "What's up, Mom?" I listened to her and followed up with a question. "The big one or small one?" I glanced over at my cousin and asked, "Mom wants to know if she can borrow your deep fryer. Theirs is broken. She wants to fry a turkey for dinner tonight."

Rachelle gave me a knowing smile, and said loud enough for my mother to hear through the phone, "Of course!"

"Yes, Mom. Yes. I'll call you when we're on our way home. Do you want us to stop and get a turkey?"

After I hung up, I looked at my cousin and laughed. "I called that one. I knew she'd be checking to see if I was really here. Notice how she called your landline on purpose?"

There was a knock at the door, and I insisted Rachelle sit down while I answered it.

"Right on time," I said as I swung the door open. Launching myself into his arms and giving him a tight hug, I said, "Thank you for coming, Grandpa."

"TECHNICALLY, tonight is our real wedding night," Christian told me as he pulled me over the console of my SUV and covered my face with kisses. We were heading back to the house, turkey fryer in tow, and had pulled over before turning up our road. "Are you sure they can keep a secret?"

"Absolutely," I assured him. "My grandfather was thrilled that we were making it official. He's an old romantic at heart. And when he drops in later unexpectedly, he'll have on his poker face. They'll think he's seeing us for the first time. They won't have a clue he married us."

"It's a good thing he did," Christian admitted as he pulled back to look in my eyes. "If you hadn't called your grandfather on the way to Rachelle's I would've been tempted to do exactly what you suggested to your mother. Driven you right down to the nearest town with a courthouse."

"Then I guess it's a good thing we have a preacher in the family," I teased. I'd already explained to Christian that I was ready to ask him if we could wait until fall to get married instead of after graduation, when my mother's final comment about my father not allowing it rubbed me the wrong way.

"I doubt we'll be able to sleep in the same room tonight." His tone was serious, and I told him I agreed.

"You're coming back to Florida with me."

Tethered Souls

"I already told you I can't..."

"Yes, you can, Mimi. You have a few days before you have to be back at school and you can miss a couple days too. Drive back to Fort Lauderdale with me and you can fly back up and head directly to school."

I chewed on my lip as I pondered the feasibility.

"Look, baby. I love that you're bold, and I love that you don't take any shit, but I'm insisting on this one. You need to come back to Florida with me. Just for a few days."

I started to see the situation from Christian's perspective. He'd watched me strut my stuff in front of our parents for the last several hours. Not backing down, going behind their backs and involving my grandfather in a clandestine wedding.

"Do you think I've somehow emasculated you by being so aggressive with everyone?"

He laughed. "No, Mimi. I don't feel emasculated because you're a strong and assertive woman. I'm proud of you for it. And last time I looked, my balls were still very much intact."

I gave him a sheepish grin.

"Honestly, they want to explode right now because I want you so damn much." He raised his hips and tugged at the crotch of his jeans. "And I want my wife with me for as long as possible," he said as he returned his butt to the car's leather seat.

I looked around to make sure that no cars were coming down the road. "Unzip your jeans." I was pretty certain I shocked him.

"Are you sure?" he asked me while simultaneously doing as I asked.

"Yeah, but hurry. If someone comes down this street and sees you in my car without me, they'll definitely stop and I don't want to get caught." Christian didn't need convincing as I leaned over and brought my mouth down on his hardness. It was awkward stretching over my console, but his release was quick.

I must've had a strange look on my face because he stopped mid-zip to ask, "Are you okay, Mimi? Are you gonna be sick? You didn't have to swallow it. You could've spit it out."

I knew he was alluding to my inexperience. This was the first time he came in my mouth. Actually, it was the first time anybody came in my mouth. The few times I'd engaged in oral sex with Lucas, he never leaked and always pulled out and came on my face. I guess it was his thing.

"I'm okay. I'm trying to figure out what it tastes like."

"It probably tastes like cum," he laughed.

"Yeah, whatever," I replied. "But there's an aftertaste that reminds me of something."

He was still laughing when he shifted the car into gear and made the left onto our graveled road.

We were talking about whether or not we should try to get his mother alone to ask her about the letter, when it occurred to me.

"Kiwi!" I shouted. "The aftertaste reminds me of kiwi. Not that kiwi tastes like semen," I clarified. "Kiwi has an aftertaste that reminds me of cum and vice versa. Is it just your cum or does all semen taste like that?"

He snorted and asked, "How would I know?" He smiled over at me, and then his face grew serious. "And so we're clear, that is a question you'll never be able to answer."

I knew what he was implying, and I didn't care. I reached for his right hand and held it tightly. I was admiring his profile when I asked, "What are you thinking about?"

He gave me a dazzling smile. "I was just thinking how I'll be insisting you go on my personalized kiwi diet."

CHAPTER 38

PINE CREEK, NORTH CAROLINA 2007

Christian unloaded Rachelle and Travis's deep fryer from the back of my SUV and carried it up to the side porch. We entered through the kitchen door, and walked in on a conversation about The Ghost. Our parents were sitting around the great room, but we could easily hear their voices from the open kitchen. I nodded toward the pot of coffee that had been brewed and asked Christian if he wanted a cup. We carried our mugs in and joined them.

"You said that before Monster died he was catching a lot of shit from his men because they didn't always agree with his rules," my father said to Uncle Anthony. "Maybe there is no Ghost. Isn't it possible that Blue wants everyone to think someone else is calling the shots so when the men don't agree with his decisions he can put the blame on this supposed Ghost?"

"It's plausible," Anthony agreed. "There is one other thing." All eyes cut to him and he said, "Blue, or The Ghost, doesn't seem to protect the gang. He lets them get caught." He leaned forward and rested his elbows on his knees. "We did what we could to protect our guys." He nodded at my father. "I don't see Blue doing that, and I know it's not because he doesn't know how or doesn't want to."

There was no time for further speculation when we were interrupted by my grandfather. "I can't tell you how glad I am to see my best girl's car out front," he announced from the kitchen. We'd been so engrossed in our conversation, nobody heard him come in through the same door Christian and I had used.

My mother jumped up and immediately started making introductions. I could see she was getting nervous about how she would explain our company and Christian's battered face, when my grandfather grabbed my husband's hand and shook it. "Looks like you've been in an accident. Anything else banged up?"

"No, sir," Christian said with a half grin.

Turning to me, my grandfather wrapped his arms around me and asked, "Were you in the same accident?" Pulling back he assessed my face and concluded, "Your bruises don't look as fresh."

I laughed and said, "I had a close encounter with a kayak that was yanked out of the back of a truck."

He kissed my forehead, and made his way around the room, shaking hands with Uncle Anthony and hugging Aunt Christy. I loved how my grandfather never made anyone feel as if they needed to explain or justify themselves. He had the ability to mind his own business and accept unconditionally. He didn't ask how my parents knew the Bears. He didn't ask where they lived and what they were doing in Pine Creek. It was his way. I remembered asking him once why he wasn't more curious about my father's old lifestyle. His answer was a simple question. "Why pry when you can pray?" He'd winked at me. "Nothing good ever comes out of prying, but a whole bushel of good can come out of praying." I couldn't think of anyone I admired more than Micah Hunter.

He captivated our company with lighthearted teasing about watching Grizz raise four-year-old twins. My father wasn't offended in the least and even joined in with some stories of his own about Ruthie and Dillon.

"Believe me, Anthony and I understand—" Aunt Christy started to say when Christian quietly interrupted her.

"Mom, can Mimi and I have a minute with you?"

"Christian, I was talking," she softly said, giving him a stern look.

"Was that Rachelle's turkey fryer I saw on the porch?" my grandfather asked my mother.

The conversation immediately went from middle-aged musings on raising small children to my mother asking my father, grandfather, and Uncle Anthony to get the fryer set up outside. It was our cue to ask Aunt Christy to follow us upstairs for a private chat.

Once upstairs in my bedroom, Christian shut the door behind us.

"What's this all about?" She was smiling. "Grizz said Anthony and Micah can set up the fryer so he can give me a private tour of the hen house. I might like to set something up like that at home. We definitely have the space."

"I'm sure my dad will give you a tour after we talk to you," I answered.

She nodded and gave me an eager smile. I was certain she was expecting us to ask her some motherly advice about our current situation. I watched the corners of her mouth start to turn downward when Christian asked, "What did you do with the letters Mimi sent me?"

She slowly nodded, and softly said, "I shouldn't be surprised that this has come up."

"You don't deny that you got the letters, read them, and obviously didn't show them to me?"

She looked at me, and then Christian. "I thought it was for your own good. And your father agreed with me." Looking back at me she said with a sympathetic smile, "And I was only doing what your mother asked of me. Cutting off contact with your family. I don't need to explain to either of you what was at stake."

"Ignoring them was one thing, Mom. But writing back to her? I still can't believe you did it, but it couldn't have been anyone else."

I could see genuine shock on her face.

"W-write back?" she stammered. "I never wrote back."

Christian gave me a curt nod and I walked toward my bookshelf. I felt their eyes on my back as I sifted through the deep shelves. My old Bible had been buried behind so many other books I wasn't sure if maybe my memory was wrong and I'd actually disposed of it. I spotted the worn binder and pulled it from the shelf. Turning back to them, I looked down as I flipped through the long-abandoned pages and retrieved the piece of notebook paper that had been pressed between them for the past five years.

I gulped as I handed the letter to Christian, not allowing my eyes to meet his. Knowing that he hadn't written the letter hadn't been enough to stave off the reminder of the humiliation and sting the cruel words had inflicted.

I watched his brows furrow in concentration. When he looked up his eyes were blazing with a fury so intense, I half expected fire to shoot out of them.

"I didn't write this, but it's my handwriting!" he spat as he thrust the letter at his mother.

Her eyes widened as she took the note from his hands. I noticed the paper slightly shaking as Aunt Christy read it. She let out a gasp and brought her hand to her chest. "You think I wrote this?" There was a swift but uncomfortable silence. "To Mimi? You think I'm capable of this, Christian?"

"I didn't write it and there is nobody else who could've." He stood over his mother with his arms crossed, glaring down at her.

She looked at me. "I'll admit that I threw all your letters away, Mimi. I'm not denying that." She turned to Christian. "But those three letters went in the shredder. There is no way anybody else, other than your father, could've seen them, let alone replied to them." She shook her head. "I'm at a loss. I don't have an explanation."

"Wait," I interjected. "I sent four letters."

"Four?" Aunt Christy asked, her blues eyes objecting. "No. That can't be right." She shook her head again slightly. "I distinctly remember reading three letters." She looked up at Christian. "You can ask your father. He'll tell you. There were only three."

"Well, if you didn't send Mimi a reply it could only mean that someone else intercepted my mail. And the only people I can think of who would've had access to it is Dad or Slade."

Aunt Christy and I both gasped at the same time.

"Absolutely not, Christian!" she whisper-shouted. "Your father or brother would never write something this horrid to Mimi. Never!"

"I don't want to disagree with you, Aunt Christy," I politely stated. "I want to believe that you didn't write it, but if it wasn't you or them..." I paused trying to articulate my thoughts. "Basically you're looking for someone who not only had access to your mail, but let's face it was someone who knew Christian well enough to emulate his handwriting. I'm not trying to be disrespectful, but it all points to one of you."

I leaned into Christian, as the heartbreak of knowing my new family was capable of something so mean-spirited and hateful weighed heavily on my heart. He pulled me in closer.

"Unless..." Aunt Christy started to say.

"She would've been able to copy my handwriting," Christian growled.

"I can't believe she didn't immediately come to mind," Aunt Christy countered.

"Who?" I practically screamed.

"The woman I'm going to kill," Christian replied in a voice so low and menacing it took my breath away.

CHAPTER 39

FORT LAUDERDALE, FLORIDA 2002

Five Years Earlier

"**H**arder! Faster!" Autumn screamed as she yanked on Christian's long hair and tried to pull his mouth to hers. She squeezed her legs tightly around his waist and locked her ankles.

"Shut up, Autumn," Christian said in a threatening whisper. "Daisy is gonna think something's wrong and come looking for you."

"I don't care," she yelled. "Harder, Christian!"

Christian immediately lifted himself up, reaching behind him and squeezing her ankle hard enough to force her to release him. "You are one stupid loud bitch, you know that?" he said before ripping off the condom and tossing it on the floor. He stood up and stepped into his jeans, pulling them up.

"You didn't think that when I tutored you over spring break," she said in outrage. "If it weren't for me, you wouldn't have graduated."

"So what? You want an award or something?" he asked without looking over at her. He buckled his belt and headed for the bedroom door. He turned around to look at her.

Autumn was a nice-looking girl. Not beautiful, but pretty in a wholesome girl-next-door kind of way. She'd been a transfer student last year, and she'd honed in on Christian almost immediately. When she discovered that she lived in the same neighborhood as him, she'd shown up one day uninvited and introduced herself to Christy. And she was more than happy to offer babysitting services for Daisy.

"I just think you could be a little nicer, Christian. I gave you my virginity. You could at least act like I mean more to you than just a lay. You've only taken me out twice, and you don't even introduce me as your girlfriend," she whined. Her face was getting red as she scooted off his bed and started to get dressed. "And you don't take your time with me. It's all about you getting off."

"I told you from the start, Autumn. You are just a lay. I don't want a girlfriend, and you knew that from day one. And fucking yeah, it's about me getting off. Why would you think it's something more? My mother is paying you to look after Daisy and I know you left her in the den watching TV. Get out of my room and take care of my little sister. You're supposed to be playing with her. Not plopping her down in front of a television set."

"You didn't seem to care about your little sister when you were screwing me!" she yelled, her voice beginning to rise.

"I didn't come looking for you," he said, his hand on the doorknob. "You heard me pull up on my motorcycle, took off your clothes, and jumped in my bed before I even came inside the house. You wanted to get screwed. I screwed you. Now get out."

He waited until she was dressed before he yanked open the door. She held her head up proudly as she started to walk past him. She stopped and turned to look at him. Wrapping her arms around his neck, she pushed herself against his body and cooed, "I didn't mean what I said. I'm sorry. You're right. You were up front with me since the beginning. I guess I'm upset that I didn't get to come. Let me make it up to you."

She tried to kiss him, but he turned his face. He roughly grabbed her by her wrists, disengaging them from around his neck and said, "No, thanks, Autumn. This has gone on longer than it should have. Don't let me find you in my bed again. Ever."

She started to object, but he firmly removed her from his room and kicked the door shut, immediately locking it. He went to his stereo and blasted his music. He dug around in his dresser until he found the hand lotion he kept stashed. He lay back on his bed and unzipped his jeans. Autumn wasn't the only one who didn't get to come. He closed his eyes and fantasized about an innocent stare from smoldering brown eyes and remembered her last words. "No. It's not too late, Christian. Trust me."

AUTUMN HAD TRIED EVERYTHING, even giving Christian her virginity. She smiled when she remembered their first time together. She was certain that he would be rough, but she was surprised at his gentleness. Unfortunately, she misread his tenderness and respect for her first time as feelings for her. He was just being nice then, and she had wanted it to be something so much more than sex. He hadn't taken her on official dates. Not even close. She manipulated it so that it seemed that way, but he hadn't asked her out. Their relationship, or rather lack of one, had been totally fabricated in her own mind. She even tried to make him jealous by sleeping with his best friend, Dustin. That had backfired. Christian didn't care. He even told her he was happy for her.

She took a deep breath and headed back to the den. She suddenly felt the need to distance herself from the house—from Christian—even if just for a short time.

"Daisy, want to walk out to the mailbox with me?" Daisy was almost seven years old and a sweet little girl. Autumn's original intentions hadn't exactly been honorable. She only offered to babysit as a way to get herself immersed in their household. And it had worked. She was certain Mrs. Bear thought of her like a daughter, not just the girl who occasionally stayed with Daisy.

"C'mon," she said, holding out her hand. Daisy jumped off the couch and took it. The Bears lived in a residential neighborhood that offered the homeowners a little more space than most developments. Mr. Bear owned a landscaping company, so their property housed a huge, separate garage, and the house was set back from the road quite a distance. They walked down the long driveway to the mailbox hand in hand.

After returning to the house, Autumn started to toss the mail on the kitchen table when she noticed a letter addressed to Christian. Daisy was busy pulling a chair up to the counter to reach the cookie jar. Autumn took the opportunity to snatch the envelope and shove it in her bag which was hanging on a hook by the kitchen door.

Christian never left his room, and when Mrs. Bear offered to drive her home, Autumn told her she'd rather walk. And she meant it. It would give her time to blow off some of the steam from Christian's rejection and harsh words. She didn't like being ignored. She didn't like being treated like a used-up whore.

She was very curious about the letter addressed to Christian. The need to read it fueled her and she made it home in record time. Letting herself in and ignoring her mother's greeting, she headed straight for her room and locked the door behind her. Kicking off her shoes, she jumped on the bed and pulled the letter out of her bag. She noted the pretty handwriting, obviously female. There was no return address, and the postmark was from some town she didn't recognize in Ohio. She carefully opened it.

Dear Christian,

I guess this will be the last letter you'll be getting from me. I don't know why I'm even bothering since you never replied to the first three. I have two theories. One, I've made a total fool of myself by telling you how I felt. That maybe I read more into our last time together, and these letters are just a nuisance, and you don't want to stay in touch with me. The other theory is that you aren't getting my letters because they're being intercepted by your parents. If this is the case, I'll respectfully ask Aunt Christy or Uncle Anthony to please not do this. If you are getting these letters and not giving them to Christian, please reconsider what you're doing. You might think it's for our own good, but you're wrong.

My mother had the babies. She swore she was the only woman in history that ran well past her due date while carrying twins. We all told her that we think the doctor may have miscalculated. It's probably a combination of both. Anyway, they are beautiful and healthy, and my mom is glowing. She's a little more tired than usual, but it barely shows. She had a boy and a girl. Their names are Dillon and Ruth. They have turned our lives upside down — in a good way.

I feel kind of stupid. Especially since I don't know if you'll even read this. I still check the email address I gave you as often as I can, but I'm wondering if maybe you're just not an email kind of guy. If that's the case, I want to give you a chance to write me a letter. You don't have to worry about it being intercepted on my end. I can guarantee that won't happen. The name and address may seem off, but I promise it'll get to me. Don't put your return address on it.

Ariel Lipman
1322 E. Highland Drive

San Diego, CA 15012

If I don't hear from you, I'll take that as a sign that one of my two thoughts about why you haven't replied to my other letters is true and I won't bother you again. I promise.
I miss you, Christian. I know it doesn't seem like I should since we hardly spent any time together since we were children. Maybe I just miss what my heart thought it saw, or wanted to see, in your eyes that night.
Love,
Mimi

Autumn read the letter three times before she neatly folded it and placed it back in the envelope. She looked up when she heard a motorcycle—it was Christian whizzing by on his Harley. She sprang from her bed, and quickly walked to her window craning her neck to see him round the corner and disappear.

So, Christian had a girl in his life. A girl named Mimi who had moved away and was trying to reconnect with him. One thing was obvious. Mimi was smart. The letter was postmarked in Ohio, yet she provided a California address. The girl was going to extremes to get in touch with Christian without revealing where she lived. Had he received the letters and was ignoring her or was it the other possibility Mimi had suggested? That Christian's parents were intercepting them? Autumn wouldn't know why they would do that, but if that was happening, they probably had their reasons. It didn't matter, though. She thought that Mimi deserved a response, and Autumn decided it was her job to give her one. She had no way of knowing if this Mimi person would recognize Christian's handwriting, but Autumn had tutored him enough to know that she could come pretty close to emulating it. She went to her desk and pulled out a piece of notebook paper. After all, Christian certainly wouldn't be the type of guy to use fancy stationery.

I CHEWED the inside of my cheek raw while I listened as Christian briefly described a girl who used to babysit for Daisy to be around him.

"I can't remember once asking her to bring in the mail, but I know that there were a few times I found it piled on the kitchen table. Up until now, I'd always assumed someone in the family brought it in." Aunt Christy blew out a long breath and ran a frustrated hand through her short blond hair.

"Who could've thought that something so hateful could've resulted from you rejecting a girl?" I exclaimed, nodding toward the letter Aunt Christy was tightly clutching between her fingers. "She must've really had a thing for you," I said to Christian's profile.

Aunt Christy started to say something when there was a light rap at the door and my mother poked her head in.

"I'm sorry for interrupting." She turned her head toward Christian and said, "Your father wants to speak with you. Should I tell him you'll be down soon or..."

I looked at Aunt Christy and watched as she discreetly folded the letter without my mother noticing. Apparently, we'd just made a silent pact that my family didn't need to be privy to our conversation. Christian's expression revealed he concurred. The past was in the past and needed to stay there. I was relieved and felt a wave of love rush over me when I recognized the look on my mother's face. She was feeling left out. She didn't belong outside with the testosterone turkey brigade, and she hadn't been invited upstairs for our private talk. Christian looked like he had more to say when I interjected.

"It's okay, Mom. I think we're done here." I inhaled deeply and the scent of the vanilla bean sachets I kept hidden around my room were oddly comforting. At that moment they felt like lungfuls of happiness.

I hadn't meant to cut our discussion short, but in my mind there was nothing more to be said. Autumn had been a vindictive teenager, and as soon as I got Christian alone I would make sure he knew I didn't want to start our marriage off with him exacting his revenge on her.

Before leaving us, Christian grabbed me softly by my upper arms and looked down into my eyes. "I want to talk more about this later. When we're alone. All right?"

"Is everything okay?" I detected the sincere concern in my mother's voice. She may not have been ready to give her blessing for our relationship, but she was a nurturer at heart.

"It's all good." I nodded at Christian, and repeated, "All good." I smiled and waved him off as my mother stepped into the room as Christian left.

"I guess it's not something I need to know about?" she asked.

"It's not a big deal, Mom. And it's not important anymore. We're all good."

She looked relieved. "I thought maybe you were conspiring to elope or something. You never did make that announcement you promised after you talked to Christian about deciding to wait until fall. You did talk to him, right?"

I didn't get a chance to reply when Aunt Christy said, "No conspiracy here, Ginny. And fall is just as good as summer. It'll be wonderful to have us all together. Especially Abby. She should be part of Mimi and Christian's wedding day. Slade, Daisy, Jason, and the twins, too!"

It was an odd statement, but I thought I caught her drift. I grabbed Aunt Christy's hand, squeezing it tightly. "I'm sure your daughter—" I paused to clarify in case my mother hadn't known or didn't remember, "and Christian's half sister, Abby, will be with us. Like my father, Tommy. They'll both be with us in Spirit."

My mother looked confused. And Aunt Christy, realizing a split second too late that I hadn't known the truth behind the name Abby tattooed on Christian's arm, blurted out, "Not that Abby."

The light behind her eyes started to wane when she recognized her faux pas, but it was already too late to turn back from the truth.

In an almost apologetic voice she said, "I'm talking about Abby, Christian's daughter."

CHAPTER 40

PINE CREEK, NORTH CAROLINA 2007

I was certain I hadn't heard her right. My knees felt like they were getting ready to buckle so I unceremoniously plopped on my bed. My eyes were focused but staring at nothing; I couldn't seem to tear them away from a dark-green candle that rested on my dresser.

I felt the bed sag slightly as Aunt Christy sat next to me and reached for my hand.

"How could he not have told me he has a daughter?" I barely whispered. "I've been with him twenty-four seven for more than a week. I've shared every secret, good and bad."

Aunt Christy squeezed my hand tightly. "I'm sorry, Mimi. I didn't know he hadn't told you about Abby. I should've realized something was off when you didn't react to her mother's name."

I cut my head sharply to the right. Her blue eyes were misty.

"Are you telling me that Autumn is the mother of Christian's child? The same Autumn who wrote that hateful letter?"

"What letter?" This from my mother who was probably more confused than I was.

I looked up at her and shook my head. "I'll tell you later, Mom." So much for keeping that fiasco private.

I stood, freeing Aunt Christy's hand from mine and approached my dresser. With my back to them, I asked, "And Christian's daughter never once came up in any of the conversations the four of you have had since our little reunion?" I turned to glare at both of them.

"No, Abby never came up," my mother admitted, glancing over at

Aunt Christy. "Then again, in defense of the Bears, we were all dealing with what I thought were bigger matters." She leaned against my bookshelf and offered, "Preventing your father from beating the life out of Christian comes to mind."

Aunt Christy stood up and walked toward me. "And we didn't make the drive up the mountain together. We were in separate cars. We'd just gotten up from taking a nap and put that pot of coffee on when you came back from your cousin's."

Sensing I didn't want her to come any closer, she stopped. "And when your grandfather was telling stories about Grizz raising twins at his age, I started to chime in about how Anthony and I had been going through the same thing with Abby, but Christian cut me off."

"Abby lives with you and Uncle Anthony?" I asked, cocking my head to one side.

"We've had legal custody of her since she was six months old," she admitted. "Autumn never wanted a child. She wanted a means to trap Christian. He was sentenced to prison before she gave birth. With him out of the picture, she had no desire to take care of Abby or be a mother."

I looked at the ceiling and clenched my jaw. "Now it all makes sense. Christian gets out of prison, it's time for him to get his daughter back, and he needs a mother for her." I shook my head in disgust. I wanted to muster some anger, but the deep sadness I was feeling smothered it. I'd been a fool.

"No!" Aunt Christy quickly came to Christian's defense. "I'm not saying that he was right to not tell you. I'm not saying that how he's gone about any of this was right. But I am saying you're wrong about the reason why."

I put my hands on my hips and thrust my jaw forward. "And how could you possibly know Christian's reason for not telling me about his daughter?"

"Because I know my son, Mimi. I know that he's ashamed. Not of Abby." She smiled sadly before continuing. "He's ashamed of not being there for her. He's embarrassed that she doesn't know him, and worse yet, she's afraid of him. She literally screams when he's near her."

I didn't have a comeback, but knowing she'd caught my attention, she continued. "Christian doesn't want you to be a mother to the daughter he hasn't been a father to. I'm sure he has big plans to have more children with you. He has loved you for as long as I can remember, Mimi. And I know he hopes that Abby will come around and that you can be a real family, but I can say for certain that he's not using you to make that happen."

My mother stifled a cough and I knew what she was thinking.

"He knows, Mom." I evenly addressed my mother. "I was up front with him about everything. Everything." I slapped my hand against my thigh in exasperation. "And I'm still having a hard time wrapping my head around all of this—that during our soul-baring moments, he failed to mention his daughter!"

"What does Christian know?" Aunt Christy asked, looking from my mother and then back to me.

"I was in a serious accident. I broke my pelvis and lacerated my uterus." I looked at the hardwood floor. "I had to have a hysterectomy. I can't have children, Aunt Christy."

"That's not true, Mimi," my mother interrupted.

I rolled my eyes. "The ovaries are separate from the uterus so they weren't removed. But I don't get periods, and I can't get pregnant or carry a child."

"But you can have your eggs extracted and use a surrogate?" Aunt Christy asked me.

"Yes, but..." I couldn't meet her eyes. "I don't plan on doing that."

"I see," was all she said. I detected a short burst of air and before I knew it, Christian's mother was hugging me. Aunt Christy was so short I could rest my cheek on the top of her head.

She pulled back and looked up at me, her eyes pleading. "Please don't let Abby come between you and Christian." She sighed before continuing. "Please give him a chance to tell you, Mimi. I heard him say before he walked out that he wanted to talk to you more. I'm guessing that's what it's about."

I blinked but didn't answer her.

"Christian has always been a ball of frenzied and misplaced anger." She addressed my mother, admitting, "I'm probably not making a good case in front of his potential future mother-in-law, but please hear me out." Looking back at me, she smiled and continued, "I used to think it stemmed from when he'd been targeted for the color of his skin when he was a child. He got past that. Then I thought he was naturally belligerent, destined to be a born troublemaker. But now I see it's not true at all. Christian is a very passionate soul. He always has been. He's very loyal to those he loves, and I know he loves you, Mimi. Do you know that I cannot remember the last time I saw my son smile before this impromptu gathering? I'm still in shock that he didn't retaliate against your father. You have always had that effect on him. You're like a balm to his soul. He's a different person with you."

"I don't want Christian to be a different person, Aunt Christy. I love Christian the way he is. I don't need or want him to change for me. And most importantly, I don't want him to be someone he's not."

I saw the relief on her face. "That's my point," she said followed by a wide grin. "I think the real Christian has been buried beneath all that other stuff. The real Christian is who I'm seeing when I watch him watching you. It's like his soul is finally being filled up with what's been missing for so many years." She made sure I was listening. "You."

I gave her a half smile and looked over at my mother. I could see the romantic in her was doing battle with her sensible side. She shrugged her shoulders slightly and tilted her head to the side. The complete opposite of her feelings from our earlier conversation, it was her way of telling me to forgive him. That was her belief even though she thought things were progressing too quickly.

Aunt Christy wore a worried expression. "I'll give him a chance to explain, Aunt Christy. If I detect anything other than what you've shared about his reason for not telling me about Abby, I can tell you now this will never work out."

"That's all I ask," she replied.

We all heard my father yell for Aunt Christy. He apparently didn't know where she'd gone. It was our cue to join the others.

As I followed both women down the stairs I was suddenly gripped by fear. I tried to figure out what I found so frightening, and it hit me as soon as my foot found the bottom step.

I was afraid that it had all been a ruse on Christian's part. That he was using me. To what extent? I wasn't sure. To win a misguided bet to marry the infamous Grizz's daughter? To play mommy to his child while he ran around impregnating other women? To make me pay for riding out of his life five years ago?

The myriad of reasons taunted me as I walked like a zombie through our great room, and zeroed in on Christian and my grandfather talking by themselves on the back deck. They spotted me at the same time, and I watched my grandfather prompt Christian to approach me.

Christian opened the slider, headed toward me with a purpose. "Mimi, come here, please. I have to tell you something."

I looked past Christian and caught sight of my father and Aunt Christy walking in the direction of our hen house. I took Christian's hand and led him out the same sliders he'd just walked through. I took him down the deck steps, the opposite direction of the hens.

"You're darn right you have something to tell me," I huffed as I angrily pulled him toward the woods.

CHAPTER 41

PINE CREEK, NORTH CAROLINA 2007

I lay in my bed and stared at the ceiling. It was a full moon, and my bedroom was shrouded in a warm glow. It was well past midnight, and for obvious reasons, sleep had eluded me. I tossed and turned as I relived the conversation I'd had with Christian after finding out that Abby was his daughter, named after the older half sister he'd never known.

My brain battled and raged over him deliberately hiding the truth, followed by sadness as to the reason why. Just like his mother had told me, Christian went into even more detail about Abby's fear of him. He explained how Aunt Christy brought her to see him while he'd been in prison. When she was an infant, he could do nothing but hold her and stare into her beautiful, tiny face as she slept. He'd even been able to give her a bottle, burp her, and change her diaper. As she got older, she would cling to Aunt Christy, screaming at the top of her lungs when Christian had tried to hold her. Christian finally told his mother to stop bringing her. And when Aunt Christy defied him and brought Abby against his wishes, Christian refused to see both of them.

"It's even worse since I got out," he'd explained. "She cries if I'm even in the same room with her, Mimi. I can't figure out why. I look almost identical to my father and she adores him. It's why I moved in with Slade for a while. I could've stayed at my parents' house, but it puts everyone on edge to see her so upset."

"I just don't see why you couldn't tell me when I asked you about the tattoo," I'd replied, thoroughly exasperated. "This looks bad. It looks like you tricked me. And now we're legally married. It's like you trapped me on purpose."

We'd been walking on the property away from the house. Christian stopped and turned me to face him. Taking both my hands, his blue eyes grew serious when he said, "The timing wasn't right, Mimi. It was so early on when you asked about the tattoo, I didn't know where we stood. As we started getting to know each other, telling you about a daughter who hates me didn't feel right. I was going to tell you on the drive to your parents' house—the original visit we'd planned before they all showed up."

"Hey," I'd jumped in, "we made the drive alone up to Pine Creek. There was opportunity."

"A drive that was already weighted by our parents' unannounced visit and you learning that your friend had died."

I'd pulled my hands away from his to cross my arms. I looked around, avoiding his penetrating gaze. I warred with myself, wanting to dredge up some anger for not just the Abby secret, but for the entire situation. I could feel his eyes on me as another thought occurred.

"I still think you should've told me before I had my grandfather marry us. It's legal now. Tell me how that doesn't sound sneaky."

"Mimi," he pleaded.

When I wouldn't look at him, he pulled me to him, wrestling with me until I was forced to look at him.

"Our marriage isn't legal. Not yet."

My eyes flew wide open.

"When you went out to the barn to get Travis to serve as a witness, I asked your grandfather if we could talk alone. We stepped out on the porch and I told him about Abby. I knew how it would look when you found out, and I didn't want you to think exactly what you're thinking. And if you remember correctly, I insisted you come back to Florida for a few days."

I nodded.

"It was so you could meet her. And if you didn't want to stay married it wouldn't have been an issue because I'd asked your grandfather not to file any paperwork to make the marriage binding. You can ask him yourself when we get back to the house."

Later that night I battled insomnia as I stared at the ceiling in my bedroom. An owl hooted somewhere out in the black night, and I rolled over on my side and yanked the covers up around my back. I'd done exactly what Christian had suggested. Upon returning to the house I immediately sought my grandfather, who confirmed everything Christian had told me.

"He said he'd let me know when and if I could file the paperwork. That's when I knew for sure that I was supposed to marry you two. Even with everything you'd told me on the phone, I wasn't certain I'd go through with performing the ceremony. Until then." My grandfather's smile was sweet and comforting.

I was finally on the cusp of sleep when I sensed him. I hadn't heard him come into my room, but I felt him. I had my back to the door and when he snuck under the covers and lay down beside me, his weight caused me to dip, rolling into him. He pulled me close and whispered, "Are you still awake, Kiwi?"

"Don't even with that name," I laughed.

"Couldn't sleep, Dreamy Mimi?" He nipped at my ear.

"Nope." I broke free from his arms and turned over to face him.

"How did Autumn get pregnant if you always used a condom? I remember you told me at the rental house that you always had them with you."

"I've never fu—" He stopped and sighed. "I've never slept with any girl without using one. Ever. I even stopped sleeping with Autumn for a while, but she was persistent. The only thing I can figure is, she whipped one out once or twice, and she had to have sabotaged it. I don't know. Maybe poked pins through the wrapper? Anyway, as you can probably guess, the first thing I insisted on was a DNA test. Abby is definitely mine so that's the only way it could've happened."

"Never went without one? With anyone?" I asked as I burrowed into his warmth, my head tucked beneath his chin.

"Until you, Mimi. You're the only woman that I've not used a rubber with. Maybe deep down inside I wanted you to get pregnant."

He felt the shift in my mood as I tried to pull away, but held me tighter and said, "It doesn't matter. I don't care if we can't have children." He kissed the top of my head before whispering, "I don't need to get you pregnant, Mimi. I just need you."

THE NEXT MORNING passed by in a blur. As we ate a quick breakfast together, Christian announced that I would be going back to Florida with him for a couple of days, and then flying back to North Carolina to retrieve my car before driving back to campus.

I was in my room, looking around for things I might want to take with me, when I sensed my father in the doorway. I turned around and stiffened. Grizz was a huge and imposing man. There was no denying my father was a bully, and although he'd never pressed me into any decisions, his demeanor alone was normally enough to persuade people into compliance.

I raised my chin and crossed my arms. "I'm going. You can't stop me from going."

He gave me a half smile and said, "I know."

He sat on my bed and patted the seat next to him.

"I can't say I understand what an eating disorder is, but what I can say is that I'm sorry if our family secrets and way of life has contributed to it."

Obviously, Mom told him. I wasn't surprised. They told each other everything. I scooched back a tad so I could face him. I hefted my left leg up and leaned on it. "It's not your fault, Dad. It didn't start with you."

"I believe that, Mimi, but I also know that the pressure we've put on you to keep our family secret must've taken a bigger toll than I'd first thought. I never once considered what you've been missing out on because of me."

"Dad, you—"

He held his hand up. "Let me finish."

I gave him an apologetic nod.

"You should've been able to bring college friends home for the weekend. You should've been able to invite us to football games and family activities on campus. Lots of things." He scratched at his chin. "All of that aside, what I'm trying to say and not doing a very good job is that I don't disapprove of Christian."

My eyes went wide at his admission.

"Your mother, who seems to be having second thoughts about her feelings with regard to this, pointed out that I was like Christian, only much worse."

I couldn't argue with that.

"I was livid at how he tricked you. But I also recognized something of myself in him. I've been watching how protective he is of you. It's all about body language, and you may not notice it, but he's like a lion poised to spring if someone so much as looks at you sideways."

"Yeah, he thinks I need him to…" I started to say.

"He's right. I know you're a strong and independent young lady. But I still believe you need someone to be your champion. I can't be. And as Christy pointed out to me, Christian is the perfect man for the job. He knows the lifestyle." He paused and narrowed his eyes. "Christian knows what's at stake."

He was alluding to our big family secret, and I had to agree with him.

"But, all of that aside, she believes he really loves you. Believes he always has. I actually get that. I was always destined to be with your mother. It's something you feel right here." He lightly tapped my heart with his fingers.

"I know, Dad, because I feel it too."

"When I was beating on him…it was anger that might have been a little misdirected. My fury was aimed at more than what he'd done." He let out a sigh and looked at my ceiling. "Mimi, it was the thought of losing you that made me see red."

"Dad, you're not going to lose me."

"Not completely. But when you think about it, I haven't had you in my life for very long. Right after we moved here you got in the car accident. You spent a lot of time in the hospital and the rehab facility. Then you went off to college, and now you'll be graduating and moving to Florida. I feel like I've lost my chance to be a real father to you. And it's my fault. It's one of the highest prices I've paid for my decisions, and one of my biggest regrets. I don't know how to make up for it, but if I could, I would."

I patted his thigh. "The best way you can make up for it is to give my marriage to Christian a chance. To trust me when I tell you I know this is right. And when it's time, walk me down the aisle so I can marry him in our church, with all of our family there."

I saw it in his expression, and I started to blush. Caught.

"Grandpa told you, didn't he?"

"I've played the subterfuge game for too long, sweetheart. I knew something was up. And your grandfather will be on my shitlist for a long time for that."

"You're not mad?" I asked, tilting my head.

"Yeah, I'm mad," he admitted. "But I also get it. If your mother and

I were in your shoes, we'd have done the same thing." He gave me a half grin. "So you can have your wedding whenever you want, and I'll walk you down the aisle and give you away."

"No you won't, Dad." I shook my head and saw what I thought was hurt in his eyes. "You'll never give me away. That implies I'll be gone. You won't be losing a daughter. I know it sounds cliché, but if anything, you'll be gaining a son. And I can only pray that you'll see Christian that way some day."

He pulled me to his side and kissed the top of my head.

"And it goes without saying..." A beat passed. "If I ever suspect that he's so much as touched a hair on your head, disrespected you in any way," he paused, "and that includes fucking around on you. I will..."

"I know what you'll do, Dad."

I shivered with the realization that my father wasn't one to make empty threats, and that he still had the means to make good on them.

Part Two

"Back Where You Belong"
.38 Special

CHAPTER 42

C hristian and I said goodbye to his parents in Atlanta, where they decided to return their rental car and fly home. We continued in the borrowed truck and almost six hours later we stopped in Jacksonville to get Christian's truck and cell phone. We hit Fort Lauderdale about five and a half hours after that, and since it was almost midnight, we checked into a hotel instead of going to Christian's parents' house.

"You said you were staying in Slade's spare room," I'd reminded him as I stretched during our last stop for gas. "Why don't we stay there?"

He stood by the pump and shook his head. "Nah," he smiled, "I can promise there won't be enough privacy for what I plan on doing to you tonight."

He made good on his promise, and we slept in late the following morning. I woke up before he did and watched him sleep. I thought about the fourteen-hour drive including breaks, and how we'd arrived thoroughly exhausted, but filled with excitement at the plans we'd made. We'd called his parents from the road only to find out that Autumn had made a rare appearance and picked Abby up. She told Aunt Christy that she'd be returning her sometime this afternoon.

"What are you thinking about?" came a sleepy voice from beside me.

"How long have you been awake?"

His eyes popped open and he said, "I dunno. Ever since you started moving around?"

"I was wondering how Autumn is going to react to our news," I answered, leaning up on my elbow.

He scoffed.

"And I'm not quite sure what her role is. I mean, your parents have legal custody of Abby, right?" I asked.

"Yeah," was all he said. "But she gets Abby every other weekend from Friday night to Sunday night. The last time she saw her was two months ago. Right before I got out of the joint."

"What's her story? Is she on drugs?" I didn't know why that last question came to mind. I guess I couldn't fathom another reason for her staying away from her daughter for so long. "Does she work? Does she have a boyfriend?" I paused before asking, "Does she still want you?"

He pulled himself into a sitting position. "Since Autumn is my least-favorite subject in the world, I'll be brief. I've never been interested enough to know her story, but I do know a little. Her family made the move to Florida after her parents were in a factory accident that killed her father and put her mother in a wheelchair. I think she loves Abby, but has no interest in motherhood. I don't know why she bothers to see her at all. I've never known her to do drugs, but that doesn't mean she doesn't. I don't know. She got a job right out of high school and makes decent money at a fancy store in the mall—don't ask me to remember which one 'cause I don't know and don't care."

He laced his fingers behind his head and leaned back against the headboard. "I don't know if she has a boyfriend—another don't care topic. And as for still wanting me? Couldn't tell you. Maybe. Probably." He shrugged his shoulders and added, "Autumn is the least of our concerns. She won't warm to you, but she also won't make a scene. She's afraid of me, but more afraid of my parents."

"How is that possible?" I asked incredulously, while scooching up to sit next to him. "Your parents are awesome people."

"My parents let Autumn know how things were going to be after we determined Abby was definitely my child. I never asked them what they told her, but I can promise you, it was enough to keep her from causing drama."

"Maybe it scared her enough into only seeing Abby once in a while," I offered, almost feeling sorry for the girl.

"Don't go there. My parents were fair, and the only reason they got custody of Abby was because Autumn's mother asked them for help.

She's a good lady; she's wheelchair bound. Autumn lived at home and tried to push Abby off on her. The poor woman couldn't handle an infant, and my parents stepped in."

I was relieved. I didn't want to think that Christian's parents were keeping Autumn away from her daughter. Apparently, that had been Autumn's doing. Still, I wasn't going to naively believe that the girl who'd manipulated a pregnancy was going to see me as anything other than public enemy number one.

"She's going to pay for writing that letter to you, Mimi. And don't say it might not have been her. I'll get the truth out of her."

"No!" I shot back. "I can understand if you want to hear the truth from her mouth, but as far as making her pay? It won't be necessary, especially after she finds out we're together. Believe me, that's enough payback for someone like her."

He sighed but didn't respond. Instead, he slowly lowered his eyes to where the duvet had fallen away, exposing my left breast. He reached for me and all talk and thoughts of Autumn evaporated.

We spent what was left of the morning making love. First in the bed, and again in the shower. Afterward, Christian told me he'd booked the room for the duration of my stay.

He took me to brunch at a small restaurant within walking distance to the beach. And it was over our meal that we talked more about the plans we'd discussed on the drive down to Florida. We decided that I would fly down every other weekend until graduation when it didn't interfere with school. We would use the time to visit with his family, especially Abby, although I watched Christian cringe at the prospect. I knew he wasn't looking forward to having me see Abby's reaction to him.

"In our free time, we'll look for a place to live for when you move down permanently," he announced directly.

I raised my coffee cup to my lips and sipped. "Are you sure you want to rent? We can afford to buy something."

He shook his head. "Let's rent for a year, Mimi. It'll give us more than enough time to decide what kind of house we want."

It was a logical suggestion, and I nodded my head as I signaled the waitress for a refill.

"And I still think you can ask my mom to help you find a therapist," he added.

I stiffened at the suggestion. During our long drive we'd only briefly talked about my decision to get help for my eating disorder. If I was going to be honest, I was so happy with our plans, I didn't want to think about it, and tried to convince him that I had it under control. He didn't buy it, and was adamant about me seeing a counselor or at the very least joining a support group.

"I'll find someone. I promise. I'm just not ready to bring your mother into it. Okay?" I pleaded.

He seemed satisfied with my answer. We spent some time driving around and I refamiliarized myself with the layout of the city I hadn't visited in a while. Five years didn't seem like a very long time, but it was long enough for me to notice the changes. There were more people, there was more concrete, and less space. After living in a tiny college town for the past few years, it felt almost claustrophobic.

"We can live further west," he assured me. "It's not as crowded. At least, not yet."

I gave him a smile and turned up the radio. "I love .38 Special," I announced while swaying to the rhythm of "Back Where You Belong."

"It's our song." He pulled into the parking lot of a strip mall.

"The lyrics aren't exactly our story." I laughed.

"Screw the lyrics. I'm only hearing the words 'back where you belong.'" He paused. "You're back with me, so it's definitely our song." He parked the truck and we got out.

"What are we here for?" I asked, looking up and down the cement walkway.

He placed his hand at the small of my back and steered me toward a door. It was a jewelry store. "You'll see."

Once inside, he gestured toward the glass cases and told me, "Pick a ring, Mimi. Any ring you want."

There would obviously be no surprise proposal. We'd already moved past that romantic formality. But Christian was still full of surprises. He patiently waited while I perused every jewelry case. The smartly dressed woman that offered her assistance after we came in the door stayed busy a few counters over, but kept an eye out if I needed her. I found myself wandering back to one display in particular. I hadn't realized she'd walked over. Breaking my focus on the case, she asked, "Is there something specific I can show you?"

I looked back at Christian who was strolling toward me. I pointed to a blue topaz ring set in white gold. The stone was small and simple, but the color reminded me of another ring.

"Ah…" the sales clerk said as her keys jangled against the case. "A beautiful selection. Blue is the rarest topaz, and this particular ring is reasonably priced at just under four thousand dollars."

I was stunned at the cost and couldn't imagine walking around with four thousand dollars on my finger. I felt Christian's breath on my neck.

"Is that the one, Mimi?" His words washed over me like warm honey.

"Yes, it's perfect. But it's too expensive, Christian."

Ignoring me, he told the lady, "You should have something in the back under the name Bear. I was in first thing this morning, and left a deposit with someone named Daphne."

She gave him a wide smile and said, "I was wondering who was going to end up getting that ring. I'll be right back." She locked the case and briskly walked to the back room.

I looked at him, my jaw slack. I had no words. Minutes later I heard the familiar clinking of her keys and turned my head to see her making her way back over to us.

Christian's lips found my right temple as I watched her delicately open a black velvet box. "I love you, Dreamy Mimi," he whispered, his breath wafting over my ear. It was then that I felt the air leave my lungs as I gazed at the most vivid blue stone I'd ever seen. It was similar to the one that had first caught my eye, slightly larger, but not too big for my finger. But that wasn't what caused me to lose my breath. The stone was surrounded in diamonds that sparkled like twinkling stars against a pitch-black sky.

"Try it on," Christian prodded.

I held out my left hand, and tried not to shake. It slid on easily.

"It's a tad loose, but we can have it properly sized and you can come back for it later today," the woman explained.

"Do you like this one, Mimi? If you prefer diamonds, you can try on some of those. I think they might even have some blue ones."

"We do," the sales clerk chimed in.

"N-no," I stammered. "This ring is perfect."

I stifled a gasp when she told him the balance due on his deposit. Without blinking an eye, Christian reached into his back pocket and took out a wad of cash. He fanned the amount due on the counter and told the woman, "It's all here."

She picked up the money and smiled. "I'll be right back to get your proper ring size."

I watched the slight sway of her hips as she approached a man who sat behind a high counter in the back. He stood when she passed him the cash.

"You snuck out this morning when I was asleep." I glanced down at my finger. "And climbed back in bed with me when I didn't even know you'd left. I really do sleep like the dead, don't I?"

His answer was a smile.

"How did you know what ring to have them hold?" I took a deep breath and added, "And how did you know I would love the blue stone?"

He reached for and held my face in both hands, touching his forehead to mine.

"I told you before, Mimi. We're tethered souls, and you're back where you belong. Where you've always belonged."

CHAPTER 43

FORT LAUDERDALE, FLORIDA 2007

We spent a couple of hours driving around neighborhoods to get a feel for where we might want to set up house when I asked Christian for a favor. Twenty minutes later, we were parked across the street from the home where I was raised. My eyes started to mist over when I announced, "I'm glad they're keeping it looking nice, but I don't like the color." I sniffled. "My dad hated brown."

Christian reached across the truck console and grabbed my hand. "I'm having a hard time keeping up with which dad you're referring to."

I could understand his confusion. Grizz was my biological father. Sometimes I referred to him as my father, other times as Dad, and always in private as Grizz. Tommy Dillion was the man who'd raised me, and was technically my stepfather. But I'd only ever called him Dad.

"I'm talking about Tommy," I said softly. "He always thought brown was boring. He was a talented architect, and hated when his clients had their homes or businesses painted brown. He said the color took away from the design. Drabbed it down is what he used to say."

Christian didn't respond, but gave my hand a gentle squeeze to acknowledge he was listening. I swiped at my eyes. "I dream about him a lot. I even fantasize that he's still alive somewhere."

"I was at his funeral all those years ago, Mimi. And so were you."

"And my mom watched Grizz die on the lethal injection table." My phone pinged and I sat up straighter, grateful for the intrusion. "It's the jewelry store."

Christian shifted the truck into drive and we left the neighborhood I'd instantly and secretly vowed to never visit again.

I never considered myself materialistic. I'd be lying if I didn't admit I couldn't stop looking at my finger. I couldn't fathom what I loved more—the color reminded me of Christian's eyes, and the ring he'd given me on a playground in 1990—or that out of all the rings in the jewelry store, I'd zeroed in on the closest match to the one he'd picked out just hours earlier.

We arrived at the Bears' home and I was more than relieved to discover that Autumn had already dropped Abby off. I was warmly greeted by Aunt Christy and Uncle Anthony, and ushered into their sizeable but comfortable great room, only to learn that Abby was napping. Minutes later, Christian and I stood over her bed, and watched her tiny chest rise and fall as she slept peacefully.

"She's even more beautiful in person, Christian," I whispered. He'd shown me pictures on his phone after we'd retrieved it from his friend in Jacksonville, but they didn't do justice to the two-and-half-year-old that slept serenely in her toddler princess bed. She had jet-black hair, just like Christian's. Except it wasn't straight like his. Thick and shiny black ringlets framed her heart-shaped face. She had light skin, and her pink lips were slightly moving as if she was talking in her sleep. Her eyes were closed but I knew they were light brown.

"I think I hear Slade and Daisy," Christian said in a low voice as he clutched my elbow and we walked out of Abby's room. His mother had told us that Slade would be coming for dinner, and she'd asked him to pick up Daisy from her dance class on the way. He'd made an excuse about not having time to stop in, but Aunt Christy was persistent and refused to take no for an answer, only telling him they would be celebrating something important and wanted him to be included.

"I'll be a minute," I told Christian as I made my way to the bathroom. I hadn't seen Slade in years. The memory of the last time we'd been in the same room, the one he was apparently standing in now, had jumped to the forefront of my consciousness. I felt like I needed to freshen up before I faced him. I looked in the bathroom mirror and saw barely perceptible smudges beneath my eyes from my mascara starting to smear. I took a tissue and wiped below each one, and then pinched my cheeks for color. I'd left my purse in the great room so I used my fingers to swipe through and fluff my hair. Satisfied there was nothing else I could do to make myself look more presentable, I headed for the room where the family was gathered.

I could hear twelve-year-old Daisy asking, "What's the surprise, Daddy?"

"It must be that Christian made it back from South Carolina unscathed." I recognized Slade's voice. His tone was sarcastic. "Unless we're not counting what happened to his face."

"Don't be rude," Aunt Christy chided. "This couldn't have turned out better if we'd planned it."

"From what you told me before you took off for South Carolina, he did plan it." Again the bite of Slade's words held bitterness.

I entered the room at the same exact time Slade sighed loudly. "I don't have time for this. I've got plans tonight. What's the big surprise?" he asked.

All eyes turned to me as I gave first Slade, then Daisy a wide smile, and sidled up to Christian.

Daisy looked like she might've remembered me, but I couldn't be certain.

"You remember Mimi, don't you, honey?" Aunt Christy asked.

I tore my eyes away from Daisy's expectant face and was met with Slade's cold stare. Confused, I clutched Christian's arm and returned my focus back to the twelve-year-old who was giving me a toothy grin while admitting, "I kind of remember her."

Sensing the tension, Aunt Christy quickly chimed in, "Daisy, do me a quick favor and check on Abby. I don't think I turned on the baby monitor and I'm pretty sure I didn't put a blanket on her. Can you do those things without waking her up?" She rolled her eyes and said to no one in particular, "Autumn didn't give her a nap. I'll probably have a hard time getting her to sleep tonight."

Daisy nodded, smiling at me as she left the room. I'd barely heard Uncle Anthony speak five words in the past few days, but it was obvious by the tone in his voice that he was not happy with his oldest.

"What's your problem, Slade?" Anthony addressed Slade's despondency.

"Why is she here?" He nodded in my direction.

All eyes turned my way, and in an awkward attempt to sum up the past several days, I did the only thing I could think of. I held up my left hand and displayed my ring while stammering, "We're to...to...together now." I cleared my throat, and looked at Christian, then Slade.

What happened next was so unexpected I couldn't say it even rivaled my father's reaction to seeing my bruised face at the rental house. I think it was an obvious assumption that Christian was going to receive the wrath of Grizz's anger. But this. This was something nobody could've predicted.

A wail resembling a war cry shattered the silence as Slade reached for the nearest object which looked like a tiara. It had been resting on a shelf, and I would later learn that it was made of iron and had been handcrafted by Uncle Anthony in his workshop over twenty-five years earlier. Slade aimed it directly at my husband's head. Christian shifted to the left as it passed by, narrowly missing him, striking a painting on the wall behind us. The piece of art fell to the floor with a loud thud, but it was nothing compared to the sound made by the tiara hitting and cracking the tile floor.

Aunt Christy screamed as Slade charged Christian, trying to ram his head into Christian's stomach. But Slade's anger and speed were no match for Christian's brawn and street sense. Towering over his older brother, Christian shoved him away with a warning.

"Don't make me kick your ass, bro."

Slade answered by taking a swing that Christian easily deflected with his left arm, while simultaneously using his right fist to connect with Slade's cheek.

Uncle Anthony inserted himself between his sons, trying to keep them apart. While taking in huge gulps of air, Slade's voice was almost unrecognizable when he barked, "I've done it the right way. All of it. Graduated high school with my associates degree. Went to college, became a lawyer. I've always respected our family, and the law. And he"—he pointed at Christian—"barely finishes high school, mutilates a guy, gets a girl pregnant, goes to prison, violates his parole, and brings home an innocent woman from his childhood he doesn't deserve?"

I was too stunned to think straight. I looked around the room and saw the same expression on his parents' faces. It was like they were seeing their eldest son for the first time.

"This is what we're celebrating? Christian committed another crime and this time gets rewarded for it? This family is so screwed up!" Slade spat, while swiping the blood from beneath his nose.

Heavy silence hung in the air as we all fumbled for coherent words that didn't come. I glanced at my husband who stood with his hands clenched into fists. His jaw tightened noticeably. I didn't think it could get worse, but I was wrong.

After checking on Abby, Daisy had run to her bedroom to get pictures of her dance recitals to show me. While she was digging out her photo album, the skirmish had woken up little Abby who toddled out to the great room. She made a soft squeak and I turned to see her standing at the hallway entrance. She was clutching a doll to her chest, and her brown eyes landed on me, Christian, and Slade. Uncle Anthony and Aunt Christy were standing off to the side, blocked by the dining room wall and hidden from Abby's view. Abby walked toward Christian, and I almost cried in relief. But it was short-lived. Realizing too late that Christian wasn't her grandfather, she stopped abruptly and let out a blood-curdling scream. Christian bent low and held out a hand to her, but she dropped her doll and ran past him, launching herself at Slade's legs. Tilting her face upward, she reached her tiny hands into the air and said to her uncle, "Uppy. Uppy, Sway."

Slade bent down and picked her up while his eyes shot daggers at Christian.

My heart ached for Christian. He grabbed my hand and, pulling me toward the front door, said, "C'mon, baby. Let's get out of here."

CHAPTER 44

FORT LAUDERDALE, FLORIDA 2007

The silence was heavy as we got in Christian's truck and headed north. I wanted to comfort him, but knew there was nothing I could say that would make him feel better. Still, I had to break the tension if only to let him know I cared.

"I'm sorry," I managed to get out, my voice raspy.

"Don't be," he answered evenly without looking over at me. "I'm not."

"What do you mean you're not? Aren't you upset at Slade's outburst?"

"Nope."

I looked at his profile and didn't recognize any sign of him lying. No tightening of his jaw, no clenching of the steering wheel.

"What about when Abby ran to him instead of you?" I asked before I could stop myself.

"I expected it," came his sound reply. He let out a long breath. "And I wasn't surprised at Slade's reaction either. Maybe taken off guard that he did it in front of you. But no, not surprised."

"Why not?" I looked over and waited for his answer.

He shot me a glance. "Because everything he said was true." Looking back out over the steering wheel, he confessed, "I love my brother and I know he loves me, but we're total opposites. Slade is a methodical planner. I'm sure he's mapped out his entire life down to where he'll vacation every summer with his future wife and kids, and where he'll spend his retirement. He's never understood my compulsiveness. My…uh…not quite sure how to describe it."

"You don't have to," I told him. "I get what you're trying to say. He sees things working out for you when you handle something differently than he would have."

"Exactly," Christian replied. "And he resents it. He would've slowly insinuated himself into your life. He would've wined and dined you, then proposed on bended knee with a traditional diamond ring."

He tapped his fingers on the steering wheel. "And there is nothing wrong with that. I admire my brother, and I hope he finds a good woman. But just because he likes to live a predictable and by-the-book life, doesn't mean he should resent me because I don't. And it's not like I haven't accepted the consequences for my actions."

I knew he was alluding to not being there for his daughter, and the time he'd spent in prison away from her.

"I guess that's part of the problem," I added. "He thinks there should've been consequences for violating your parole and abducting me."

"Yep. And again, he's right, and I'm not mad that he was upset," Christian quickly added. "However, I am mad that he showed his ass in front of you. And he would have in front of Daisy, too, if Mom hadn't sent her off."

I nodded in agreement. Before I realized it we'd arrived at our destination. I couldn't tell where we were because we'd apparently driven down a back alley and were now parked behind a business. What kind of business, I didn't know.

"Where are we?" I asked while scanning around me. I spied two dumpsters to our left, and an unusually large pile of tires to our right.

Christian opened the console between us and started rummaging through it. "Axel's garage."

"Where you work?" I asked as he muttered under his breath while digging for something.

"Yeah."

"What are we doing here?" I asked as I took another look at our surroundings. It was almost spooky. There was one light over the only door to the building, and it made clicking sounds as it flickered on and off.

"Found it." He was holding up a tool. "We're breaking in," he told me after opening his door and jumping out. He looked over at me. "You coming?"

I flung open my door and jumped out of the truck. "Wouldn't miss it."

"DIDN'T KNOW I MARRIED A REBEL," Christian teased as he expertly picked not one, but three locks that opened the back door to the garage.

I stood with my hands on my hips and sardonically asked, "Why do I have a feeling this isn't the first time you've broken in here?"

"Because it isn't." He chuckled, opening the door and flipping on a light before waving me in.

"What are we stealing?" I followed behind him, and looked around for hidden cameras.

He stopped and turned around. "Mimi, do you really think I'd bring you with me to commit a crime?"

I shrugged my shoulders and looked away, embarrassed. I wouldn't let myself think about how quickly and without reservation I'd agreed to accompany him to what I thought was a real break-in. "What are we here for?"

Ten minutes later, I had my arms wrapped around Christian as we sped through the night on his Harley. Apparently, he kept it at Axel's garage, and since he didn't have his own key, he had to break in to get his bike.

We ended up at what appeared to be a trashy biker bar in a not-so-nice part of town. It didn't turn out to be as bad as I thought. The Alibi was actually a decent place inside, and I was grateful the waitresses were wearing shirts. I'd watched Christian shirk off Tina at Chicky's, but I had no clue how he'd react if a woman shoved her breasts in his face. I knew it was acceptable in the biker world, but by now, Christian should know it wasn't acceptable to me. He'd assured me infidelity would never be an issue. Once again I wrestled with how easily I'd assimilated into what I thought was going to be an illegal break-in, followed by my nonchalant acceptance of what at first appeared to be a seedy juke joint, but ended up being a biker hangout.

This wasn't me.

Or was it?

When we'd first arrived I was getting admiring glances from some of the men, and I immediately noticed a change in Christian's demeanor. They noticed it too. It was as if a crackle of electricity swept through the small pub, and all eyes respectfully turned the other way. Without even uttering a syllable, Christian Bear established a boundary that no one dared cross.

I never understood my father's overbearing and aggressive protectiveness of my mother. I'd always thought it was attributed to one of two reasons. The first and most obvious was that Grizz was naturally intimidating and pushy. The second, I surmised, was because he lived in fear of losing my mom again, and would do everything in his power to prevent that from happening.

But in watching my twenty-three-year-old man threaten men twice his age with only a glance, I realized it wasn't either option. Both man and beast instinctively knew not to mess with a grizzly bear cub if its mother was around. And that was the same type of energy Grizz and Christian exuded. The same type of natural panic that one might feel if up against a grizzly. I smiled at the ironic comparison.

We spent the next few hours listening to music, playing pool, drinking beer, and laughing with a few of Christian's friends. Some of the men were wearing leather jackets and the patch was unmistakable —my father's old club. The name and design were different, but I knew who they were based on Christian's explanation.

The women weren't as friendly, but I knew to expect that after hearing some of my mother's old stories about when Grizz had taken her to the motel. I was sipping on my beer, listening to Christian and a bar regular comparing prison stories, when the woman I'd been casually chatting with leaned over and whispered in my ear, "Krystal is harmless. She's had her eye on Christian since before he went to prison. Even made a point of visiting him there."

"Am I being that obvious?" I stared back at the woman sitting next to me. She'd introduced herself as Chili, and I guessed she was in her late forties, maybe early fifties. The bright-red dyed hair that she kept piled on top of her head may have hidden the gray, but it couldn't erase the obvious lines on her face that came with hard living.

"Nah. But I recognize the looks you're trying not to give her."

I took another swig of beer and set it down with a sigh. "Yeah, just like I recognize the looks she's trying not to give Christian."

Chili waved her hand nonchalantly, the bracelets jangling around her wrist. "You've got nothing to worry about. He couldn't care less. Even before he went to prison, and for the short time he's been out, he's never brought a woman here or to any of his other hangouts. You're the first."

She leaned sideways toward me, close enough that our temples touched. "That tells me you'll be the only one." She smelled of cigarettes, beer, and sickly sweet perfume.

I pulled away and gave her a huge smile. Raising my beer, I said, "I'll drink to that." Our bottles clinked, and we both downed the rest of our brew in one long swallow. Chili signaled Krystal to bring another round, when Christian shouted toward the bar, "Krystal, three more."

I looked over at him, surprised that he'd been paying attention. "Chili's right, you know?" he said with a smile. "You're the only one. And you always will be."

Christian didn't even look at Krystal as she delivered our beers, deliberately trying to make small talk to get his attention. When he wouldn't acknowledge her, she bent down between us and whispered loud enough for me to hear, "I have a message for you."

He continued his conversation with the ex-con barfly as if he hadn't heard her. She jabbed at his right shoulder. She raised her voice this time, saying, "Christian, I have a message for you." There was a pause, and I was certain he was purposely ignoring her when she said a little louder, "From Blue."

This got my husband's attention and he finally turned around to her and snapped, "What is it?"

She slapped her tray against her hip and rolled her eyes before answering him. "I can't give it to you here. Meet me in the storeroom."

She walked away with a bounce in her step, and peeked back over her shoulder to see if Christian was following her. He stood up, bent over, and kissed the top of my head, saying, "I'll be right back, baby."

I watched as Krystal disappeared down the hallway that led to the restrooms, and wondered if there really was a message from Blue or if this was a ploy to get my husband alone. Or both. I was getting ready to excuse myself when Chili nudged me with her elbow. "Don't just sit here."

I hadn't planned on it.

"Follow them," she said before returning her eyes to the hallway.

"You read my mind," I answered as I stood so quickly my chair almost fell over.

"Second door on the right past the ladies' room," she said to my back as I strode toward the rear of the bar.

It was easy enough to find the door to the storage room. I stopped long enough to catch my breath, but not long enough to let myself think about what I would find on the other side. I only knew that I would either be beside Christian in our hotel room bed tonight or sitting next to a stranger on the first flight home. I slowly turned the door handle, and prayed there wouldn't be a noise to announce my intrusion. I was able to crack it just enough to go undetected and hear the conversation between Krystal and Christian.

I heard Krystal say, "There is no message, Christian. It was obvious you needed rescuing from that woman you brought here. I've missed you the past couple of weeks. I thought we'd be spending more time together after you got out of prison."

"You thought wrong, Krystal. And I'll never need rescuing from Mimi. She's my wife."

"Your wife?" Krystal was astonished. "You got married?"

"Yeah, I got married." Even though we'd never gotten around to asking Micah to officially file our paperwork, Christian and I still considered ourselves wed.

"Does your wife know I've blown you every time you've stepped foot in this bar?"

I heard him scoff before saying, "Mimi knows that I've been with other women. She also knows I won't be anymore."

"Just because you're married doesn't mean we have to stop doing what we were doing," she cooed.

I heard her heels clicking against the aged floor and could only assume she was approaching my husband.

I held my breath as I waited for Christian's response. He didn't give one, and my heart sank at what was about to happen. Then I heard Krystal give a small cry, "You're hurting me, Christian. Let go of my wrists."

"Keep your fucking hands off me and I won't have to hurt them, Krystal."

"Fuck you!" she cried.

I'd heard enough. I quietly closed the door. Not knowing if I would be caught walking away, I ducked into the ladies' room. I was splashing cold water on my face when the door behind me opened. I looked up and saw Krystal's reflection in the mirror. She was rubbing one of her wrists. She gave me a dirty look and said, "Your husband is an asshole."

Tossing the paper towel in the garbage, I swung the door open, and gave her a wide smile. "Consider yourself permanently relieved of blow job duty, Krystal." I tilted my head to one side. "At least where my husband is concerned."

I didn't give her time for a retort as I let the door close behind me. When I returned to the table, Christian stood up and pulled out my chair.

"I ran into your friend in the restroom," I said as I took my seat.

"She's not my friend," he answered.

"What was the message that was so important?" I batted my eyelashes innocently.

"There was no message, and I'll tell you about it later, Mimi."

After that, Krystal avoided our table. The rest of the evening passed without incident.

Later in our hotel room, I was sitting on the bed cross-legged when Christian asked, "What are you doing?"

He'd just come out of the bathroom after showering and drying off. At the moment, he was standing in front of me completely nude and stuffing a Q-tip in his ear.

I couldn't help but laugh. Returning to the object of my attention, I said, "I'm looking at my ring. I still can't believe you picked it out."

He tossed the used cotton swab in the trash and crawled up the bed toward me, hovering over me until he had my back pressed against the pillow behind me.

"Believe it, Mimi," he said before giving me a long, lingering kiss. He made his way down my body, removing my clothes as he went.

Later, wrapped in his arms, I ran my fingers against his chest. I asked him to tell me about the conversation with Krystal.

And he did. He told me word for word everything that was said in the storeroom.

"I know," I confessed without looking at him. "I followed you. I was listening." I held my breath and waited for his reply.

"Good," was all he said before tilting my chin up. Our eyes locked and he said, "I'm glad you were listening, Mimi. At least you know I'm telling you the truth."

I asked why he would take me to a bar where I was bound to run into a woman he'd obviously been screwing around with. His answer made sense.

"Krystal is a whore and nothing more. I never thought twice about what it would look like to you. I've told you before, I've never had a girlfriend, let alone a wife. I'm sorry if it made you feel bad."

I waved him off and told him I had no problem handling Krystal. But something else occurred to me. "You also said that you had to stay away from the motorcycle club as a condition of your parole. I saw men in there that I know are from that gang. They wore patches." I leaned up on my elbow and looked down at him.

"I was having a beer with my wife and some friends. Some of the men you met tonight are mechanics at Axel's garage and have nothing to do with the club. I can't say who is going to be at what bar or if they have any gang affiliation. I wouldn't be in violation unless I was caught at an official meeting or a crime scene with them."

He picked up my hand and kissed it. "I won't deliberately risk screwing this up, Mimi. I've waited too long to be with you."

I must've had a worried expression on my face because he added, "It's why I purposely chose The Alibi, and didn't even think about Krystal."

"Because it's not a known hangout?" I asked.

"No," he corrected. "It's because it lives up to its name."

I didn't understand, so he went on to explain that the owner of The Alibi was an ex-biker named Ken who'd served time in prison, and had no intention of ever going back. He established the bar as a neutral zone for people like Christian who were out and had conditions to their parole. "The police can raid The Alibi any time they want. They might find ex-cons or people who regularly engage in criminal activity, but they won't find anything illegal going on there. No prostitution, no drugs, no gambling, and specifically, no cameras."

"What's so important about no cameras?" I asked with a suspicious tone.

He laughed. "It's kind of how the bar originally got its name. Back when Ken first opened it, people that were committing crimes started saying they had an alibi if they were caught. All they had to do was tell the police they were at Ken's bar, and he always verified it for them, whether it was true or not. Ken proved his loyalty to his biker buddies without participating in any way. They're very serious about protecting him so they help enforce the 'no illegal activity' rule. Without surveillance cameras, the police don't have a way to dispute someone's alibi."

"I saw two men fighting in the parking lot when we were leaving," I informed him.

"There will always be bar fights. Two guys even died there. But it was their own doing, and not tied to anything illegal. I won't take you back there if it makes you feel uncomfortable."

"I didn't feel uncomfortable." If anything, I felt a little too comfortable, and my brain was trying to process why. I wondered if it was because I was with Christian. Or something else.

Christian mistook my silence as I mulled things over for something else.

"I'll have Krystal fired," he told me.

"No!" I shouted. In a calmer voice, I told him, "I don't want the girl to lose her job because of me. I'm not threatened at all by her, Christian, and if I was, I'd handle her on my own."

My answer seemed to satisfy him. I reached over and turned off the light. I was exhausted and on the brink of sleep when he said, "I forgot to tell you that Chili thought you looked familiar."

"What?" I popped up. The room was dark and I couldn't see his face.

"Yeah," he commented. "She said you looked familiar, but she couldn't place you. I think she was around during the old days when Grizz had that motel out on State Road 84. I'm pretty sure if they hadn't changed up the club patch with your mother's likeness on the jackets, she'd have guessed who you were."

"What jacket with my mother's likeness?" I asked.

"Axel has an old one in his garage. I'll show you when I take the bike back and get my truck."

CHAPTER 45

FORT LAUDERDALE, FLORIDA 2007

I stared, slack-jawed as Christian held up the old biker jacket he'd retrieved from the bottom drawer of a metal filing cabinet. It was Sunday morning, and after breaking back in to return his motorcycle to the garage, I followed him into the office.

I held my hand over my mouth, stunned at the image staring back at me. I had no doubt I was looking at a reflection of my mother that was at least thirty years old. Below the club name was a skull with horns, wearing a sinister smile. A naked woman, who I knew to be my mother, was draped seductively across the top of the skull, its horns hiding her private areas. The woman had brown hair, big dark eyes, and was wearing a choker with a peace sign.

"She still has that peace choker." My voice was barely a whisper.

"If you had bangs, you'd be a dead ringer. I can't believe you've never seen one of these."

He folded it and returned it to the drawer.

"I can't believe it either," I confessed. "And believe me when I tell you I did some snooping when I was younger. Then again, Bill has done a great job burying Grizz's past, and it's not like either father kept one hanging in the closet."

I would later find out from my mom that my brother Jason had seen the jacket years ago, but had never mentioned it. Still reeling at the discovery of the image that used to terrorize South Florida so many years ago, I wasn't sure what bothered me more. That my sweet and loving mother's likeness had been the living illustration for brutality, or that it didn't bother me as much as it should have.

I silently wrestled with that thought as I followed Christian out the back door and asked him, "Does Axel know how vulnerable his garage is? Maybe your motorcycle is safer parked on the street than in a garage that can be so easily broken in to."

"Nobody messes with Axel's garage. They know better," Christian told me as he opened the truck door and watched me climb in.

Before we'd left our hotel room and exchanged the bike back for his truck, Christian and I had a long phone conversation with his parents, and decided to give a family gathering another try.

We arrived at their house shortly after leaving the garage. and I noticed a motorcycle parked in their driveway. When we got inside I was introduced to Jonas and Lucy Brooks. They seemed like a lovely couple, but as mismatched as a sumo wrestler and a kitten. She was a tall, thin woman with extremely pale skin, and straight brown hair that brushed the top of her shoulders. Her thick glasses couldn't hide the intelligence that shone in her eyes. She barely uttered two words when we were introduced. He was the exact opposite. Huge and boisterous, Jonas Brooks grabbed me and hugged me like he'd known me all my life. He told me that he didn't go by Jonas, and that I should call him Brooks. He reminded me of a Sasquatch. He was gigantic, and had a thick head of brown unruly hair and a beard down the front of his chest. He had some facial tattoos that could best be described as alarming.

"Lucy and Jonas live in Naples and were over here visiting their son, Isaac," Aunt Christy explained. "He moved here a couple of years ago. He's just a little older than Christian." She nodded at Christian and turned to address Lucy. "You need to call Isaac and invite him over here."

"Oh no, Christy," Lucy softly said. "We're not staying. We just dropped in to say a quick hello. Besides, you have good news to celebrate." She nodded toward my left hand, then looked up and gave me a sweet smile. "It's a family affair."

"All of you are family," Aunt Christy said, taking both of Lucy's hands and squeezing tightly.

After a few more minutes of gentle prodding, and Aunt Christy getting nowhere, we waved goodbye as Jonas and Lucy climbed on their Harley and sped off, the loud pipes reverberating off the asphalt.

"They seem like a lovely couple," I commented as I followed Christian and his parents back into their home. "I guess they're bikers?"

"Oh yeah," Aunt Christy laughed as she signaled me to follow her into the kitchen. "And you'd never guess it, right? She's a distinguished scientist with the CDC."

"Really?" I couldn't hide my surprise.

"She cures diseases for a living, and he owns a bait shop. Isaac is good friends with Christian. I guess you haven't had a chance to meet him yet?"

Shaking my head I told her, "No. Pretty sure I haven't met someone named Isaac." I cocked my head to the side and said, "For such an odd couple, they sure seem happy."

Aunt Christy reached into the refrigerator and pulled out a bowl. Setting it on the counter, she said, "They are, but they got off to a rocky start."

"How so?"

"It's a long story, and as you can probably imagine, she resisted him at first." She paused and blew out a breath while pouring ingredients into the bowl. "Jonas used to ride with Anthony's crew. He was with us one time when I ran into Lucy at a restaurant." She shot me a quick glance and said, "I went to high school with her and her twin brother, Lenny. I hadn't known then that Jonas already knew Lucy, but she didn't remember him." She swiped her arm across her forehead before continuing. "Apparently she'd made an impression on him. He did what Christian did to you. Abducted her. He tricked Lucy and took her to a cabin in the Everglades. No modern plumbing or electricity." Aunt Christy shuddered. "For weeks. It might've even been a month."

"Oh no!" I interrupted. "Did he? Did he?" I couldn't find my voice.

"Take advantage of her? Sexually assault her?" she asked.

I could only nod.

She gave me a long, slow smile. "No. He didn't do either of those things."

My eyes widened as I waited in anticipation to hear what Jonas Brooks could have possibly done to that sweet, mild-mannered woman.

"He kept her only long enough for her to teach him how to read."

I could've been knocked over with a feather.

Aunt Christy didn't elaborate further so I began to share the details about Christian's secret visit to the jeweler yesterday morning. A few moments later we heard voices coming from the great room.

"That must be Slade," Aunt Christy stated. "Listen, Daisy has Abby out back." She nodded toward the tall glass windows in the breakfast nook. I peered closer and could see the two girls sitting in a huge sandbox. Daisy was obviously too big for a sandbox, but I could see she was thoroughly enjoying keeping her niece entertained. As if reading my thoughts, Aunt Christy added, "Daisy is Abby's favorite person in the whole world. I was hoping maybe you could go out back and try and start over with Abby before Daisy brings her inside?"

She didn't need to ask me twice. I found my way to the glass doors, and before heading out turned and asked, "So, do you think you'll set up a hen house?"

"A what?" she asked as she dried her hands on a dishtowel.

"My father showed you our hen house. Are you still thinking about getting some birds?"

"Oh." She laughed. "No. I don't think they're my cup of tea."

After shutting the door behind me, I cautiously headed toward the girls. Daisy immediately jumped up and came at me for a hug. "I'm sorry you didn't get to see my photo album yesterday," she shyly admitted. I hugged her and noticed Abby watching us.

"I am too," I answered sincerely.

"Listen, Daisy," I whispered. "Do you think you can introduce me to Abby before we go inside? I'm afraid I didn't make a very good impression yesterday."

"Mom told me Slade started it. It wasn't your fault, Mimi. It wasn't Chrissy's either."

"Chrissy?" I asked. "You mean Christian?"

"Yeah, Christian," she answered with a mischievous smile.

An introduction to Abby wasn't necessary because she'd wandered over to us. She was grinning, trying to hand me a shovel.

I squatted so I was eye level with her. "Do you want me to dig with you?"

She looked at Daisy who gave her a smiling nod. Abby took my hand and led me back to her sandbox, where I sat and played with her while Daisy perched on the edge.

Abby babbled while I chatted with Daisy, and before too long something occurred to me. It was obvious that Abby trusted me because Daisy did. Could it be something so simple? I dared to hope.

"Daisy, do you know where Christian's been for the past three years?"

"I'm twelve, Mimi, not two," she said with a smirk.

"Of course," I told her. "I'm sorry. I still remember you when you were six. It's hard for me to wrap my head around you being a teenager soon." I scooped a shovelful of sand in the bucket. "Did you ever visit him there?"

"A couple of times. Mom took me, but I cried for days afterward. It made me too sad to see Chrissy in jail." She shrugged her shoulders.

"I understand. I wouldn't want to see him there either." I hoped I'd never have to.

"Has he visited here a lot since he's been out?" I swirled my finger in the sand.

"Not really. Mom told me that he stopped coming because it upset Abby so much."

"Did Christian visit when you were here with Abby?" I asked, my heart getting optimistic.

She slowly shook her head. "I think he only came by a few times when I was at school." Her eyes got wide with excitement when she added, "He did pick me up at the bus stop twice to take me to McDonald's." She rolled her eyes. "My girlfriends all crush on him. It's gross!" She made a face like she was gagging.

I choked back a laugh. "And when he dropped you at home?"

"He didn't. Both times, Daddy met us and brought me home."

"So, what I'm hearing is that Abby hasn't seen you with your brother?"

She shook her head slowly. "No. I guess not."

"Daisy, I have an idea. Do you mind doing a little experiment with me?"

After stomping off all the sand, the three of us found Aunt Christy in the kitchen. Abby ran to her grandmother who picked her up and held her over the sink so she could wash her hands. I explained our plan, and I could see the light of hope in Aunt Christy's eyes.

The idea was for me and Aunt Christy to lead Abby into the living room where Daisy would be hugging on her brother.

"Do it up good, Daisy," her mother prodded.

"I know how to love on Chrissy," she replied with a roll of her eyes as she left the room.

I peeked around the dining room wall and saw Uncle Anthony sitting in a chair absorbed in something on his phone. A petite and attractive brunette was sitting on the edge of the couch, smiling up at

Daisy who was clinging to Christian. Daisy had her arms wrapped around his waist while he stood talking to Slade. I noticed that Christian affectionately rubbed his hand up and down Daisy's side while she clung to him. Slade was standing to Christian's right, nodding at something Christian was saying. It was obvious they'd buried the hatchet during the time I'd spent out back with the girls. I was relieved.

"Who's the woman?" I quietly asked Aunt Christy.

"Her name's Erin," she whispered back as we walked toward the living room, with Abby between us and tightly holding our hands. "We've never met her before."

We hadn't been noticed yet, but we both smiled triumphantly at each other over Abby's head as we watched her eyeing Daisy. She seemed startled at first to see Daisy hugging on Christian, but she looked more confused than upset.

Erin stood when she noticed us. Introductions were made and Abby still hadn't moved toward Daisy or Christian, but she also hadn't cried or run away. It was a start.

"Are you Slade's girlfriend?" Daisy innocently asked, a little too loudly.

"Uh, no," Erin started to say.

"She's a close friend," Slade interjected. He looked uncomfortable with the admission and stammered. "She's more than a friend, really."

We watched Erin shake her head and smile. "We're very good friends. That's all."

The highlights in her bobbed hair shimmered, and her freckled nose crinkled when she smiled. I immediately realized what was going on. They were sleeping together, and Slade was being a gentleman. He didn't want his family to think he'd brought his side piece. An older one at that. Instinct told me Erin wasn't trampy. I smiled warmly and extended my right hand, still clutching Abby's with my left.

I made small talk with Erin and Aunt Christy, while Christian shared some of our future plans with Slade. Daisy continued to hug Christian's side while trying to get Abby to walk toward her. Even though I was listening to Erin and Aunt Christy, I kept glancing down at Abby for her reaction. She looked hesitant, but not afraid.

"I think this is going to work," I whispered toward Aunt Christy, my heart hopeful.

I'd spoken too soon.

Aunt Christy had asked Erin how long her and Slade had been friends and wanted to know if there was any chance they were more than that. I tried not to smile. It was so obvious Aunt Christy was digging for information on Slade's love life, I was almost embarrassed for him.

Erin's face grew serious, and she leaned toward us so the men wouldn't hear her.

"We really are just friends. I'm his emotional support right now while he tries to mend a broken heart."

Unfortunately, Christian had kept an ear tuned to our conversation, and assumed the worst. He thought that Slade's outburst the day before wasn't because of the reasons we'd originally assumed.

The little bit of progress we thought we'd made with Abby immediately dissolved when Christian grabbed Slade by the collar of his shirt, and angrily accused him of harboring feelings for me.

We were back to square one.

"I CAN'T UNDERSTAND why you would think Slade has feelings for me." I blew out an exasperated breath. "It looked like we were making progress with Abby."

We were driving back to our hotel, and I was grateful that the day had been salvaged, but frustrated that we'd have to start over with Abby. She still wouldn't go near Christian, but continued to keep a curious eye on Daisy who'd made it a point to show her brother even more affection, especially after he'd grabbed Slade. At least there was a chance.

He shrugged nonchalantly and said, "I heard that woman…"

"Erin," I interrupted.

"Whatever," he said. "I heard Erin say she was only there to help him get over a broken heart. It made me think that his outburst yesterday had more to do with you than me getting away with all my shit."

I sighed, exasperatedly. "I'm glad it didn't go any further than you grabbing him. And he handled it better than I would've expected. Especially with such an embarrassing admission. I know Erin never intended for anyone other than me and your mother to hear her comment. She seems like she cares about him."

Ignoring my observation, Christian glanced over at me. "I told you before, Mimi. I'm hotheaded. Some would even say a monster."

I reached for his hand and said to his profile, "I know what a monster is, Christian. You don't even come close."

"I hope I don't prove you wrong, baby."

"It doesn't matter if you do," I told him.

"You're not what I expected, Mimi." "Street of Dreams" by Rainbow was playing on the radio and he pulled his hand away from mine to turn it down.

"How so?" I blew at a lock of hair that had fallen from my ponytail into my face.

"You're not as much of a goody two-shoes as I originally thought. It wouldn't matter to me anyway. It's just the background check the P.I. did on you didn't bring up any flags that would make me think you were anything other than a straight-laced honor student."

I could understand his comment. "I'm not a party girl, I take my classes seriously, and I've purposely stayed away from anything that could've brought unwanted attention to me or my family. And let's not forget I was dating a criminal justice major." Yeah, I could see why he thought that. "I don't know," I admitted while turning my head away and looking out the passenger window. "Maybe I was too careful because of Grizz." When Christian didn't reply I added, "I didn't want to do anything that would bring notice to myself and potentially bring notice to him." I glanced at him. "But I guess I always felt like I missed out somewhat. I feel so free with you, Christian. I feel like I can be myself."

"I wouldn't want you to be anything else, Mimi."

I reached to turn up the radio when his next question stunned me.

"Do you like Grizz?"

"Why would you ask me that?" I was incredulous.

"You seem to enjoy challenging him." He raised his eyebrows as he drove. "I still wonder if you would've asked Micah to secretly marry us if your mother hadn't told you Grizz would've forbidden it."

"Oh, that!" I huffed. "Yeah, I like Grizz. I love him. But I guess there's something in me that doesn't like seeing him get his way all the time." I pondered for a moment. "I guess it's no better than Slade being ticked that you abducted me and got away with it."

He laughed. "It does seem that way." He turned thoughtful when he asked, "Do you think Grizz was mad that you had Micah perform a ceremony at Rachelle's house?"

"Yeah, he told me he was," I admitted. "But when he was talking to me, I knew he was making an effort to not let it show. I recognized what was simmering behind his eyes. But he held it back."

"Why do you think he held back?"

"Because he thinks he owes me, and as weird as it sounds, this is his way of paying me back." I looked over at him. "By giving you—us—a chance."

"And he won't tell your mother what you did? What you asked Micah to do, even though it's not yet official?" Christian cussed under his breath when he caught a red light.

I nodded. "I asked him not to, and I think he'll honor my request."

"Request? Or test?"

"It might be a test," I confessed somewhat sheepishly.

He shook his head with a smile. "My Dreamy Mimi is a tough chick. I mean, c'mon, the man gave the cemeteries in South Florida more business than they needed, and here you are challenging and testing him."

"Does that bother you?" I teased.

"Bother me? Nope," he said, pulling into the hotel parking lot. "It gives me a raging boner."

CHAPTER 46

FORT LAUDERDALE, FLORIDA 2007

I had one day left with Christian before I had to fly to North Carolina to retrieve my car and head back to school. Ideally, I would've spent it in bed with him, but when I woke up the next morning, reality started to sink in, and he immediately detected a shift in my mood. I didn't get a monthly period, but because I still had my ovaries I was subject to the same hormonal mood swings that most females dealt with. But something inside told me it wasn't hormones. This was all me.

We'd just finished the big breakfast he'd pre-ordered from room service the night before. Instead of making love, I slunk off to the bathroom while he made a phone call to his parole officer. It was the first time I hadn't invited him to shower with me, and after finishing his conversation and giving it more thought, he barged into the bathroom, his eyes more concerned than accusing.

I'd just turned off the shower and pulled the curtain back. When I realized why he'd rushed in, I told him, "I would've locked the door if I was purging."

He gave me a half grin before getting serious. "What's going on, Mimi?"

I shrugged my shoulders, dried myself, and bent over to wrap my hair in a towel. When I stood up, he'd walked toward me and said, "You can tell me."

I pulled one of his clean shirts over my head, struggling to get the towel through the neck opening. He helped me and when our eyes met, he asked, "Is it Lucas? Are you worried about having to go back and deal with him?"

"Lucas," I scoffed. "I can handle Lucas."

"What is it, baby?"

"I'm torn, Christian," I told him. I thought I saw a myriad of emotions flickering in his eyes. Concern, worry, anger. Love.

I skirted around him and left the bathroom. I could feel him behind me. Once I got to the adjoining room, I flopped down on the small sofa, crossed my legs, and looked up at him.

"I can't remember the last time I was so happy," I confessed.

He smiled, his relief obvious. "Torn over what then?"

I took a deep breath. "That it's all an illusion." I remembered my mother's words about the honeymoon phase of a relationship. They haunted me. "That I'll go back to school and you'll go back to work, and we'll get so caught up in real life that this will seem like a dream." I looked away, not wanting to meet his eyes.

"Has it all been just a dream for you, Mimi?" he asked, his voice calmer than I'd expected.

"Yes, but the best dream I've ever had, Christian. I don't know how you and I will handle real life. All we've done together is make love, ride the motorcycle, spend time with our families, and shoot some pool at The Alibi. And it's been the best time of my life."

"Are you thinking that after you graduate and so-called real life kicks in, we won't have anything in common? Nothing to keep us anchored?"

I shrugged my shoulders and looked at him sadly. "I don't want to think that, but it's a possibility." I didn't want to tell him that other than the things I'd mentioned, I was wondering what kinds of activities we would do together. It was as if he was reading my mind.

"What kinds of things did you do with Lucas?"

"Studied, went out to eat, went to the movies. I would go to his games."

"Mimi, I'm sure we'll go out to eat and to the movies." He gave me a crooked smile before adding, "I highly doubt I'll ever have an occasion to study with you." He paused and his brows furrowed. "But I'd shovel shit for the rest of my life if I knew that when I got home at night, you'd be there. Even if you wanted to sit on the couch and watch TV, that would be good enough for me. I want to be with you, no matter what we're doing." He gave a thoughtful pause before adding, "Or not doing. My love for you isn't based on a list of things we do or don't have in common."

"You're right," I told him. "I feel the same way. I'm just over-thinking."

He sat next to me, and made me extend my legs so he could drape them over his lap. I leaned back against the arm of the sofa and watched as he caressed my thigh. He gave me a serious look and said, "Say them."

"Say what?" I asked, not sure what he was talking about.

"Our vows," he answered softly. "We've said them to each other every night since we stayed at the rental house. Say them again this morning."

I smiled at him, and a love so intense filled my chest, it warmed my blood. Christian had insisted on repeating our spur-of-the moment vows every single day, and now I knew why. At first, I had a hard time remembering them, but he had a memory like an elephant, and helped me fill in the blanks. "You have to go first," I prompted. "You always go first."

After the last words, tears swelled in my eyes, and one formed, overflowing and trickling down my left cheek. Sitting with my legs across his lap, lost in the depths of his soulful blue eyes, the words caused a physical reaction in my chest. The same feeling I'd had on the deck that night when we'd first recited them. Knowing that our impromptu oaths hadn't been rehearsed, but came straight from our hearts that night in the snow, only validated them further. Warmed by the memory, I knew once again where I belonged, and any doubt or conflicted emotions I thought I'd had no longer existed.

"Thank you for reminding me," I said before bringing his hand to my mouth and kissing his rough knuckles.

"I'll always remind you," he said with a smile.

He casually removed my legs from his lap and stood up. "C'mon," he said, extending his hand.

"Where are we going?" I asked.

"Not to a study session," he said with a smirk.

"You can't hurt me, Mimi. Harder!" Christian yelled as I did my best to punch the heck out of the pads he'd strapped around his forearms and was holding up in front of me.

"I'm not used to having gloves on. It feels weird," I whined.

We were in the back room of a gym run by one of Christian's friends. I'd rolled my eyes when we'd first pulled up. I'd confessed to him early on that I was not a fan of exercise, so I'd hoped maybe we were there so he could lift weights, something that had never interested me either. Of course, I wouldn't mind watching him pump iron. Me? I'd rather lie naked in a bed of fire ants.

I went at him with everything I had, but it still wasn't enough. He continued to push me until I was on the brink of exhaustion, my shirt saturated with sweat. I slowed down attempting to catch my breath. He knew I needed to rest and stopped prompting me for a minute.

When I got my second wind, he suggested, "Think about something or someone who makes you mad. It'll give you a reason to come at me, Mimi."

Left jab. Right cross. *Thump-thump!* I didn't know what I was doing but at least he'd told me what the hits were called.

"You're not focusing," he barked. "Aim for the middle of the pads."

Left. Right. *Whack-whack!* I started to like the strong thudding sound my gloves were making.

"C'mon, Mimi. Who or what pisses you off the most?"

Left. Right. Getting faster.

"Ed does." My voice came out hoarse.

Left and right in more rapid succession.

"What did this Ed do to make you mad?" he goaded.

When I didn't answer, Christian probed further. "Did Ed steal your lunch money when you were a kid? Tease you in high school? Run you off the road?"

"He says horrible things to me," I panted.

Christian broke my rhythm by grabbing both my wrists.

"Who the fuck is Ed?" he asked through clenched teeth.

Pulling my arms from his grasp, I took a step back and rested my hands on my hips. "Ed isn't a real person. It's what I call my eating disorder."

He nodded, and after readjusting the pads on his forearms, held them up. "You wanna beat the fuck out of Ed?"

"More than anything."

I saw the challenge in his eyes. "Let's go. Don't stop."

Left. Right.

"Your arms are getting tired. Push through it, Mimi."

Left and right. Hitting harder.

"Why do you hate Ed so much?" he pushed.

Left and right. Harder.

"Because of the things he says to me and how it makes me feel," I sputtered.

"Keep going. You're doing great."

Jab and a cross.

"What does Ed say to you, baby?"

"He says I'm weak." It came out in a squeak.

"What else does he tell you?"

"He says I'm ugly." It was barely a whisper. I was utterly breathless and already spent.

Jab and a cross.

"He tells me I'm a failure," I huffed.

"Pretend I'm Ed, Mimi. Give me your best. Hit me anywhere."

"If you were really Ed I'd hit you below the belt. Like he hits me." My voice was a low growl.

"If you hit me where you want to hit Ed, you lessen your chance of us making love again before you leave tonight."

He was right so I went for his jaw, but he dodged me easily.

"You need to channel the anger, Mimi," he said with a lazy smile. "Or you're wasting your energy."

I bent over and placed both gloved hands on my knees, gasping for breath. I looked up at him sideways and said, "You're purposely... trying to rile me. Trying...to make me mad."

"Yep. Doesn't it feel good?" he asked, as he bent and placed his hand on my back.

"Doesn't what feel good?" I stood up straight and leaned backwards, trying to stretch.

"Using all that energy to beat the shit out of Ed and let him know he's not gonna win this fight or any fight with you?" he said as he stood up straight.

I smiled as I wheezed. "Yeah...it kinda does."

CHAPTER 47

SOUTH CAROLINA 2007

I slowly unpacked my bags and looked around my dorm. It was the first time I wished I had an apartment off campus. An apartment with a huge bathtub so I could soak my aching muscles. A reminder of the workout I'd done with Christian just yesterday appeared when I woke up at my parents' house this morning. It was almost midnight by the time Jason and Micah picked me up at the airport last night, and drove me home to get my car. I could've made the couple of hour drive to school then, but because I'd missed the chance to give the twins their birthday gifts, I decided to get a good night's sleep and leave for campus first thing in the morning.

I was awakened at six thirty by two rowdy four-year-old children climbing on my body, causing more agony than they'd intended. They knew what it took to rouse me from sleep, and enjoyed interrupting my dreams a little too much.

My brain craved coffee while my body screamed for a pain reliever. My father seemed unusually quiet as we sat down at the breakfast table. A short while later, Ruthie and Dillon opened the gifts I'd brought them. After fussing over their new toys, they each took one of my hands and led me downstairs to their bedrooms in the basement to show me the rest of their presents.

I hadn't realized how much I'd missed them. I was caught off guard when another face popped into my head. It was heart-shaped and framed with black curls—Abby. How was it possible to love a child I barely knew? To miss her as much as I missed her father?

My oohing and aahing over all of their birthday treasures made the

twins happy, but my inevitable drive back to campus loomed. I reluctantly headed back upstairs and saw that my mother had already
cleaned up after breakfast.

"Where's Dad?" I asked.

"He's checking your car—under the hood, tire pressure. You know
your father. He wants to make sure everything looks good before you
drive back to school."

I nodded my understanding.

After pouring us both a second cup of coffee, we took advantage of
the kids staying busy downstairs, and sat in rockers that faced the
huge glass sliders. I told her all about my visit to Florida as we looked
out at the spectacular mountain view. I could still see concern in her
eyes, but there was no judgment or worry.

"I saw Dad's old club jacket," I said without any prompting. We
hadn't been talking about motorcycle clubs or gangs. It bubbled up
out of nowhere. She gave me a small smile, a faraway look in her
eyes.

"Jason saw it once a long time ago. I'm surprised he never said
anything. I guess he forgot about it," she confessed.

"What did you do with it? Does Dad still have it?"

She shook her head. "Your father..." She paused to clarify before
continuing, "Tommy told me he would take care of it. I don't have a
clue what he did with it."

I brought the mug to my lips. "You still have that peace choker."

She placed her hand to her neck. Even though the choker wasn't
there, the memory obviously was.

"Was life back then so horrible?" I questioned.

"Truthfully?" she asked.

"Yeah, Mom, Truthfully," I shot back.

"Yes. For some it was an awful way of life. Especially for the
women who were trapped because of their addictions. It's not a life I
would wish for anyone."

Her eyes filled with warning. I knew her sentiments were directed
at me. Just as Uncle Anthony's comments about Blue not protecting
his gang members had been a harsh warning for Christian. What did
they think we were? Ten years old?

Her face softened when she said, "But for me, no. I had everything.
Your father was respected, and because of that I wanted for nothing."
Her voice turned wistful as she looked back at the view. "I was loved

and provided for." She sighed. "My biggest problem back then was thinking it was my job to change him."

She used both hands to bring her mug to her lips. After taking a sip, she said, "And you know he's still the same person he was back then. Yes, he's definitely made changes for the positive. But deep down inside, he's still the man who had me abducted when I was a teen."

I knew what he'd done to Myrtle Blye's grandson-in-law, Tom Deems. I also knew he hadn't totally behaved himself since then. I could only nod.

"If that's the way it is with you and Christian, Mimi, you need to accept it now. You won't be able to change him. If you're looking for a chance to do that, you need to face the truth now instead of later."

I knew what she was trying to tell me. All the years she'd wasted worrying about Dad, trying to look the other way, pretending things didn't happen while convincing herself that her positive influence would make him a better person, had all been for naught. Yes, he definitely was a better person now. There was no denying that. But he was still the same person.

"That's where you and I are different, Mom." I reached over, placing my hand on her arm. "I'm not looking for a chance to change Christian."

She gave me a questioning stare.

"I just want a chance to love him."

Now, standing alone in my dorm room, I was faced with the reality of how dull and colorless my life had been. How had I lived for four years in the same room and never once thought to hang up a poster, throw a bright pillow on my bed or put a couple of potted plants on my shelves?

I looked at the one framed picture on my nightstand. Lucas had been looking at me, while I smiled for the camera. To the casual observer, they would have no doubt they were seeing a man in love. I knew better. Outward appearances were so deceiving. Scoffing, I grabbed the picture, and tossed the entire thing—tainted frame and all —in the garbage can. It landed with a loud thunk that resounded off the empty walls.

I picked up my bag and slung it on the bed. Even my bedspread screamed boring. I robotically sat down on the soft mattress and suppressed a groan. It seemed my body was almost in as much pain as my heart. I couldn't believe how badly I already missed Christian. He'd driven me to the airport less then twenty-four hours prior, but there was an emptiness in my chest that seemed to echo off my ribs.

I realized then that other than a quick reply from him after I'd texted to let him know I'd landed, I hadn't heard from him. I'd texted again as soon as I'd woken up, and again before I'd said goodbye to my family and left for school. He hadn't replied.

I reached for my phone at the exact moment it pinged with an incoming text from Christian. "Sry baby didnt charge phone and didnt no it died."

I smiled and started to send a reply when a second one came through.

"Imissu"

I started to text him back and thought, screw this...I want to hear his voice. My phone rang before I could complete the thought.

His voice was like medicine to my aching heart. As I listened to him, I lounged on my boring bed with its bland colors and felt sunshine returning to my world.

I told him that I'd stayed the night at my parents' instead of driving to campus, and how the twins woke me up by pouncing on me. I shared that I'd never realized before how depressing I found my dorm room, and that it already felt like an eternity until my graduation. He told me that today was his first day back at work, and he'd already gone head-to-head with Axel over his work assignment. Christian preferred to work on the bikes in the back, but Axel needed him to work on the cars. I could hear the trepidation in his voice when he told me he was going to his parents' tonight for dinner, and was going to make another attempt at getting close to Abby.

I reminded him to take small steps with her, and he reminded me to pull off the Band-Aid when it came to Lucas. I didn't need the reminder. Lucas had returned to campus two days ago and had started calling me to find out when I'd be arriving. I'd ignored his calls and sent a text that said I would talk to him sometime today.

A knock at the door interrupted our conversation. Before I could say goodbye to Christian, I heard a soft feminine voice ask, "Mimi, are you back? Are you in there? I saw your car."

It was Tiffany. A so-called friend from two rooms down. We shared two classes, and apparently, my soon-to-be ex-boyfriend. She was one of the girls highlighted in the report from Christian's detective. It said that Tiffany was known to have regular trysts with Lucas. I should probably thank her.

I told Christian I had to go.

He told me he loved me. I said, "I love you too," at the same time I opened the door. Tiffany's fake smile became an immediate frown. Did she think I was talking to Lucas and was jealous?

"Was that Lucas?" she asked after composing herself and pasting on another smile. I didn't answer fast enough because she quickly added, "We were wondering when you would be back. Classes started two days ago."

I didn't invite her in, but leaned against the doorjamb, my arms crossed. "Yeah, school officially started two days ago, but I don't have a class until today."

"Oh, right," was all she said. Her eyes widened and she asked, "Is something wrong? Are you okay?"

I gave her a steady look. "Things couldn't be better, Tiffany."

Without warning, Lucas peeked his head around the doorframe. Neither of us had seen him coming.

I saw her pout when Lucas shoved her aside and rushed at me through my dorm door. He pulled me into a hug, and started rambling about how much he'd missed me.

I pulled away, giving him a tight smile. Without looking at Tiffany, I said, "I need a few minutes alone with Lucas."

He realized something was wrong.

I watched as Tiffany flounced back to her room. Lucas stepped further into my room and started to shut the door when I held out my hand to stop it from closing.

"This won't take long," I assured him. I intended to take the high road, and not bring up his indiscretions. For starters, I would've broken it off anyway, but I didn't see any reason to let it get nasty by throwing the other girls in his face. Still, I had no intention of apologizing for breaking up with him.

"What's going on, Mimi?" His eyes were warm, concerned.

Bleh.

"There's no easy way to do this, so I'm going to go with honesty." I was being sincere, and he saw it on my face.

He squinted his eyes, and tried to reach for my hand. "Honest about what?"

I brushed his hand away and stuck mine in my pockets. "I ran into a childhood friend during break. We rekindled our relationship. It's serious." I wasn't going to share any details about what happened. Breaking up with Lucas was going to be enough fodder for the gossip whores. I didn't want to throw Christian in the mix. "I'm with him now, Lucas." I gave him a level look. "I'm not trying to hurt your feelings, but I think we both know this"—I waved a hand between us —"could never have worked."

I watched his expression go from one of shock, to surprise, to anger in less than five seconds.

"You're dumping me?" His anger was striking and evident.

"I'm breaking off what wasn't meant to be." I'd let my guard down, thinking this would be a civil conversation. But he slammed the door shut before I could stop him. He stalked toward me, and was only inches from my face when he asked, "Is this a joke, Mimi?"

I refused to step back. I crossed my arms, and looked him square in the eyes. "I'm sure Tiffany will help you get over it." So much for taking the high road. "And Tessa. And Blakely. Should I go on?" I'd been shocked at how much the P.I. had uncovered in such a short time, but Christian explained how the compensation had been commensurate with the quick turnaround he had required of the man.

Lucas turned his back on me and walked toward the bed. I could tell by the rise of his shoulders he was taking deep breaths, trying to calm himself.

"You know…I was going to propose to you on graduation night." He spun back around, and stood with his hands clenched tightly at his sides. "I figured it would be the one and only time I'd get to meet your family. I was going to ask your father's permission first, and then get down on my knee when I accepted my diploma on the stage."

I was more shocked he had the audacity to ignore my accusation of infidelity than that he'd intended to propose. I didn't bother to comment that a proposal was ludicrous since we weren't in love, or that he wouldn't have met my father that night anyway.

"You're not going to deny you've been screwing around behind my back?" I threw at him.

"Of course I screwed around. I wasn't getting it from you!" he spat.

His eyes were pleading as he started to walk toward me, saying, "I would never cheat on you after we were married, Mimi. Never."

I immediately recalled a conversation I'd had with Christian. It was what I referred to as deal breakers in a relationship. I had three, and one of them was infidelity. I wondered if Lucas would violate the other two. I didn't have to wait long.

I shook my head. "You cheated, Lucas. And that's cause enough to break up with you. But the truth is, I don't care because I'm with someone else now. I have no hard feelings. I want only good things for you."

"You fucking bitch!" Spit flew from his mouth as he ranted. "Who is the asshole? I'm going to kill him."

I had to stifle a laugh. The thought of Lucas messing up Christian was absurd, but I didn't want my amusement to show. The last thing I wanted to do was give Lucas, or anyone at school, details about Christian.

When I didn't answer right away, he got closer. "You're lying," he sneered. "There is no other guy."

I shrugged my shoulders. "Believe what you want." I skirted around him and opened the door. Gesturing with my hand toward the hallway, I said, "It doesn't have to be like this, Lucas. We can still be civil."

"You've been a prick tease for months, Mimi. This is going to be anything but civil." The contempt in his gaze stopped me short, but I regained my composure. "You've made me look like a fool."

"And screwing around behind my back with my so-called friends hasn't made me look like a fool?" Not that I cared.

He ignored my question, narrowed his eyes, and shot me an angry look. "No one would blame me. You give the worst blow jobs ever!"

This did make me laugh. "Yeah," I agreed with him. "I've been told." Christian hadn't worried about my pride when he eagerly gave me pointers on how to improve my technique. "But I've gotten a lot better," I snidely said. I got all mushy inside thinking about the next time I would be able to use my skills on Christian. My last comment didn't go unnoticed by Lucas.

He was already out the door, and spun around to face me. "You're gonna be sorry, Mimi." His voice was low and threatening.

"I'm already sorry I wasted my time on you," I scoffed. "Goodbye, Lucas."

I shut the door in his face, plopped down on my bed and sent Christian a text. "Lucas. It's done. All good."

There was no way I would go into detail with Christian about Lucas's reaction. In addition to cheating, Lucas had violated another one of my deal breakers. I could never be with a man who verbally abused me. I'd heard every imaginable form of profanity come out of Grizz's mouth, but not once, not once was it ever directed at my mother. And they'd had their share of heated arguments and disagreements. He'd never called her a bitch or any other names. He never told her to fuck off or go fuck herself. He never disrespected her verbally. Not once. And last, but in no way least, I would never be with a man who raised a hand to me. If I'd shared the things Lucas had said, and the threat that followed, I had no doubt I'd be causing Christian to violate his parole, and get hauled back to prison. Besides, I wasn't afraid of Lucas. I saw him as nothing more than a mean girl with a penis.

I mechanically unpacked my bag, and stopped short when I caught sight of what was at the bottom. Carefully removing my Bible, I sat down on the bed, clutching it to my chest. "I'm so sorry, Father," I said out loud.

In a quiet voice, I poured out my heart.

"You answered a prayer that had been buried in my heart for years. You brought true love back into my life, and allowed me to unburden my soul with secrets that have been weighing on me forever. And my way of thanking You was to deny my vow of celibacy that night at the rental house without a second thought. It was Christian, who probably hasn't stepped foot in a church since he was a kid, who respected You that night, by insisting on a wedding under Your splendor. Not me." I let out a long sigh before adding, "And I've probably used more colorful language in the last two weeks than I have in years. I know it hurts Your ears. I'll do my best to reel it in."

I leaned back against my pillows, and thought about how easily I'd gotten caught up in the world and had too easily forgotten about the Word. Christian had even offered to take me to church Sunday morning, and I'd brushed him off. I quietly perused the pages and settled on Scriptures that always brought me comfort. I fell asleep with my Bible on my chest, and peace in my soul.

CHAPTER 48

SOUTH CAROLINA 2007

W hen I'd woken up from that nap almost two weeks ago, I'd immediately made my airplane reservations. Not for that coming weekend, but the following one.

I threw myself into concentrating on my classes. I shared with the few friends I still trusted about Camp Keowee's closing and running into my childhood friend. They seemed genuinely happy for me when I showed them my ring. I saw two of them exchange quick glances, and I knew what they were thinking. I instantly resented them, and did my best to avoid them after that.

I was so over people, my parents and Christian's family included, for judging how quickly we'd fallen in love. What none of them realized or understood was that our love for each other had always been there, and was inevitable. Not one person had walked in our shoes. Therefore, not one person had a right to judge our relationship.

I stuck with the three friends who were genuinely happy for me. Sandy, Jeanie, and Marilyn now sat in my dorm room for a late-night study session that included pizza and gabbing. We'd met in Sandy's room last time, and it was my turn to host.

"I still think you should've reported Lucas, Mimi. The campus police aren't going to do anything, but maybe the real police should know." This comment came from Jeanie who was with me when I discovered my tires had been slashed a few days ago.

I shook my head. "I can't prove it was Lucas who cut my tires."

"It had to be him," Sandy chimed in. "Ever since you broke up with him, he's been harassing you."

"What'd I miss?" Marilyn asked with a mouthful of pizza.

"Lucas has been hassling Mimi," Sandy answered. "He's slipped her threatening notes."

"And just yesterday, someone spray-painted 'Mimi is a whore' on the back side of the library." Jeanie reached for another slice and added, "It could only be him or one of his lame friends."

"And to make matters worse," Sandy continued, "he has some kind of protection. One of his criminal justice cronies must know somebody with campus security because"—she used air quotes to finish her sentence—"'unfortunately, our cameras didn't pick up anything.'"

It was all true and I knew Lucas was behind it. This was the first time the four of us had been together to talk about it. However, I couldn't tell my friends the reason I'd avoided contacting the real authorities was because I didn't know if the police would call my parents. If that happened, certainly Christian would find out. Not good. I'd even lied on the report filed by my vehicle assistance program, telling the man who changed two of my tires, "I don't want my parents to worry because I'm engaged in a battle with mean girls. Would you say that I hit a deep pothole that blew out two tires?" He'd agreed.

"Something needs to be done about this," Marilyn said between bites. "He can't keep doing this for the rest of the school year."

I nodded my agreement. "Or maybe his wrath will just fizzle out." What I hadn't shared was that if it didn't, I would take some counter-measures of my own. I didn't want to get into a battle with Lucas, but I would if he didn't back down. I would sleep on it, and make a decision about the best way to proceed.

Our conversation was interrupted by my cell phone pinging. I reached for it and saw it was from Daisy. I wondered why she was texting me so late? I couldn't stop the smile that lit up my face. My heart melted at the picture that came through with a text that said, "I took this tonight."

"Let us see," Jeanie piped in, as I reluctantly handed her my phone. I could've stared at the photo all night and immediately knew it would become my screen saver. It was a candid shot of Christian and Abby. She was leaned back against his body, and they were both looking at a book that Christian was obviously reading to her.

"I can't even," Jeanie sighed while placing a hand on her chest. "He looks so hot in glasses."

Tethered Souls

"I didn't know he wore glasses." Sandy swiped the phone out of Jeanie's hand. "And I still think she is the most beautiful child I've ever seen."

Christian's baby steps with Abby had turned into huge elephant strides thanks to Daisy. He'd made a point of having dinner with his family almost every night since I'd left, and it was paying off. The only time Abby seemed to waver was when given a choice between her father or grandfather, and we'd speculated maybe that had something to do with her fear of Christian in the beginning. Maybe her little mind couldn't wrap itself around seeing the two of them, who bore such striking resemblances to each other, but were obviously two different men. Maybe confusion had added to her prior reluctance to be anywhere near Christian.

I stared dreamily into space while my three friends oohed and aahed over Christian and Abby. Because they'd so warmly and excitedly received the news of my engagement, I'd let my carefully guarded walls down and shared more about Christian and his daughter. They knew I'd be moving to Florida, and that Christian was a mechanic and had a daughter from a previous relationship—if you could call it that. I trusted them to keep these details private. I would miss Sandy, Jeanie, and Marilyn, but promised myself and them that I would stay in touch after graduation.

A couple of days later, I met Sandy for lunch before heading to my one o'clock class. I found my seat and was taking out my books when I realized I didn't have my phone. I sighed when I remembered leaving it on my bed. I had two more classes before I could go back to my dorm and text Christian. I noticed then that there seemed to be a subtle buzz of activity around me. I slowly scanned the room and saw a couple of people talking to each other in whispers while shooting looks my way. At the same time, Tiffany plopped down in the empty seat on my right, and leaned toward me, her eyes blazing with excitement.

"Have you heard, Mimi?" she huffed, her breath coming in quick waves.

After I broke up with Lucas, Tiffany made quick work of trying to take my place. His coldhearted rebuff was all over campus. I felt sorry for the girl, and even though I hadn't invited her into my fold, I didn't have the heart to be mean to her.

"Heard what?" I cast a wary glance around the room.

"Your ex is in some deep shit," came a masculine voice from behind me.

I turned around and made eye contact with Rob, a nice guy who'd borrowed my notes in the past.

"Lucas, three of his criminal justice friends, and a guy who works for the campus police are all in hot water." Tiffany didn't give me a chance to reply when she named the three friends, who I'd known, and the guy from the campus police, who I'd never heard of. "They've been caught cheating. Apparently, their campus police friend helped them get the answers to their midterms for all of their classes. Lucas and his friends cheated on every single exam. It resulted in their immediate expulsion, and the guy who works for the campus police was fired. It's all over school." Her eyes were as wide as saucers. "They think a teacher may have even helped them, and that there might be more students involved too. Isn't it crazy?" I could see the satisfaction in her expression, and I had to agree. I'd been praying for an easy resolution to my situation with Lucas. I'd battled retaliating, and had truly wanted to come up with a solution that would just make him go away. I looked heavenward and whispered, "Thank you."

"And to think I felt sorry for the guy when I heard yesterday that his car had been stolen," Rob chimed in over my shoulder.

I leaned back in my seat and tried to suppress a smile. Something about karma and her unavoidable bitchiness sprang to mind, but I didn't voice it. Instead, I silently thanked God for answered prayers.

CHAPTER 49

I t was my wedding day. Not the one under the stars and snow at the rental house during my spring break. And not the secret one at my cousin Rachelle's house almost a week later. It was the wedding I'd spent the last few months planning. The one where my father would be walking me down the aisle. The one where Christian would be standing at the altar, waiting for me to say our vows with our closest family and friends in attendance. Of course, all of them with a few exceptions, didn't know that we'd already been married— twice. We chose to go through with this formality for several reasons, the first and most important being that we wanted to have a ceremony where our loved ones could take part. I'd had my grandfather hold off on filing the paperwork for our hasty nuptials at Rachelle's house. It made sense, and was a lot easier to just fill in the details using today's date.

Rachelle didn't object when I asked Daisy to be my maid of honor. Besides, Rachelle had asked if she could play the piano during the ceremony. Slade was Christian's best man, Jason was an usher, and Ruthie and Dillon would each hold one of Abby's hands as the three of them walked down the aisle.

I stood and walked to the full-length mirror. I was alone in the bridal waiting room at our little church. I was told the mirror had been installed back in the seventies to accommodate brides, as was the small couch that sat adjacent to the church secretary's desk. The sofa showcased a loud floral pattern that had seen better days. Then again, it was over forty years old. I wondered how many brides had sat on it.

I looked at my reflection in the mirror. My silk gown was simple, with a round neck and long sleeves. It was summer in the mountains, but the air was cool. The sleeves were made of a thin sheer material that was overlayed with a pattern of intricate lace. I had my hair pulled back and gathered at the nape of my neck. One of my cousins had braided an elaborate design through my thick brown locks, weaving in baby's breath and pearls since I'd opted not to wear a veil. The only jewelry that adorned my body was my silver cross necklace, pearl drop earrings that had been a wedding gift from my husband, and a gaudy blue synthetic stone that hung from a silver chain and rested between my breasts and against the white silk of my gown.

I liked what I saw in the mirror, but was angry with myself for what I'd done to make sure the dress wouldn't be too tight on my wedding day. For as many times as Christian had taken me to the gym to do battle with Ed, I'd allowed my eating disorder to win when it came to my wedding gown.

I still had some time to myself so I glided over to the worn sofa, picked up my bouquet, carefully sat down, and reflected on the last few months.

Though not physically draining, thinking about all that I'd managed to accomplish was mentally exhausting. Prior to graduating, I'd spent two long weekends each month in Florida with Christian where we'd found a lovely home to rent with an option to buy. It was a three-bedroom, two-bath, ranch-style house with a two-and-a-half-car garage. It sat on an oversized lot and butted up to a small lake. The back yard showcased an enormous tree where the previous renters had erected a solitary swing.

After that, we partially furnished our new home. I graduated college with honors, and moved out of my dorm. I shipped my belongings to Florida, planned a wedding, and still squeezed in time to see Ruthie and Dillon earn their yellow belts in karate. I should've been worn out, but I was too excited about the future to be anything but floating on air.

I was more than relieved that Lucas never bothered me after he'd been expelled from school. I'd heard through the grapevine that after his expulsion, things had gotten even worse for him. I didn't ask for details because I didn't care. I was grateful that he'd been too preoccupied with his own unfortunate circumstances to hassle me anymore.

I remembered having a small concern that Lucas might crash graduation, so I'd insisted that nobody, not even my mother or grandfather, attend. They were reluctant to agree, but I was adamant. I'd spent four years living cautiously so as not to bring attention to my family. The last thing I wanted was a potential confrontation with an angry ex-boyfriend. And of course, Christian couldn't be there due to his parole limitations.

The graduation ceremony was recorded so my family would be able to pop in a DVD and watch me and a thousand other students walk across the stage. And it wasn't like graduation was a lonely affair. Sandy's parents were there. Not only did they invite me, Jeanie, and Marilyn to a celebratory dinner at a five-star restaurant, but they rented us a suite in the ritziest hotel in town for our last night together.

I sighed and studied my bridal bouquet as a special memory from graduation night warmed me from the inside out. I'd been in line, getting ready to go up the few steps to the platform to accept my diploma when the hair on my neck bristled with electricity. I knew he was there. I felt him so vividly, it was as if my lungs tingled with the recognition that I was breathing the same air as him. The auditorium was big, but my eyes immediately zeroed in on the solitary figure casually leaning against an open doorway on the opposite end of the massive space.

It was Christian.

After accepting my diploma I broke with protocol, and instead of returning to my seat I headed straight for Christian. I threw myself at him, and he caught me and spun me around.

"I'm so proud of you, Mimi. I could never miss this." His hot breath caressed my neck as he held me aloft.

"But your parole?" I asked as he set me back on my feet.

"I have permission to be gone two days. I got here in time to see you walk across the stage and I'll leave tomorrow. You already told me about your plans with your friends, and I'm not interfering with those. All I'm asking is that after they fall asleep, you sneak down to room 204." He handed me a keycard. "I'll be waiting for you, sweetheart."

"I'll be there," I whispered breathlessly.

My daydreams were interrupted by Rachelle who opened the door and peeked her head inside.

"Ten-minute delay," she informed me. "Don't ask how, but Ruthie managed to already get her dress dirty. We need ten minutes to get her cleaned up. Your parents will come see you in a few minutes."

Not the least bit surprised by the announcement, I nodded and smiled.

"Oh, and your husband is the hottest groom I've ever laid eyes on. Don't tell Travis I said that," she said with a goofy grin.

"Cell phones and cameras?" I asked.

"Everyone is respecting your wishes and leaving them in a basket. They know they'll get them back after the reception." She quietly closed the door.

I was relieved. It wasn't like we'd invited a ton of people to the ceremony, but I didn't want to take any chance of a picture getting posted on social media. My cousin, Scott, was not only an exceptionally talented photographer, but a trusted friend. I knew he wouldn't share anything I didn't want him to. I planned on making sure everyone would get a wedding picture of me and Christian in the thank you cards I intended to send.

Only a few minutes passed when my mother let herself in the room.

"Christy is helping get your sister cleaned up. I wanted to have a few minutes alone with you." She took a seat beside me on the sofa.

"First, I want to tell you how proud I am of you, Mimi. You've gone above and beyond, not only with your grades, but with all the planning, and moving." She waved her hand in the air. "Everything. You've been like superwoman!"

I knew something was coming. "But?" I asked, tilting my head to one side.

"I hope it wasn't at the expense of your health. You've assured me you've been taking care of yourself. I want to make sure you continue."

She was talking about my eating disorder. I'd tried to squeeze in a few sessions with a therapist while at school, but I'd been so preoccupied and busy with everything else, I'd be lying if I said it helped. "I promised you I would talk to someone, and I did, Mom. And I'll make it a priority as soon as I get settled in Florida."

She nodded, and I saw that a mist started to form in her eyes. "You're sure about this, Mimi?"

"I've never been more sure about anything in my life, Mom." And I meant it.

"I know it's been a few months now, but you and Christian haven't been together the whole time. Are you still sure this isn't just infatuation, Mimi?" Her eyes were warm as she reached for my hand.

Squeezing her hand, I said, "When I think of infatuation, I think of immediate desire." I shook my head. "I read somewhere that it's like one hormone calling to another."

She smiled at me.

"But, love. Love is friendship that has caught on fire. And Christian is my best friend, Mom. He always has been. I just didn't let myself remember it. I don't know if many married couples can call their spouse their best friend." She nodded her understanding. "The article also said that infatuation is filled with insecurity, whereas love is a mature acceptance of our defects. It allows you to be yourself, and know that you are unconditionally loved. Flaws and all. I totally agree."

I watched as she waged a battle within herself. She was genuinely happy for me. She'd even admitted that considering our family's secret, and long history with the Bears, Christian was the best choice for a husband. She just needed to make sure I wasn't settling because of it. A moment passed before a wide smile broke out on her face, and she pulled me toward her. "I'm happy for you, Mimi." She squeezed me tightly. "Truly happy."

"Thanks, Mom," I whispered in a hoarse voice as a wave of unexpected grief descended on me.

She released me and stood up. She was smoothing out her dress when she saw my face.

"Mimi, what's wrong, honey?"

She reached for my hands after I laid down my bouquet and stood up to face her. "He should be here, Mom. He should be part of this day."

"I miss him, too," she admitted.

We were talking about the man who'd raised me until his untimely death in 2001. Tommy.

"My heart hurts, Mom. I just wish he could be part of this somehow," I explained.

"I already anticipated this, Mimi. And Rachelle and I have a surprise for you. It's why she agreed to play the piano. I hope you don't mind, but we've changed up the music a little bit. I'm afraid it's not going to be very traditional," she said somewhat sheepishly.

My tears threatened, but didn't spill over as my father came in the room and told us, "Ginny, you need to let Jason escort you down the aisle. Everything is ready." I was relieved. I didn't want to ruin my makeup before the ceremony even began.

Her eyes got wide as she remembered something. Turning to me she asked, "You said that after Micah starts with the traditional vows, you and Christian are going to say your own. Do you have them written down?"

I shook my head. "I didn't need to write them down, Mom. They're permanently etched on my heart."

She gave me a curious look before I added, "Just like Christian is permanently etched on my soul."

I LOOKED up at my father, and admired his strong profile as we stood in the church vestibule and waited for Rachelle to play the piano to announce our entrance.

Without looking at me he said, "I love you, Mimi. There isn't much I can give you except my blessing. I hope that means something."

"It means more than you could know, Dad. And you'll see. Christian will prove himself. I know he will."

He looked down at me and his smile was genuine, but his eyes conveyed that Christian better.

I clutched his arm tighter and whispered, "And I love you too."

So much for not wanting to ruin my makeup. Mom was right. The piano selection she had chosen wasn't traditional, but was exactly what I needed to feel like my other father was with me on this special day.

I glided down the aisle on Grizz's arm to the piano interlude at the end of "Layla" by Derek & the Dominos. It had been Tommy's favorite song, and after his death in 2001, I'd played it in tribute to him at my piano recital. Rachelle had slowed it down a bit for today's occasion —perfect.

When I got to the altar, Christian was waiting for me. He stepped over to shake Grizz's hand, and wiped my tears with his thumbs. I'd purposely asked my grandfather to leave out the part that asks who gives this bride, because like I'd already explained to my father, he wouldn't be giving me away. I would always be his daughter.

Before I knew it, we'd gone through the first part of the traditional marriage ceremony, and Micah was telling the guests that it was now time for Christian and me to recite our vows.

I looked up at Christian, and swallowed the lump that had started to form at the back of my throat.

Without removing his eyes from mine, he began: "I, Christian Bear, take you, Mimi, as my wife." He smiled, and my heart melted.

"I, Mimi Dillon Hunter, take you, Christian, as my husband."

"I felt you in my soul before I knew how to even form words, Mimi. You've always lived there, warming my cold places, bringing light to my dark spaces."

I swallowed thickly now just as I had done that night under the stars and snow.

Filled with emotion, I began: "I never knew how lost I'd been until you found me, Christian. My world wasn't one of darkness or light, but somewhere in between. Dull and without color. You've brought me into the sunshine and made everything bright."

"I will always love you, Mimi." He reached for my left hand. "I will always cherish you, protect you, listen to you, be faithful to you, put your needs before my own."

"I will always love you, Christian." I squeezed his hand. "You'll always have my love, my loyalty, my faithfulness, my heart." I paused and brought his hand to my chest. "My soul."

"I'll never lose you again, Mimi. Never."

"I'll never be lost again, Christian."

Micah continued with the traditional vows, and I drifted in a dreamlike state for the rest of the ceremony. My grandfather had just told Christian it was time to kiss his bride when Abby, who'd been sitting quietly on Aunt Christy's lap, made her way up to the altar and wedged herself between us. We broke from our kiss to look down at her smiling face. It couldn't have been more perfectly timed if we'd planned it. My grandfather saw his opening and took it.

Addressing the congregation, he said in a booming voice, "And now, I present to you, Christian, Mimi, and Abby." He paused for comedic effect. "The three Bears."

CHAPTER 50

FORT LAUDERDALE, FLORIDA 2007

I sat at my desk and casually perused the old photo album. I reached for a carrot and crunched loudly as I turned the page, getting lost in local history as I thought about the last few months.

After our wedding, I returned to Florida with Christian and began a new chapter in my life. The summer had been fraught with challenges. Abby's mother, Autumn, was one of them.

Christian and Aunt Christy's suspicions that Autumn had intercepted my letter to him and sent that hateful reply had been accurate. She'd denied it at first, but after finding out that Christian and I had reunited, she couldn't hide the disappointment that her wickedness hadn't worked. She'd been livid, and her first tactic had been to lash out at me. I knew how to deal with mean girls. I laughed at or ignored her nasty comments and snide remarks. And of course, her crude insults were directed at me when nobody else was within earshot. Autumn immediately slipped into the role of dutiful mother, showing up at the appointed time to take Abby every other weekend. After finding out the day we'd planned to get married, she went so far as to ask her lawyer to petition a judge so she could get special permission to have Abby that weekend. She'd made up some stupid reason, but her petition had been denied.

I'd asked Christian once, "What is behind her obsession with you?"

He'd shrugged his shoulders and said, "She must be into guys who treat her like shit, because I don't think I've ever been nice to her."

"Do you have any friends you could introduce her to?" I'd asked sarcastically. "Someone who would treat her worse than you did? Maybe it'll distract her enough that she'll back off." Christian knew she'd mouthed off to me, but he also knew I was adamant about him not interfering. I wasn't afraid of Autumn. Annoyed, yes. But she wasn't a real threat.

"Isaac Brooks," he'd said, interrupting my thoughts. "I could introduce her to Isaac. He treats women pretty crappy."

After hearing sordid tales about Isaac's love life, and then finally meeting Jonas and Lucy Brooks's son, and seeing him in action, I had to agree. I shook my head. "I could never do that to the mother of your child. Even if it's Autumn, nobody deserves him," I confessed. As much as I wanted to make Autumn go away, putting her in the hands of Isaac Brooks was tantamount to putting a bull's-eye on her forehead and sending her into a shooting range. Isaac was a notorious womanizer who left a trail of broken hearts everywhere he went.

The phone rang with a loud shrill and I jumped. Reaching for it, I picked up the receiver and said, "Bascom-Little Family House and Historical Museum. This is Mimi."

"Why aren't you answering your cell?" Christian asked, frustration oozing from each syllable.

"Because it didn't ring," I told him while simultaneously reaching for my phone. "Oops," I said before he could reply. "I forgot I turned the ringer off while I was adding up receipts."

Upon arriving back in Fort Lauderdale, I'd immediately started looking for a full-time job, but Christian was against it. He told me to use the summer to settle in. I could work full-time if I wanted, but he'd rather I use the time to take care of priorities. I knew what he was talking about and finally relented.

I needed to find someone to talk to about my eating disorder. It had gotten out of control in the months leading up to my graduation and our wedding. I couldn't continue to ignore it. I hadn't yet made any new friends in Florida so I reluctantly approached Aunt Christy for help. She listened to the same story I'd told Christian, and had the same reaction. No judgment, only concern. She helped me find not one, but three therapists.

"You should make an appointment with all three, Mimi," she told me. "And keep seeing whoever you make a connection with." She'd been right. The first two were strikeouts, but the third was a charm.

Not only did I like her, she'd given me the lead for the part-time job opening at the museum.

"Are you?" Christian asked.

"Uh...hmm?" I'd been daydreaming and only half paying attention to what he'd said.

"Are you going to yoga after you see your therapist tonight?" he repeated.

My dislike of formal exercise had never waned. And even though I still enjoyed sparring regularly with Christian at his friend's gym, I found that I craved something else. My therapist had suggested yoga, as there was a small workout center where they held classes in the same building as her office. Unfortunately, after only taking a few lessons, it had closed. I'd yet to find a new place.

"I know it's been weeks, but I haven't found another place yet. At least not one that I like."

"Yoga classes are a dime a dozen." His words were confident. "You'll find another one."

"Yeah, I know." I paused before asking, "Why did you ask?"

"I know it's not our regular night, but I was wondering if you minded if we got Abby tonight? She could come to our house instead of going to my parents'."

I smiled. "I never mind, Christian. You know that."

"I know," he answered. "But, if you go to yoga then we can't have dinner together. It'll be too late for her."

"That's okay. It's not like I was planning on it. I can start looking for a new place another time."

"There's something else." His voice floated through the phone with an air of apology. "She's at Autumn's mother's place, and you'll have to pick her up. I have to work later than usual."

I'd forgotten that instead of getting Abby on Friday night and returning her to Aunt Christy and Uncle Anthony's home on Sunday night, Autumn had asked to pick her up on Saturday night and return her tonight, Monday. Ugh.

There was a loud chime indicating that someone had come into the museum.

"It's not a problem. I'll pick her up, Christian," I assured him. I let him know someone had walked in before hanging up.

I closed the photo album, tucked it under my arm and made my way to the front of the museum. The Bascom-Little Family House and

Historical Museum was exactly what its name implied. It was one of the oldest homes built in Fort Lauderdale, passed down several generations. The entire home still contained furnishings from as far back as the early 1900s.

I smelled moth balls before I saw her. I approached the elderly woman with a smile on my face and said, "Welcome to the Bas—"

"You must be Miriam Bear," she interrupted. She was hunched over and leaning on a cane. She cocked her head to one side, looking me up and down.

"Yes, I am. Please call me Mimi. And you are?" I tried to raise the inquisitive eyebrow that never cooperated.

"Mrs. Winifred Truncle," she cackled. "The Truncles have been in Fort Lauderdale longer than the Bascoms. I'm on the board that approved your employment." She paused for effect. "Miriam."

She spoke with an air of superiority that amused me. It was ninety degrees outside yet she wore an antiquated lavender dress that fell to her ankles, and a mink stole that had obviously been retrieved from a closet that had been doused in moth balls.

I started to thank her when she said, "It's hot in here!"

It wasn't hot, more like stuffy, but it wasn't due to the temperature.

"What kind of last name is Bear, Miriam?" she asked me.

"It's Native American," I replied proudly. I placed the album on the table next to her, and opened it to a random page to better display it. She peered down, then looked back at me. "That's what I thought when I voted to approve your application. But you don't look Native American."

"I'm not," I answered kindly. "My husband is half Cherokee and half Seminole."

"A mixed marriage!" she spat.

Her uppity nature had amused me. Her nasty reaction to my mixed marriage shocked me.

"I had no problem giving my approval for a Native American employee. I believe in that, you know? Giving opportunities to minorities." She raised her chin in indignation. "But I don't believe in mixing the races. That's how King Solomon fell out of grace with God. He married women outside of his own ethnic group. It was displeasing to God." She took in a deep breath and waited for me to react. Did she think I was going to throw myself on the mercy seat of

Winifred Truncle and pray for her forgiveness for marrying a Native American? It was laughable.

Like I'd told Christian that night at the rental house in South Carolina, I wasn't good at Scripture memorization, but I had studied the Bible. And I knew that God's command for King Solomon not to engage in an interracial marriage was not because of skin color or ethnicity. Rather, it was because God didn't want the Jewish people to intermarry with cultures that worshipped other gods. What a sad and twisted interpretation of God's Word Madam Truncle had used to fuel and justify what could only be summed up with one word—racism. I was beginning to wish there had been a job opening at the Stranahan House instead of here.

Apparently, she considered my delay in responding as acquiescence, and she focused on the album I'd returned to the table. "You should know Fort Lauderdale's history if you're going to be of any value here."

I'd been doing my best to bite my tongue. I liked this job, and because I hadn't seen Mrs. Truncle before, I highly doubted she came by regularly. I started to tell her that I'd been familiarizing myself with all of the literature and historical items in the home when she thumped her finger on the album.

"That used to be a family-owned mercantile. It's a furniture store now," she huffed. I peeked down and saw that it was a page toward the back of the book that I hadn't seen. She flipped to the next page and let out another disgusted breath. "A gentleman's club that's now a gas station. Not even a regular gas station. It's one of those that has a restaurant inside. If you can even imagine!"

I glanced down at the beautiful building and nodded in agreement. The architecture couldn't be appreciated with gas pumps and a hamburger sign that screamed for attention. She flipped another random page and I saw her face redden. Looking down at what had incited her, I had to blink twice to see if what I was looking at was real or a figment of my imagination.

I knew the history behind the picture, but clamped my jaw shut and let Mrs. Truncle ramble. With a bony finger she thumped the black-and-white photo several times before sneering, "There's a car dealership there now. It's just as well. It's one landmark I was glad to see go. Should've been called the hotel of horrors."

I knew why she thought that, but the word was out before I could stop it. "Why?" I squeaked.

I stooped lower to inspect the picture while she spoke. It was in black-and-white but I could imagine the colors of the sign that boasted The Glades Motel. Below it stood a balding old man, his pants high on his waist and a cigarette dangling from between his lips as he tried to smile for the camera. The picture was obviously taken by a tourist who'd wanted a memento of where they'd stayed. But the man and the sign weren't what caught my attention. Winifred Truncle's rant rattled around my head as I focused on another figure. Standing behind the old man, off to the right, with a rake in his hand, was a young boy. He looked like he'd been caught unaware and had been prepared to turn his head away, but the picture had been snapped before he could. I had no doubt I was seeing Grizz as a child. I also had no doubt there was no other picture anywhere in existence like it.

"Are you listening to me, Miriam?" she snapped.

"Yes, I've been listening," I said, shaking my head. "I'm sorry, actually, I didn't hear the last thing."

She gave me a hard stare and repeated, "I was saying that my dear friend had a granddaughter who fell in with that bunch of miscreants. They drugged her up, used her, and killed her."

I looked back at the picture and gulped.

"Her name was Miriam. Just like you." Her voice sounded softer.

I knew who Miriam was. Moe, my namesake, silently screamed through my head. Yes, she'd died, but it was from an overdose. Of course I hadn't had anything to do with it, but I felt a wave of sadness and shame.

"And all I can say," Mrs. Truncle continued, "is that I am grateful that my friend and Miriam's parents died before they found that poor girl. Do you know where they discovered her?"

I could feel a wave of heat as it made its way up my spine. She was right. It was hot in here.

"After holding her prisoner and torturing her for years, he murdered her and buried her on her own parents' property. What kind of cruel and evil mind would do that to a family? To put their dead child's body right beneath their noses?"

I looked at her and I didn't see anger in her eyes. I saw sadness.

"Like I said, I'm glad her parents and grandparents didn't live to see it. Of course Miriam's sisters know. They still have to live with what that horrible man did to her." Her voice had lost its bluster. She turned and headed for the door. "Thank the good Lord he's dead now. Of course, God only knows how many demon seeds he planted all over South Florida while he rained down terror. You be careful out there, young lady. You never know when you might be looking evil right in the eyes." She slowly turned around and headed toward the door.

I heard her cane thump as she walked down the steps without shutting the door behind her. I started to close it when I heard her muttering to herself, "The Lord is slow to anger and abounding in steadfast love...but He will by no means clear the guilty, visiting the iniquity of the fathers on the children, to the third and fourth generation."

I remembered when I'd first learned about my biological father, Grizz, and how I'd refused to call him anything other than the evil sperm donor. And that was exactly what feisty Winifred Truncle had just implied. Her head would've exploded if I'd told her she was staring into the eyes of his demon seed.

I watched as her driver helped her get into the back of a black Cadillac Sedan that had to be older than me. Closing the door, I grabbed the album and went back to my desk. I didn't have any museum visitors for the rest of the day. During that time, I managed to carefully remove the last tangible remnant of my father's childhood, and replace it with a picture from the same era that I'd found in a box.

After closing up the museum I headed for my car, and reached for the flyer that had been tucked under my windshield wiper. It wasn't until I got inside that I unfolded the thick paper.

WHORE was scrawled in bold black letters.

Could this day get any crappier?

CHAPTER 51

FORT LAUDERDALE, FLORIDA 2007

I crumpled up the paper and threw it in my purse. "You could've just waited to hand it to me when I pick up Abby later," I said to an invisible Autumn. It was the second nasty note I'd received on my windshield in the past two weeks. I found the first one when I'd come out of the grocery store just over a week ago. It had simply read, HE'S USING YOU.

The museum didn't have surveillance cameras, and I wouldn't bother to ask the grocery store if they had any. I already knew who was writing the notes, so it was a moot point. I was convinced Autumn was more bark than bite so there was no way I would involve Christian in something so adolescent. Once she got it through her thick skull that Christian and I were a permanent couple, she would slink away and stalk some other poor soul.

I stopped for coffee and still arrived at my therapy appointment fifteen minutes early. The office complex was a modern structure with a bright and airy atrium in the center. I sat on a bench and enjoyed my coffee as I watched people bustling around me. I stared at the large corner space that used to be the gym where I had taken a few yoga classes and wondered what was going on behind the glass walls that had been covered with brown paper. A remodel had been going on for weeks with no sign of who would be occupying the space. I hadn't been speculating for more than a minute when the glass door opened and two men walked out. The older of the two was laughing and he stepped aside as the second man turned around to lock the door.

"You got it, Nick?" I heard the older one ask. He had a thick head of silver hair and a neatly trimmed beard to match. I saw that he was wearing blue jeans, sneakers, and a T-shirt that said, "Diamonds in the Rough."

The sensors in my head started to fire all at once. I watched and listened as the one called Nick replied, "I got this, Roger." Remembering what Christian had told me after admitting to attacking the man who'd attempted to rape me, my brain made the connection between Diamonds in the Rough and Nick Rosman. He turned around at that exact moment and our eyes connected.

Look down. Maybe it's not him.

It was wishful thinking. My eyes betrayed me as I looked below his shoulders and saw the artificial limb. Instead of glancing back up I kept my eyes lowered as I concentrated on the coffee cup I had balanced on my left knee. I saw a pair of loafers come into view. I slowly raised my head when the person standing in front of me asked, "Are you Mimi Dillon?"

"Hello, Nick," was all I said as I met his eyes. Having him stand over me felt a bit too submissive, so I stood up. "Or do you go by Elliott?"

"It's Nick," he whispered breathlessly. "Mimi, I've waited a long time to talk to you. I have so much to tell you. So much to say to you."

Just then the older man sidled up next to Nick and asked, "Friend of yours?"

Nick didn't take his eyes off mine as he replied to his friend, "This is Mimi. I've told you about her."

I chanced a peek at the older man who formed an O with his mouth. He obviously knew the story. Extending his hand, the man said, "Roger Kincaid, but my friends call me Jolly Roger."

Before he could pull his hand away I replied, "Mimi Bear. Nice to meet you, Roger."

"Bear?" Nick asked, his head cocked to one side.

I held my head high when I answered, "Yes, Bear. I'm married to Christian. I guess Roger knows Christian's story too?" My eyes wandered to Nick's prosthetic arm.

"Married?" Nick asked. He took a step back and swiped his hand through his hair. "Whoa. Wasn't expecting that one."

I studied him and watched as he tried to make sense of what I'd just told him. He broke out into a wide smile and said, "I could see you marrying the older one. The one who beat me up that night. What was his name?"

"Slade," Roger said before I could. Apparently he knew that part of the story too.

He shrugged his shoulders sheepishly. "Unusual name. Easy to remember."

I nodded my agreement, and waited for the awkward silence to descend. But it didn't. Nick immediately launched into an apology for what he'd done to me so many years ago. He explained that he even tried to find me after my family moved, but to no avail. I listened, mesmerized, as he delved into a story that I knew he'd shared with others by how articulately he described it. A story about a misguided and angry teenager, who didn't die from his injury, but was close to dying from despair. He made sure I knew he had no hard feelings for Christian by telling me, "If Christian hadn't done what he did to me, I wouldn't have paid any attention to Roger when I met him. I wouldn't have found God. I would still be wandering aimlessly looking in the wrong places for happiness." His eyes misted over when he added, "Truthfully, I probably would've killed myself."

Apparently, Nick's friend and mentor had become an ordained minister, evangelizing and saving souls while in prison. Upon his release, Roger prayed that God would show him his next assignment. And according to Roger, God did. Nick and Roger met while standing in line at a Taco Bell. Roger honed in on Nick's desperation and sadness, and invited him to a prayer meeting. Just like Christian had told me, Nick had received a substantial amount of money from the Bears, and the two new friends embarked on creating a non-profit organization that would provide not just counseling to troubled young men, but education, housing, and other forms of rehabilitation.

I pointed to the area behind them. "Is that what this is? Headquarters for Diamonds in the Rough?"

"Oh no," Roger chimed in. "I don't think the other businesses would appreciate us having our Diamonds in the Rough crew in the vicinity. Let's face it, most of the boys we deal with are criminals." He stuck his hands in his pockets and rolled back on his heels. "This is an offshoot of that program, and it's a bit different. For starters, it includes girls."

I grinned, interested in what he was saying.

"We don't even have a name for it yet," Nick added.

BETH FLYNN

"But it's for the younger kids. From kindergarten through middle school," Roger told me with a wide smile. "It's an after-school mentoring program that helps them deal with bullying." He nodded toward Nick and said, "Nick's fiancée, Rachel, is going to run it."

My smile got wider, and I focused on Nick. "You're engaged? Congratulations." And I meant it.

"She's a wonderful woman. I'd like you to meet her, Mimi." He paused. "Anyway, we've been trying to get the funding for almost a year now, and a few weeks ago, an anonymous donor offered this space, and some money."

"It's an answer to our prayers," Roger said with a smile.

Nick then answered my unspoken question. "The money I got from my settlement is all gone. It was a huge figure, but it went to a good cause. Thanks to this"—he held up his prosthetic limb—"a lot of young men are leading productive lives instead of wasting away behind bars."

I took a deep breath and measured my next words very carefully. "I'm truly glad you see it that way, Nick." I looked down at the ground. I didn't know why, but I couldn't bring myself to apologize on Christian's behalf. If there was ever going to be an apology, it needed to come from Christian. Not me.

As if sensing my internal struggle, Nick asked, "Mimi, can I ask you for a hug?"

I looked up and saw nothing in his eyes that indicated anything other than sincerity. Yes, a misguided teenaged Nick had deceived me all those years ago, but I believed he'd turned his life around for the better. I believed he'd found his place of peace.

I nodded and we embraced. After pulling back, I asked him, "How is your grandmother? How is Edith?"

"She's doing well," he told me. "She insisted on moving into an assisted living facility. She's happier than she's ever been. You wouldn't believe the place. It has everything—its own golf course, movie theater, restaurants. It's like its own little city. I still live in her house."

"I don't want to be the one to bust up this happy reunion, but we gotta head out, buddy," came Roger's friendly reminder.

"I have to run too," I added, looking at my watch. I was already five minutes late.

"Will you stop in and meet Rachel once we're all set up?" Nick asked.

"Yes, I promise," I assured him.

Roger grabbed my hand with both of his and shook it so hard I thought my watch was going to fly off my wrist. "Nice to meet you, Mimi. So very nice." His eyes disappeared when he smiled. He really was Jolly Roger.

"Nice to meet you too, Roger."

I watched them walk away, and I tossed my empty coffee cup in the garbage before heading for the stairs. My therapist was going to have a field day when I told her who I'd just run into and the story behind it.

CHAPTER 52

After my appointment, I saw a text from Aunt Christy inviting us to have dinner at her house. She'd experimented with a new Crock-Pot recipe and said she had enough to feed an army. Christian hadn't been lying when he said his mother wasn't a very good cook, but she managed to turn out some decent one-pot meals. I texted Christian who said he would meet Abby and me there, but would probably be a little late.

I was grateful that Autumn wasn't at her mother's house when I picked up Abby. Autumn did everything she could to avoid Christian's parents, including leaving Abby with her disabled mother knowing that the Bears would have to pick her up, since the woman was bound to a wheelchair. I had no doubt if she knew I was going to be the one to get her daughter she would've done one of two things. Insisted on dropping Abby at our home as a means to snoop, or waited at her mother's place to give me a hard time.

We'd just finished Aunt Christy's rendition of what I think was supposed to be beef Stroganoff when Daisy asked to be excused from the table.

"Can I give Abby her bath?" She pushed in her chair, and then picked up her plate to carry it to the sink. Before either Christian or I could answer, she added, "I'll put her in her jammies so you don't even have to get her ready for bed when you take her home."

I loved how much Daisy loved her niece, but I also knew that Christian had been reveling in playing the role of dutiful father, and he'd done it spectacularly. I saw the hesitation on his face, at the same time Aunt Christy chimed in, "You're on kitchen duty, Daisy. And I'm sure Christian and Mimi want to take Abby home soon. You can give her a bath tomorrow night when she's back here."

Even though the court had given primary custody of Abby to Christian's parents, we still brought her to our home as often as possible. She had her own room, which Christian and I decorated with Daisy's help. Abby's room even had an extra bed for her aunt Daisy for when she wanted to stay over.

Daisy didn't argue with her mother and started gathering the empty plates from the table. Abby was sitting in her chair playing with her noodles, not even paying any of us the slightest attention.

I watched Daisy leave the dining room with an armload of plates.

"Won't be much longer when she won't be making those kinds of offers," came Uncle Anthony's deep voice. We all looked at him. "Pretty soon it's going to be about boys and makeup. I'm surprised it's not already." I could see by his expression that he was already preparing himself to mourn the loss of his soon-to-be teenage daughter. I was inclined to agree. I'd noticed the way Daisy had looked at my brother Jason, and my cousin Scott, when she was visiting for our wedding.

"Daisy is different," Aunt Christy interjected. "She's very family oriented. She prefers us over her friends."

Uncle Anthony raised an eyebrow.

"How was work? What's new with you two?" Aunt Christy asked, purposely changing the subject.

After Christian described a difficult repair which only Uncle Anthony understood, I whipped out the picture I'd taken from the museum and passed it around the table. All three of them agreed it was Grizz in the old photo. Of course, I left out the part about Winifred Truncle's disapproval of mixed-race marriages, and the nasty note I'd found on my windshield. I started to tell them about running into Nick and his friend Roger when Aunt Christy banged her hand on the table, yelling, "What? You're telling me he's in the same building as your therapist? Where you go every week?"

Apparently Abby wasn't accustomed to seeing her grandmother angry, and she made a small squeak. We all looked over at her, but she only had eyes for her father.

"Dabba," she said, while reaching for him. It was the first time she'd called Christian anything. I almost cried as I watched Christian lift her out of her seat and place her on his lap.

Turning back to Aunt Christy, I told her everything that Nick had told me.

"I don't like it. It doesn't feel right," she said.

"It's not for you to like or not, Owani," Uncle Anthony interjected.

"It's okay, it really is," I added, casting a sideways glance Christian's way. He hadn't commented yet, so I wasn't sure where he stood on the issue.

"Look, they've been working on the place for weeks now and I haven't seen them. I was sitting on the bench across from the space at the precise time they were leaving. It was so random. Odds are slim that I'll ever run into Nick again, considering I only have therapy appointments once a week." I took a breath and looked at my husband. "Are you okay with this? Do you think this will be a problem?"

He shook his head slowly. "As long as he doesn't have any misguided notions that you'll be getting chummy or that we'll be double-dating with him and his fiancée, I don't see it as a problem."

"Considering a condition of your parole is not having any contact with your victim, I don't see any double-dating in your future anyway," Uncle Anthony scoffed.

"I think it's too weird, and way too much of a coincidence," Aunt Christy added as she placed her elbows on the table and leaned forward to address us. "What if Nick is up to something?" She leaned back and drummed her fingers on the table. "What if he's trying to get revenge for what Christian did to him?" She grabbed a salt shaker and nervously fiddled with it. She didn't give anyone a chance to answer when she looked at me and added, "I'll offer to relocate your therapist, and I'll make it worth her while. You said you told her about meeting Nick so she'll understand why it's so important. Right, Mimi?"

The Bears lived well below their means in their quaint neighborhood, but they didn't have to. It was no secret that Christian's mother was an heiress, and worth millions. And his father had amassed a small fortune of his own through lucrative criminal endeavors when they'd lived on Florida's west coast. In her mind, Aunt Christy's solution was simple. She would write a sizeable check to my therapist to entice her to find another office. I didn't think it was necessary and apparently neither did her husband.

"Owani, listen to what you're saying." All eyes shifted to Uncle Anthony as he reached for his wife's hand. Gently removing the salt shaker from her grasp and setting it aside, he continued, "Do you really think that Nick Rosman used up all the money he got from us on his charity while waiting for Mimi to show back up in Florida, banking on her marrying Christian? During which time he waited over a year for funding for his new non-profit, only accepting their money if they offered to put him in a building where he knew Mimi had an appointment once a week, in the hopes that he would run into her? All so he could exact revenge on Christian?"

She blinked a few times before answering. "When you say it like that it does sound a little outlandish," she admitted.

"A little?" Christian added.

"Fine," she conceded. "So, it's ridiculously outlandish. I know I'm overthinking it, but I'm also a mother. We have a bad habit of imagining worst-case scenarios."

I reached over and touched her arm. "I appreciate you looking out for me, Aunt Christy. But I felt no threat from Nick. And I highly doubt I'll run into him often or even at all."

"I LOVE YOU SO MUCH, MIMI," Christian whispered, his breath hot against my ear.

We were making love. He was on top and inside me, and after a few gentle thrusts he raised up on his elbows and looked down into my eyes.

"I love you too, Christian," I said while brushing his hair back over his shoulder.

"You don't seem like yourself. Is everything okay, baby?" His concern reflected back to me in his eyes.

I looked away and concentrated on his bicep, the muscle bulging under his weight.

"Is it Nick?" he asked. "If it is, I don't need my mother's checkbook to get rid of him."

"It's not Nick," I assured him. The last thing I wanted Christian to do was have another confrontation with him. Especially one that would no doubt send Christian back to prison.

"Is it what that fossil said about Grizz?"

He knew me so well. "Maybe," I said, a little sheepishly.

"You're not evil, Mimi. You're not Grizz's demon seed." His voice was angry as he slowly removed himself from between my legs and settled down next to me. "And you aren't going to be punished for things he did."

"I know that," I said, looking over at him. I'd been thinking about how Winifred Truncle had misinterpreted Scripture by insinuating that God would punish Grizz's children for his sins. I knew that wasn't the case so it didn't bother me. But something was itching me and it had nothing to do with Winifred.

"He looked so young and innocent in that picture," I said, my voice thick with emotion. "And he'd already experienced so many horrors. I wonder if my father would've turned out differently if the old man who'd let him stay at the motel hadn't been a pervert, but someone Grizz could've looked up to?"

"I guess you'll never know," he quietly whispered.

"I don't believe he was born evil, Christian. He knew evil because he lived with it every day, but he wasn't born that way."

"I'm sure you're right, Mimi. Does any of that matter now?"

"I guess not," I answered. "I'm just wondering if, you know..." I couldn't get the rest of my question out.

"If you're too much like him?" he asked.

I turned toward him. "Why would you ask me that?"

"Because you've mentioned more than once that it bothers you that you weren't appalled when you saw your mother's image on the jacket. And that you should've objected when you thought I was breaking into Axel's garage to steal something. You've dropped little hints like that. I think you're trying to figure out who you are."

"Maybe you're right." I stroked the side of his cheek with the back of my hand. "Who am I, Christian?" I asked. My eyes were starting to burn as I pulled them away from his and stared at the ceiling.

"You're Mimi Bear." He talked to my profile as his left thumb teased my nipple. "My wife and the woman I've always loved. You've walked a straight line for so long, you're punishing yourself for feeling the smallest thrill at doing something you consider bad."

"Possibly," I conceded. "Maybe that's it."

"And you like that people are treating us differently at The Alibi," Christian added. "You're feeling the excitement that comes with a sort of notoriety, or whatever you call it."

He might've hit the nail on the head with that revelation. We'd visited The Alibi a couple times a month since I'd moved to Florida, and it didn't take long for word to get around that Anthony Bear's son had married Grizz's daughter. Like Mike had told Sal at Chicky's, Christian and I were seen as biker royalty.

Old and new members of my father's gang slowly migrated to The Alibi, leaving their regular haunts behind. Chili practically fell apart in my arms when she asked me if it was true. She hadn't remembered that my mother was pregnant with Grizz's child when she married Tommy "Grunt" Dillon.

"I should've recognized you," she'd cried. "You look just like your mother!"

Engaging in conversations with some of the women from back in the day bordered on downright uncomfortable. The last thing I wanted to hear was that my father was the most well-endowed man they'd ever slept with. Yuck. The next time I saw Chili, she gave me her old club jacket. "You should have this," she offered.

I glanced over at my open closet. I could see the black leather sleeve peeking out. Maybe Christian was right. Maybe I was enjoying my newfound popularity a little too much.

I didn't have long to ponder the thought as Christian's hot tongue replaced his thumb, and my nipple hardened even more. I arched into his mouth and moaned loudly.

That's when we heard her. We'd shut the bedroom door, but it didn't catch so she quietly pushed it open and snuck up on us. We scrambled to get under the covers as Abby toddled toward the bed, her footed pajamas scratching against the hardwood floor. She tightly clutched her blanket in one hand, and two chess pieces she'd swiped from the game we had set up on our coffee table in the other. I kept forgetting to put it up when she came over. After she left we would find chess pieces in the oddest places. She was fascinated with them. I was grateful she had no interest in eating them. I still had a lot to learn about childproofing a home. I'd been in college when my parents had to do that for Ruthie and Dillon.

We both took turns momentarily distracting her so we could get dressed. A few minutes later the three of us were snuggled in the bed, Abby softly snoring between us.

"I'll carry her back to her bed," Christian said as he slowly rose from the mattress.

He was sitting with his back to me getting ready to stand when I told him, "No, it's okay. Let her sleep between us tonight. She's never crawled in bed with us before. It's sweet," I whispered over her head.

He turned around and said, "I'm not a parenting expert at all, but everybody I know who has kids says once they get in bed with you, you'll never get them to stop."

I slowly nodded my head in understanding, but couldn't help my objection. "I know, but maybe just this once."

Christian lay back down and faced me, his back to the edge of the bed. "What did I do before I found you, Mimi? How did I exist?"

"Probably the same way I did," I quietly answered. "Barely."

We'd eventually settled in, repeated our vows, and I was about to fall asleep when I remembered something. "Thank you for making the bed today," I whispered into the black night.

I felt his movement on the other side of the mattress when he asked, "Huh? I didn't make the bed. I leave before you do so you always make it."

"But I didn't make it this morning. I was running late. When we climbed into it earlier it was made up, right?"

"Yeah," he answered.

"So I figured you came home for lunch or something, and saw that I didn't get a chance to make it so you did," I replied with a little more snap than I'd intended.

I heard him yawn before saying, "I've only stopped home twice for lunch since we've lived here, and I don't remember it ever crossing my mind to see if the bed needed to be made."

"Who made our bed? Do you think someone broke into the house?" I sat up and switched on the light.

"Ack! Mimi, that's too bright. I was about to fall asleep. Turn it off," he grumbled.

"Not until I get to the bottom of this," I said, giving him a stern look.

He blew out a sigh and replied, "And when this person broke in to make the bed, do you think they emptied the dishwasher and did a load of laundry too?"

Ignoring his sarcasm, I frowned in concentration trying to remember if I'd managed to make the bed. I couldn't conjure up a specific memory because it was jumbled together with every other time I'd done so.

"It's one of those robotic things you do, right?" he asked. "Like brushing your teeth and combing your hair. I got to work once and started to braid my hair before I realized I'd already done it."

Christian's long hair was a hazard around engines so he always wore it in a braid while working at the shop.

I nodded. "Yeah, I guess so." I slipped under the covers and turned off the light.

"Mimi?"

"Yeah?"

"Remind me before I leave for work tomorrow to put out the paint and brushes we bought."

"Why?" I asked.

"Maybe whoever broke in will come back and paint the spare room."

"Ha ha," I said dryly. "You're not funny."

As I drifted off to sleep, I couldn't help but compare Aunt Christy's notion that Nick had acquired the office space near me only to exact revenge on Christian to my "bed-making break-in" speculation. My assumption was just as ridiculous as hers. I flipped over on my stomach, and pulled my pillow over my head.

CHAPTER 53

FORT LAUDERDALE, FLORIDA 2007

The next couple of months flew by, bringing the good and the not-so-good with them. First, and most important to us, was the news that Christian's parole had been revoked. Christian had been called to a special hearing where he was told that due to the high volume of parolees and the lack of officers to manage them, some cases were being considered for early termination. Christian's was one of them. Christian and I, on the other hand, believed it had nothing to do with that. We didn't think it was a coincidence that my parents had no sooner inquired about our Thanksgiving plans, where I informed them that Christian would have to submit the proper paperwork and hope for the best, that a special committee had requested his attendance a few weeks later. We both surmised that both sets of parents conspired to grease the wheels of justice by placing the perfect amount of money in the right bank accounts.

I'd done as I'd promised and stopped in at Nick's new charity, which he ended up calling Little Gems, and met his fiancée, Rachel. She knew who I was, and just like I hadn't been able to bring myself to apologize for Christian's assault on Nick, she didn't apologize or make excuses for what Nick had attempted to do to me. I instantly liked her, but knew our acquaintance couldn't go beyond an occasional greeting when and if we crossed paths at the office complex.

Jolly Roger on the other hand, made more of an attempt to befriend me. I'm pretty sure he watched for me and made sure we ran into each other. He was never obnoxious or intrusive, only gentle-spirited and kind. I knew what he was trying to do, but it would never work, and I said so. He was under the misguided impression that Christian and I could actually be friends with Nick and Rachel. I finally told him in a kind way that he was wasting his time. I genuinely liked Roger and found myself occasionally arriving early to my appointment to talk to him for a few extra minutes each week.

As for Nick, I hadn't seen him since that first time.

Mrs. Truncle never again graced the museum with her presence, at least not when I was working. I was thoroughly enjoying my job, seeing my therapist regularly, thriving with Christian in the boxing ring and by myself with yoga. We'd gotten into a groove with Abby. Life was good, but not perfect. Then again, I hadn't expected it to be.

In addition to working out the kinks that are expected in a new marriage, I'd had to secretly continue to deal with Autumn's harassment which only got worse after Abby started to call me something resembling my name. Unfortunately, Mimi and Mommy were a little too close, and Autumn was furious. She even accused me of trying to replace her. I denied it. Just like she maintained her denial of the offensive notes I still found on my windshield. She'd recently upped her game when she left one on my car while it was parked in front of my house. I was beginning to wonder if turning the other cheek had been a bad idea. It might've been time to tell Christian about the extent of her nastiness.

The bed-making intruder never did come back to paint our spare room, so we continued to work on making our house a home while dealing with the aggravating darts life threw at us. I tried not to scream when Christian decided to help me with the laundry and combined my hand-washable delicates with his greasy work shirts. And he tried not to lose his temper when I unknowingly filled my gas tank with diesel fuel, almost damaging my car beyond repair.

My parents had shipped me the piano my dad, Tommy, had bought for my eighth birthday, and I was delighted when Daisy asked me to teach her how to play. I'd also taught Christian how to play chess on the set I'd displayed. The one Abby continued to be fascinated with. It was another gift from my parents that had been passed down from Tommy. I was told it was the same chess set he'd used to teach my mother to play back in the seventies. The same one I used to see in Mom and Tommy's bedroom when I was a child. I used to sneak in there and play with the pieces when I wasn't supposed to.

I hadn't really had an opportunity to make friends anywhere.

Certainly not at my job, since I normally worked alone. I had coffee with a few girls from yoga, but it never went beyond that. I was grateful when I'd managed to make a new friend, through Christian's connections at The Alibi where we'd pretty much turned into regulars. It was a typical Friday night and the owner, Ken, told me he had a surprise for me. During my first visit to the bar months prior, I'd noticed an old piano that had been pushed up against a wall. When a few of the regulars heard that I knew how to play, they insisted I treat them to a song. But it hadn't been possible. The piano had no life left in it.

I watched as Ken ceremoniously yanked a bright white sheet off a brand-new piano. "I'm sorry it took so long for me to get a new one. Will you play for us, Mimi?" A couple of the patrons started cheering me on so I sat down on the bench and started banging away to songs I thought they'd like. And they did. After about three, one of the guys asked me if he played a couple of songs on the jukebox, could I play the piano parts? I told him I would try. He picked the right artist, because I loved Bob Seger and knew almost all his music. I'd just finished "Roll Me Away" and was headed back to our table when I saw someone come in the door. I knew I would run into Blue eventually. I just didn't know when. I hadn't made eye contact with him so I headed for the table and sat down with my newest and closest friend, Debbie.

"You are so talented, Mimi." She took a long sip of her beer. "I want to be you when I grow up."

The comment was funny because Debbie was in her early forties. She hadn't been part of my father's old club, and I was grateful and relieved that she didn't have any sex stories to share about him. Her boyfriend, Joe, hadn't joined the gang until right after my dad went to prison so he hadn't personally known Grizz either. Debbie and Joe had met a few years back. She hadn't even known Christian because he'd been in jail when she had hooked up with Joe.

Even though they were older than us, Christian and I both enjoyed the couple's company. So much so that we'd started seeing them outside The Alibi. At first, it was hard for me to believe that Joe was part of the motorcycle club. He was so quiet and mild-mannered, it was hard for me to imagine him as someone who was moving up the ranks. Even though he made a good amount of money through the club's illegal activities, he still worked a day job for an audio company that specialized in setting up home theaters, surveillance, and alarm systems. What Joe lacked in conversation, Debbie more than provided. But not in an obnoxious, annoying sort of way. She was obviously proud that he was considered one of only a few who would be in line to replace Blue one day, but her life didn't revolve around the club. She worked full-time for Blue waitressing at his restaurant, Razors.

"You were great, babe," Christian told me as he nodded toward the pool table.

I thanked him then shook my head. I didn't feel like shooting pool.

"You two go," Debbie chimed in, waving Joe and Christian away from the table. After they left, she leaned toward me and asked, "Has she been behaving herself?"

I rolled my eyes. "No. I got another one two days ago."

Debbie was the only person I'd told when Autumn started leaving her hateful notes. I didn't even tell my therapist because I was afraid she would insist I report her harassment to the police.

"I already suggested you have a surveillance camera installed on your property. Joe will hook you up with a deal." She took a long drag on her cigarette and added, "Besides, I told you it might not be Autumn." I watched as she gave Krystal, who was on the other side of the bar, a dirty look.

I shook my head. "I don't need a surveillance camera to know who's behind it, Debbie."

"As long as you come to Joe if you decide to get one," she reminded me. "You'll come to him first, right?"

I nodded, and she scooted slightly closer to me. "So, what did it say?" she asked, concern in her voice.

I took a deep breath, reluctant to share what was scrawled on the last note. I'd found it on my windshield before I left for work, which meant Autumn must've watched the house and waited for Christian to leave before leaving it there.

I took a sip of my beer and set the bottle down on the table, concentrating on placing it perfectly on the cardboard coaster. Without looking at Debbie, I repeated the scribbled message.

"He fucked me last night?" she whisper-yelled. "What does that even mean?"

"I can only assume she watches the house enough that she saw Christian leave the night before, and she tried to mess with my head." I looked over at her then. "You know, to make me think that he was out screwing around when he was supposed to be helping Joe fix his bike."

Debbie quickly looked away, and I knew I'd said something that had made her uncomfortable. "Christian was at your house working on Joe's motorcycle, right?"

She shifted in her chair. Shaking her head slowly, she said, "Christian hasn't been to the house to work on Joe's bike. I didn't even know anything was wrong with Joe's bike."

I was visibly shaken, and Debbie knew it. Christian had never lied to me, and I was beginning to wonder if hanging with his old biker friends was a good idea. Maybe he was missing out on the freedom he'd become accustomed to. Maybe marriage wasn't what he thought it was. Maybe I wasn't enough after all.

"Mimi, don't." I felt Debbie place her hand on my forearm. "I'm sure Christian has a perfectly good explanation for where he was."

I pasted on a smile and said, "I'm sure you're right."

Then her eyes got very serious. "You cannot tell Christian what I just told you," she pleaded.

I was surprised by her request, and was going to ask her why when she continued, "This is what the life is like, Mimi. More than likely, Christian asked Joe to cover for him and Joe forgot to tell me. If it gets back to your husband that I slipped, even if it was accidental, it could be bad for Joe and me. The guys don't betray each other's confidences."

I swallowed back my reply.

"Please?" Her eyes looked watery when she added, "Like I said, he probably has a reason, but if you decide to confront him, I'm begging you to come up with another way you could've found out. Don't bring me and Joe into it. Please, Mimi."

I assured her that I had no intention of dragging her and Joe into my marriage.

In an attempt to change the subject, she nudged me and nodded toward a table a few down from us. My uncle Blue was talking to a few men. He made eye contact with me, raised his beer and nodded. I gave him a small smile, and prayed he didn't come over to the table. I didn't feel like making small talk with a man I'd believed to be my biological uncle for the first half of my life, and hadn't seen since Tommy's funeral over six years ago. Not that I'd ever had an issue with Blue. I just wasn't in the mood.

"People are talking, Mimi," Debbie said.

I looked over at her. "About?"

"About Blue chasing his dick all the way over to Louisiana after some piece."

She could only be talking about my mother's twin sister, Jodi.

"So?" I asked, showing only mild interest, while focusing on my beer bottle.

"Soooo," she said with an exaggerated drawl. "Everyone has been saying for a while now that he might step down. I can't believe you haven't heard this already. Talk is that Christian might be in line to take his place."

I snapped my head up, and narrowed my eyes at her.

"Especially since his parole has been revoked." She twirled her hair, looking nonchalant as she glanced at the pool table where Christian was bent over, getting ready to make a shot. "He has nothing to stop him from being part of the gang anymore."

I let her words sink in. I hadn't once thought about Christian joining the club again. But the more I looked around me, the more I saw how the crowd had changed since we first started coming to The Alibi. I could see why she'd made the assumption.

"You want that, right?" Debbie's question broke through my thoughts.

"Want what?" I asked.

"For Christian to step up as prez?"

I didn't get to answer her because Christian, Joe, Isaac Brooks, and two men I'd never seen walked over and joined us. After sitting in the chair to my left, Christian draped his right arm around me and said, "Mimi, this is Nigel. He's from down under." He hesitated and shook his head. Gesturing with his beer toward the other guy, he added, "Can't remember your name, dude."

The man said his name, but I was only half listening and didn't catch it.

"Down under?" I peeked around my husband to get a better look.

There was a round of laughter and Isaac piped up, "Yeah, we got an Aussie in our midst and it's a good thing he has that accent or he'd never get laid. I've stood next to him in the john and his pecker gives new meaning to the word wee.

"Why are ya sussing out my cock? If you don't shut your mouth,

I'll smack you in the fucking head with it." Nigel's accent was strong and I could see why women would find it appealing.

I listened to the banter, and tried not to let Debbie's earlier revelation about Christian's unknown whereabouts bother me.

The next thirty minutes passed uneventfully, until it was obvious that Nigel had reached his alcohol limit. Up until that point the conversations had been jovial, but his comments started to take on an angry edge. Thinking to put him in his place, Debbie jokingly said, "Nigel, you need to show some respect. You don't want to say something to offend Christian. He might be your new boss if the rumors are true."

Nigel, who sat next to Christian, leaned sideways in his chair and looked Christian up and down, saying, "So I heard. I wanna apply for the job me self."

"I didn't know Blue was taking applications," Isaac said with a laugh.

I was watching Christian, trying to gauge if he had any reaction to the rumor when Nigel's next words sent a chill up my spine.

"Seems to me like the only fuckin' thing someone needs to do to be considered for prez is stick their cock in the infamous Grizz's long-lost daughter."

I'd witnessed my father attack Christian at the rental house. I'd watched Slade assault Christian at his parents' house. Other than a quick punch to Sal's jaw at Chicky's, I'd yet to see my husband make the first move.

What happened next could best be described as surreal. I'd never seen a human being move so swiftly. With an animalistic roar and terrifying speed, Christian stood and pulled Nigel up with him. He slammed him hard on our table. Bottles, drinks, and plates flew everywhere. Nigel had no time to react or defend himself as my husband expertly used his fists to inflict a punishment that was barbaric. Christian could've knocked Nigel out in one hit, but he didn't do that. He deliberately aimed where he could do the most damage without giving him the benefit of unconsciousness. He wanted Nigel to feel each blow. I thought I heard bones breaking and wondered if it was Christian's hands, or Nigel's ribs and face.

Joe and Isaac immediately jumped up from the table, but didn't try to pull Christian off Nigel. Nigel's nameless friend stood to the side, mouth agape. I looked around to see if anyone was going to intervene, and that's when I was mortified to discover that nobody cared. Some of them looked over, but went back to their drinks. A few of the women hooted and hollered. Out of the corner of my eye I noticed one gal, who'd been cheering on the fight, get grabbed by her hair and pulled back to her seat with a reprimand from her man to "Shut the fuck up."

My eyes pleaded with Isaac and Joe to intervene, to stop Christian before he did further damage. They both deliberately looked away from me.

I watched in shock as Christian reached into his back pocket and pulled out a switchblade. He opened it and held it to Nigel's neck.

"Apologize to my wife," Christian ordered, his voice low and menacing.

"Sorry. I'm sorry." Nigel's voice came out garbled. It was obvious he was choking on his own blood.

Christian closed the blade, returned it to his pocket, and started punching him again.

That's when I felt him at my side. I looked up and saw Blue. He didn't look down at me, but after exchanging a look with Isaac that I couldn't decipher, said one word. "Enough."

It took Joe, Isaac, and two other men to pull Christian off Nigel, and by then, he had lost consciousness. I prayed he wasn't dead.

Blue nodded to the other two men and to Nigel's limp body draped backwards over our table. "Get him out of here."

He looked at my husband who was breathing heavily, and still on an adrenaline high.

"He disrespected Mimi," Christian said, his tone fierce, eyes still blazing.

"What do you want done with him?" Blue asked.

Wait. What? What else needed to be done? If anything, the man needed to be taken to a hospital.

Christian didn't answer right away and Blue asked another question. "Does Nigel need to take a trip?"

I knew what that term meant. A trip meant Nigel wouldn't be returning. Ever.

That's when I realized to my horror that a man's life was hanging in the balance. A simple decision made by my husband and enforced by Blue could make a human being disappear forever.

My world felt like it was crashing down on me and I started to feel dizzy.

Since moving to Florida I'd been harassed and stalked by Autumn. I'd been called a demon seed and a sinner by Winifred Truncle. I'd come face-to-face with the man who tried to rape me when I was a teenager. And Christian had lied to me about his whereabouts a few nights before. I'd been so caught up in the celebrity of the biker world, I hadn't seen what the lifestyle entailed. And now, a man's life was going to be determined by either a yes or no from my husband.

As the vertigo retreated I spun around and headed for the exit, vowing never to set foot in The Alibi again.

CHAPTER 54

FORT LAUDERDALE, FLORIDA 2007

"It's the lifestyle our parents lived, Mimi. And I can assure you both of our mothers saw worse. Tell her, Mom," Christian said to his mother.

It was two nights later, and we'd purposely invited Christian's parents to dinner at our home *sans* Daisy and Abby.

The past two days had been fraught with unspoken tension between me and Christian. When he tried to explain what I'd seen had been mild compared to what happened at other biker bars I'd refused to listen, insisting that he could've done anything other than almost kill Nigel for the slight. My comment angered him.

"What he said was more than a slight, Mimi," he growled. "Saying something derogatory about you was the worst thing he could've done. Even if I hadn't heard it, but it had gotten back to me, I would've done the same thing."

I countered with, "Are you sure it wasn't you who was slighted?"

"You think I care what he thinks about me being considered as prez? Which is a bullshit rumor by the way. I don't even know who started it."

I'd been terribly upset by what I'd seen, but I'd understood Christian's explanation. The truth was I'd been dragging my anger out longer than necessary for another reason. Not wanting to betray Debbie's confidence, I'd been struggling with coming up with how I could've known about Christian not being at Joe's that night. I'd wanted to confront him, but not at the expense of something coming down on my new friend and her boyfriend. I was in a quandary.

Interrupting my thoughts, Aunt Christy sternly replied to Christian, "Our old lifestyles have nothing to do with today or your marriage." She stared at his battered knuckles as she passed the peas to Uncle Anthony. "Personally, I think you should step back from The Alibi. Make some new friends. Besides, if you're telling me that since you two started hanging there the riff-raff has been showing up more regularly, it's all the more reason to pull back. You can certainly find another place where you can drink beer, play pool, and eat wings that doesn't involve a biker club."

"That won't be a problem," I countered. "I don't care if I never step foot in that place again." I went on to tell them about the man who'd violently grabbed his girlfriend by the hair.

"I'm surprised you haven't seen more of that, Mimi," Uncle Anthony told me. "It's very common in that setting for the men to abuse their women. Even share them with other men. You, your mother, Christy, and very few others are rare exceptions."

I knew he was right based on some of my mother's stories.

Aunt Christy set her fork down. "What about that nice guy you work with, Christian? What was his name? The one who you stopped hanging with because his wife tried to fix you up with her girlfriends."

I glanced over at Christian who rolled his eyes. "Glen," he said before reaching for his glass. "He's cool. So is Susan, but I didn't like when she tried to set me up. They invited me out to eat twice after I got paroled, and both times Susan brought one of her friends along."

"I'm sure she only expected you to enjoy their company and a meal with them, Christian," Aunty Christy said with a slightly sarcastic tone. "I doubt you were required to propose."

I brought my napkin to my lips as I tried to stifle a smile. God help the woman who'd been set up on a blind date with my husband. He probably treated her so miserably she developed a complex.

"Glen and Susan might be a good suggestion though, Mom. They're a nice couple, and have nothing to do with bikers. However, they do ride." Christian looked thoughtful for a moment. "And Glen and I have a lot in common. We both prefer working on bikes more than cars." Then he looked at me and said, "You'd like his wife, Mimi."

"Did you bring him along to Joe's the other night?" I stabbed a piece of chicken with my fork and without looking at Christian, I asked, "You know, when you went to his house to work on his bike?"

My eyes cut to Christian's. "Nah. It wasn't a big job."

We'd cleaned up after dinner and I was carrying a tray of coffee with lemon cake into the living room when I heard Aunt Christy ask, "What is that?"

I looked where she was pointing and broke out in a wide grin. "That's the white queen we're using until we can find the one we think Abby hid," I laughed. I looked over at the chess set that was up on a shelf. I'd gotten in the habit of keeping it out of Abby's reach, but she must've snuck the queen away before that and I hadn't noticed until Christian and I recently started a game.

"Is that the...?" she started to ask.

"The candlestick from Clue? Yes, it is." Daisy had brought the board game with her during one of her visits and left it.

We made small talk while we ate our cake and drank our coffee.

"Are you two still considering buying the house next door?" Aunt Christy asked.

She was referring to the place next to ours that had been vacant and for sale since before we'd moved in. I'd told Christian that maybe we should look at it. I'd offered to make an appointment with the realtor one Saturday when Christian dragged me out our back door and over to the empty home. I looked around nervously as he easily broke into one of the rear sliders and ushered me inside.

"I don't know why they bother to lock it. Abby could've broken in," he'd grumbled before closing the door behind me.

We'd walked around inside, our voices and footsteps echoing off the cool tile floors. The only room that was carpeted was the living room. We sat down and compared it to the place we were renting. At some point, the conversation turned toward the hopes and dreams we had for the future. We must've sat there cross-legged on the carpet for an hour. That was a month ago. Before my husband decided he could lie to me.

I'd obviously taken too long to reply because I heard Christian tell his mother, "No. It was a nice house, but Mimi said it had a smell. It had been too lived-in or something like that."

"A smell?" Aunt Christy asked.

I nodded. "It was weird. I thought maybe it was the carpet because you know how they can carry odors." I shook my head. "But we sat on it and it was new." I shrugged my shoulders. "I don't know. It smelled kind of like somebody was still living there, which obviously no one is."

"You have to go with your instinct," Aunt Christy said before taking another bite of cake.

Yeah, my mind answered. *Like the instinct that says maybe I won't be buying a house with Christian after all.* The thought made my heart ache.

My expression must've hinted at my melancholy, and Aunt Christy noticed because she spun the subject back to The Alibi, and more specifically, Blue.

"Hmm," she said with a bit of a smug attitude, "what made Blue decide to grace The Alibi with his presence? I thought you told me he hangs at his restaurant, or The Red Crab or the HVAC headquarters?"

Christian shrugged his shoulders. "I dunno. Maybe he's been there when Mimi and I weren't around and decided he liked it."

"Maybe The Ghost told him to go there," she replied in a mock spooky voice.

"The Ghost that might not even be real," Christian replied. "Doesn't matter though. Blue's okay."

"Whatever." Aunt Christy rolled her eyes, waving her coffee mug toward Christian and me. "Ghost, no ghost, I'm glad you two saw the light before you got sucked in."

I couldn't have agreed with her more, but I still wasn't certain where Christian stood on the subject. I noticed that his parents eyed him, waiting for him to say something, and when he didn't, I changed the subject.

The conversation turned to Abby and how much Christian and I wanted her to live with us. Even though Aunt Christy would continue to watch Abby during the weekdays when I worked, and the occasional evening when we wanted to go out, it wouldn't be the same as having their granddaughter living under their roof. Although saddened by the prospect, Christian's parents understood. After discussing it a little more we all agreed that it still might be too soon, and that we should probably consult an attorney to see if it had the potential to stir anything up with Autumn.

I pray I won't be consulting an attorney for another reason, I silently mused.

We brought up Thanksgiving and Christmas and how my parents wanted us to visit for at least one of those holidays. And of course, we wanted to take Abby with us. I could see by Aunt Christy's expression that she wasn't keen on the idea, but she understood.

Christian's parents left. I was cleaning up the last of the dessert dishes when he came up behind me. Before wrapping his arms around my waist, he gently pulled my hair off the back of my neck so he could place tender kisses there. I automatically stiffened, as visions of him kissing another woman in the same manner floated around in my brain.

"You haven't been yourself for a couple days, Mimi. What's wrong?" he whispered.

"Nothing," I said a little too quickly. I turned off the water and stepped out of his embrace.

"You're not being honest." He was so close behind me I could almost feel his breath at my ear as I approached the open doorway that connected the kitchen to our tiny dining room.

I spun around and crossed my arms in front of me. "Think hard before you accuse me of being dishonest. Are you sure you want to do that?"

His eyes narrowed. "What's this all about?"

I looked around the room, avoiding his gaze. I'd backed myself into a corner. There was no way I could confront him about the other night without betraying Debbie. I looked back at my husband and made the difficult decision that my marriage was more important than my friendship.

"If I tell you something, do you promise me that you won't ask me where I heard it?"

He nodded.

"No." I shook my head. "I need more than that from you, Christian. You have to promise me, like all the promises you made at the altar, that you won't pick at this or retaliate."

"Yeah, okay, Mimi." He scrubbed his hand down his face. "I promise. Now tell me."

"Where were you the night you were supposed to be fixing Joe's motorcycle?"

His eyes widened. I knew the second he realized how I knew because he couldn't mask the fury behind his baby blues.

"Debbie has a big fucking mouth," he spat.

"I never said I heard it from Debbie, and you promised you wouldn't ask," I cried.

"I don't have to ask," he sneered. "I told Joe to cover for me, and that would've included her."

He wasn't denying that he lied. He was more concerned about Debbie's betrayal. I immediately jumped to her defense. "Maybe Joe never told Debbie." I could feel the hairline cracks in my heart, and I hadn't even gotten to the part where I would demand to know where he'd been and who he'd been with.

"Even if Joe didn't tell Debbie he was covering for me, she should've known better." He scowled. "I don't know how your conversation went down with her, but if you hinted that I was with Joe that night, she should've nodded her head and changed the subject. It's an unspoken rule, Mimi, and Debbie knows better. The same would be expected of you if the roles had been reversed."

"I never heard that rule, and Debbie is relatively new to the lifestyle, Christian."

"She's not that new, Mimi," he replied, his tone calmer.

"Maybe she really cares about me, Christian. Maybe she cares more about my friendship than that stupid club."

"It would appear so," he said. "If I were to tell Joe about this, he'd be pissed. It makes them look bad."

"And?" I asked. "Where were you? And don't lie to me, Christian. I'm not going to be that wife. The one who will forgive you for cheating. So, if it's happening, you need to tell me now because I am not going to hang around for years and pretend not to know or care."

I couldn't be certain, but it looked like he was trying not to smile. "Yeah, I remember. Cheating was one of your deal breakers."

"This isn't funny, Christian." I thrust my chin in the air.

"No, it's not. I'm sorry, Mimi." He grabbed the back of his neck and tilted his head sideways. "I was with Blue and Isaac. I didn't even tell Joe. I just told him to cover for me in case it ever came up, which it obviously did."

"Blue?" I hadn't realized how tense I'd become until I felt my muscles start to relax. "Why were you with Blue and Isaac? And why couldn't you tell me about it?"

"I asked Blue to help me stage a little show for you." His eyes grew serious. "I know you've been having a hard time discerning your feelings about the MC lifestyle. We've talked about you being caught up in the whole club thing. I get it. That kind of living, that kind of power can come with a high. The crew at The Alibi has been relatively mild compared to other places, and I know you saw a couple of spats, but they were nothing compared to reality."

"You had Nigel say those horrible things so you could beat him up in front of me?" I wasn't sure if I was angry or grateful.

"No," he said through a clenched jaw. "That wasn't how it was supposed to go down."

"And?" I motioned for him to continue.

"Isaac was supposed to engage me, and I was going to say something shitty to him, and he was going to pound on me. Nigel was never in on it. It was just me, Blue, and Isaac." He reached above his head and used both hands to grab the doorframe. Leaning toward me, he continued, "But when Nigel said what he did..."

I could see flames of fury in his eyes. "I could've killed the son-of-a-bitch."

I was stunned by the confession, and upset at the beating Christian had given Nigel. But then another thought occurred to me. "You weren't cheating on me," I said with a relieved sigh. "And you were willing to take another beating." A wave of love rushed over me. "For me."

He let go of the doorframe, walked toward me, and pulled me up against his body. "Don't you get it yet, Mimi?"

"Get what?" I asked breathlessly, while the heat and hardness of his body pressed against mine.

"How totally in love I am with you?"

A hard squeezing fluttered in my chest and only got more intense when he added, "I can't remember ever loving anyone but you, Mimi. Ever."

His lips came crashing down on mine. Christian's mouth felt hard, desperate. I wrapped my arms around his neck and let him swallow me whole. I groaned and tried to pull away, thinking to lead him to the bedroom, but he wouldn't let go of me. I reached for his belt buckle but he swatted my hands away.

He broke from our kiss long enough to say, "No. Just this."

And that's what we did. Kissed. I lost track of time as my husband and I made out fully clothed in the doorway that separated the kitchen from the dining room. His deliberate denial of what my body craved only heightened my need. He must've sensed when my legs started to weaken because he picked me up and carried me to the bedroom. He gently laid me on the bed and stood over me, pulling his shirt up over his head. I sat up, and once again reached for his belt buckle. He didn't slap my hand away this time as my hands quickly and expertly removed his jeans.

Giving me a wicked grin, he asked, "Did it work?"

As I was getting ready to take him in my mouth, I looked up.

My head was fuzzy, so I shook it and asked, "Did what work?"

"The little show Nigel inadvertently participated in. Are you still fascinated with the club?"

His head was bent as he watched me, his long hair threatening to cover the ripped abs that always caused an ache only he could appease. At that moment, I lost all reasoning. Coherent thought wasn't an option.

"What club?"

LATER, I scooted out of his arms and told him I wanted to take a bath. He said he would join me in a few minutes.

In the bathroom, I pinned up my hair, lit some candles, turned on the faucets, and reached under the counter for my favorite bubble bath. I realized that the bottle was empty, so I set it on the edge of the tub and reached for another one. Empty. I blew out an aggravated breath and reached for the third and last bottle.

"What the frig?" I said, frustration dripping off each word.

"What the frig what?" I heard Christian ask from behind me. I hadn't noticed him as he came up behind me. I held up the third empty bottle, waving it in the air. "Why would I put not one, but three empty bottles of bubble bath away?"

His eyes ran up and down the length of my body, memories of what had just happened in the bedroom causing the corners of his mouth to tug upward in a devilish grin.

"Christian," I demanded. "Did you hear me?"

"How should I know, Mimi?" He shrugged. "When was the last time you took a bath?"

I chewed on my lip as I tried to remember. "Two, maybe three weeks ago. And that doesn't have anything to do with it."

"It's obvious you put them away thinking you had more. I don't see what the big deal is." He wandered over to the tub, placing his hand under the water, testing it. "Daisy spends the night here. Maybe she takes baths and used it up."

It was a reasonable assumption. Daisy had spent several nights at our home, and I never questioned or noticed whether or not she took a bath or shower while she was here. I grabbed my bath salts and after sprinkling them in the water, looked over at Christian and noticed he was frowning down at the tub.

"What's wrong? Too hot for you?"

"No," he told me. "I just know that every time I've taken a bath with you, my hair is so long, half of it gets wet. I don't feel like drying it or going to bed with wet hair."

"I have a solution," I told him while I reached in one of the drawers for a hair tie. "Kneel. You're too tall for me to do this."

After he got down on one knee, I grabbed all of his hair and twisted it into a bun. He stood up and eyed himself in the mirror.

"You put my hair up in a bun," he said evenly.

"I know. I recently saw Grizz do it. My mom told me he does it to aggravate my grandfather, but she kind of likes it. She calls it a man-bun."

"I look ridiculous," Christian told me while simultaneously reaching for the hair tie to pull it out.

"Don't!" I cried while grabbing for his hands. I looked sideways at him. "You know, on my father, I didn't get it. But you look good. Leave it in. For me." I batted my eyelashes exaggeratedly. "Please?"

He didn't answer right away, but stepped into the tub, and after sitting down and motioning for me to follow him, said, "Anything for you, Dreamy Mimi."

CHAPTER 55

FORT LAUDERDALE, FLORIDA 2007

I t was about a month after our dinner with Christian's parents, and Aunt Christy's suggestion to widen our friendship circle had been spot on. I immediately warmed to Glen and Susan, and I knew they liked me too. We'd only met up with them twice before she invited me to her book club which met every Wednesday, and was more of a girls' night out since very few of them had time to read a book a week.

Christian had decided to spend his Wednesday evenings with Glen working after hours at the garage for some overtime that Axel doled out in cash. It was strange. Both Christian and I had wealthy parents, and never had the financial burden that so many young couples faced. We could go to either set of parents if we ever needed monetary help. I knew the Bears had given Slade a condominium as a graduation present. They'd made the same offer to Christian and me as a wedding gift. We hadn't turned them down, but put it on the back burner while we did what Christian originally suggested, which was to rent for a year before deciding on anything permanent. In the meantime, we paid our bills using our money and still managed to live quite comfortably.

We hadn't been back to The Alibi in almost a month, and I didn't miss it at all. However, I did miss the loss of what I thought was a solid friendship with Debbie. She'd started making excuses and turning down a couple of my invitations to meet up with them for dinner. I'd tried to meet her for lunch, and she was always too busy. When she turned down my offer to grab a quick coffee, I swiftly real-

343

ized that she hadn't been my friend. Even though she'd kindly asked about my situation with Autumn every time I called her, I figured it might've been more gossip-fueled than concern for my welfare.

As he'd promised, Christian never confronted the couple about Debbie not covering for his lie, so I knew she wasn't upset about that. I think our supposed friendship took a nosedive because Christian and I were no longer the proverbial cool kids at The Alibi. Debbie may have pretended not to care about the biker hierarchy, but it was now obvious to me that it hadn't been true. She cared more than I'd thought, and if she and Joe weren't going to be seen hanging with biker royalty—as Christian and I had come to be known—they didn't have time for us. I guess it was better that I found out sooner rather than later.

It was a cool Saturday afternoon in November and Christian and I were heading over to Glen and Susan's to discuss the possibility of the guys going into business together. Since they preferred repairing bikes over cars, they'd been toying with the idea of opening their own shop.

It was Autumn's weekend to have Abby, but more than likely she left the little girl with her handicapped mother. Even though the woman was wheelchair bound, now that Abby was no longer an infant, Autumn's mother was able to manage her visits and welcomed the child with open arms. I knew it was only for two days, but I missed my stepdaughter. I couldn't imagine what my father felt spending fifteen years away from me while he was in prison. Children had a bigger impact than I'd ever imagined. I laid my hand on my abdomen and tried not to mourn the child I would never carry.

Christian was driving my car when we stopped for gas at my regular station. I pulled my reward card out of my wallet and handed it to him with a reminder: "Don't put in diesel like I did," I teased.

He rolled his eyes before lowering our windows, turning off the engine, and swiping the card from my hand. Once he started the pump he leaned in my window and asked, "Is this where you always get your gas?"

"Always," I answered without looking at him. I'd been texting with a lady at the museum who wanted to know if I'd be interested in working full-time for two weeks while another employee recovered from surgery.

"And you never get gas anywhere else?" he probed.

I sent the message I'd typed on my phone and looked up at him.

"This station is convenient to home and work, and has the best prices. Why?"

"Because there aren't any diesel pumps at this station," he replied while scanning the other kiosks. "You never get gas anywhere else?"

"I can't say that," I answered. "I'm sure I've stopped at other stations, but it's not the norm. I'm a creature of habit," I said with a shrug. "You know that."

We spent the afternoon with Glen and Susan and were saddened to have to turn down an invitation for Thanksgiving at their home. I told them we would be spending it with my grandfather in North Carolina. Early on, I'd handled casual inquiries about my family by telling them they lived in Montana. After a time, Christian had privately reminded me to be careful. "I understand why you've stuck to the Montana story, Mimi, but what are you going to do if you actually say it to someone who's familiar with Montana, and starts asking deeper questions?"

His observation was accurate and I considered it a miracle that it hadn't happened yet. I would remember to ask my parents for their thoughts and advice when I saw them at Thanksgiving.

After finishing up at Glen and Susan's, we headed home with a plan to go for a motorcycle ride together the next day. I was getting ready to ask Christian if it would be a good time to give Slade his surprise present when my phone pinged. I must've made an uncomfortable sound because we stopped at a red light, and Christian looked over at me.

"Who is it?" he asked.

"Rachel."

"Who is Rachel?" He tapped his fingers on the steering wheel and scanned the intersection, only half interested.

"It's Nick Rosman's fiancée."

"Yeah, right," came his reply.

"She wants to know if I can have lunch with her next week. She's already asked like four or five times and I've always made excuses. I think she wants to be friends. I guess she's seen me talking with Jolly Roger so maybe she feels it's okay."

"Do you want to be friends with her?" he asked. He turned his head toward me and tucked his chin against his right shoulder, his blue eyes looking at me over the top of his sunglasses.

"Not necessarily. And it's not because she isn't a nice person. It doesn't feel right." I glanced at the light and told him, "It's green."

"You're too nice, baby," he said as we proceeded through the intersection and approached our neighborhood. "Some people and relationships aren't meant to be. They're like dead skin. After a while, if you don't slough it off, it starts to itch. When it starts to itch it annoys and distracts you. You've gotta scrape them off, Mimi, before they take you away from what's really important. How many hours have you wasted fretting over how to tell this girl you aren't interested?"

I'd already known that Christian saw the world in black and white, but it became more obvious since I'd moved to Florida. Christian either liked someone or he didn't. A potential friendship was something he wanted to pursue or drop. He didn't waver with what-ifs or maybes. I remembered his advice when I had to break up with Lucas at college. "Rip the Band-Aid off," he'd told me.

"You're right," I informed him when we pulled into our driveway. "I'll let her know, and I'll tell her why I don't think it would be a good idea." I thought about the embarrassment I would've saved myself in pursuit of Debbie's friendship if she'd been honest with me about not feeling the need to stay friends. We no longer fit into her and Joe's world, just like Rachel and Nick had no place in mine and Christian's.

I asked Christian how much longer it would be before he gave Slade the surprise he'd been working on.

"I'm thinking about asking him over tonight."

"It's ready?" I asked.

"I want to give it a once-over, but yeah, it'll be ready. I know it's last minute, but can you check and see if he wants to come by?"

"What should I tell him?"

"Tell him the truth." He grinned at me. "That it's a surprise."

"Give me your phone." I held out my hand. "Mine is almost dead. I need to charge it." He handed it over and I stuck it in my pocket.

I went inside and found my charger while Christian headed to the garage. I called Slade from Christian's cell phone, and when he didn't answer I sent a text.

I caught up on chores and reflected on how in spite of the loss of our friendship with Debbie and Joe, things had been looking up. For starters, Autumn's harassing notes had ceased. I hadn't seen her in over a month, which was fine with me. And when I mentioned her to Aunt Christy I was told that she'd heard through Autumn's mother, that Autumn had finally found a love interest. Mrs. Truncle had never again visited the museum, and I was enjoying my job more than ever. I was making good progress in my eating disorder therapy and had even joined a support group that met weekly. I'd only been once, but it was nice knowing they were there if I felt the need to share outside of my weekly visit with my therapist.

Finally feeling settled and confident in my new life was having another positive effect on me. I didn't seem to be as scatterbrained as I'd been when I'd first moved here. Adjusting to a new husband, step-daughter, family, job, therapist, had weighed heavier than I'd thought. I guess I'd been so overwhelmed, I couldn't seem to focus on what I was doing, and I'd started to believe I really was Dreamy Mimi. Yes, I was proud of myself that it had been over a month since I'd done something ridiculously stupid. Like putting a gallon of milk away in the cabinet instead of the refrigerator. Or washing my car and leaving the hose on all night.

I looked over at the chess set and the candlestick that replaced the white queen we'd never been able to locate. I would have to say that the missing queen was the biggest regret in my lapse of responsibility. When we'd discovered Abby's fascination with the chess pieces, I was certain I'd made it a point to put it out of her reach. But I'd obviously not stayed on top of it because it came as a surprise when Christian and I discovered the piece was gone. I knew it would show up one day, but until then, it nagged at me.

The distinct ring of Christian's phone brought me out of my daydreams. I slammed the dryer door shut and pulled the phone out of my back pocket. It was Slade. He told me he was supposed to have dinner with Erin, but he knew she wouldn't mind if they stopped by.

I headed out to the garage to tell Christian when I saw him walking up the street toward our house. I left the garage and strode across the lawn to meet him. When he got closer I could see he had a scowl on his face.

"Where were you?" I asked, puzzled by why he'd left without telling me and wondering where he'd gone.

He tilted his head back over his shoulder and said, "Tom wanted me to look under his hood."

Tom was one of our neighbors. He and his partner, Richard, were interior designers and had introduced themselves after we'd moved in. They'd offered their assistance in decorating our home, and after I told them we weren't certain about buying it, they settled for helping me select some colors for the rooms.

"Is it something that's easily fixable?" I asked Christian.

He looked distracted and asked, "Huh?"

"Whatever is wrong with Tom's car. Were you able to help him out?" I asked while trying to keep up with his long strides as he returned to the garage.

"Yeah," he replied as he headed back inside.

"Slade said yes to the invitation. He's taking Erin out to dinner, but said they'd stop by on the way."

"Okay," he muttered before returning his attention to the gift he'd been working on for Slade.

"I DON'T KNOW what to say."

It was hours later and Slade was standing in the garage, looking at the Harley-Davidson Christian had restored for him.

"I didn't know you rode a motorcycle." Erin ran her hand over the leather seat.

"I don't," Slade said. "At least I haven't in a long time," he corrected. I could see excitement that he couldn't disguise. "It's the hundred-year anniversary model," he said reverently. He swung his leg over the seat, careful not to kick Erin in the process. "And a hard one to find."

His comments led me to believe that Slade may not have ridden a bike in years, but he still loved them.

His eyes roamed over the front as he clutched the handlebars and said, "It's been so long, Christian. I don't know if I remember how to ride."

"I could've given you your old one," Christian commented. "I'm sure Dad has it stored somewhere. But if you'd wanted to ride that one, you would've already. I found this for a steal because the guy managed to mangle it. I knew when I saw it you would like it."

Christian reached for a photo that had been sitting on the shelf. He handed it to Slade. "This is the before picture."

Slade's eyes widened as he looked up at Christian. "This is the bike I'm sitting on?" he asked as he waved the photo in the air.

Christian nodded.

"I don't think I ever realized how talented you are, Chris."

"What do you say?" Christian asked. He was hopeful, struggling not to let it show. "Mimi and I ride almost every weekend that we don't have Abby. Why don't you start coming with us?"

I could see Slade nodding as if chewing on a thought. "Yeah, I think I will, bro. It'll be good for me." He got off the bike and reached for Christian, pulling him into a man hug and releasing him. "Thank you." He waved toward the bike. "For this. It means more than you could know.

"And thank you, Mimi. I know he wasn't spending time with you if he was working on this." He thumped the seat with his fingers. "Thank you for that."

I was sure part of Slade's decision to accept the gift and ride with us was based on how he'd heard from his parents that Christian had been staying away from the club. But I also felt there was more to it. Regardless, it was a way for the brothers to start rebuilding their relationship.

I turned to Erin and asked, "Would you like to see the inside of the house? I haven't done much except for paint because we're renting, but it still feels like home."

Her answer was a smile followed by, "Lead the way."

I escorted Erin inside and I listened as she oohed and aahed over some of my minor decorating decisions. It turned out she had a background in interior design, and wholeheartedly agreed with Tom and Richard's color suggestions.

I'd shown her the bedrooms and was coming down the hall when Christian appeared. "I'm taking Slade next door. He's thinking about buying a house as an investment. We won't be long."

I waved him off as Erin followed me toward the kitchen. It turned out that Erin was a super sweet woman, and someone I hadn't considered as a potential friend. Then again, why would I? I'd only seen her the one time at the Bears' home. I'd heard through Aunt Christy that Slade occasionally hung out with her, but that they weren't officially dating. My curiosity got the best of me and I couldn't stop myself from probing further.

"Are you and Slade a thing or not?"

Without missing a beat, Erin said, "Slade and I are good friends and bed buddies." There was no embarrassment or shame in her comment.

"Nothing more serious?" I reached for a pitcher. I thought I would whip up some margaritas to offer them before they left for dinner. "You two sure seem well-suited for each other." I was being honest.

She shook her head with a grim smile. "Slade and I have a simple relationship. The truth is, we both carry a torch for someone else."

I stopped mid-stir and looked at her. She was standing next to me, and had started slicing the limes I'd laid on a cutting board. She felt my stare because she launched into a sad tale about the man who owned her heart. A man she couldn't be with until she handled an undesirable situation concerning the ex-husband who'd cheated on her, and his manipulation to make her life miserable. I could understand that. She didn't want to start out a new relationship with an old one hanging over her head.

"He's a horrible, mean-spirited person. It's been going on for over a year. He can't get past our divorce. If it weren't for our children, I'd have moved out of the country. And I've tried everything legally to make him go away, but it's not working."

As if reading my thoughts, she added, "Slade has been so good with the legal advice. Unfortunately, I seem to have hit a road block."

It made more sense now. Their friendship, although genuine, had been born of need and convenience—physically, emotionally, and technically. Which raised a question.

"Slade?"

She stopped cutting limes and looked over at me.

"The torch he carries. Is it for the same person you alluded to all those months ago when we met at his parents' house?" I asked.

Her mouth turned downward as she nodded. She told me about a librarian named Bevin that Slade had shown interest in several months before, and how Erin had felt responsible for inadvertently kiboshing the potential romance.

"If I hadn't worn his shirt, he wouldn't have smelled like me," she said as she scraped the limes from the cutting board into a bowl.

"It was obviously a misunderstanding," I tried to reassure her.

She shrugged her shoulders and said, "I thought so too. But he was so wracked with guilt over having slept with me less than an hour before going to her house, he justified her rebuff."

She shook her head and said, "Slade can have any woman he wants. I'm sure I don't have to tell you that he's a catch. Yet he's fixated on this one girl who turned him away."

I had to agree. My brother-in-law was not just handsome and intelligent, but a decent and good human being. His mother had confided that she'd never seen Slade act the way he had when Christian first brought me home. I wondered if he was stinging even back then over the woman Erin was talking about. Maybe his frustration at his own situation is what caused him to lash out at Christian.

"I thought maybe he was getting past it. He'd gone the whole summer without seeing her when she didn't accept the temporary position at the law library. He took a couple of women out but told me their conversations never went beyond where they worked out, what they wore, and what they drove. Slade felt like Bevin was a woman of substance. Someone whose discussions wouldn't be based on materialistic things." She walked the cutting board and knife to the sink and started rinsing them. "Apparently this girl made one heck of an impression on him." Shaking out her hands and reaching for a dish towel, she added, "And I don't think they've even spoken much."

"I can see that," I agreed as I reached for glasses. I grabbed three because I knew Christian would want a beer. "I think Slade is very insightful and probably puts a lot of value in first impressions. And she obviously made one. You said you thought he was getting past it. What happened?"

"I met him for lunch about a month ago. I've never met him for lunch before, Mimi. Not once." She rolled her eyes. "The most we've done is grab coffee, and an occasional dinner. And that's only when I don't have my kids. Like tonight. So it's rare."

"Sorry," I said as I nodded toward the button on the blender. She waved me on, and after I turned off the blender and started pouring the mixture into our glasses, she continued.

"I had a client near the courthouse. I thought I would take a chance and see if Slade wanted to grab a sandwich. It turned out Bevin was at the restaurant, and after Slade discreetly, or so I thought, pointed her out to me, I could tell her friend said something to her."

"Did Slade talk to Bevin?" I asked, riveted to every word.

"No." She shook her head. "I think the friend noticed me because immediately afterward, Bevin jumped up and couldn't get out of the place fast enough. I told him to go after her, but he didn't want to make a scene."

"Sounds to me like Slade needs to pull his big boy shorts up and talk to the woman," I said. For goodness' sake. Christian had literally abducted me. The least Slade could do was approach the woman for a conversation.

I was getting ready to say that to Erin when she said, "Slade is the consummate gentleman. He doesn't want to force himself on a woman who isn't interested."

"I think you and I know that by the way Bevin ran out of that restaurant, that she is interested. Don't we?"

"Yes!" Erin practically shouted. "That's what I've tried to tell him. I've never seen a more intelligent, attractive guy be such a doofus when it comes to women. Especially when he could probably have any one he wanted."

"I'll drink to that," I said as we clinked our glasses together. I agreed. My brother-in-law would be any girl's dream. Especially if they ever caught sight of him on his new Harley.

"Drink to what?" came Christian's deep voice from behind us.

I turned around and said, "To it being margarita time!"

CHAPTER 56

FORT LAUDERDALE, FLORIDA 2007

Twenty Minutes Earlier

After letting themselves in the vacant house, Christian and Slade slowly climbed the steps to the attic. "What is that smell?" Slade spat.

Christian swung the flashlight around the empty space and fixated on a far corner. As they got closer they could see that someone had been there. There was an old sleeping bag with a shredded pillow. Critters had obviously been pulling the stuffing out to make nests. Off to the side was a Bunsen burner that sat on what looked like a fishing tackle box. Garbage was strewn everywhere, including empty cans that carried the stench of uneaten food. Christian kicked at one with his foot and said, "Whoever's been staying up here probably left prints on these cans." He bent down and scanned the area. "And I don't think he's been here for a while."

"If you can sneak back over here with a plastic bag and get a few, I can get them dusted," Slade offered while scanning the area. "Chances are it's just some vagrant who needed a place to sleep and thought it would be fun to mess with your heads."

Christian swung around and gave Slade a hard glare. "No. This is more than that. Whoever this fuck is, he's been targeting Mimi specifically. Something seemed off this morning when we stopped for gas and she brought up accidentally putting diesel in her tank. After seeing her regular gas station, it just didn't make sense. Not to mention a lot of the newer diesel nozzles won't fit in a regular gas tank. And it's not just the diesel. There's been a lot of stupid shit happening at our house. I chalked it up to forgetfulness. Damn. I even teased her about it." He shook his head in disgust. "It's obviously been more than that and it's one of the reasons I wanted you to stop by. I was gonna ask you for some help."

While Mimi gave Erin a tour, Christian explained to Slade how his neighbor, Tom, had approached him and said there was something he should see. Tom had Christian follow him back to his house and showed him video of what his surveillance camera had picked up.

"I'm sorry for not coming to you with this sooner," Tom said apologetically. "Richard and I never have cause to look at it. I had it installed a while ago before you and Mimi even moved here when a neighbor's kid was breaking into houses. That kid was sent off to military school and we haven't had a problem since. I don't know what made me decide to look at it today, but I'm glad I did. Some of this footage goes back months."

Christian leaned closer to the screen and squinted his eyes as he watched a hunched figure in a black hoodie approach Mimi's car with a jug. *The diesel in her tank.* He also watched as the man went around the side of their home and disappeared from view. *He let himself in through a window out of camera range,* Christian thought. There was footage of the intruder near their front bushes, where the hose was neatly wrapped around its holder. *The flooding incident.* Each time, the lone figure came into view from the back side of the vacant house. Of course, he could've been weaving his way through back yards and skirting around the lake to get to their home, but Christian's gut told him the person in black had been squatting in the empty house next to theirs. Mimi had detected a smell when they'd let themselves in to check out the house. Was the stranger lurking about even then? The last shot of the man was curious and was from just over a month ago. He'd approached Mimi's car, on the driver's side, but Christian couldn't tell what he was doing. He couldn't remember Mimi telling him anything unusual about her car. Maybe the guy had gotten spooked and run off before doing any damage.

"That's the last time he shows up," Tom informed him. "I have no footage of where he's specifically coming from. Nothing of him walking down the street. My best guess is he comes from a block over and makes his way around your lake and through the back yards. Or maybe he's slumming at the vacant house next to yours."

Christian nodded. "Yeah, you can easily get into that house through the back slider. I'm gonna check it out." He stood up straight and pinched his nose between his fingers. "I appreciate you telling me about this, Tom."

"I didn't want to tell you in front of Mimi." He paused thoughtfully before adding, "I didn't want to scare her."

"No," Christian quickly interjected. "You did the right thing. I'm not going to tell her just yet. Will you keep an eye on your footage and let me know if anything else shows up?"

After agreeing to do so, they'd exchanged cell phone numbers.

A loud crash brought Christian back to the moment.

"Sorry," Slade said sheepishly. "I wanted to see if there was anything in the tackle box that could provide a clue as to who's living here." He stood up. "It's empty."

"Someone is purposely messing with her," Christian said through a clenched jaw.

"Any idea who it could be?" Slade asked.

"Shit, man. It could be so many people."

Slade raised an eyebrow.

"An old enemy of Grizz's. A woman that he rejected for Mimi's mother. The boyfriend she dumped in college." He scrubbed his hand down his face in frustration. "There was an old bitty where she works who told her that some woman who Grizz killed years ago still has sisters that live around here."

Slade let out a low whistle. "I get the biker connection, but do you think sisters of one of Grizz's victims would know who Mimi is?" he asked.

"Nothing would surprise me," Christian confessed. "It could even be Nick Rosman's fiancée. Maybe the woman is pissed at me and wants to take it out on Mimi."

"What about Autumn?" Slade asked.

Christian nodded. "She'd be the most obvious." He paused before adding, "We're assuming it's a guy, but I couldn't tell from the video. And I can't shake the feeling I know this person. It's the walk, the gait. It's familiar."

"So other than the diesel in her tank and a bunch of other stupid shit, this person hasn't tried to hurt Mimi." It wasn't a question, but a statement. "And whoever's been doing it, hasn't done it for a month or so."

"It would seem that way, but I can't take any chances. When my gut told me something wasn't right at the gas station this morning, I was gonna ask you to find me a legitimate guy who can watch Mimi for me. I didn't want to go to anyone in my circle, including Blue or our parents, because if it's someone who's close to us, I don't want them to know I'm on to them.

"You couldn't possibly think it's our parents?" Slade asked incredulously.

"Of course not," Christian chided. "I don't want them involved. You know them. Mom especially. You'd think raising my daughter would be enough to keep her busy, but she's always looking for a project. She wouldn't approach this subtly."

Christian's eyes snapped to Slade's, and his expression grew dark. "I don't want Mimi to know about this. I want to handle it and get rid of the person without her even suspecting. She's tried so hard since we moved here, and I couldn't bear for her to think she has an enemy. Especially if it's someone who's been holding a grudge over something Grizz did."

Slade nodded his understanding. "I have a guy for you. He's good. She'll never know he's keeping an eye on her. He's expensive."

"We're leaving in a couple days to spend Thanksgiving with her family. I want him to watch her until we leave, and resume when we get back which will be a week from tomorrow." Christian scoffed. "And since when has money ever been an issue?"

They left the attic, and before they got to the house Christian whispered, "I'll get a couple cans to you as soon as I can sneak back over without Mimi knowing."

"Why don't you invite us to stay for dinner and we can run back over when the girls are busy?" Slade asked.

"Sounds like a plan, bro," Christian said as he gave Slade a slap on the back.

CHAPTER 57

I t was only a couple of weeks after we'd returned from our Thanksgiving visit and I was spending my lunch hour daydreaming about our trip to the mountains. I could've tried to finish my Christmas shopping, but I wouldn't have been able to make it to my favorite mall and back in an hour. I took a bite of my sandwich and browsed through the pictures on my phone. I came to one that had me almost spitting out my food. I laughed out loud at the picture of my little sister trying to hold Abby on one hip, while a tote bag that contained Ruthie's favorite baby doll and a karate trophy dangled from her shoulder. Four-and-a-half-year-old Ruthie, the quintessential badass girlie girl, had no business trying to carry around three-year-old Abby, but she'd tried to for almost our entire visit. It was comical to watch her as she attempted to play nursemaid to her new niece.

Christian and Abby had blended so seamlessly into my family during our short visit, I secretly wondered if it would ever be possible to live near them. I absentmindedly touched my stomach and remembered the heartfelt offer my cousin Rachelle had made to Christian and me.

"Travis and I have talked about this, and we're both in agreement. If you ever think you want to have a baby, I'd consider it a privilege to be your surrogate. I have easy pregnancies, and I'd make sure you were part of everything. It would be an honor carrying your child for you."

I'd cried in Christian's arms that night, not only because I'd been

357

so moved by Rachelle's offer, but because it brought back a memory from our childhood, and something Christian had said to me on a hot Florida playground almost twenty years earlier.

I was able to shake off the melancholy feeling that memory evoked and thoroughly enjoyed the time we had with my family, and before we knew it we were driving back to Florida.

I sighed when I considered how in recent months Abby seemed to blossom and had turned into a real chatterbox. Just two days ago, and for the first time ever, she'd cried when Christian took her back to her grandparents. She'd wanted to stay with her daddy. My heart melted when he told me about it. I was beginning to think that maybe it was time to have another custody discussion with Christian's parents and an attorney. I still hadn't crossed paths with Autumn in months, and had even forgotten to ask Aunt Christy about her. But she'd stopped harassing me, leading me to believe that maybe she'd finally moved on.

I reached for a piece of celery and crunched on it as I thought about how the past two weeks had gone by in a blur. Between Christmas shopping and temporarily working full-time, I'd barely had a minute to think.

Which was how I surprised even myself when I accepted a lunch invitation from Blue. He'd called my cell about ten o'clock my first morning back to work after the holiday and apologized for the last-minute invitation. I was so caught off guard I couldn't even think of an excuse not to, so I agreed. His restaurant, Razors, was just a few short blocks from where I worked, so I could easily make it there and back on my lunch break.

The hostess led me toward a table tucked away in a cozy corner. I followed her, my eyes scanning the room as I tried to imagine what it looked like when it was a biker bar back when my father owned it. I couldn't conjure up an image. The professional-looking men and women having power lunches over mineral water and California veggie plates were in total contrast to scary-looking bikers who were waited on by topless women.

The lunch had been pleasant enough, even with the sidelong glances I noticed coming from Debbie. I hadn't spoken to her in ages, and I wondered if she was worried that I might mention to Blue how she'd cut me out of her life. Not that she had anything to worry about. Blue wouldn't care one way or another.

"Your aunt Jodi hates me," Blue told me.

I'd just taken a sip of water and carefully measured my words. "She hates all bikers."

"Yeah, I know," he said as he leaned back in his chair. "I'm crazy about her, and it's probably because she hates me. I seem to have developed an affinity for women who despise me."

His comment was so random and sincere I couldn't suppress a giggle.

"I hope you're not going to ask me for relationship advice," I told him honestly. "Aunt Jodi is an enigma."

"She haunts me, Mimi. And don't think it's not fucking weird that I see myself fantasizing about Ginny's identical twin. The dyed blond hair and blue contact lenses can't hide that she is the spitting image of your mother. Grizz would be doing somersaults in his grave if he knew I lusted over someone who looks exactly like his woman."

And you'd be doing somersaults out of your chair if you knew Grizz was alive, which is probably one of the main reasons my aunt Jodi has been pushing you away.

We continued to make small talk and it wasn't contrived or forced. I hadn't really known Blue while I was growing up, but the few times I'd had an occasion to see him, he was always kind to me. I asked about his sons, Timmy and Kevin. My half brother, Jason, and Blue's youngest son, Kevin, were actually half brothers. Although I don't think either of them knew it or if they did, it wasn't something either felt they should pursue.

"Kevin is in the military and barely speaks to me," Blue told me. "Not that we've had a falling out," he quickly corrected. "He's just one of those kids that doesn't stay in touch. When we do speak, we're good."

"And Timmy?" I politely asked.

"Timmy is married to a lovely girl and has two boys." I detected sadness in his expression. "They're in Orlando and I see them as often as I can." His demeanor changed and he immediately perked up. Perhaps I'd misread the sadness as nothing more than missing his family.

We were interrupted by Debbie who said, "I'm sorry to intrude. Mimi, I meant to say hello when I saw you but this place gets crazy during lunch."

I smiled and told her I understood. She turned to Blue and said,

"You have a phone call in the office. It's a realtor and she's pretty excited. She thinks she has a buyer for Razors."

"Tell her I'll call her back," Blue replied without even looking at Debbie.

She told me it was nice seeing me, excused herself, and strode toward the office.

"You're selling your restaurant?" I asked. *Maybe the rumors about Blue stepping down from the club had been true.* He answered my unspoken thought. "I want to be closer to Timmy and his family. I'm not getting any younger, and let's face it, it's closer to Louisiana too."

Closer to Aunt Jodi.

His eyes grew serious and he leaned across the table. "Mimi, there's something I have to say to you. It's something I should've said to your mother years ago before she moved away." He tugged on his beard. "Something I hope you'll tell her and Jason for me." He cleared his throat before adding, "Something I hope you'll forgive me for."

I sat up straighter. "Of course. What is it?"

"It's my fault Tommy was murdered."

I didn't know what to say so I stared, not understanding.

"I'm the one that called him that morning."

"The call the police couldn't trace? They thought maybe it was from one of the kids from the shelter where he volunteered."

Shaking his head he said, "No. It was me. I'd heard something unsettling on the street that concerned you and a boy you were dating."

"Nick Rosman," I interrupted.

Nodding he said, "Yeah, him. I'd heard what he'd tried to do to you, and I thought Tommy should know. I'm the reason he deviated from his normal route on the way to work."

I tried to blink back the tears as the pain of Tommy's death slammed into my chest. After swallowing my grief I reached for Blue's hand across the table. "It's not your fault. You aren't responsible. The man who shot him is responsible."

"It is my fault. I should've handled that piece of shit, but I didn't. Instead, I settled on giving Tommy a courtesy call. If he'd asked me to do something, I would have. But the fault is mine. I shouldn't have had to ask him if he needed me to handle Nick. I should've just done it. I'm sorry, Mimi. Please tell your mother and brother for me." A moment passed and he added, "Umm...does she know about Nick? What Christian did and why he did it?"

I could only nod.

"Christian did what I should've done." He shook his head slowly as a thought came to him. "Your husband is like a different man now. He's changed so much from when he used to hang with the club before he went to prison. He's calmer, more focused. You've been good for him, Mimi."

I sniffled and said, "We're good for each other."

Lunch with Blue was last week, and after reassuring him that he didn't need to apologize for something he hadn't done, I had strolled back to the museum, enjoying my walk along the tree-lined streets. I remembered having the distinct impression I was being watched, and not for the first time, but I shook it off. Seeing Debbie, and reliving Tommy's death, had made me feel vulnerable. *Everything is perfect now,* I told myself. *Things are finally going my way.*

My cell phone rang, pulling me from the memories of our holiday visit and the lunch with Blue. I'd been so startled I banged my knee on the desk while jumping up to retrieve it from my purse.

It was Christian telling me that he would be working late again. In the couple of weeks since we'd returned from the mountains, Christian had been racking up a lot of overtime at the garage. I guess he'd forgotten that it was Wednesday night and I would be going to girls' night out at Susan's.

"I figured," I told him. "It's Wednesday night. Tell Glen I said hey."

"I guess all this overtime is making me lose track of time," he confessed. "I'll see you tonight, sweetheart. I love you."

"I love you too," I replied.

The rest of the afternoon passed uneventfully and it was finally time to lock up the museum. Employees parked out back, but I still used the front entrance because the back door key was fickle. Some days it worked and some days it didn't. It was easier to leave through the front, and walk around the side.

After making sure everything was turned off and the museum was secure, I locked the front door and stood on the wide veranda observing the one-way street. The majority of homes were still occupied residences, and the adherences to bylaws concerning their exteriors added to the ambience and cozy feel of the neighborhood. The hair on my arms stood up and the same feeling I'd had last week of being watched returned. I shivered in spite of the unseasonably warm December air, and quickly walked down the steps, around the side of the museum and directly for my car. I spotted it immediately and with a heavy heart removed the paper from beneath my windshield wiper. What was scrawled on it hurt almost as much as thinking Christian had been cheating on me.

BARREN BITCH!!!

Autumn had struck again. I'd been so hopeful that she'd finally given up and was going to let me live in peace that I hadn't thought about her in weeks. When she'd started missing some of her weekends with Abby, I hadn't concerned myself with the woman who didn't concern herself with her own daughter. I hadn't asked Aunty Christy so I didn't know, but could only assume that Autumn's new beau hadn't worked out so she once again turned her wrath and jealousy toward me.

I crumpled the note and tossed it on the seat next to me as I started the car. I was getting ready to back out when I froze. What my eyes landed on brought an immediate wave of adrenaline that felt like fear, but quickly transformed into a rush of anger so intense I could hear my heartbeat as it pounded in my ears.

Hanging from my rearview mirror was one of Abby's hair ribbons. And dangling from the end of it was the missing white queen from our chess set. Autumn had used blood red nail polish to paint most of it red. The only white part that wasn't covered had four letters written in thin red marker—my name. Mimi.

So that's where the missing piece went. Abby must've somehow smuggled it out of the house after one of her visits, and Autumn found it during one of her rare weekends with her daughter. The queen dangling by its neck at the end of a rope indicated that Autumn had decided to step up her game. How dare she threaten me, and use precious Abby's hair ribbon and her love of our chess pieces to do it! I was furious.

I threw the car into reverse and jammed on the brake before almost taking out a decorative lamp post. I shifted into drive, and blasted out of the parking lot so recklessly, I didn't realize until I almost had a head-on collision that I'd turned the wrong way down the one-way street. After mouthing my apology to the other driver, I kept going the wrong way until I was finally able to make a turn onto a two-way street.

I was done tiptoeing around Autumn and her hatefulness. I was finished with turning the other cheek. It was time to confront her, and let her know this crap had to stop. And if I had to get Christian involved to make sure it did, then so be it. I knew where she worked so I would go there first. *I hope you know how to defend yourself, Autumn, because my blood won't stop boiling until I've splattered some of yours.*

CHAPTER 58

FORT LAUDERDALE, FLORIDA 2007

I had to rely on the breathing techniques I'd learned in yoga to calm myself as I made the drive to the fancy boutique in the mall where Autumn worked. I'd purposely avoided this mall because I never wanted to run into her, so once I got inside I would have to rely on a directory to help me find her store.

I snatched the queen off my rearview mirror and stuck it, along with the crumpled note, in the pocket of my sweater. I'd just locked the door and was getting ready to stick my keys in my back pocket when I realized my car had been locked when I left work. How did Autumn manage to get inside it at the museum?

I had to bite the inside of my cheek to keep myself from screaming when I remembered the set of spare car keys that went missing months ago. Maybe Abby's fascination with swiping chess pieces had morphed into something more. I shook my head to clear away the thought. *No. My keys and chess piece? Those are too specific.*

I saw red when the truth became obvious. All of the parts started to fall into place at the same time. The empty bottles of bubble bath. The milk in the cupboard. And so much more. Autumn had been in my house.

My feet pounded so hard it felt like the pavement shook as I barreled into the mall, and instead of looking for a directory I asked the security guard I passed where to find the upscale shop. When I got there, I stopped and took deep breaths. I couldn't see Autumn through the glass displays, but that didn't mean she wasn't in the back. I approached the first woman who looked like an employee. She gave me a polite smile, but I wasn't fooled. She had snob written all over her. I didn't give her a chance to speak. "I'm here to see Autumn. Is she in the back?"

Her eyes narrowed in displeasure, and she shook her head slightly. The clothes she'd been straightening were ignored as she clasped her hands together and replied, "Autumn decided to take her vacation during the busiest two weeks of the year."

Yeah, so she can focus on stalking me.

"Do you know if she's vacationing locally?" I asked, trying to hide my disappointment at not being able to strike while the iron was hot.

"No. I didn't ask and she didn't offer. Maybe Britney can help you."

A woman who'd obviously been eavesdropping on our conversation made her way over. "Are you a friend of Autumn's?" she asked sweetly. Her name tag identified her.

If Britney was Autumn's friend, she would've heard about me, and might not be cooperative.

"I am!" I lied with a smile. "We haven't talked recently." I paused and tried to look dumb. "Obviously, since I didn't even know she was on vacation. But I recently lost all the numbers in my phone, and since I was shopping here I thought it was the perfect time to drop in and say hello."

I could only hope my earlier angst hadn't shown on my face, and that Britney believed me. Apparently she did because she reached into her pocket and pulled out her phone. "I can forward her number to you." She handed me her cell and said, "Here. Just send it to yourself."

The number was displayed. I already knew Autumn's cell phone number, and had no intention of forwarding it to my cell phone from Britney's.

I started punching in a random number when Britney's next comment caught me by surprise.

"I hope she's not in the subway when you call her," Britney giggled.

I looked up sharply. "The subway?"

"Yeah," Britney replied. By now the other woman had lost interest in our conversation and had walked away. Britney glanced over at her and looked back at me. "Carol has never liked Autumn. Thinks she has a dark side."

I couldn't agree more.

"And is a rotten mother," Britney added. "But I know she's a good mom. It's not Autumn's fault that her daughter's new stepmother has turned the little girl against her."

Now I've heard it all. I had to battle an eye roll.

"You said something about a subway?" I interjected. I was anxious to put the conversation behind me, but the subway comment had stumped me.

"Autumn called me from New York today." She tilted her head sideways before continuing. "Her new boyfriend's family is there, and they're visiting. She was in the subway, and the trains were so loud I could barely hear her."

"Autumn called you today?" I repeated.

She nodded.

"From the subway in New York City?"

"Yeah. I've always wanted to go there. It sounds like the most romantic place in the world. I mean, I know there's crime, but the subways sound so cool."

I could hear Britney still babbling to herself as I headed for the exit.

CHAPTER 59

FORT LAUDERDALE, FLORIDA 2007

I sat in my car and stared out the windshield over the steering wheel. The puzzle pieces that I'd so intricately placed together were no longer fitting. *Think, Mimi.*

Okay, so Autumn hadn't been in my house. The misplaced spare keys, the empty bottles of bubble bath had all been on me. But someone had stolen that chess piece. Who? It had to be someone who'd been in my home. And it had to be the same person who'd been writing the notes. But who, other than Autumn, hated me enough to say such awful things?

Autumn certainly did, but she wasn't even in Florida. *She could've had an accomplice,* I mused. Could the bubbly Britney have helped her? No. I couldn't see it. And if I let myself think about it, how much animosity had Autumn really inflicted on me? Other than nasty comments and snide remarks that had always been directed at me out of earshot of others, what had she done? Did I see guilt in her expression when I'd confronted her about that first note? I couldn't remember.

I reached into my pocket and pulled out the crumpled note. I smoothed it against my steering wheel and stared at the painful words.

BARREN BITCH!!

All caps, just like before. The same handwriting. The same slant. The same colored marker. But something was wrong. What was it?

And then it hit me. Autumn had called me a bitch to my face, but she'd never implied she had any knowledge of my inability to carry a child. She had no way of knowing. And I wasn't barren. I had ovaries. I couldn't conceive or carry the baby in my own body. Who, other than my family, knew this?

I shook my head in an attempt to clear away the cobwebs and tried to instantaneously dredge up every conversation I'd had with every person since moving to Florida. It was too much to wrap my head around.

I needed to tell Christian. This was something I could no longer keep from him. I was driving home when I remembered it was girls' night out at Susan's. Christian would be at the garage with Glen. I was at a red light when the memory slammed me so hard I gasped out loud. I *had* told someone.

One person knew that I'd had a hysterectomy. Susan had been complaining about how much Glen's parents were pressing them for grandchildren, even though both she and Glen had agreed before getting married that they didn't want kids. I remembered her saying that it would be so much easier to shut them up if either her or Glen were sterile. I liked Susan, and I wasn't offended by the comment, but I did want to offer her some words of wisdom. I didn't go into the details of my surgery, just that it was an emergency hysterectomy, and that Christian and I wouldn't be having children which is why we were so grateful for Abby. I kindly told her she should be glad she was able to have a baby in the event she and Glen ever changed their minds. She seemed truly mortified and wouldn't stop apologizing.

Someone honked behind me and I proceeded through the light. *How long had I been daydreaming?*

But why? Why would Susan hold a grudge against me? Heck, I didn't even know her when I got the first note.

But Christian did. He worked with Glen. What if I was targeted because of something work-related with Christian? I shook my head. That didn't even make sense. Why would they be interested in going into business with us? Christian and I were going to front most of the money. What if they planned on somehow sabotaging the business and then finding a way to keep it for themselves?

"You watch too many crime shows," I said out loud. "The idea is ridiculous."

Someone stalking you is ridiculous too, but it's happening.

Okay, so what if this isn't business-related? After all, I'm the target. And then it occurred to me. The women Susan had tried to set Christian up with. What if this was more personal than I thought? Could she have known about me before I even met her? Was she trying to drive me away to get back at Christian for rebuffing her friends?

There was only one way to find out. I looked at my watch. I would be thirty minutes late, but girls' night out, here I come.

CHAPTER 60

FORT LAUDERDALE, FLORIDA 2007

I stood in front of Susan and Glen's house and pasted on a smile. I was glad I was the last one to arrive because I wanted to be the first to leave and wouldn't have to worry about being blocked in. I knocked on the door and took a huge breath. One of the regulars opened it, and after exchanging air kisses, waved me in with an almost empty wine glass. I scanned the room and didn't see Susan.

"Sorry I'm late," I said to the seven pairs of eyes that greeted me. There was a round of warm smiles and hellos. "I can't stay. I need to talk to Susan quickly though," I hastily informed them. I waited for someone to hint at where she might be.

A brunette who was new to the group, and whose name escaped me, provided the answer. "She should be a few more minutes. She's in the guest room helping her sister put her daughter to bed."

I frowned. I knew Susan had a sister, and an infant niece who lived in Georgia, but I didn't know they were visiting. Susan had recently shared with the group that her sister was a recluse who didn't drive, and barely left her home. She wasn't in an abusive relationship. She had a good and kind husband who did his best to encourage her to be more social.

One of the women started to offer an explanation. "We got started without Susan. We were lucky she still had book club tonight."

Another woman lifted her glass to toast. "Both of them could use a glass of wine." There was a murmuring of agreement from the others.

"What's going on?" I asked. I had no clue what they were talking about.

"Susan's sister agreed to a visit, but we all know she doesn't drive, and she most definitely doesn't fly. Her husband couldn't get away from work to bring her down here so Susan drove to Georgia yesterday to get her. They left early this morning to come back, and according to Susan they spent at least five hours in bumper-to-bumper traffic." She gestured to two of the ladies. "We offered to call off girls' night, but Susan told us to get started without her while she helped her sister get the baby settled."

"Oh," I squeaked. I had seven eyewitnesses that basically told me it would've been impossible for Susan to be behind the note and chess piece I'd found earlier. Unless of course, she hadn't really spent the day driving from Georgia and decided to include her phobic sister and infant niece in her plan. It sounded ludicrous even in my own head.

"Even though they're exhausted I think Susan wants her sister to have some girlfriend interaction since she's taking her back before we meet up again," the brunette whispered.

"I can't stay, but since I was nearby I wanted to say hello," I lied. "Will you tell her for me?"

"Of course."

"Yes."

"We'll miss you."

I barely heard them as I turned around and walked out the front door.

Christian, my heart cried. *I need Christian.*

I robotically climbed into my car. My emotions were all over the place. None of it made any sense. Then again, maybe I'd been trying to put a puzzle together that had been missing a few pieces. I was almost at Axel's garage and still wracking my brain for a reasonable explanation.

A million thoughts shoved each other out of the way as they clawed to the top of my brain one at a time. Maybe Nick's fiancée, Rachel, was behind it all. *Yeah, and Jolly Roger is her happy accomplice,* I inwardly sneered. Maybe Susan had someone else sending the notes and planted the chess piece. What if it was one of the women who my father had rejected for my mother? Christian might've casually mentioned my surgery, and it could've made its way around the biker gossip circle without either of us knowing. *No. Christian didn't make small talk, especially about something so personal that concerned me.* What if it was one of Moe's sisters? Except there was no explanation as to how they could possibly have known about Grizz's daughter moving back to town or about my hysterectomy. Then again, maybe somehow they had known, and the barren comment was a stab in the dark that hit home. My head was spinning with outlandish possibilities. There were too many unknowns to pursue this on my own. I needed my husband but dreaded his reaction after finding out how long I'd kept this a secret. He would be angry with me for not coming to him immediately. And I couldn't blame him.

I let out a wary but relieved breath when I saw his truck. Knowing that I wouldn't have to deal with this alone lightened my predicament. I parked but didn't leave the car right away. I took a moment to collect my thoughts. Christian would demand a succinct timeline, and I needed to make sure I could explain it properly.

Unfortunately, my brain wouldn't cooperate. When I started remembering the circumstances surrounding the hateful messages, my mind wandered back to possible suspects, and the last note in particular. It had been so personal it could've only come from someone close to us. Someone who had access not only to intimate details of our life, but to that chess piece as well. Someone who might've been jealous of our happiness. I didn't want to think it. God knows I didn't mean for the name to pop into my head. But as if on cue, my phone rang. It was him. I almost didn't answer, but curiosity got the best of me. When had he ever called me on my cell phone? I only had his number because we'd exchanged them early on, but neither of us had ever called the other. Until this moment.

"Slade?" I answered.

There were no pleasantries or small talk. I had to pull the phone away from my ear when he barked, "Mimi, where the fuck are you?!"

I stiffened at the tone in his voice. "Not that it's any of your business, Slade, but I'm at Axel's. I just pulled up to see Christian."

There was a pause on his end, and he sounded like he was catching his breath. "You're with Christian at the garage?" he panted.

"I will be in less than sixty seconds," I practically spat.

"Why isn't he…"

I didn't let him get the rest of his sentence out as I disconnected the call and blocked his number. I didn't want Slade bothering me while I explained to Christian that I had a stalker, and there was a distinct possibility that it was his older brother.

CHAPTER 61

FORT LAUDERDALE, FLORIDA 2007

I found my way into the garage and followed the sound of "The Spirit of Radio" by Rush to the area where I knew Glen and Christian were working. I didn't see Christian and waved my arms to get Glen's attention. He stood up and smiled. After turning down the radio he said, "What a nice surprise, Mimi."

"Hi. I'm sorry to bother you guys but I need to talk to Christian. Is he in one of the other bays?" I absently glanced around the garage. Axel's was a huge structure housing at least twenty separate garage bays. Some had cars, others contained motorcycles, and some were empty.

Glen shook his head slowly. "You missed him, Mimi. He left right after work."

"Left?" I asked. "But his truck is out front."

"He's been taking his bike," he said while using a rag to wipe his hands.

"Taking his motorcycle?" I was confused. That last Sunday we rode before the Thanksgiving holiday, Christian detected a problem with his bike and had left it at Axel's. I was under the impression it wasn't safe to drive while he waited for a hard-to-find replacement part. Taking it when? Taking it where?

"Yeah, when he leaves here at night he rides his bike home," Glen informed me.

No, he doesn't.

I put my hands on my hips. "You think he's been driving his bike home when he's finished with his overtime?"

"You mean Wednesday nights?" he asked, barely interested as he returned tools to their chest. "He canceled with me last Wednesday, and tonight."

I felt instantly nauseous.

"Not only Wednesday nights," I said stiffly. "Almost every night since we've been back from the Thanksgiving holiday."

Glen tried to disguise his surprise, but it was of no use. It was obvious that Christian hadn't been working overtime. And he was leaving his truck here and making Glen think he was riding his motorcycle home. He was going somewhere else on his bike, returning it back to Axel's, getting his truck and driving that home. He must've gotten to work before Glen because it was obvious Glen hadn't realized all the trouble my husband had undergone to swap out vehicles.

But why?

Only one explanation surfaced. I knew he wasn't out joyriding. He was swapping his truck for the motorcycle behind my back for a reason. And I knew what it was. He was hanging with his old gang. Which bar, I wasn't sure, but I would try The Alibi first. And I wouldn't be calling him to let him know I was on my way. Besides, he hadn't answered when I called to let him know I was heading to Axel's. I gritted my teeth. This was a confrontation that needed to happen face-to-face.

I swung around and headed for the exit.

"Mimi," Glen called out. "Hey, are you okay?"

"No, Glen. I'm not," I growled as I slammed the door behind me.

CHAPTER 62

FORT LAUDERDALE, FLORIDA 2007

I pulled into the parking lot at The Alibi and immediately spotted Christian's bike. The notion that I was right wasn't as comforting as I'd hoped. I was downright miserable. I'd parked in the only spot I could find in the back with a cluster of cars. Like Christian's, most of the bikes were parked in a long row out front. He obviously wasn't trying to hide that he was here. Then again, The Alibi was out of the way. I'd never had an occasion to drive by.

I'd been battling my inner demons since I'd left the garage, and couldn't come up with a feasible explanation for anything that had transpired since I'd locked the door at the museum only hours before. But something deep inside told me it was all connected. I just didn't know how. The only thing that made sense was that Christian had given me the option to walk away from the biker lifestyle, but hadn't wanted to give it up himself. So he kept it from me. How the hateful notes and chess piece tied in remained a mystery.

I nodded at the few people who recognized and acknowledged me as I made my way to the door. Once inside, I stopped and slowly perused the room. "Tightrope" by Stevie Ray Vaughan was blaring so loudly I couldn't hear myself think, and I wondered how people were even having conversations.

I spotted him almost immediately, and my heart sank. He was sitting at a table with his back to me. And Krystal, the waitress who'd avoided us after our first visit, was sitting on his lap. She had her arms wrapped around him, and was whispering something in his ear.

Through blurred vision I noticed Debbie. She was sitting across from Christian, giving him a death stare.

It was obvious that he'd been cheating on me, and my friend hadn't been avoiding me because we were no longer part of the biker scene. I had no doubt my husband had ordered her to stay away from me. I would've preferred a shotgun to the chest over what I was feeling. A mixture of anger, shame, sadness, and self-condemnation descended on me all at once. Debbie spotted me and started to rise. She was walking toward me when I turned around and headed back out to the parking lot.

Foolish, stupid, naïve, dumb. It was about the gang. It was about being Grizz's daughter. That's all I was to Christian. A trophy to display in front of his criminal friends. He wanted it all and had manipulated me into believing he loved me since we were children. It had all worked out to his advantage. He had a mother for his child, and he was vying for the spot of club leader. And he had me over a barrel. I was stuck. All he had to do was tell Blue that Grizz was alive. Tell anyone for that matter, and my world, as well as my family's, would disintegrate.

He had to be behind the nasty notes, the chess piece. To what end? To make me think I was crazy? *Gaslight*, an Alfred Hitchcock movie where the husband kept convincing his wife she was insane, came to mind.

"Mimi! Mimi!"

I heard Debbie's boots crunching on the gravel as she ran up behind me. "Mimi, I'm so sorry you had to see that."

"Go away, Debbie," I said without looking at her, my car yards away.

"You just have to accept it, Mimi. It comes with the territory," she whined.

I swung around, my fists balled so tightly I was certain my nails were drawing blood from my palms.

"I don't have to accept anything, Debbie, and if you think you do then you aren't half the woman I thought."

I could tell she didn't like that comment because she took a step back and tried to compose herself. My words must've raised her hackles because after a moment she thrust her chin at me and said, "You must be a lousy lay or he wouldn't have needed to start coming back here."

I let the comment slide and asked, "Exactly how long has he been a regular?"

"Right after Thanksgiving," she spat. "Coming around like he owns the place. I guess you told him about Blue selling Razors and he had to come back and show his ass. Couldn't handle the thought of someone else taking over your father's old club."

She was right. Blue's impromptu lunch invitation was the day after we'd returned from our Thanksgiving holiday. And I'd told Christian about it that night. But I was so caught up in describing Blue's heart-felt apology, I'd forgotten to mention the call from the realtor.

Peace settled over me that could only be described as heaven sent. Christian wasn't here because he wanted to be the club leader. And he wasn't here to get laid. Christian loved me. He'd always loved me, and he reminded me of it every single day. I saw it in his eyes, I felt it in his touch. He could dissect my thoughts with a glance. He knew me better than I knew myself. And if he knew me that intimately, then I knew him too. And I knew he wasn't here because he wanted to be. Debbie had said he started coming right after Thanksgiving. Right after our visit to the mountains. What if he was here because of something to do with my father? What if he was letting Krystal on his lap for show? I preferred that scenario over the others and decided I would walk back in and ask him to come home.

"Have you even heard a word I said?" Debbie screamed at me.

"No, I guess I haven't. I'm going back in and getting my husband, and I'm going to ask him to come home with me." I shook my head slightly before adding, "Using the club as an excuse to step out on your woman isn't acceptable." I didn't know why Krystal was sitting on Christian's lap, but I also didn't believe that he was cheating on me, and only made the last comment as an encouragement to Debbie. She shouldn't be putting up with Joe being unfaithful, if that was the case.

"Then you're as brainless as you are barren," she huffed. "No woman tells their man what is and isn't acceptable."

"What did you just say to me?" I asked, my eyes narrowed.

"You heard me," she spat.

"You called me barren. How would you know that?"

"Because I told her." The voice wasn't familiar and I spun around and recognized the man who'd been with Nigel the night Christian had beaten him. He was leaning up against the car next to mine. His arms were crossed, and he was smoking a cigarette. What was his name again?

"Shut up, Dennis!" Debbie yelled.

Yes, that was it. Dennis.

There was a nervous edge to Debbie's voice when she asked, "And what are you even doing here? I thought you were arrested."

"Yeah, can you believe it? First time ever. And I've been sitting in there for almost eight days without a friend in the world to bail me out." He spit on the ground.

Debbie looked at the ground where he'd spit and said, "You should've called Nigel."

"I was in Tallahassee begging money off me sister. I lost a lot of income because of you and that fuckin' show you wanted to put on."

I immediately recognized the Australian accent. Turning to where the voice came from I saw Nigel walking up from between the cars. He stood with his hands in his pockets and cocked his head to one side. In a mocking voice he said, "You'll probably have to take a couple of punches to make it look real. But it'll be worth it. I'll make sure when Joe is club prez you'll move up the ranks."

Debbie began to stutter, and took a few steps back.

Before she could reply, Nigel said, "He put me in the fucking hospital. I couldn't work, and Blue tossed me out on me ass so I'm no longer part of the crew."

"You...you can be part of the club again when Joe gets promoted," she stammered.

"You don't think I haven't heard on the street about Bear showing back up here? He's gonna be prez and you know it. It all backfired on you. Even the notes you had Dennis leaving on her car didn't work." He paused and nodded toward me before finishing. "You said they would be a distraction and get under her skin enough so she wouldn't want anything to do with the club. You said that Bear loved her enough to walk away. Apparently, Grizz's daughter doesn't scare so easily and had a little more backbone than you'd anticipated."

"It was you," I interrupted, as my eyes cut to Debbie. "You were the one trying to railroad me this whole time. All because you thought Christian was gonna be made club leader?"

"Not because I thought it!" she cried. "Because I knew it. And you were so stupid, Mimi. You immediately thought Autumn was sending the notes. I tried to play along. I even hinted more than once that they could've been coming from someone here." She waved her hand back toward The Alibi. "But you were so focused on that stupid bitch, you could barely see past her."

That part was true. I was certain the hateful notes were from Autumn because she'd sent that letter so many years ago.

"All of this because you want Joe to take over the club for Blue?" I slapped my hand against my thigh. "You could've asked me, Debbie. You could've just been up front and asked if Christian was interested? If anyone is stupid, it's you."

"I did ask you, Mimi. I was always dropping hints, but you never said a word. You just smiled and pretended like you couldn't have cared less."

I could feel Dennis and Nigel's eyes on us as Debbie and I went to war with words. Dennis even jumped in and cleared up some things that had been nagging at me. If this was just a small fraction of what it would be like to live the club lifestyle, I was more than glad I was out. Still, none of this explained why my husband was inside with Krystal on his lap.

"Enough of this bitching!" Nigel yelled. "I'm here on unfinished business."

I stiffened because I knew what was coming. He was mad for what Christian had done to him and I was going to be on the receiving end of his wrath. I scanned the parking lot. Not a soul in sight. I was a decent runner, but was I fast enough to get to the back door of the bar, and if I did, was it unlocked?

A couple of options were scrambling around in my head when Nigel walked menacingly toward Debbie. She placed her hand on her chest and said, "Wha..? What do you want?"

"I only came here tonight to tell Christian about your little scheme, and then ask Blue to take me back in the club. But having you right here in front of me with no witnesses." He paused and looked around the parking lot. "I think me plan has changed." His tone was low and menacing making his Australian accent even more pronounced.

He wasn't targeting me or Christian. He was after Debbie.

"Mimi is a witness," she said with more bravado than I knew she felt. "And why are you coming after me? It was her husband who beat you senseless. If anything, you should be taking it out on her."

Gee, thanks for that, Debbie.

"You're the one who told me to pick that fight with him. I'd never seen Bear in action before, and neither had you. You should've done your fucking homework. He beat me within an inch of me fuckin' life, and based on what you told me to say, he had reason to."

Then Nigel looked at me and said, "I was supposed to hurt Christian to scare you away. I think we all know how that shitstorm ended."

"You can't touch me," Debbie managed to squeak out. "Mimi will see everything."

"She has more reason than I do to want to see your arse in that boot," he countered as he pointed to an old Oldsmobile sporting a huge trunk.

I felt a shift in the air at the same time Dennis said, "Trouble."

Just like when I'd been getting ready to go up on stage to accept my diploma, I felt him. I didn't have to turn around to know Christian was coming up behind me.

Chaos descended as I tried to wedge myself between Nigel, Debbie, and an outraged Christian who came barreling at us with Joe and Isaac in tow. There was some initial shoving and shouting, but it was squelched before it got too out of hand.

Blue and some of his men had pulled up on their bikes at that point. He quirked a finger at me and said, "Come here." I walked toward him, grateful that I would be given a chance to explain without any bloodshed. Christian started to follow, but Blue said, "Not you. Not yet."

I heard Debbie snicker.

I don't know if it was her snicker or Blue's words that infuriated Christian. He stomped toward me and Blue and growled, "Nobody gives me orders. She's my wife! Not yours!"

Two of Blue's guys grabbed Christian, but Blue held up his hand to stop them. "It's okay. He's right."

Blue gave orders for his men to escort Nigel, Dennis, Debbie, Joe, and Isaac through the back door of The Alibi to wait in the storeroom. The same storeroom where Krystal had invited Christian all those months ago. The reminder of what I'd seen less than twenty minutes earlier slammed into my chest.

Christian and I followed Blue to the back office of The Alibi. Apparently the bar's owner, Ken, had no problem with Blue using it.

After closing the door behind us he hefted his hip on the end of the desk and pointed to two chairs.

"Who wants to tell me what the fuck that was in the parking lot?"

I raised my hand. "I'll go first."

CHAPTER 63

FORT LAUDERDALE, FLORIDA 2007

Neither man interrupted as I unloaded on them the events of the past several hours. As I'd suspected, Christian was furious that I'd never told him about the notes left on my car. And I was upset that he'd not told me about the video our neighbor Tom had showed him of the grainy figure who'd been living in the attic next door. Instead, Christian asked Slade to hire someone to watch me when he couldn't be with me.

"You could've come to me," Blue interjected, giving Christian a hard look. He turned his gaze on me. "And you could've too."

Christian shook his head. "My gut told me he was connected to the club, but I didn't know how. I'm not saying I didn't trust you, but the less people who knew I was looking for someone, the better."

Blue nodded his understanding.

Christian explained why he lied about the overtime. He'd basically been hanging at The Alibi to see if he'd recognize the man in the video. He hadn't seen a face, but he was certain that if he saw the walk, the mannerisms, it would trigger a memory. But that didn't happen because Dennis hadn't been back to the bar. I could see disgust in his eyes as he realized his ability to recollect details had failed him this time.

"When I first got here, I saw Krystal sitting on your lap."

"It was all part of the ploy, Mimi. I had to make it look like I wanted to be here."

"Exactly how much did you make it look like you wanted to be here?" I asked.

He knew what I was asking, and he reached for my hand. "Not that much, baby." He kissed my hand. "Not what you're thinking. Not even close."

"Debbie was shooting you daggers with her eyes when I showed up. I thought it was because you were cheating on me. Now I know it's because she was angry you were coming around again."

"And she's the one who put the note on your car today?" Blue asked. "And put the chess piece inside?"

I nodded. "Yep. Razors is close to the museum. I walked there the day you invited me to lunch. She must've run over on her break today and gone through the alley to the back parking lot."

"Which was probably why the P.I. never saw her, right?" Blue asked Christian.

"Was he at the museum today?" I scrunched my nose.

"I just finished telling you he follows you, Mimi." Christian rubbed a frustrated hand down his face.

"Which explains why I felt like someone was watching me since we got back from Thanksgiving." I rubbed my arms as if to ward off a chill.

"Except you lost him today when you tore out of the museum going the wrong way!" Christian yelled. "He tried your usual places before he called Slade to let him know something had upset you, and you got away from him."

That was true. I'd gone to the mall. And I'd been thirty minutes late to girls' night out so the P.I. had missed me. That explained why Slade called me in a panic wanting to know where I was. And I'd hung up on him. I dropped my head, too ashamed to meet my husband's eyes.

"Did Slade call you? Is that why you came out to the parking lot when you did?" I asked without looking up.

"He tried calling and texting, but I didn't hear it." Christian blew out a frustrated breath. "Tonight was the night Ken decided to replace their old jukebox with a fancy sound system. Slade finally called the bartender who told me to check my phone."

That explained why I thought the music was unusually loud.

"What I'm hearing is that Mimi has been getting nasty notes on her windshield since you two started hanging here?"

I nodded at Blue. "And the night Christian planned to stage the fight with Isaac coincided with Debbie's plot to have Nigel pick a fight with Christian to scare me off."

"I remember it was her comment that caused Nigel to say what he did," Christian remarked.

"Exactly!" I said as I sat up in my chair. "And things were quiet for a month because we stopped coming here. There were no more notes and no weird things happening at the house."

"What weird things?" Blue asked.

"Before you and Christian showed up in the parking lot, Dennis, the man living in the attic next door, told me a little bit more of what he'd been doing."

I told them how Debbie denied any involvement in Dennis's decision to live next door. After the first time he left the note on my car at the grocery store, he followed me home. When he noticed that house was empty, he decided staying there was more convenient than his back seat. He left his car parked a few streets over and nobody was the wiser.

"He's homeless?" Blue asked.

"Yes, and he would let himself into our house when we weren't there." I sensed Christian stiffening. He'd already told me how our neighbor's tapes revealed the stranger's intrusion, but Christian hadn't understood his motive.

"Dennis wasn't trying to mess with us. He was just sloppy. When he was explaining the events that had occurred, I asked about our bed. Apparently, he took a nap and made it afterward." I made a mental note to go home and have a bonfire in the back yard with our bedding. "He listened to our CDs and put them back in the wrong cases. He stole food he didn't think we'd miss. He accidentally put the milk away in the cupboard when he thought he heard one of us pull up. And he apparently availed himself of our huge tub more than once because he used all my bubble bath. He thought throwing the empty bottles away was too obvious so he put them back under the counter." I shuddered. *How many times had I climbed into the tub after he'd used it?*

"He put diesel in your gas tank, Mimi!" Christian spat.

"A misunderstanding," I assured him. "He was making his way through the yards one night when he came across a full gas jug in someone's open carport. He thought he was being nice by filling up my tank to pay us back for the stuff he'd been using." I sighed. "He said that's all it was, and I believe him."

I waited for one of them to say something, and when neither did, I piped up. "When you think about it, if Dennis hadn't been living next door, we wouldn't be sitting here now. Even though Debbie wasn't involved in him stalking our home, she was still secretly targeting me." I gave Christian a pleading look. "You seeing Dennis on the video fueled you to come here. You would've eventually figured out what she was doing." I knew Christian wanted to get his hands on Dennis. I didn't want that to happen.

Circling back to Debbie's motive, Blue looked at me and asked, "This only started up again after Christian started coming back to The Alibi without you?"

"The notes did. I don't think Dennis has been in the attic for a while now." I looked at Christian who nodded his agreement. "And think about it. Not only did Christian start coming back here, but you invited me to lunch at your restaurant. Debbie had to have been thinking that you were lining something up for Christian to step into your shoes. You must know that there's a buzz about you leaving."

"What did she mean by barren bitch on the note?" Blue asked.

I quickly explained about my surgery. I told Blue that Dennis had been in the attic listening the day Christian and I walked through the vacant house, and ended up sitting on the carpet and discussing our future. We'd talked that day about our dreams, and if we wanted to give Abby a little brother or sister. And of course, we touched on my inability to carry a child, and whether or not we might want to pursue adoption or seek a surrogate. That conversation had happened before my cousin Rachelle made her offer. And apparently, Dennis had heard it all and reported it back to Debbie.

Just thinking about Dennis eavesdropping from the attic made my skin crawl.

Blue didn't say anything, but I knew his thoughts were racing. It was a lot to take in. But it also wasn't that big of a deal. Let's face it. I never felt like my life was in danger. All of Debbie's tactics had been to upset, not harm. Yes, it had caused me months of aggravation and brought to light a ripple in my marriage—Christian and I had both kept things from each other under the misguided notion that we didn't want to worry or burden the other. We both vowed in front of Blue not to let that happen again.

Blue tugged on his beard. "I'm not hearing anything that points to Joe's involvement."

"I don't think he knew," I said before looking over at my husband for reassurance. I knew that Joe and Blue went way back. After my father went to prison Blue had given up his job with the phone company and had gone into the home security business. Blue was the one who'd introduced Joe to his current job.

"Doesn't sound like it," Christian added.

"Debbie and Dennis will be dealt with," Blue informed us.

"But it's all over. It was a childish scheme on her part. I'm not happy she put me through this, but truthfully the relief in knowing it's over is enough for me to walk away from this." I swiped my hand through my hair. "And Dennis didn't do anything wrong."

"Yes, he did," Blue corrected. "He invaded your privacy, and he saw what was written on the notes he delivered. He knew who he was messing with." He gave my husband a respectful glance. "You have no say in this, Mimi. They'll both be dealt with."

I cast a pleading look Christian's way, but he sat stone-faced.

"Now, to change the subject."

I looked back at Blue.

"The rumors are true. I'll be stepping down soon. But not until I deal with this mess." He cut his eyes to Christian. "After I get this shit handled, you want my job?"

CHAPTER 64

The Ghost

I t was time for me to pass the gauntlet. Especially after realizing how terribly I'd failed Christian and Mimi. Then again, there had been no obvious signs that would've flagged me. The woman who had been harassing Mimi, and the man who'd been infiltrating their home hadn't used any high-tech devices that would've alerted me and my associate to their situation. Instead, they'd used old-fashioned tactics that didn't include cell phones, video cameras, or computer searches. Besides, I'd had my attention focused elsewhere.

I attributed my failure to my lookout for more plausible threats. The most obvious in my mind had been Nick Rosman. However, I couldn't dig up anything that revealed he had vengeance in mind. But I also didn't want to leave it to chance that something might've been missed. Nick and his jolly sidekick Roger Kincaid still needed to be watched. I continued to have all of them, including Mimi's ex, Lucas Paine, monitored. I'd known even more about Lucas than the detective Christian had hired. Even if Christian and Mimi hadn't ended up together, I would've still found a way to expose Lucas. After intercepting his texts and viewing the easily-hackable college security cameras, seeing footage that showed him defacing the library with graffiti and slashing Mimi's tires, I knew it was time to take him and his cohorts down. Convinced of his continued hatred toward Mimi, I was still having him monitored all these months later.

I sighed as I reached for my coffee cup. After inhaling its rich aroma I closed my eyes and took a healthy mouthful, savoring the flavor as it made its way down my throat.

I thought back to when I'd first decided to become The Ghost. It was purely selfish on my part. I'd never agreed with Anthony's decision to let Christian join Grizz's old club. Anthony thought the club would provide Christian with discipline. I disagreed. It was a parent's responsibility to discipline their children. And I took my responsibility as a parent very seriously.

I told Anthony about my intentions. He didn't believe me at first, and almost dared me to try. I was up for the challenge and my first visit had been to Bill Petty's home. I knew that Bill ran a sophisticated computer program that allowed him to play watchdog to Grizz and his family. I also knew that his talents were being wasted at his day job. As the heiress of a high-end automobile conglomerate, and thanks to my vast real estate holdings, I'd accumulated more wealth than I could spend in ten lifetimes, so I offered Bill a monetary incentive he couldn't refuse. Besides, his wife, Carter, had a big heart for animals, and the money I was providing would be well spent.

After reassuring him that I wasn't a criminal, I asked him to do a thorough investigation on Blue. I'd heard that Mickey "Monster" Moran was dying and Blue would be stepping up as leader. What kind of an incentive would Blue need to work for me?

It turned out to be a sad one. Blue's oldest son, Timmy, had a child who'd been born with heart problems. Blue made good money from his restaurant and criminal endeavors, but he didn't make the kind of money needed for the child's care. Truth be told, Ghost aside, if I'd heard what was going on with Blue's grandson, I would've given him the money anyway. I knew what it was like to lose a child.

I laughed to myself when I remembered how I thought I would bring an air of sophistication to the motorcycle club. I started out by referring to myself as Verkozen, or "the elected one." I thought it was a clever name, but it bombed, and I quickly became known as The Ghost.

I was responsible for moving the club's headquarters from a run-down warehouse to the HVAC company. It was simple enough. I bought the place under a phantom LLC and stationed the men there, even providing training for those that wanted to work. It slowly became a requirement. I didn't want loafers, I wanted people who could prove their willingness to earn a living apart from their illegal endeavors.

To convince Blue that The Ghost knew how to manage a motorcycle club, I turned to my husband for advice. When Anthony told me he didn't want any part of it, I remembered something. A conversation that I'd had with Carter after Grizz and Ginny left South Florida. Grizz had killed a man in North Carolina. It was the only time Ginny had violated her own no-contact rule. She'd been so upset, she'd called Carter to share her concern about what Grizz had done.

I realized then that Grizz needed something else besides the Montana air to calm his inner beast. That was when I still thought they'd moved there. I contacted him through Bill, and told him that I was looking for a partner. I would run the business side of things, and he would occasionally be consulted on gang tactics and activities. He wouldn't be getting his hands dirty, but he would still be involved from the sidelines. He immediately agreed, but I wouldn't bring him in until Ginny was on board.

My sweet friend didn't want to see her husband battling the hidden demons that threatened to surface. One dead extended relative was enough as far as she was concerned. Grizz was in. Bill created an encrypted chat room where I could contact Grizz for advice. We never discussed anything personal. If it hadn't been for Mimi's letter to Christian, I would've never known that Ginny was pregnant with twins.

I grimaced when I remembered our visit to their mountain home after we met up with Mimi and Christian. Grizz had offered to show me his chicken coop, and Anthony had cast a wary glance my way when I'd agreed.

Grizz had been so angry with me, the hens immediately sensed it and scattered. But I stood my ground. I wasn't afraid of Grizz.

"If you were a man, I'd turn your face into hamburger meat, Christy," he'd barked. "You and Bill knew long before that kid's death at Mimi's camp hit the news that your son went after my daughter. And you both deliberately kept it from me."

I didn't deny it, and it was indefensible. All I could do was thank him for not telling Ginny that I'd known about Christian's actions well before they found out. I also did my best to reassure him that Mimi was never in any danger. Bill had intercepted Seth's rental reservation and put Christian and Mimi in a home that had surveillance. When I saw Mimi coming out of the master bedroom with bandages on her forearms, and the look of anguish on my son's face for having caused them, I'd told Bill to kill the surveillance. I'd already known Christian would never hurt her, and I'd been right.

But Grizz was right too, and I deserved his wrath. I'd made sure Bill kept an eye on Christian after he'd been released from prison, and I'd heard from Bill the moment Christian had Seth looking for Mimi. I knew my son and believed it would only be a matter of time before he started looking for her. There had been no delay in the facial recognition program, like Bill had suggested that day he dropped by our house. That visit had been staged for Anthony and Slade's benefit. At that point, I hadn't kept Anthony in the loop, and he'd been furious with me. Especially after realizing how close Grizz lived to the rental house.

My original and only intention as The Ghost had been to protect my son. To give him a job with the club that didn't involve breaking bones. But I would soon learn that a mother's arms could only reach so far. His decision to attack Nick Rosman hadn't been club-related. I had to swallow my pride, and let Christian serve out his prison sentence. That's when I decided that I would let all of the gang members suffer the same fate. If they stepped out of line and did something that warranted prison, then so be it. It was the discipline a mother would hand down to her child, so I told Blue that if they deviated from the club's directives, they were responsible. I guess I really was a mama bear.

I only used my position for good. At the same time Christian had been scheming to see Mimi, it had come to my attention through club activities that the man Slade had been prosecuting was actually innocent, and a dirty attorney on his defense team was sabotaging his client by withholding information.

Slade had told me about the girl he'd seen in the library and I used her to open a dialogue with him. I'd ascertained that she'd been looking for her biological father, and I used that knowledge as a trade for her to slip Slade that note. I felt badly about what Bill quickly uncovered concerning Bevin's father. It was a tragic story, but one she had a right to know.

Tossing thoughts of Bevin's sad family history to the side, I reflected on how proud I'd been that Slade had done the right thing, exposing the dishonest defense attorney. I knew he would. I'd recently discovered there was a fire in him that had been squelched his entire life. It's strange how for the longest time I believed my sons to be as different as fire and ice. I'd been wrong. Slade and Christian are both fire. They just wear it differently.

Christian wears his on the outside for everybody to see. His flames were always wildly exposed. That is until Mimi came back into his life. She brought with her a new sense of purpose for him. His love for her and Abby, tamed his fire. It's still there, but it's more of a wild glow instead of a blazing inferno.

Slade wears his fire on the inside where nobody can see it. He's lived his entire life by the book because he has a high sense of morals. But his fire is eating him alive. The flames are always there, burning him from the inside out. I'd always suspected it, but hadn't seen it until he threw my tiara at Christian and attacked him during Mimi's first visit. Slade has always tried to be the studious son, the thoughtful man who was always respectful concerning everything he did. I've watched him slowly simmering since he started working for the state. He's being exposed to injustices for what he believes is the right side of the law and it's eating away at him.

I told Anthony that I was finally passing the torch. Blue was still club leader, but there was a possibility that Christian might step up to take over. And if he did, I wanted someone watching out for him. And I knew who I wanted it to be.

"Owani, are you coming to bed?"

I looked over at the father of my children. We'd been married for almost thirty years, and my body never failed to react to his deep voice or smoldering black eyes. "Be right there, Anthony."

HIS MOTHER WAS RIGHT. He'd been a powder keg ready to explode. He'd spent his entire life striving to do what was right. Only to come to the sad realization that he'd always tried to deny.

Rotten human beings were everywhere. Even where they shouldn't be. They wore name tags that deceived. The rich got richer, and the poor got persecuted, and he was tired of seeing it. He watched too many defense attorneys get the bad guy off with a slap on the wrist. And if it hadn't been for his mother, he would've watched a crooked defense attorney railroad an innocent client right in front of him. How many others were out there like that?

He'd listened wide-eyed as his mother sat him down and explained what she'd been doing from behind a computer for the past five years. He couldn't believe it. But after listening to how she managed to manipulate certain situations for good, he could only stare slack-jawed at her business prowess. Then again, he knew she hadn't accumulated a fortune through ignorance.

Blue's motorcycle club may have been involved in a high-priced call girl ring, but in managing them, his mother was able to take down several pimps who'd been dealing in the sex slave business. The club was involved in drugs. What biker gang wasn't? But Christy had exposed an executive at a pharmaceutical company who'd had his own team of lab rats stealing high-priced medications and replacing them with placebos. Which meant that the people who really needed the drugs were taking capsules filled with sugar and baking soda.

He'd grabbed the back of his neck and given his mother a sideways glance.

"When did you first think I would be a good replacement?"

She looked at him, her bright blue eyes filled with intelligence and pride. "When Christian took Mimi. I knew your father and I would be going after him, and I'd pestered you all week to stop by. When you called and said you were coming, I let Bill know he needed to show up."

"Why?"

"I wanted to see how you would react to the whole situation. Especially finding out Grizz was alive. You handled it well."

Slade nodded, and she continued, "But it was a bad call on my part. Waiting too long to step in with Grizz living so close was just plain stupid. Your father was furious with me. Which is why I want you to take over. You have a good head on your shoulders, son. The fire that's been burning in you now has a place to go."

"And you still think that? Even after I hurled your tiara at Christian?"

"Yes," she smiled. "It only confirmed that you needed an outlet. You can use this for good, Slade. I did."

And that's what Slade had done. He'd agreed to do it on a trial basis, and his first order of business had been to discreetly and nonviolently handle Erin's crazy ex-husband. She was now free to be with the man she loved.

In the quiet comfort of his condo and with his laptop under his arm, Slade grabbed a beer and headed for the couch. He opened his computer and stared at the keystroke that would activate the robotic voice that allowed him to anonymously give instructions over the phone.

His mind immediately cut to thoughts of Bevin and how he'd tried to approach her several times in the past few months, but she either rebuffed him or scampered away like a frightened rabbit. He thought long and hard about the woman who'd intrigued him all those months ago, and pondered what it was about her that he couldn't move past.

Slade's fingers hovered over the keyboard as his brain fired off a dozen scenarios he could use to bring Bevin to him. If she'd agreed to do The Ghost's bidding for his mother, he could certainly get her to do his without her even knowing it.

He slowly closed his laptop and shook his head. No. He'd promised his mother and himself that he would only use The Ghost's influence to maintain a protective eye on the family, keep the motorcycle club on track and use his knowledge of the law for good. He wouldn't use it to stalk a woman. He would have to figure out a way to get Bevin Marconi to come to him without deception or subterfuge on his part. It might've been fun to watch her awkwardly approach him under orders from The Ghost. But he would remember what he'd done to achieve that, and he never wanted to look in her eyes and know that he'd manipulated her into a relationship with him.

A relationship he would continue to pursue. Only not from behind the anonymity of a computer.

CHAPTER 65

FORT LAUDERDALE, FLORIDA 2008

Christmas and New Years passed uneventfully, and I couldn't have been more thrilled. No nasty notes or misplaced household items. Our lives were back on track, and I was more optimistic about the future than I'd ever been. Blue still hadn't sold Razors or resigned from the club. The Christmas present he'd had delivered to our home hung in the back of our closet next to the leather jacket Chili had given me. It came with a note that simply said, *Property of Grizz.*

It was my father's old club jacket. The one Tommy had been tasked with disposing of when he thought Grizz had died by lethal injection. I realized that even though Tommy had battled with Grizz for my mother's affection, he still couldn't bring himself to destroy a piece of history that belonged to the man who'd fathered me. Instead of throwing it away, he'd given it to Blue.

I'd watched as Christian tried it on before returning it to our closet. Just because it was a perfect fit didn't mean it was meant to fit perfectly in our lives. Christian had turned down Blue's offer to take over the club. He promised me that giving up the lifestyle was nothing for him. He told me Abby and I were his priorities, and I believed him. He knew I had no intention of being my mother, who pretended not to see the harshest aspects of that world. Or his mother, who used her money to make things better for the women who'd succumbed to that life. I was too selfish. I didn't want to share my husband with a biker club. I kept both jackets only as a reminder of our legacy, not as a reminder of what some thought should be our destiny.

Christian's parents, along with Autumn, had readily signed the paperwork granting Christian and me full custody of Abby. Autumn was expecting another baby and had settled in New York with her new boyfriend and his family.

Christian's parents and Slade listened as we sat them down around the kitchen table right before Christmas and explained everything that had secretly transpired since my move to Florida. Aunt Christy shivered when I told her about the harmless oaf who'd been living in the attic next door, letting himself into our home.

"I remember you saying you detected a smell when you went through the house. Too bad I hadn't been with you. My nose would've led me right up those attic stairs," she announced proudly. We didn't disagree with her. Christian's mother had the keenest sense of smell of anybody I'd ever met.

"What do you think was behind Debbie's offer to have Joe set up surveillance cameras at your house?" Slade asked.

I smiled at my brother-in-law who'd readily accepted my apology for being so rude. He'd only been trying to help the night I'd so callously hung up on him.

"Was it maybe her backup plan in case the nasty notes didn't spook you? Like if she knew more about your habits she could use them against you?" he asked.

I gave him a noncommittal shrug. "Probably. Maybe. I don't really know, but that's a solid guess."

Aunt Christy jumped in and said, "I still think you two should've known better than to keep this kind of thing from each other and from us. We're family. We could've helped."

"Christian told me about the guy in the attic," Slade interrupted. "And before I forget. About those prints you wanted lifted from the cans we found there..." Slade looked at Christian. "Two sets came back."

Everyone glanced Slade's way and waited for him to reveal the owner of the fingerprints.

He looked at Christian and smiled. "Yours and Dennis's."

Of course Christian's prints were on the cans. They were stolen from our house. Mine were probably on some of them too.

"Why did it take so long?" Christian asked.

"Surprisingly, Dennis didn't have an arrest record until recently.

And even though they inked him, the prints didn't get submitted to the database right away," Slade explained.

"That's the justice system for you," Aunt Christy commented. She gave Slade a look I couldn't decipher before excusing herself to put on a pot of coffee.

Three Months Later

It was a lazy Sunday afternoon. I'd spent the morning at church with Aunt Christy, Daisy, and Abby while Christian and his father puttered in our garage.

We were now home, and while Uncle Anthony was inside helping Daisy with homework she'd brought with her, Aunt Christy was fixing a snack for Abby. In the few short months that we'd had custody of Abby she'd transitioned full-time into our home without a hiccup.

Even though Autumn didn't want to pursue a relationship with Abby, didn't mean that her mother didn't want one with her granddaughter. We included Abby's maternal grandmother in as many family gatherings as possible. Christian would be leaving soon to pick up Autumn's mother, but there was still enough time to enjoy each other's company beforehand.

We strolled hand in hand and enjoyed the warm breeze rolling off the lake as we made our way around it.

"I'm so glad we decided to buy this house. It fits us perfectly, don't you think?" I asked him.

"I like it too, but like I told you before, Mimi, home for me is wherever you are." He raised my hand to his mouth and softly kissed it.

"Do you miss it? Do you miss them?" I was talking about the club, the lifestyle, and the friends Christian had so easily dismissed.

"I have you. I have my daughter." He stopped walking and looked thoughtful. "And I have my motorcycle. Don't need anything else," he said with a dazzling smile.

I stepped in front of him and wrapped my arms around his neck. I gave him a crooked grin and said, "Marriage and fatherhood suit you." I raised up on my tiptoes and playfully nipped at his chin.

His face grew serious as he took mine between his hands and said, "Marriage and motherhood suit you too, Mimi. Should we tell them today or wait to see if it works?" He kissed the tip of my nose before letting his hands fall away.

"If an opportunity presents itself, we say something. If not, we don't. Let's wait and see how it goes," I told him.

I slowly brushed my hand over his shirt, and asked, "Is it still sore?" I was referring to the tattoo he'd gotten. It was a chest piece that boasted Dreamy Mimi.

"Nah," he teased. "It hurt more when it wasn't there. When you weren't there."

I tilted my head sideways, an invitation for him to explain.

"When you were missing from my life, it hurt more"—he thumped his fist against his chest—"than the sting of a tattoo needle."

I was pretty sure I sighed. My husband may have been an alpha male with a mean streak, but he was also the most romantic man I'd ever met.

We resumed our walk and reflected on our decision not to open up a motorcycle repair shop with Glen and Susan. It had nothing to do with them. They were still our best friends. After hearing that both men were considering opening up their own businesses, Axel made them an offer they couldn't refuse. He made Christian and Glen co-managers for the motorcycle repairs and their new responsibilities also came with hefty raises.

"I feel relieved that we're not opening up our own shop," I blurted out. "Owning a business comes with a lot of responsibility. I think it would take time away from us."

He nodded his agreement.

"The new neighbors seem nice," I added, changing the subject. "But, their teenage son looks like he might be a problem."

"Not for us," Christian scoffed.

I gave him a sideways glance.

"I had his number from day one. Already set him straight." I recognized the rigid line of his jaw and smiled. Just like my father had told me, I would need a champion. I'd never felt so safe, so cherished, so loved in my entire life. And Christian had been right about that .38 Special song. I was back where I belonged.

We walked the rest of the way in silence and came upon Aunt Christy and Abby coming out of the house.

Christian still had time before he had to pick up Autumn's mother, so Aunt Christy and I sat on the grass and watched Christian push Abby on the solitary swing that hung from a huge shade tree that almost swallowed up our back yard. The sun was glistening off the lake as a family of ducks slowly quacked their way past us.

"Can you believe we're finally going to meet Bevin today?" Aunt Christy whispered. She looked at her watch in anticipation.

"Yes!" I replied a little too loudly. "I'm looking forward to meeting the woman who has mesmerized Slade for so long."

"Me too," Aunt Christy said with a hopeful grin. "I hope we're not too much for her. I hope she'll feel welcome."

I knew that Aunt Christy was more than excited at the prospect of Slade finding someone, but she had reservations about Bevin's mother disapproving of Slade because of Uncle Anthony and Christian's criminal histories.

"We'll make her feel like family," I assured her.

Her answer was a worried smile so I decided to share something that I thought would cheer her up.

"Christian and I have talked about it and decided we want to try and put a baby in Rachelle's belly."

Her scream caused the ducks to scatter and Christian to give us a questioning look. "You told her?" he asked me over Abby's head.

I nodded as Aunt Christy pulled me into a rough hug. I explained that there were no guarantees, but she ignored me and said she couldn't wait to witness the birth of her second grandchild. Sadly, Autumn hadn't allowed her to be part of Abby's birth. When Christian and I told Rachelle that we wanted to accept her offer, her only stipulation was that Christian couldn't look at her privates. "He can be in the room and cut the cord, but no peeking at my lady parts," she told me in her smooth Southern drawl. We didn't have a problem with that request, and I was certain Rachelle wouldn't have an issue with Aunt Christy being there.

"There are a lot of ifs, and we're getting ahead of ourselves, but we're going to be optimistic," I told Aunt Christy as she broke from the hug to wipe her eyes.

After she composed herself our conversation circled back to the decision to buy our home. Aunt Christy was surprised that I wanted to live here despite Dennis's secret home invasions.

"I guess I'm shocked that you're not freaked out about it or spooked," she admitted while gazing at Christian and Abby.

I explained that I was never one to be spooked or superstitious. I went by feelings, and my gut told me this was our home.

"I'm glad." She gave me a wide smile, and then her expression changed. "There was something I don't remember asking you."

"About?" I asked while fiddling with a blade of grass.

"Back to Debbie. So, I can understand how she'd managed to pilfer your spare set of keys and the chess piece the few times she was at your house."

"Yeah, it's how she got into my locked car at the museum. When she hung the white queen from my rearview mirror."

"But what was the significance of the white queen?" she asked, cocking her head to one side. "Debbie knew Abby had been swiping the pieces, but why did she target that one specifically?"

"I'd told her a story," I replied. I looked up at my husband who winked at me. "I guess she was holding onto it in case she felt the need to bring out the big guns. Which she obviously did after Christian started showing back up at The Alibi after Thanksgiving."

"What story?" Her brows crinkled with curiosity.

"The story about one of our weddings," I answered with a cheesy smile.

"One of your weddings?" Uncle Anthony asked. He and Daisy had walked up behind us. Apparently they'd finished Daisy's homework.

"Yeah, the most important one," Christian answered without taking his eyes from mine.

"Do tell," Aunt Christy suggested, her eyes wide with curiosity.

"I'm sure you'll remember some of it," I told her with a smile. "You were there."

EPILOGUE

"I'll push you on the swings, Mimi. C'mon!" Christian ran toward the swing set, his black braid swaying behind him. He was enjoying every minute of his play date with Mimi and fantasizing about being her hero. He would push her as high as she could go because it would be the perfect opportunity to show off his muscles. There weren't any kids on the swings so he would have her all to himself. He couldn't stop grinning.

Mimi glanced at her mother, and after receiving a smiling nod of approval, she bounded happily to her best friend.

"You have to promise not to push me too high, Christian!" Mimi called out as she excitedly trotted behind him toward the swing set.

"I promise, Mimi," Christian yelled back at her.

When they tired of the swings they happily made their way hand in hand to the huge slide structure.

"Mimi, do you want to get married again?" Christian asked as they followed each other through the maze of jungle gym tunnels. He stopped crawling and turned around, accidentally kicking Mimi in the face. She looked startled but not hurt.

"I'm sorry, Mimi! I'm sorry. Did I hurt you?" he cried as he tried to wiggle closer to her in the small space.

She gave him a wide grin and said, "Yeah, it kind of hurt, but not bad."

Christian looked relieved and started to turn back around when she answered his earlier question, "I forgot to bring my ring with me. I didn't know if you wanted to play wedding again."

Christian had given Mimi a plastic ring that he'd won at a carnival and she'd worn it every time they saw each other.

"That's okay," he told her as they ventured out of the maze and were now standing in a small cube-shaped part of the structure that had open windows. He proudly pulled something out of his right front pocket. "I got this one for you out of the claw machine. It has a bigger diamond!"

Mimi's eyes got wide as she gazed at the new ring, the big blue artificial stone overshadowing the tiny plastic gold band it was attached to.

"It's so beautiful, Christian," she cooed. "Did you get it because it matches the color of your eyes?" she asked adoringly.

"No," he answered matter-of-factly. "I got it 'cause it was the only one in the claw machine."

"Let's get married by the water fountain this time," Mimi told him.

"Why?" he asked as he returned the ring to his pocket and scooted into the tube that would eventually deliver them to the ground.

"Because I'm thirsty," she told him as she gave him a shove and jumped in behind him.

After taking turns at the fountain, they made their way to a small shaded area, waving to their mothers as they went. Still within their protective view, Christian yanked his white T-shirt over his head and handed it to Mimi. The first time they had played wedding, they got some help from Christy who showed them how they could turn a shirt into a makeshift bridal veil. He purposely selected a white one that morning when getting dressed for their play date.

While Mimi tucked her hair up under Christian's shirt, he picked some flowers that may or may not have been weeds.

The wedding preparations were complete, and it was time to take their vows.

Mimi looked at Christian adoringly and said, "I will always wear my ring and be your bestest friend ever. And I will be your wife and live with you when we get older, and we get jobs, and you make us a house." Mimi paused while she contemplated her next words. "And if we go to the doctor and he puts a baby in my belly, I will be the mommy, and you will be the daddy when the baby comes out."

She smiled big at Christian and waited expectantly for his response.

He took a deep breath and said, "I will always win more rings for you. I will win ten hundred rings with different colored diamonds, and you can have one for every day. I will be your husband, and I will make you a house, and I will eat soup every day if that's all you can cook. And if the doctor doesn't put a baby in your belly, then I will put one there. I don't know how, but that's how I think babies get in the mommies' stomachs. The daddies put them there. That's what Slade told me, but he didn't know how either." He paused before shyly adding, "And you'll belong to me, and I will love you forever, just like my daddy tells my mommy."

He started to reach into his pocket to retrieve the ring when they heard a voice say, "It's called screwing, you idiots."

They both looked over to where the snide remark came from and realized they had an audience. A boy who seemed to be a few years older than they were had stopped to observe them on his way to the water fountain.

"So, are you and your squaw gonna live in a teepee?" the intruder sneered while swiping at his sweaty face with his arm. "Wait, she can't be your squaw. She's a pale face, and you're too dark."

Mimi looked back at Christian with a puzzled expression. He was staring hard at the older boy when Mimi asked, "What's a squaw?"

"It's a dirty injun's wife," the boy laughed. "You are an injun, right?" he sneered at Christian. "You have a long braid and dark skin. Where do you keep your bows and arrows?"

Christian broke his gaze from the bully to gauge Mimi's reaction to the taunt. It wasn't the first time he was singled out due to the color of his skin. Whenever his mother, a striking blonde with light skin, took him and his brother, Slade, out in public, the stares were obvious. Most people weren't rude, but they were curious. Slade favored Christy. He didn't have her white-blond hair, but he did have her lighter skin tone. Whereas Christian had his father's straight jet-black hair and dark skin. The only thing he'd inherited from his mother was her intense blue eyes. He'd once heard a classmate's mother ask Christy how old he was when she adopted him. He was the only dark-skinned student in his class and had already been in several lunch-room and recess fights. Just because he was different.

And even though the bullying he experienced was only verbal, he was the one getting into trouble because he responded physically. Like he was going to now.

From across the other side of the playground, Christy knew the minute Christian was going to strike. She and Ginny had spoken for a few moments with the harried woman who had earlier unloaded her three children out of a minivan. She introduced herself as Linda and explained to Ginny and Christy that they were on vacation from Illinois and visiting her parents. Her boys were getting antsy, so she brought them to the playground to let them tire themselves out. "I had to get my boys outside to play because that one," she nodded toward the boy talking to Mimi and Christian, "can be a pistol and needs to run off some of that wild energy. He's nothing but trouble when he's not exhausted."

Christy had no way of knowing what Linda's son was saying to Mimi and Christian, but when she saw Christian's hands clenched at his sides, she stood up to walk toward them. When Christian rushed at the boy and knocked him over, Christy started running.

A very pregnant Ginny looked at Linda and clumsily stood up from the bench, a worried expression on her face. The woman waved off her concern, saying, "I don't know what my kid said to her kid, but I'm sure my boy is getting what he deserves. He's rotten to his little brothers too, so I have no doubt he's the one who started it."

A short time later, Christian followed his mother to their car and kicked at the asphalt as she unlocked it. Ginny had explained that she was getting tired, so she decided it was time to head back to their home on the other side of the Alley. Christian was torn between his conflicting emotions. Feeling guilty for disappointing his mother and cutting the play date short, and elated over Mimi's confession about her secret game. He now sat in the back seat as Christy headed for home.

Christian thought about how his mother had pulled him off the bully. How the bully's mother never even came over to see if her son was okay, and how Christy had walked the boy to the water fountain and helped him clean up his bloody nose. Christian noticed when Ginny started slowly making her way over to them. He looked up and saw that Mimi was staring at him.

She must have dropped her bouquet while he was fighting. Mimi was now removing his T-shirt that served as a veil and held it out to him. He took it from her and pulled it over his head, realizing that he felt the need to cover his dark skin. All of a sudden, he wanted to try and hide it from her.

As if sensing his discomfort and remembering the bully's cruel taunts Mimi quietly told him, "I like your dark tan, Christian. It reminds me of the black king."

He blinked at her, the curiosity in his eyes prompting her to continue.

"My mommy and daddy have a special board game in their bedroom. Daddy is teaching me to play it. It's called chess. And there are different pieces, and they're different colors. There's a black king and queen and a white king and queen. Sometimes I go in their room when I'm not supposed to, and I play with the game, but I don't play the game Daddy is teaching me. I made up a different one."

She shyly looked at the ground before continuing. "I give all the pieces names. The black king's name is Christian, and the white queen's name is Mimi. And I play wedding with them. And all the other pieces in the game are their family."

She looked at him then, the gentleness, kindness and innocence of a five-year-old girl immediately warming and comforting his angry and bruised six-year-old heart.

Smiling now in the back of his mother's car, Christian reached into his front pocket and pulled out the ring he'd forgotten to give Mimi. He would hold on to it until he saw her again. Then he would marry her and do like he said at their wedding that had been so rudely interrupted. He would love her forever and she would belong to him.

Christy mistook his quietness for melancholy. "Don't be so upset, honey," came her soothing voice from the front seat. "Aunt Ginny just got too tired to stay and they have a long drive home."

He tucked the ring back in his pocket before asking his mother, "Do you think Mimi will marry me again?"

"Of course she will, Christian. You're best friends." Her words were comforting. "If you asked her to marry you a hundred times I bet she'd always say yes."

"How do you know, Mommy?" he asked.

"Well." She hesitated while trying to think of an explanation that would reassure him. "You and Mimi are..." She paused and thought carefully. "Tethered souls," she offered and immediately realized he wouldn't understand. She was right.

"What does that mean?"

"It means that your hearts are connected to each other," she softly said.

BETH FLYNN

He sat a little higher so he could see his mother's face in the rearview mirror. "You mean stuck together? Like with handcuffs?"

Christy started to laugh. The previous night they'd been watching a sitcom where the zany wife had unwittingly secured herself to her husband with a pair of old handcuffs. "No, sweetie. I don't think you can attach hearts with a pair of handcuffs like we saw on television last night." She brushed a hand through her hair and tried to explain. "Nobody can actually see what you and Mimi feel in your hearts for each other."

"What about a rope?" he interrupted, wide-eyed. "Maybe even an invisible one since nobody else can see it? That way it can be a secret. Just me and Mimi will know about it. And you too, Mommy."

"Yes, an invisible rope." She smiled. "But only you and Mimi can feel it. It's a very special connection."

"What if it breaks?" His voice sounded worried.

"It can't break," she replied, trying to soothe his little heart.

"Why not?"

"Because like you said, it's invisible, which means it's special."

She peeked in the rearview mirror and saw him nodding as if trying to understand.

"So me and Mimi will always be teh... tethered so...souls?" he stammered.

"Always, Christian. Always."

THE END

412

BONUS CHAPTER

FORT LAUDERDALE, FLORIDA 2007

Bevin Marconi lay on her bed and stared at the ceiling as she contemplated her life. The last several months had brought more heartache than happiness. She ran her hand over the smooth fabric of her duvet and remembered the first time, many months before, when she'd laid eyes on Slade Bear during her temporary stint in the law library at the courthouse. And the hollowness in her chest that memory resurrected was made even bigger with the reminder of another loss. The relationship with her mother.

As much as she loved her job as a librarian at Citrus Acres Middle School, she'd been happy with the break from the kids as well as the extra money she'd been able to make at the law library during their spring break. She'd stared dreamily at Slade from afar, not daring to even make contact with him. Guys like Slade Bear didn't notice girls like her.

He was every woman's dream. She'd immediately started digging around for any information she could find. It was easy to locate an address for him. He lived in a condo on Fort Lauderdale beach. She knew he drove a white Porsche because she'd seen him leaving the courthouse in it.

After probing a little deeper, it was easy to find his brother's mug shot. Slade and Christian Bear looked nothing alike. It was obvious they shared Native American heritage based on Christian's photo, but the only thing that hinted at Slade's ethnicity was his strong cheekbones. Where Christian had long, straight, black hair, Slade had collar-length, light-brown hair that curled at the ends, and was unruly enough to be fashionable, but didn't look unkempt. Christian's face was clean-shaven, but Slade had looked like a movie star who always needed a shave. Christian's eyes were a piercing blue. Slade's were light brown, with flecks of gold. She hadn't been able to get a real good look until she purposely knocked his folder off the table. And whereas Christian's mug shot showed him to be six foot two inches, Slade stood eye to eye with her at five foot eleven.

A little more investigating turned up details about his parents, showing that Christian had obviously inherited his father's genes, while Slade had received his mother's. Either way, they were a handsome family. Despite Celeste Marconi's warning to stay away, she'd been intrigued, and jumped at the chance to have an excuse to talk to him.

It had all started with an anonymous email from a stranger. It occurred just a couple days after she'd started there, and the stranger's offer coincidentally involved Slade Bear. It was a simple exchange of information. She would be told the identity of her biological father, and all she had to do was slip a note to Slade the next time he used the library. She'd been so shocked by the offer she never stopped to wonder how someone would even know that she'd been trying to find her father, with disappointing results. At first she'd haggled back and forth with the unknown person, citing all the reasons why she couldn't interfere. Noting especially how dangerous it would be for Slade's career. But the person had assured her that it would be for a good cause. The defendant in the case Slade was prosecuting was innocent, and was being railroaded by someone on his own defense team. Slade Bear would either prove to be a person of integrity or not.

Bevin, who'd walked a straight line her entire life, couldn't deny the thrill that came with being part of something so covert. She easily convinced herself that she would be righting a wrong. And besides, slipping the information to Slade would serve another purpose. She would find out whether she was attracted to a person of high moral standing. Or not.

It turned out that Slade Bear was an upstanding person. He'd done what was right despite the possibility he could've been disbarred or become a pariah in the public defender's office. But neither of those things happened. The defendant had been acquitted, and Slade moved on to his next case. But Bevin hadn't moved on.

The stranger had done as promised, and almost immediately

provided her with irrefutable proof of the man who'd remained name-less and faceless her entire life. Once when she'd tried to drag his identity out of her mother, a melancholy look had appeared in the judge's eyes. Celeste Marconi was a hard woman, who'd never married, and never dated. The rumors about her sexuality had been spinning around the courthouse for years. But Bevin knew differently. She knew that somewhere deep down, her mother had carried a torch for the man Bevin had never known for more than twenty years. She'd always believed that her father must've been married to someone else at the time.

When she confronted her mom with the proof of her father's iden-tity, the stoic judge broke down and wept.

And that was when Bevin learned the horrid truth. She'd been the product of rape. Not just any rape. It had been a gang rape. Celeste Marconi had been a twenty-two-year-old law student when she was coming out of a convenience store, was grabbed from behind and dragged into the shadows.

"It all happened so fast," she explained to Bevin. "There were three of them, and I knew they belonged to a motorcycle gang based on jackets that two of them wore. It had a scary- looking skull with a naked woman across the top of it. I only caught a glimpse of it when they rode away on their bikes. I couldn't see the name, but they would be in the news a few years later when their leader was arrested for kidnapping a teenage girl."

Bevin listened, transfixed as her mother described a nightmarish scene. Apparently, the two older gang members were initiating a newer member who hadn't earned his right to wear their patch.

"It was dark. There were shadows, and I didn't get a good look at any of their faces. I heard one of them call the nastiest one, Monster. Monster was the first one to rape me. He was the worst. The most brutal. The second one had a tattoo of a scorpion on his left forearm, and the third one"—she paused and swallowed—"the third one was obviously the youngest, and didn't want to do it. I remember him telling the other two that he didn't know rape was part of the initia-tion." She stopped to blow her nose and said, "They told him they would kill us both if he didn't do it."

Bevin shuddered at the thought of the terror her mother had endured.

"The last guy, the youngest one"—she had to stop for a moment again—"he got on top of me, and kept whispering in my ear how sorry he was. The other two were laughing so they couldn't hear him. But I heard him. He even told me he was going to pretend to bite me on the neck and that I should cry out to make it believable. I remember him telling me the better show we put on, the quicker it would be over."

Celeste looked at her daughter and swallowed thickly. "Each time he pushed inside me, he whispered he was sorry. Each time, over and over again. I'm sorry. I'm sorry. I'm sorry. Until he was finished." She swayed back and forth as if in time to his thrusts.

"Did you go to the police?" Bevin softly asked her mother as she reached for her hand.

"No." Celeste shook her head. "They took my purse. They knew who I was. When I first found out I was pregnant, I wanted to get an abortion, but I couldn't bring myself to do it. As the years went by, I used my job and the access it provided to my advantage. I was able to identify the men through mug shots. Even though I hadn't seen their faces clearly, the system provides identifying marks, like tattoos and birthmarks, as well as street names. I hadn't seen your father's face, but I'd noticed he had a large birthmark on the side of his neck."

"Which one is my father, Mom?" Bevin asked.

"He's serving two consecutive life sentences in prison for murder," she answered.

"I know that," Bevin snapped. "I know his real name. Was he Monster or scorpion tattoo guy or polite rapist?"

"The last one," Celeste said, as she averted her eyes.

Bevin let go of her mother's hand and walked away. Turning around, she crossed her arms and said, "You care for him. Don't you?"

"Don't be ridiculous!" her mother snapped while jumping up from her seat. Apparently the memory of that horrible night had vanished and she was back in the role of authoritative judge.

"I'm not being ridiculous. You felt something for him. Even though he was raping you, you somehow romanticized that he didn't want to. You've clung to that for years. What I can't figure out is, why?"

"Shut up, Bevin!" her mother spat.

Ignoring her mother's reprimand, Bevin continued, "It makes so much sense now. How you shut yourself away from any potential real relationships. You use him as an excuse to not get involved. Some-where deep down, you've developed feelings, whether imagined or real, for a rapist." Bevin paused and looked thoughtful. "What is so special about him? How has he kept this hold on you for so many years?"

Ignoring her daughter's questions, the judge sternly corrected, "He was never a rapist."

"He's not just a rapist, Mom." A second passed before Bevin added, "He's a murderer and you've been in love with him for almost twenty-five years. What a waste of your life."

The last comment had earned Bevin a slap across the face, and she hadn't spoken to her mother since.

It was after that encounter that Bevin decided she might give Slade Bear another chance. After all, she was certain there was disappointment in his expression right before she'd closed the door in his face the night he'd come to her home. But she was also cautious and had asked a friend to do some light, non-invasive surveillance on Slade. The results had been heartbreaking. When Bevin saw a picture of the beautiful woman who'd accompanied Slade to a coffee house, and later back to his condominium, memories of the bullying she'd endured for being the biggest kid in middle school came plummeting down. Her friend had taken only two pictures of Slade and the pocket-sized woman that Bevin was certain smelled of Chanel No. 5. But those two photos had been enough to send her in a downward spiral of depression. She'd declined the offer to spend her summer working in the law library. It was the best and only way she would be able to avoid not just her mother, but Slade Bear.

Instead, she'd spent the summer volunteering for a public library reading program, taking cooking and stained art classes, and doing some DIY around her bungalow. She'd even joined a gardening club with two teaching friends that also had their summers free.

She made herself accept invitations to go on a few dates. They were nice guys, but they didn't have light-brown eyes with gold flecks or a cavernous dimple in their left cheek. In spite of her date fails, she'd found her spirits had lifted and she was starting to feel her confidence returning. Until one of her new garden club friends invited her to have lunch at a cafe near the courthouse. School had been back in session for over a month, and it was an optional teachers workday. The students would have the day off, and the teachers were given the choice as to whether or not to work or take off a day as well. In retrospect, she should've used the day to organize her library shelves. And more importantly, she should've known better than to agree to meet so close to where both her mother and Slade worked. She'd convinced herself that a whole summer had passed and she was starting to feel like herself again. Besides, what were the chances she'd run into them —her mother always ate in her chambers and Slade spent most of his lunch hours in the library.

She thought she'd dodged a bullet until her friend said, "Whatever you do, don't look. One of the hottest guys I've ever laid eyes on is staring at you."

That was the first time anyone had said those words to Bevin, and she knew without asking that Slade Bear must've been in the restaurant. She was struggling with whether or not to turn around when her friend's next words decided for her. "Oh, wait. He's with a woman."

"Is she small enough to fit in my pocket, and has short highlighted hair?" Bevin whispered.

"Yeah, " her friend replied. "How did you know?"

The same way I know she smells like Chanel No. 5, Bevin thought.

The waitress had returned with their change, affording Bevin the perfect opportunity to flee. She didn't look over her shoulder as she made a beeline for the exit, her friend awkwardly trying to keep up. Once in the parking lot, she spotted the white Porsche. She got into her car and drove away from Slade. Apparently, a whole summer hadn't been enough to heal her obviously still-bruised ego.

I hope you enjoy this excerpt from Better Than This, the third spin-off from the Nine Minutes Trilogy.

Prologue
The Disgusting Pig

Everyone knows life can change in the blink of an eye, but what they don't know is if it will change for the better...or worse. A devastating car crash resulting from a blown tire. A winning lottery ticket bought with your last buck. A backyard pool without a childproof gate. Faulty house wiring that causes a fire erasing every tangible memory of your existence. Or in my case, catching my younger sister in bed with the man I'd given the best of my yesterdays and had promised all my tomorrows. All unforeseen circumstances we don't have control over. Or do we? Did the car owner know he had bald tires and drove on them anyway? Did they know the risk when they hired an unlicensed electrician to save a couple hundred dollars? Did I ignore the obvious signs that my marriage was deteriorating? Or did I see them and choose to pretend they didn't exist? So again, I ask, were these unforeseen circumstances? Or choices?

My story is as cliché as they come, and my experience couldn't add anything different or special to marriages across the world. Safe marriages, routine marriages, comfortable marriages. Even happy marriages.

I gave Richard what I believed were the best years of my life, accepting a childless union with the man who I thought could give me everything except children. It's not that Richard didn't want kids. It was that he couldn't have them. I knew that when we married, and it didn't matter. We were happy. At least I thought we were. Looking back now, I can see that it was an illusion we worked hard to create. We both needed something perfect to make up for our flawed and imperfect pasts. Doesn't everybody do that? Toward the end, we'd become nothing more than roommates. Talk about banal, right? Good friends who shared the morning paper over coffee and croissants and made it a point to play tennis at least two evenings a week. We shared household responsibilities, the remote, and little else. It was a business relationship, not a marriage. Our home, our routines, our lives were as sterile as his testicles.

Richard wasn't a bad guy. Unless you count sleeping with my sister as bad. It's strange how I've managed to forgive him. Once I forged through the grief, I was able to look back with more clarity. Richard had brought neatness and order to my life I thought I needed. And it worked. But only for a while. We knew something was missing and we both ignored it. Until she showed up.

My baby sister, Frenita, who at seventeen decided to call herself Fancy after the Reba McEntire song, had been down on her luck and asked to stay with Richard and me until she got back on her feet. Down on her luck, meaning her man of the hour, month, or year had dumped her. Fancy never worked a day in her life. She was a professional mistress who targeted men of financial means. At fifty-two years old, I considered myself an intelligent and savvy woman and never in a million years would've believed she'd target my husband. But she did. In the end, I'd wanted nothing more to do with her, but because she was my only living relative, I wouldn't allow myself to lash out. She was still my little sister, so I settled for distancing myself in place of vengeance.

Instead of staying in Greenville, South Carolina, and living with daily reminders of their betrayal, I went home. Pumpkin Rest was three hours away, where our elderly grandparents raised Fancy and me. A sleepy little hamlet in the northern end of South Carolina with one intersection and very few residents, it was a place where I wasn't reminded of the geometrically faultless straight lines of our luxury condominium in Greenville. Pumpkin Rest didn't have condos, car washes, cafés, or state-funded pristine parks. It couldn't boast of organic grocery stores, gyms, or fast food restaurants. The one intersection affectionately referred to as the crossroads, housed a small grocery store, gas station, diner, and pharmacy now turned hardware store.

I hadn't realized how much I'd missed it until I sought refuge in its quiet splendor. As badly as I'd wanted to escape the dusty and lonely roads of my youth, I'd never felt more alive than when I stepped on the porch of my childhood home for the first time in too many years to count. After not being able to keep up with the mortgage, the couple who'd purchased it after my grandmother's death eventually forfeited it to the bank. It remained abandoned and neglected until I bought it last year.

I glanced down at my hands. The age spots there were even more evident since I'd been working in my yard and kept forgetting to wear gloves. That wasn't entirely honest. I'd made a deliberate choice—there's that word again—not to wear gloves. I'd missed the feel of the rich, dark earth between my fingers and under my nails. Memories of Richard's soft and perfectly manicured hands dragged themselves up from the recesses of my brain. Hands that didn't like to get dirty. Hands that belonged to a man who insisted we buy a condominium so he wouldn't have to bother caring for a lawn or paying someone to care for a yard he didn't need.

I tossed a weed into the bucket beside me and stood up. After removing my floppy hat, I swiped my arm across my brow. It was a scorcher, and my back had started bothering me. I glanced over at the front porch and saw the dip in the roofline where a beam sagged. A gutter perilously dangled by a thread thanks to the previous night's rainfall. I cocked my head to the side and glanced at the siding that was so worn, the original wood peeked out at me like a forgotten friend. *It'll all get fixed in good time,* I told myself as I stretched while enjoying the melodic sounds of nature.

Other than my childhood best friend, Darlene, that's what I'd missed the most about Pumpkin Rest. The lack of human noise. The town was devoid of traffic, sirens, stores that blared music, and people talking loudly on their cell phones. I'd picked the perfect place to heal, to regroup, to rethink my life and my future. I was experiencing the epitome of contentment and couldn't fathom anything that could disrupt my retreat from the rat race.

I was about to resume my yard work when I stopped and looked around. I'd heard what I thought was a lawnmower. Impossible. Other than the Pritchard farm at the end of my dirt road, I had no neighbors. And the last of the Pritchards had died off, leaving no heirs. That wasn't entirely true. Two brothers were the rightful owners. The oldest, Kenny Pritchard, went to prison the same year their father died, leaving the youngest brother, Jonathan, a legal ward of the state. Kenny was killed years later in a prison fight, and the developmentally challenged Jonathan wasn't in a position to claim his property, leaving no one who wanted to assume responsibility for a dilapidated old farmhouse. I took a deep breath and shoved aside the grief that still rose in my chest when I let myself think about the

Pritchard family. I'd considered buying the property to guarantee my solitude but saw no need as nobody in their right mind would want to live out there. The sound was getting louder when I realized that lawnmowers didn't rumble.

I turned around and watched as a motorcycle slowly made its way toward me. He must've missed or ignored the Private Road and Dead End signs. I walked to the edge of my yard to warn the solitary rider that the road didn't go through and that he should probably turn around in my gravel driveway. As he effortlessly glided past the front of my house, spewing dust behind him, I eyed his muscular and heavily tattooed arms. He was wearing a black do-rag on his head, and the sun bounced off an earring in his right ear. Dark glasses hid his eyes as he gave me a curt nod with a chin that boasted a neatly trimmed beard.

I raised my arm to motion him to stop at the same time my eyes landed on his gas tank. They widened as I recognized the image emblazoned there. That's not a...? Why yes, I think it is! *What a disgusting pig,* I mouthed. It was obvious he'd caught me because I saw a hint of a smile before he continued his way down the road to nowhere.

"So, my disgust amuses you?" I said out loud as I watched his back, a thick braid swaying between his shoulder blades. I snorted and squatted to resume my gardening. I'll show him. When he finds out there's nothing at the end of the road except for a run-down farmhouse and neglected fields, he'll have to turn around. And when he does, I won't even bother looking up when he passes by. I smugly returned to my yard, concentrating on a patch that I intended to clear so I could plant vegetables.

After twenty minutes I had to use the bathroom and busted a move getting in and out of the house in two minutes. I didn't want to miss my chance to ignore him. The thought made me laugh at myself, and I returned to my weed pulling. Another twenty minutes passed, and I started to wonder if I'd missed him. I couldn't have because I'd watched from the bathroom window.

Two hours later (I know this because I kept checking my watch), I was forced inside by an afternoon rain shower, but I carefully kept an eye on the front of the house. I fell into bed that night exhausted and convinced myself that I'd somehow missed his return from the

Pritchard farm. I didn't know if it was from the yard work under the relentless sun or my constant but obviously ineffective vigil that caused me to collapse into bed utterly spent. My last conscious thought before falling into a deep and dreamless sleep was, *what kind of man has a vulgar display of female genitalia painted on his motorcycle?*

A NOTE FROM THE AUTHOR

Eating disorders, such as bulimia, binge eating disorder, and anorexia, are serious illnesses that involve extreme emotions, attitudes, and behaviors surrounding food, exercise, and body image. Eating disorders often hide in plain sight, so whether you have serious concerns or just an inkling about yourself or a loved one, please seek help. Eating disorders have the highest mortality rate of any mental disorder but recovery is absolutely possible and early intervention greatly improves the chances of success. Seeking help takes strength and courage, and there are many compassionate people and organizations devoted to helping those who struggle.

If you, or anyone you know is struggling with an eating disorder, help is available. Please know you are not alone and seeking professional help is important for recovery. To learn more about eating disorders please visit:

https://www.nationaleatingdisorders.org/
or call 1-800-931-2237

TETHERED SOULS PLAYLIST

"Roll Me Away" by Bob Seger & The Silver Bullet Band
"I Disappear" by Metallica
"Sweet Life" by Paul Davis
"I Saw the Light" by Todd Rundgren
"Linus and Lucy" by Vince Guaraldi Trio
"Count On Me" by Jefferson Starship
"Something in the Air" by Thunderclap Newman
"I Want You to Want Me" by Cheap Trick
"Back Where You Belong" by .38 Special
"Time Has Come Today" by The Chamber Brothers
"Seminole Wind" by John Anderson
"Bad Time" by Grand Funk Railroad
"Feelin' Alright" by Joe Cocker
"Street of Dreams" by Rainbow
"Run Through the Jungle" by Creedence Clearwater Revival
"The Weight" by The Band
"The Spirit of Radio" by Rush
"Tightrope" by Stevie Ray Vaughan & Double Trouble
"Layla" by Derek & the Dominos
"Piece of My Heart" by Janis Joplin

ACKNOWLEDGMENTS

Acknowledgments are always the most difficult part of finishing a novel because I can never seem to find the words that adequately describe the level of appreciation I feel for the dear family and friends who contributed to bringing this story to life.

I always like to thank my heavenly Father, first and foremost. Thank You for the imagination You so lovingly bestowed on me. And for giving me the opportunity to spill my daydreams onto these pages that found readers because You brought people into my life who've helped me navigate publishing and social media.

Just like it takes a village to raise a child, it takes an army to get a book published. I have so many people to thank. Each person contributed in a special way. Whether it was legal or medical advice, beta reading, editing, proofreading, cover design, map design, photography, keeping my social media wheels turning, being a muse for my MILF or just holding my hand in friendship and love, you each played an important role in bringing Tethered Souls to fruition. My thanks go out to:

Adriana Leiker, Alyson Santos, Amy Donnelly, Beth's Niners, Cheryl Desmidt, Darlene Avery, Dr. Stacy Waltsak Lexow, Eli Peters, Elle Christensen, Erin Noelle, Jay Aheer, Jim Flynn, Judy Zweifel, Kate Sterritt, Kathleen McGillick, Katie Flynn, KC Lynn, Kell Donaldson, Kelli Flynn, Kim Holden, Leylah Attar, Nicole Sands, Nisha E. George, Scott Dry, Jr., and Tracy Justice.

If there are any discrepancies or errors in the medical or legal aspects of the story, they are a result of my creative license and do not reflect on the professionals who so patiently provided their knowledge.

Any deviation from Native American culture or values was spun strictly from my imagination, and no disrespect is intended.

ABOUT BETH FLYNN

Beth Flynn is a fiction writer and USA Today Bestselling Author who lives and works in Sapphire, North Carolina, deep within the southern Blue Ridge Mountains. Raised in South Florida, Beth and her husband, Jim, have spent the last twenty-one years in Sapphire, where they own a construction company. They have been married thirty-six years and have two beautiful daughters, an adored son-in-law, and a lovable Pit bull mix named Owen.

In her spare time, Beth enjoys studying the Word, writing, reading, gardening, and motorcycles, especially taking rides on the back of her husband's Harley. She is a ten-year breast cancer survivor.

Keep in Touch With Beth

Beth Flynn
    P.O. Box 2833
    Cashiers, NC 28717
    USA

Email: beth@authorbethflynn.com

Website: www.AuthorBethFlynn.com

Twitter: @AuthorBethFlynn

Facebook: Author Beth Flynn

Facebook Group: Beth's Niners

Instagram: bethflynnauthor

Pinterest: beth12870

Goodreads: Beth Flynn

ALSO BY BETH FLYNN

The Nine Minutes Trilogy

Nine Minutes (Book 1)

Out of Time (Book 2)

A Gift of Time (Book 3)

The Nine Minutes Spin-Off Novels

The Iron Tiara (Book 1)

Tethered Souls (Book 2)

Better Than This (Book 3)

Made in the USA
Coppell, TX
16 March 2022

75090230R00246